A Promise Kept
Mallery Malone

I0658277

Chapter One

Ireland, 1016

Conor mac Ferghal welcomed death.

He pushed a dying raider from the point of his sword, moving closer to the thick of the fighting that centered on two giants on a mist-shrouded hill. Their dress and the wicked-looking battle-axes they wielded bespoke their Viking heritage. Even in the heat of battle, Conor admired the way the fair-haired warriors worked together, standing back to back and holding their own despite the odds against them.

And the odds were against them, Conor knew. His admiration of their skill would not stop him from vanquishing them. He would have vengeance, and he would give no quarter. He wasn't known as the Devil of Dunlough because of his charity.

A shout cut through the screams and groans of the wounded and dying. "The Angel of Death! The Angel of Death comes!"

Everyone, friend and foe alike, seemed to halt as a form materialized from the cloying mist. A pale horse broke through, bearing a rider wrapped head to toe in bleached garments that seemed to make rider and horse more apparition than reality. The conical iron helmet and sword gleamed in the weak afternoon sunlight as the pale warrior drove the horse up the hill to the Northmen.

"Stand your ground, men," the Devil called, crashing the hilt of his sword into a raider's face. "Remember what befell our village. Leave the supposed Angel of Death to the Devil of Dunlough!"

The pale warrior now stood beside his companions, wielding the shimmering sword in graceful, deadly arcs. As he drew ever closer, Conor noticed how the taller two men protected the smaller. Their leader, perhaps? The Viking's conical iron helmet, with nose and eye guards, concealed from Conor all but a pair of startling lavender eyes that blazed with hatred and a chin devoid of even the slightest beard.

Very few of the Northmen went without beards. A youth, then. Conor refused to feel compassion for him. Becoming a warrior meant preparing to fight and preparing to die. He had seen younger ones than this meet their end in battle, mere boys who did not deserve death. This one did. Pushing to the forefront of his men, the Devil engaged the enemy.

The young Viking moved with a lethal ease that belied his years, parrying the blow Conor dealt him. He smiled as the familiar bloodlust coursed through his veins. It was always thus, when he found an opponent worth his skill and concentration. The darkness would come later, after the blood had dried.

The two combatants matched each other blow for blow, neither uncovering a weakness in the other. This one would not go down easily. The thought had no more than crossed Conor's mind when one of the Viking's companions stumbled. The youth buckled, thrown off balance as the other

Northman fell at their feet. When the young Viking turned to the fallen man, Conor seized the opportunity, slashing his adversary deep in the thigh.

The resulting cry of pain was so feminine that Conor checked the killing blow that would have bit deeply into the leather tunic and cleaved the man in two. It was a futile effort. The tip of his sword pierced the pale leather and embedded itself in the Viking's side. He gave Conor a look of utter disbelief before slumping to the ground, his hand stretched toward his fallen companion.

Conor took a deep breath, seeking the freshness of the early spring breeze over the smell of blood and death as he scanned the field. His opponent had been the last to fall. Even now his men availed themselves of whatever riches they could glean from the fallen among their enemies, a curious mixture of Irish and Northmen. Satisfied that all was secure, he knelt beside his fallen enemy. With a sense of foreboding, he removed the iron helmet. What he saw stole his breath.

The Viking was not the untried youth he'd thought, but a woman, the most striking woman he had ever seen. The helmet had obscured a heart-shaped face with high, sharp cheekbones and near translucent skin. Hair so pale it was almost silver was pulled into a plait as thick as his wrist. Her brows were gossamer wings, as were the sooty lashes that fluttered against her cheeks. A blade-thin nose perched above full, pouty lips and a defiant chin that reduced her features from ethereal to fascinating. The skin was pulled taut across her cheekbones and throat, an indication of the unkind life a bandit led. Even in unconsciousness there was a guarded demeanor to her expression that gave her an air of otherworld mystery.

"A woman!"

Conor glanced up. Ardan, his second, stood beside him, protecting him as always. Ardan was a hardened warrior with a ruddy, weathered face and red hair sprinkled with gray. He had the unswerving loyalty of one whose life had been saved many times by the man he gave allegiance to. A man of few words but great wisdom, Ardan had been Conor's friend since the younger man's days in fosterage, and one of the few people he trusted without question.

The surprise on Ardan's face matched his own. "Yes, it is a woman."

Ardan spat down the hill. "You've strange luck with women trying to kill you."

"True." Conor let the comment pass. If any other than Ardan had said the same to him, that man would not get home under his own power. "At least this one had the decency to meet me face to face on the field of battle, unlike my dear-departed wife."

He fingered the scar that ran down the left side of his face, a gift from his late wife. "This land will fall into the sea before I let a woman put an end to me."

Seeking a pulse, Conor touched the fallen woman's neck, wondering at the frisson of awareness that coursed along his fingertips. He found her life-beat. It was there, but weak.

As he brought his hand away, his fingers brushed a neck-chain. He pulled it free of her tunic to discover an exquisite crafted cross hanging on a braided silver chain with a gilded Hammer of Thor. He grinned in spite of himself. 'Twas obvious the woman meant to be well prepared when she left this world.

Tucking the pendant back into the woman's tunic, he lingered over the satiny feel of her skin. So delicate to be so deadly. He shook his head to clear it of such inane poetic thoughts and rose to his feet.

"Is she?" Ardan asked.

"Dead? No. The Angel of Death? I believe so."

Ardan cursed under his breath, a long and colorful sentence that would have stunned Conor with its length in other circumstances. He felt the urge to curse himself.

The Angel of Death.

Conor had dismissed the stories as colorful tales spun by bards at the royal court. The idea of a woman, Viking or Irish, garbed completely in white and riding into battle was impossible to believe. Yet the proof lay before him.

Ardan regained his composure. "Why would herself attack our village?"

"A good question." Conor's voice was flat. "The village has naught to offer but cottages of fishermen and the tenants who raise tribal cattle. Even the Irish riding with her and her Northmen should know that our treasures, such as they are, are kept close to the dun."

He looked down at the unconscious woman. "The stories call the Angel a defender of the defenseless. Perhaps the stories are false. Unless someone sent her."

If Ardan was surprised by Conor's statement, he did not show it. And why should he, Conor thought. After all, someone was always after the Devil of Dunlough.

Ardan prodded one of the mail-clad Vikings with his foot. "Her man could be one of these two."

For an inexplicable reason, the idea that the legendary Angel had followed her lover into battle made Conor's jaw clench. He forced himself to calm. "You could be right, Ardan. They were defending each other."

"This one lives yet."

The Devil wiped his blade on the second Viking's breeches, then sheathed it. "Bring them," he ordered, calling for his horse. With an ease that belied his size, he swung astride. "Send for the priest to bless the dead and dying. If the Angel and her companion survive the journey, I will have Gwynna tend to their wounds."

"You won't execute them then?"

He shook his head, steadying his mount with a quiet word. "Someone sent the Angel of Death to slay me. I would have answers from her before she dies."

Ardan issued orders, then swung aside his own mount as the famed warrior and her still-living companion were thrown over a horse without ceremony. "Where do you think she's from?"

"I don't know," Conor replied. "There are Viking strongholds aplenty here. Sitric Silk-beard holds Dubh Linn, and more Northmen control Waterford, Wexford, Limerick and even Dun na Ghall to the north. She could be from any of those."

A frown shaded Ardan's features. "If she was, we would have heard of her before Clontarf."

Clontarf. The word caused a chill deep in Conor's soul, even two years later. Clontarf, where the tenuous peace that the High King Brian Boruma had forged through decades of warfare had been shattered with his death. Where Irish and Viking fought against Irish and Viking for the ultimate control of the island.

Where Conor had lost his soul and gained a kingdom.

"Have a care with our war-prizes," he told a thin, red-haired youth as he secured the Vikings to the mount. He turned his own mount towards home and away from the mesmerizing figure. "We've a way to go, and more war bands could be about."

Ardan drew alongside him. "Think you she was sent by Ulster?"

"It is probable," Conor answered. "There's little love lost between us, though you'd think with the other three kingdoms as well as Connacht fighting old Máel Sechnaill for the High Kingship, they'd have more sense than to send their men to sure death against us."

"Who said that Ulstermen had sense?"

The men around them laughed at the joke, and Conor let them have their mirth. They'd had little to laugh at over the last two years that he'd been ruler of the *tuath* and chieftain of the tribe. He knew he was a prize worth catching for his many enemies. Near six and a half feet tall, he towered over his men. With his penchant for wearing black while his men wore the saffron yellow warrior's *leine*, his dark brown hair that was almost black, and the ever-present scar, many thought him more demon than Irishman.

It did not bother him, the moniker that he'd acquired. Devil he was, through and through. And despite the name, despite the scar, men of the tribe flocked to Dunlough for the honor of serving the mac Ferghal. Flocked to fight beside the man who threw them into battle again and again, a man who made himself a target, the center of many battles. It was his duty, he told himself. He fought because he had to, and he fought with a zeal that went beyond the typical Gaelic zest for life.

No one knew what that zeal cost him.

He wrenched his thoughts back to the present as the dun came into view. Bards often said Dunlough was cradled in the bosom of Eire, and he agreed. Hidden in the northwest of Connacht, bounded by rugged, rocky hills to the north, crystal lakes and streams to the south, the mountain Slieve Torc to the east, and the ocean to the west, Dunlough was as wild and glorious as its people. The dun itself sat on a verdant hill surrounded by earthen walls. A stream ran around the base of the wall and cascaded down the hill where it joined a larger river on its way to the dark *lough* that gave the dun its name.

Oh, people had laughed when his father's father and his father before him started adding stone to the timber and thatch. They stopped soon enough when they came to seek solace from raids by Vikings and Ulstermen alike.

The dun had grown to a considerable size over the last two centuries. Its solid construction ensured that the people of Dunlough were well protected. Indeed, the remoteness of the northern part of the kingdom protected it from the brunt of the trials and tribulations that encompassed the rest of the island.

Of late, the warriors of Dunlough were riding out to challenge raiders, not armies. Rumors spoke of the *Gaill-*

Gaedhel, the "foreign Irish", riding again. Mercenaries descended from the mixing of Irish and Viking blood, their ferociousness had caused them to be called "the sons of death". They cared little for who they attacked as long as plunder was to be had.

That thought had Conor drawing sharp on his reins. Sons of death and the Angel of Death. Were they related? His village had been attacked. The Angel of Death was nearby.

Coincidences were not something that Conor had much faith in. If the woman was truly the notorious Angel of Death, why was she in Connacht? Why attack his poor village? Why look at him with such hatred in her eyes?

He would have been well within his rights had he slain the Angel in battle. But the Viking female had captured his curiosity. No, she would not die soon.

The Devil was a patient man. He would find the answers he sought. When he did, all the angels in heaven and hell would not keep this angel safe.

Chapter Two

"How many dead?"

Abbott Brochadh folded his hands. "Four. Two more may die before sunrise. One lost an arm, one an eye and two are lame."

Conor's hand clenched around his tankard as the priest recited the names. Each man's face floated before his eyes, settling into his memory. Dunlough's warriors were a fierce and proud group, unafraid to face death in defense of their homes. Conor's people would celebrate their fallen heroes tonight. He would not participate, nor did his people expect him to. The *bhean sidhe* would be wailing on Slieve Torc tonight, and there Conor would be.

Repressing his guilt with thoughts of retribution, he thanked the priest. When the holy man took his leave, he turned to Ardan. "Has my sister seen to our fair-haired guests?"

Ardan took a deep swallow of his ale before replying. "Lady Gwynna and Old Aine are with the white witch now. The brother could still die."

"Brother?" Conor sat forward, his tankard crashing against the table. "Why claim you such a thing?"

"Old Aine is certain."

If the old healer believed it to be so, it was enough. Rising to his feet, he moved to the hearth, digesting the news. A brother. That would certainly explain the horrified look on the Valkyrie's face when the man slammed into her during the battle. 'Twas apparent she cared for him. That care could be a weakness, one that Conor would exploit most ruthless to acquire the answers he sought.

Ardan turned on the bench to face him. "Are you certain we have captured the Angel of Death?"

"'Tis certain she fits the rumors we've heard for the last several months. Know you another female warrior riding about our land?"

"You should have beheaded her when you had the chance."

Conor raised an eyebrow. "In her condition? It would not have been fair."

"There was no need to be fair. The accursed witch wanted to kill you!"

"True, but there must be more here than we see. Besides, if the Viking female is the Angel of Death, she is worth much more to us alive than dead."

"And if not?"

"Then she will pay, in one manner or another, for what she did to our village."

He gestured for Ardan to follow him as he turned to the door. They walked down a short stone corridor to a thick wooden door. Clasping the braided cord around his neck, Conor pulled out a key, fit it to the lock and threw open the door. "Come, Ardan, and tell me what you think of these weapons."

The older man followed Conor into the room, a small, circular chamber lit by two well-placed torches. The only piece of furniture was a narrow wooden table that occupied the center of the room. But it wasn't the table that drew the eye.

It was the weapons.

They hung everywhere, these instruments of death. Great battle-axes, broadswords, short-swords, spears. Bows and arrows and shields. By any standard it was an impressive collection. What made it extraordinary, Ardan knew, was that every last weapon had once belonged to one of Conor's enemies.

Only four swords, grouped alone near the door, had not belonged to adversaries. They belonged to Conor's elder brother and three nephews, all lost in the great battle two years prior.

Ardan approached the table. It held a striking array of weapons: a broadsword, two short-swords, two great axes, and a rune-etched leather quiver full of arrows. A leather sheath with a long knife and leather scabbards and baldrics for the swords. A chainmail shirt and helmet with mail attached at the neck were at the bottom of the pile. All were covered with dried blood.

"Fine craftsmanship," Ardan said in approval, fingering the runes on the scabbard. "More than a mercenary raiding fishing villages could afford. Unless they were stolen?"

"I do not think so." Conor pulled free the broadsword. The blade gleamed in the torchlight, catching the runes etched upon it. A grand amount of silver wire chased a massive purple crystal on the pommel.

"Look at this jewel," he said, turning the pommel to Ardan. "The Angel's eyes are the same color."

"You noticed the color of her eyes while she was trying to kill you?"

"The eyes are the windows to the soul. You yourself taught me that to read eyes is to read my enemy's intent."

He replaced the blade. "I was not so caught by the unusual color of her eyes that I wasn't aware of her hatred. And it was hatred, Ardan, as if I had personally wronged her."

"Have you?"

Perplexed, Conor shook his head. "I have never seen the Valkyrie before today, and I've not fought Northmen in two years."

They left the weapons room, returning to the hall. "There must be more to the Angel of Death and her brother than the fables we have heard," Conor said. "I would have you find those answers. Start at the village. Discover all you can about our guests."

He moved to the main hearth. "You have two days. Get a good night's rest and set out at dawn."

"Two days?" Ardan's incredulity shone through in his voice. "Do you mean to summon a law-giver to decide the Angel's fate?"

"No."

Conor's voice grated above the crackling of the fire. "I will decide the Angel's fate. It is possible our friends to the north are responsible for this day. If so, you will discover the truth soon enough. If not, once the Angel realizes I hold the very minutes of her life, she will tell me what I seek. I promise you that."

Ardan left. Conor stared into the flames, fingering the scar on his cheek. For the second time in his life, a woman had tried to kill him. The first time had been his wife, but she had been near insanity. This woman, the Angel of Death, was far from it.

He remembered the look in those amethyst eyes as she swung her blade toward his skull. Hatred and the white-hot desire to kill.

He had never seen the Angel of Death before, and as far as he knew, she had never seen him. In fact, the latest tales about her had come from the south, near Limerick. So why had she been so intent upon killing him? Had he killed someone she knew, someone she loved?

Conor shook his head. He felt neither love nor hate for the fair-haired foreigners. Northmen were well and embedded in the fabric of the island, intermarrying with nobles and freemen alike, establishing trade and even fighting with the Irish against their kindred. And to be sure, there were just as many natives committing deeds as heinous as those contributed to the Northmen. He did not go out of his way to kill anyone, foreign or native, save an Ulsterman foolish enough to cross his border. Perhaps the Valkyrie's morals were not so noble.

Leaving the fire, Conor headed deeper into the dun. He stopped at a stout door flanked by two guards, one of whom opened the door for him. The chamber inside was little more than a cell, its only luxury an anemic fire burning in the minuscule hearth. The smell of burning peat failed to dampen the scent of blood and sweat and pain.

Two more guards and Conor's sister were by the pallet on the floor. The sentries looked as if they had been in a scuffle. Their tunics were in disarray, scratches and welts covered their faces and arms, and both had more than a little blood on them. Gwynna applied a cloth to her patient's forehead. Old Aine sat on a stool near the hearth, asleep.

When Conor moved toward the pallet, Gwynna climbed to her feet. He felt a momentary pride. His sister was a gifted healer, having learned herb-lore from the oral histories of generations of Dunlough and Druid women like Aine. Danu knew he'd put her skills to test on more than one occasion and would again.

Blood drenched the front of her dress and her face was pinched with fatigue. Concerned, he led her to the room's only chair and poured her a cup of wine. He nodded toward the guards. "I take it that your charge did not submit willing to your care?"

Gwynna pushed a lock of hair from her forehead. "She awakened while the guards were carrying her in. She thought they were taking her to be executed and 'tis certain she does not wish to die."

"Fought like a hellcat, she did," one of the guards added. "Beg pardon, milady."

Amused, Conor folded his arms as Gwynna glared at the guards. "You both will be after a bit of ale," he observed. "Help yourself to the barrel, and tell Cook to prepare a meal for Lady Gwynna and Aine."

The guards made a hasty retreat. Conor poured his sister another cup of wine, which she gulped with a sigh. "That is an extraordinary woman you have captured." She patted her face dry with a clean cloth. "She threatened to consign me to the bowels of the Viking Hel if I took her leg off. She also threatened me with further horrors if I did not save her brother."

Noting the wry pout to Gwyn's mouth, he asked, "What did you do?"

Aine stirred herself then. "True to your blood, she was," the old woman said, her eyes the color of moss. Her hair was pure white, her lively face unlined. She could have been thirty or sixty or two hundred. In Conor's twenty-five years, Aine had always been old.

The Druid woman got to her feet. "Gwynna told her that if she could not lie still, she would shave her bald."

A tired smile of remembrance lit Gwynna's face. "It worked."

Conor coughed what passed as a laugh from him. Gwynna joined in, then hushed him with a glance to the pallet. "She sleeps for now. Let's keep it that way, so I do not have to threaten her more."

"What of the man? The one you believe to be her brother?"

Gwynna didn't answer him at once, causing him to swing towards her. Her cheeks were flushed, as if with fever, and she appeared flustered. "Gwyn?"

She jumped, startled. "I have done my best, with Aine's help. But his wounds are dire. I will return to him when I am done here."

Moving to the makeshift pallet, Conor stared down at his would-be slayer. With the dirt and blood bathed away, and the pain eased by slumber, the warrior's beauty shone through. The luminous quality of it struck him like physical blows. Pale curls that had escaped the braid were stained gold by candlelight. Those full lips would be devastating in a smile, even with the defiant chin jutting above the slim neck. He knew her skin to be as smooth as satin. Did her lips taste as sweet as they looked?

He shook his head, disturbed by his winsome and over-whelming reaction to this woman. "I can see why they call her Angel."

Aine returned to the bed, Gwynna beside her. One gnarled hand touched a pale cheek. "The Angel of Death. Among her people, such a one is gifted with the ability to see signs and portends, and prepares the dead for their final journey."

"How do you know of such things?" Conor asked, surprised.

The old woman gave him an enigmatic smile. "It is my calling."

Her voice filled with pity as she gazed down at the pale woman. "So young to have such a name."

"How old do you think her to be?"

"No more than our Gwynna, I would say, a score of years or so. She is not new to the warrior's way. Her arms are strong enough to handle a sword, and she has calluses on her hands."

"What could have happened in her life to make her take up the sword?" Gwynna asked.

Conor stared at his sister. "What do you mean? 'Tis obvious she enjoys it, else she'd not have ridden about Eire these last two years."

Gwynna shook her head again. "You may know the way of a warrior, brother, but I know the way of a woman. Look

at her. Her beauty is undeniable. Her manner is that of someone accustomed to being obeyed. I am sure she is of noble
lineage, despite the lash marks."

"Lash marks?"

Solemn eyes regarded him. "She has several old scars.
Some are on her back, and another trails along her left arm
to her wrist."

"Perhaps she was an unruly slave."

It was Aine who answered. "I'm doubting that, my lord. I
do not believe she was born here. No one knew of the Angel
before last year, and 'tis certain a woman like that would be
memorable. She probably came from Denmark or Anglia."

"Betrothed to a powerful man, and one she did not favor," Gwynna added, clearly taken by the tale. "Perhaps her
brother was banished for some reason and she left with him.
What else could make her turn from a life of wealth and priv-
ilege?"

Conor frowned. His sister's words had the effect of making the Viking woman more human, and he didn't like it.
"We will find out soon enough, if she wakes."

"Her left arm deflected most of the blow to her side,"
Gwynna informed him, "but the wound was still deep, as was
the gash on her leg. After I convinced her of my skill, she allowed me to stitch the wounds. When I finished, she shuddered once and slipped out of consciousness."

He couldn't help but admire a woman with such mettle.
Most women became queasy at the sight of blood. He
doubted if even his sister could quietly watch someone stitch
her up.

Ruthless, he dampened his growing regard for the Viking. Admirable or not, she was responsible for many lives this day, including the people in the village. "Will she live?"

When Gwynna nodded, Conor strode to the door. Yanking it open, he beckoned the two guards inside. "Take the Viking to the pit and put her in chains."

Gwynna was aghast. "Conor, you cannot mean that. She is a wounded woman!"

He swung to face her. "A woman who tried to kill me and did kill several of our people, or did you forget? Even now she should be dead."

"And why is she not?"

Aine's quiet question halted his diatribe and movements. How many more would question his actions? It was his right to destroy her. Yet when and why had he made the decision to spare her? It could not be that he was taken by her comeliness. He knew firsthand how treacherous a beautiful woman could be.

"The Angel of Death is a prize many have sought," he finally said. "She will be of use to Dunlough."

Aine's mossy eyes measured him, and Conor wondered what she witnessed. "You'll do what you must, and well we know it. But remember this, Conor mac Ferghal: with this woman, things are not always as they appear to be."

Conor inclined his head, acknowledging her words and the tone in which she'd said them. Christian or pagan, one did not fail to give Aine the respect that was her due. Her utterances were always full of wisdom when they could be understood.

"I will remember what you say, but neither of you will gainsay me in this. She is not called the Angel of Death for sport. Until I know the truth about the Valkyrie, she is to be a prisoner."

Chapter Three

Pain.

It was the first thing she was aware of. Agonizing pain that arced up her legs to her side then to her arm. Endless, unrelenting waves of pain that hammered at her will.

Erika welcomed the pain. At least it kept her from dwelling too much on her failure.

Without opening her eyes, she sensed her surroundings. Her neck, legs and arms were shackled together, with just enough length in the chain to allow her to lie in sparse straw. She wore only a thin shift too small for her and a blanket riddled with holes. Stalks of straw pierced through the threadbare material and into the skin of her legs and back. Tightness surrounded the aches in her right leg, left arm and left side. Bandages.

Someone had treated her, Erika realized. Why go to the trouble of healing a prisoner? Why hadn't the tall warrior killed her when he had the chance?

She remembered the hill. She saw Larangar take a thrust to the chest. A cold certainty told her that her dearest friend was dead. But what of Olan? What of her twin?

She struggled to remember. After his mail broke, deflecting a blow meant for her, several arrows had hit Olan. Yet she could still, weakly, sense her twin in the back of her head, the sense that told her he was alive.

Lars dead, Olan near death, herself captured—and to what purpose? She had failed in her duty, failed to destroy the vile creature that ravaged the poor village they had ridden through. She had promised the villagers vengeance, and she had failed them.

The failure cut deeply. Never before in her life had she been unable to fulfill a vow she'd made.

Mentally she cursed her fate. In her mind she could still see him, the towering warrior who was her nemesis. As tall as Larangar and Olan—who were considered giants—her personal demon had been dressed completely in black, with dark hair spilling past his shoulders, eyes like thunderclouds and a menacing scar that ran from his left temple through his close-cropped beard to his chin. He fit closely to what the Irish monks described as the Christian devil.

Erika ground her teeth in frustration, for a moment close to tears. Angrily, she brushed them away. Tears would not save her, not from a man heartless enough to ransack a village full of women and children. She forced herself to remain still, even though the pain made her want to writhe and scream in agony. Her mind raced with plans, for she knew that while there was breath left in her body, there was still opportunity for vengeance.

She would make the Devil pay for what he did. Or she would die trying.

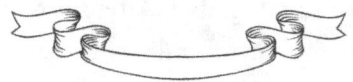

BY THE FEEBLE LIGHT of a single torch, Conor watched the Valkyrie feign sleep. The earthen room, scarce large enough for both of them, had no windows and only one heavy, ironbound wooden door. Light was not a common occurrence for the occupants of this pit. Yet the light found her, illuminating the silvery braid and pale skin, making her seem an apparition.

The shift Gwynna had found for her was too thin and too small. He could see the supple length of her legs beneath its hem. Even in the sputtering light, he noticed the flat stomach and a surprising small waist for so tall a woman. He could also see the firm, high breasts that pushed against the flimsy fabric of the bodice.

How long had she walked the warrior's path? Years, 'twas certain. Her grace with a sword could not be learned in a year's time. Yet if a sword did not protect a man at all times, truer than true it would not protect a woman. How many men, he wondered, had she given herself to when her sword proved useless?

He felt the desire that had sprung alive in him and shook his head, erasing his sudden need. He had been too long without a woman if he was attracted to this bloodthirsty wench.

His anger returned as he remembered the faces of the dead. "Open your eyes, Angel of Death," he ordered. "I know you are awake."

Against her better judgment, Erika obeyed the harsh command. Every part of her body ached, even her hair. Opening her eyes only intensified the torment. But she would look upon the face of evil and prove herself unafraid.

Her devil, she discovered, was a man.

He sat on a rough-hewn bench. A torch protruded from the packed earth of a wall, casting meager light between them. It was enough. His legs were well muscled and covered with dark hair. His *leine*, a knee-length tunic made of soft wool, did nothing to conceal the girth of his shoulders and chest, broad enough to support the strength evident in his powerful arms. She could not see his face clearly, obscured as it was by shadows and dark sheets of hair that hung past his shoulders, but she could see his eyes.

Unnerving.

His eyes glinted in the dim torchlight. Erika would swear she saw both the lightning of Thor's hammer and the fires of the Christian hell burning in their depths.

She was doomed.

"Are you the one called Angel of Death?"

The Devil's voice rumbled deep and harsh as he spoke fluid Latin. She barely quelled the shudder that snaked through her. It was easy to believe that she had entered eternal punishment. She had failed to protect the poor of this verdant land, a land that she had fallen in love with at first sight. Now she would have to pay for that failure with her very life.

Every extremity shrieking in protest, Erika struggled to a sitting position. Flames of pain danced before her eyes, stealing her breath. She might well die this day, but as long as her heart beat, she would fight the man before her.

Defiant and proud, Erika raised her chin, the heavy iron collar biting into her neck. Even that small act caused pain to radiate through her. Through gritted teeth she finally answered him in Gaelic. "My name matters not. You need only to know that I am your enemy."

A low sound wafted toward her. It took a moment to recognize the noise as laughter because it held little in the way of mirth. "I admire your courage, but it will not do in the stead of sense," the dark warrior admonished her. "I know you are my enemy. I would have you tell me why."

Erika's temper climbed, driving her to her feet despite her agony and the heavy chains. "You dare to question the cause for enmity between us?" she asked, disdain rising like bile in her throat. "You, who are the embodiment of all I hate about this land?"

The harsh accusation brought Conor to his feet. He stepped forward, out of the shadows. "You would do well to guard your tongue, Lady Death. Men have died for less than your insult."

To his surprise and secret pleasure, the Valkyrie did not recoil at the sight of his ravaged features. She thrust her face forward, her eyes sparking with fire and passion.

"Are you so easily wounded, Devil, by words alone?" she asked. "Prepare to be slain, then, for I have more darts to let fly!"

Conor growled. He had never struck a woman on purpose in his life. He was not about to begin, no matter how much she goaded him. "I warn you again, Viking wench, to guard your tongue. The sole reason you yet live is to answer my questions!"

The pale-haired woman had the temerity to laugh. "Then you would do well to attempt to kill me now. For I have nothing more to say to you than this: pray for God to cleanse the blood of innocents from your hands, for if I am able I will send you to Him for judgment!"

For a lightning-quick moment, Conor almost laughed. *Attempt* to kill her? He could snap her neck with one deft twist of his hands. Attempt indeed! Then he registered the rest of her vehement declaration.

Settling his hands upon his hips, lest he fit action to thought and take her beautiful head from her shoulders, he summoned the iron calm that had served him for years. "What do you accuse me of?"

The earthen chamber fell silent, save for the muffled sputter of the torch and the Viking's own tortured breathing. Conor could see perspiration beading on her forehead and lip, and her nostrils flaring with each labored breath. He knew resolve alone kept her upright.

"I will use whatever means necessary to gain the answers I seek," he told her in a voice chilling in its softness. "I will have answers."

The mercenary refused to answer him. Conor could do naught but stare at her. How comely she looked, glaring in pure Viking defiance. He wondered if she knew how her breasts pushed against the delicate fabric of her shift when she breathed.

"Where are my belongings?" she demanded. "And my—my companions?"

"The pain makes you rude, Angel," he admonished her. "Your weapons are locked away safe. Most of your garments are ruined, but more will be procured for you. If you need them."

So, she was to be left with nothing. Erika knew then that she would die. She could accept that. It had always been the destination at the end of the path she had chosen. But by Odin, she would take this despicable cretin with her when she left this world!

Despicable or not, her adversary was not unpleasant to look upon. She thought the men in her homeland were giants, but this man matched the size of many a Viking warrior. There was an air of masculine grace and prowess about him that was unmistakable. Just looking at him caused something to thrum deep inside her. Those gray eyes bored into her own, digging beneath her surface.

The pain made her more than rude. It made her fanciful as well. Blinking to clear her thoughts, she demanded, "Will you tell me the fate of my companions?" Her jaw clenched as she jerked her eyes away from him to stare at the wall. She would not ask again.

She heard him take a foundering breath. Would he tell her? "The elder Northman is dead," he said bluntly. "The younger man still clings to life, but my healer is not optimistic."

Larangar. She wanted to shriek at the grief that welled inside her. Another two days, and her close-kin would have been on a ship bound for Anglia. She clung to the belief that he had found his way to Valhalla and was even now drinking with their fathers. She could not bear it if he was denied. Then his blood would be on her hands, as surely as if she'd felled him herself.

Pushing the anguish away, Erika summoned anger as her shield. Weakness spread through her with each breath. If she wanted to vanquish this ignoble cur, she would have to do it now.

"You wish to know what I accuse you of," she said heavily. "I accuse you of being a thief and a coward and a murderer!"

"What?" His roar of outrage could flatten the stoutest of men. Even Erika was not immune to it. Her legs crumpled beneath her, and she collapsed nerveless onto the coarse straw.

"You would feign ignorance of your heinous deeds?" she demanded, wheezing as stars danced on the periphery of her vision. Her arm pressed against her side in a futile effort to staunch the pain that throbbed with every heartbeat. "You—you murdered the women and children of that village for nothing more than fish, pelts and a few pieces of silver!"

"How dare you accuse me of raiding my own village?"

"I have seen Irish as well as Viking attack villages and monasteries," she answered, gasping. "Your protest means little to me. Devil or no, I will kill you. You will pay for what you have done."

She pushed him too far. Infuriated, Conor swooped down on her, grabbed her by the shoulders and pulled her upright. It was no small accomplishment—though slight of build, the Viking had weight to match her height. He brought her close until a mere breath separated them.

"What *I* have done?" he echoed, his anger blazing like a summer squall. "You are the one who will pay for what you have done!"

She stared at him with eyes as hard as the amethysts they favored. "Threatening wounded women—that is so like a coward," she sneered. "Is that how you earned your name?"

"Woman, you try my patience!"

"What will you do? Kill a defenseless woman? Surely you have more honor than that, Devil?"

Unthinking, Conor backed her against the wall. "What would you know of honor, Angel of Death?" he asked, his voice brutal with rage. "You and your *Gaill-Gaedhel* attacked one of my villages while most of its men were away. Women, old men and children had to defend their selves and their homes against a band of ravening outlaws that you led."

The amethyst eyes widened with shock. "Who are you?"

"I am Conor mac Ferghal, chieftain of Dunlough. That village is part of my *tuath*, and its people of my tribe."

"That village...belongs to you?" she whispered, her voice numb.

Conor was thunderstruck. "You admit to raiding my village?" he roared, giving her a savage shake. "I should kill you now!"

If possible, she became even paler. Her eyes became glazed even as she stared at him. When she spoke, her tone was soft, breathless, but the words were like daggers. "You lie...men call you Devil. Only a man with such a name would hurt those pathetic souls."

Forgetting her grievous wounds, he gave her another vicious rattle. "You are the one responsible for the deaths of my people. You are the one who will pay. Do you understand me?"

Her only answer was a moan. Conor watched in horror as the Viking's eyes fluttered shut and she went limp in his grip.

Chapter Four

Erika jerked her eyes open and attempted to surge to her feet, her hand automatically reaching for her sword. Pain slammed into her like fists, pummeling her senses. The breath fled her lungs like a startled bird, taking a moan with it.

"Ease, lady, ease."

Fingers pressed against her shoulders, pushing her back to the sparse straw. It was a measure of her weakness that she did not, could not, fight the gentle touch. Raising her eyes, she sought the owner of those hands.

A tall, slender, dark-haired woman, no more than twenty, gazed at her with brilliant green eyes and a concerned expression. Erika had no idea who the woman was, but her voice and touch were familiar. Healing, comforting. A healer.

She held a cup of water to Erika's lips. "You must be thirsty," the strange woman said in halting Norse.

Erika was surprised almost to the point of tears to hear her native tongue. She drank in the refreshing liquid, letting its coolness revitalize her. "*Go raibh maith agat,*" she said in Gaelic. "Thank you."

The woman set the cup on the ground beside her. "I am Gwynna. What is your name?"

Erika almost refrained from answering, but there was no harm in telling the healer her name. "I am Erika, also called Silverhair. Where am I?"

Emerald eyes bored into her. "Dunlough, in Connacht. You do not remember?"

Struggling to shake the effects of the nightmare and the pain, Erika closed her eyes. "I remember a tiny village, littered with burning homes and broken bodies," she whispered. "I could not ride by without giving aid—"

"You were trying to help them?" The healer sounded astonished by that fact.

"Yes. How could I not? My brother and I always help wherever we can..."

Her hands clutched at the other woman's arms as memories crashed against her senses. "Olan! Tell me, what has happened to him!"

"Olan?"

Erika nodded. "He is my twin brother. Hair near as pale as mine, but eyes of blue." The ebony-haired woman grew still, and Erika feared the worst. "He is dead, gone from me."

"His wounds were grievous, but he lives," the healer hastened to assure her. Startlingly enough, color suffused her cheeks. "Each day brings him further into the land of the living."

Joy welled inside Erika at the other woman's words. But with the joy also came fear. "I must go to him," she said, struggling to rise. "The Devil will come for me—"

Darkness danced before her eyes. The healer easily pushed her back against the blanket, chains and all. "When you are stronger, you may see him," Erika was told. "But only when he is out of danger."

Shaking her head, and wincing even at that effort, Erika subsided. "Olan is not out of danger, and neither am I. The Devil is going to kill me."

"If Conor wanted to kill you, you would be dead now."

"How can you be certain?"

"I am his sister."

Shock raced through Erika. "You are sister to the Devil of Dunlough? B-but he is a raider and you are a healer! How can you be sister to such a man?"

Gwynna smiled. "Conor has been called many things, but he is not a raider. He is ruler of these lands, including the village. If he raids, it is against Ulster, to the north."

"Oh, no." Chains rattled as Erika covered her face with her hands. "He truly is a *jarl*?"

"That means ruler, doesn't it?" Gwynna asked. "Yes, Conor is ruler in Dunlough."

Erika groaned, despair gripping her. "Sweet Freyja! I promised the villagers that I would bring them the head of their enemy.

"I was going to bring them the Devil's head!"

"SHE THINKS I RAIDED my own village!"

In a fit of temper, Conor threw his tankard against the nearest wall. Wolfhounds, soldiers and servants scrambled to freedom. Only Gwynna remained with him in the great hall, her arms crossed as she observed him. She knew his temper was never directed at the innocent.

Of course, he didn't believe the Angel—Erika—was innocent. In his eyes, she was but another woman out for his blood.

Gwynna would never admit it to him, but she feared for her brother. He was a warrior, true, and his fighting skills legendary. There had been a gentler side to him once, one that made him smile easy and laugh often.

That was before Aislingh betrayed him.

Shivering despite the fire, Gwynna remembered that night, just over a year ago. Conor's bellow of pain had roused the entire dun. She had met Ardan at the door of Conor's bedchamber. Inside, they'd found Conor's wife, writhing on the floor, a blade protruding from her stomach. Conor stood on the other side of the chamber, holding his bleeding face in his hands. He had spurned aid until Aislingh was cared for. She'd died cursing him. He refused to tell them what had transpired. But he didn't have to.

Everyone knew that redheaded babes did not run in the ruling family's line. Most of Dunlough's people had auburn, sable or midnight hair—no one had tresses the color of fire, not even the babe's mother.

As Gwynna mended her brother's face that night, she had looked into his eyes and seen the emptiness in them. Aislingh had carved more than Conor's skin out of him.

There were other things, things that the siblings never talked about, that had forged Conor into the man he had become. Things like the deaths of their older brother and his sons, which had thrust Conor into an unwanted position of leadership. Dunlough needed that man, it was true, but Gwynna despaired of ever seeing her brother free of care again.

"Erika did believe you to be the one responsible for the ravaging at the village," she finally said. "I disabused her of that notion."

Conor ceased trampling the rushes into the smooth earthen floor and swiveled toward her. "Erika?"

"Erika Silverhair is what she calls herself," Gwynna replied. "That is her given name. And yes, the wounded Viking is her brother, Olan Strong-wolf."

Surprised out of his temper, her brother retrieved his tankard. "How were you able to get information from her?" he demanded, sitting at one of the tables.

Crossing to the door that led to the kitchens, Gwynna called for ale, bread and cheese. She joined her brother at the table. "For one thing, I did not attempt to rupture the wound in her side," she informed him with a touch of asperity.

It was the closest she ever came to chastising him. One side of his mouth twitched, the closest he ever came to a true smile. "Forgive me, sister, but the Angel sore tested my patience. What else did you learn from her? Did she confess her sins?"

Gwynna shook her head. She waited until the returning servant set down her platter and left before continuing. "Erika was distressed to learn that you rule Dunlough. She told me that she promised the villagers that she'd bring them back the head of the man who had wronged them. She intended to bring them yours."

Laughter exploded out of him, but not the kind Gwynna wanted to hear. "She promised the villagers my head? Why would herself do a foolish thing like that?"

"Because she is who she says, and she does indeed ride about our fair island protecting those unable to protect themselves."

A snort answered her. "You expect me to believe that the Angel and her war band just happened to be nearby when someone attacked our village? And somehow, the true raiders managed to escape us both?" Conor shook his head. "No, that is too much to credit, Gwyn. I must have more than the Angel's word."

"The tales are true."

The siblings turned as one to see Ardan enter the hall, followed by an old woman, a younger woman and a small boy.

Conor stood. The women bowed, then cowered behind Ardan. The boy gazed at him with unabashed curiosity. Conor focused his attention on his friend, noticing his fatigue. "Sit down before you fall down."

Ardan refused, rubbing the side of his face with a beefy hand. "The story I have to tell keeps me upright."

He pulled the women in front of him. "This is Múireann and her son Gil, and this is Eithne. I would have them tell you in their own words what happened that day in the village."

Conor gave what he hoped was a reassuring smile but felt more like a grimace. "I would be honored, Good-mother, if you would tell me what befell the village."

The old woman bestowed him a tremulous smile. "It was like a nightmare, my lord, sure it was. Our men had put out to sea hours before, leaving us defenseless. The thieves came out of nowhere, it seemed. They were only there to terrify us."

Conor grew still. "Why do you think that?"

"They didn't go into our homes, they just set 'em afire. They trampled our cattle and young. I prayed for deliverance, for any God to hear. It was only when I called upon Danu that I was answered."

The old woman glanced around, as if unsure if her blasphemy would earn her trouble. When Conor urged her to continue, she said, "A fog had gathered around our village, thick as wool. Deep in its heart we could hear the sound of pounding hooves, like a great number of warriors charging. Then the fog parted, and out she rode, like one of the *sidhe*."

Conor did not have to ask who "she" was. Even if he wanted to, the woman, in true Gaelic fashion, warmed to her tale and would brook no interruption. "She was a terrible vision, a specter dressed all in white, astride a giant pale beast that breathed smoke. With a cry that chilled the hearts of the evil, she thundered into the village, laying waste to the raiders with powerful swings of her mighty sword. Unable to withstand so great an opponent, the cowards turned tail and ran."

"Which direction?"

"To the north." The answer came from the younger woman.

Folding his arms across his chest, Conor shared a look with Ardan. If the tale were true, it would prove that the Angel was savior and not destroyer. The true culprits could very well be Ulstermen.

He had to be sure. "Describe the person who helped you."

Again, the younger woman answered. "I am sure she was Viking."

"And you are sure the Viking was female?"

"Yes, all the others wore beards and loose hair. This Viking was beardless, and had long, pale-colored hair in a decorated plait that hung to her waist. But then she took off her helmet, and I was certain."

The old woman, not to be outdone, picked up the thread of the tale. "She must have been sent by the gods, my lord. Never before have I seen beauty such as hers. And her eyes, they were the color of rainclouds at sunset. She fairly glowed with inner fire as she promised to return with the heads of those who had wronged us."

The younger woman stepped forward again, capturing Conor's attention. "My lord, the lady did help us. If she had not appeared when she did, more of us would be dead."

Thanking them, Conor called for a servant to take them to the kitchens to be fed before they were escorted back home. When they were gone, he moved to the hearth, hoping the flames would order his thoughts.

Amethyst, not red, was the color he saw.

It was difficult to keep the woman from intruding upon his thoughts. Erika Silverhair. Erika meant "forever strong" in her language. It suited her. He had never known a woman so vibrant and alive with untapped energy and passion. How defiant she had been despite the obvious pain she endured.

How unbowed, despite the fact that she faced death and he was her only salvation.

How she fired his blood.

Heat surged through him, but the fire from the hearth was not the culprit. He walked to the table, reaching for the ale. "What else can you tell me about our guest, Ardan?"

The other man settled onto the bench opposite Gwynna. "I happened upon a wandering bard at a *bruidean* on the southeast road. He wove an incredible tale of the Angel of Death."

He paused, refilling his tankard. "She killed a man with her hair."

Gwynna gasped. Even Conor had to raise an eyebrow at that. "I did not credit you for a jester, old friend."

Ardan set his drink down. "The bard swears he saw it with his own eyes. A man was attacking a child who was refusing him at the top of her lungs. It was said that the Angel took down her braid and looped it around the man's neck in the blink of an eye. Jerked him right off his feet. He died facedown in the dust in the middle of the lane. No one lifted a finger against her. In fact, she was feasted.

"There are other stories, all the same. When she attacks, it's to defend those too weak to defend themselves. She and her brother take hires from merchants and nobles who need extra protection. At the start of each hire, she has to challenge their best with whatever weapon they choose, to first draw of blood. From what I heard, she's never lost a challenge. And all her kills have been honorable."

Conor's lips twitched. "You seem disappointed, Ardan, to discover that the Angel fights fair."

"A female warrior is unnatural."

Gwynna's back straightened with an audible crack. "It wasn't so long ago that the women of Connacht fought alongside their men in battle. And 'tis certain the way of things that many have need to fight now."

Ardan dipped his head. "My pardon, my lady."

Conor joined them at the table. "Our Gwynna is more apt to trust than most."

Conor swallowed deep of his ale, then turned to Ardan. "Anything else?"

"Just that she has made more enemies than allies during her time here. Her sense of justice had pricked the ire of many a *boaire*."

So, the cattle lords may have put a price on her head. Interesting. "If we are to credit these tales, and I believe we should, that means that someone else attacked the village. Who?"

"Ronan of Ulster."

The sound of his enemy's name sent an icy rage through Conor. "This smells of his hand. It is sly and underhanded, and he craves the blood of innocents."

Ardan stood. "When?" was all he asked.

"We will return, measure for measure, what Ronan has dealt to us," Conor said, his voice cold. "That I promise you. But first, you will take yourself off to rest, Ardan. You deserve it."

The warrior left. Gwynna turned to Conor. "What of Erika?"

"What indeed?" Conor had no intention of giving the Viking her freedom. He doubted she would leave anyway, especially without her brother.

"Let us go see the Valkyrie."

They left the hall and went outside. Rains had swept through with their usual quickness, leaving a fresh crispness in their wake. The breeze that gamboled a continuous dance over the hills carried the warm promise of summer. The people of Dunlough went about their daily duties with laughter and song, and the younger children darted between the circular daub-and-wattle houses that hugged the outer boundary of the dun.

Pausing, Conor took a deep breath and closed his eyes, letting the spirit that was Dunlough infiltrate his senses. He loved this land, from the top of Slieve Torc to the depths of Lough Dun.

A bellow of pain shattered the pastoral peace. It came from the direction of the earthen cell. Conor and Gwynna broke into a run, several men following them.

Chapter Five

Angel crouched in the cool earth, a length of chain in her hands. She had rested fitfully since the healer had left, knowing the Devil, *jarl* or no, would come for her again. So she was prepared when the cell door opened and the young warrior entered.

She had not been prepared to see him drop his belt and lift his tunic to reveal his hardened member.

That moment of surprised hesitation had almost cost her. But the fool took a moment to gloat over his supposedly helpless victim, and that gave her time to palm her hidden weapon, a miniature dagger. When he reached for her, Angel plunged the sharp blade into the back of his hand.

"Demon-spawned bitch!" her would-be rapist screeched, stumbling back from her as she rolled into a crouch, chains hissing. With a grunt of pain he pulled her dagger free of flesh and bone and dropped it to the ground. He clutched his bleeding hand to his chest. "You'll pay dear for that!"

The warrior drew his leg back to kick her. Angel felt the fierce storm of the berserker fit gathering within her. She prepared herself to take the blow even as she readied herself to lunge at him. Then hell erupted.

The Devil strode into the chamber, dominating the small space with his presence. Grabbing the younger man by the back of his tunic, the Devil effortlessly flung him against the earthen wall.

On a lower level of her mind, Angel registered the Devil's intervention and marveled at it—and the obvious fury in his face. But the berserker fit had her deep in its clutches. Only blood would appease it. Snarling, she leapt to her feet, her hands curved into claws—

And was immediately engulfed in an implacable embrace, caught against an equally implacable chest. The Devil had caught her. Infuriated, she struggled against him. Moving one of the massive stone *cromlechs* would have been easier. Through the blood pounding in her ears, she heard her captor speak.

"Rhuaidri." The Devil's voice was a controlled blast of fury. "I will excuse you because your youth and your grief are great. Remember that you will not have a second chance to disobey my commands. Now get out before I let the Angel finish you."

Her quarry was going free! Shrieking with outrage at being denied retribution, she struggled with all her might. Dimly she heard the Devil order everyone out, but the berserker in her demanded blood, drowning out rationality. She was turned, chains and all, and suddenly her opened mouth was pressed against the Devil's throat.

Shock drove everything else from her mind. She had never been in a man's embrace before, never had her senses assaulted in such a manner before. Never *tasted* a man before. Erika pressed her lips together against his throat, his flavor stinging her tongue. He tasted of salt and strength.

The sensations pierced through her berserker fit, leaving her aware of nothing but the man. Without conscious thought, she leaned into him, breathing deeply. His smell was that of grass and horse and ale and maleness.

How could a man smell of such goodness and be so evil? Perhaps he wasn't reprehensible, after all. Could she have been so fundamentally wrong?

When the Valkyrie's mouth fastened to his neck, Conor went stock-still. Having been denied the blood of her attacker, would she rip out his jugular in retribution?

Then her lips closed against the pulse at the base of his throat, scalding him. Conor would swear that it was a kiss. Her body relaxed against his as she inhaled deep. The harsh breath pushed her breasts against his chest, the flimsy fabric doing nothing to conceal the contour and feel of her body from him. Long and lean she was, with just a hint of softness to her sharp edges. A month of good food and kind living would round her out, making what was desirous now a torment later.

It was all he could do not to groan aloud. The Valkyrie nuzzled at him the way one of his wolfhounds asked for a pat on the head. Was this the same woman who had just screamed because she wasn't able to kill a man? Why did that not seem to matter anymore?

Conor had been aware of the Angel as an adversary, a warrior and a prize. Now he was aware of her as a woman. And that made her even more dangerous.

Dangerous. Conor had to remind himself of that. This was not a meek maiden, despite the way she clung to him.

She was a warrior in a woman's flesh, a warrior as ruthless as he.

Erika shivered as the bloodlust left her veins. The Devil—Conor, she reminded herself—held her away. Staring into his eyes, she felt something unfathomable surge up from her toes and launch itself at him, charging the handbreadth of air between them.

He licked his lips. Erika watched in fascination as his tongue swept from one side of his mouth to the other. Did he taste the same things she had?

Belatedly she realized that he was speaking to her. "Erika? Did he hurt you?"

Blinking out of her stupor, she glanced up at him. The silver of his eyes was dark with genuine concern and another indefinable emotion. "I did not give him the opportunity," she replied, and couldn't resist adding, "Does that disappoint you?"

Light gleamed in his silvery eyes. "It does not. Does that disappoint *you*?"

Erika was amazed at his bantering tone. He couldn't be evil. Not evil at all. Why was he called Devil? "Why did you stop him?"

Thunderclouds gathered in his features. "I have done many things, but condone rape is not one of them."

"But you let him go!"

His jaw hardened. "Rhuaidri lost his brother in the slaughter at Dunlough village. Grief can drive a man to madness, and rash action." Had that happened to him, Erika wondered. Still, she understood. She had only to look at the last seven years of her life to know how grief drove a person. "It is the same for a woman."

"You need not fear crossing paths with him again."

A rush of warmth swept through her, engulfing her senses yet again. He was protecting her! Only Olan and Lars had ever tried to protect her before. Tightness settled in her chest.

He cleared his throat. "And...you no longer need to fear for your life, Lady Erika. I know you tried to help my people, not harm them."

That obviously was not an easy thing for him to admit.

Again she stared into his eyes, struggling for truth against the wariness. He still held her loosely in his arms and the awareness of it, of *him*, was sweeter than honeyed mead. "Are you truly lord of that village?"

His eyes were solemn. "I am."

She sighed, the last of her rage sifting from her. It was difficult to release, especially against someone she had attempted to kill days earlier. "I am sorry," she whispered, knowing it was inadequate but knowing no other way to convey how she felt about the loss of his people.

Conor believed her. Her expression, her luminous eyes, declared more than words the sorrow she felt. "How did you come to be near Dunlough?"

The startling lavender gaze shuttered. "We were on our way to Donegal, to find a ship to take Larangar to Anglia. When we saw the raiders attack, we stopped to help."

Despite the fact that it put her life in danger, despite the fact that safety lay a few hours away, Erika had stopped to help people she did not know. "Why?"

She stared at him in surprise. "We could not ride by while innocent people were being hurt. Even the defenseless should have someone to defend them."

Conor knew he had just been given insight into what drove the Valkyrie. Had there been a time when she was without defense, and no one was there to aid her? His thoughts returned to the moment he'd entered the chamber. Remembering how defenseless Erika had been filled him with unaccountable anger.

Except that she had not been defenseless. Releasing her, Conor turned to retrieve her dagger. Straightening, he hefted it in his hand, testing its weight and balance. The dagger was truly a work of art. It was a miniature of her broadsword down to the purple crystal set in the crosspiece.

Erika watched a humorless smile lift the right side of his face. "It would behoove me, I think, to remember never to invoke your fury, Lady Death," he said, balancing the blade on the tip of a finger. "Do I want to know where you hid this?"

Her cheeks flamed. "It is a hair brooch." She pulled the thick braid of hair over her shoulder, parting the strands to reveal a pale leather sheath woven within. "I would have used it to kill you, when the opportunity arose."

He stepped away from her then. For the first time, Erika hated what she was. She waited for words of disgust or condemnation from him.

There were none. Instead, he held the dagger, hilt-first, out to her. "Do you still wish to kill me?"

Taking the dagger, Erika gave his question the weight it deserved. She could sense the beginning of a fundamental shift in her world, a shift she wasn't sure she was prepared for.

But there was one thing she was sure of. She looked at Conor. His stance was relaxed, open, his hands hanging loosely at his sides. Despite the weight of the chains, Erika could have easily plunged the blade into his heart before he could raise his hands to defend himself. Looking into his eyes, she realized he knew it too.

Reversing the dagger, Erika handed it back to him. "Nay, I do not wish to kill you. Do you wish to kill me still?"

A laugh escaped him, brittle and dry. "Is everything a challenge to you, Angel?"

Her chin jerked up. "Life is a challenge, Devil. I must constantly battle it for what I want."

"And what do you want?"

"Survival and freedom, for myself and my brother," she replied without hesitation. She looked down at the chains encumbering her. "I would give anything to be free."

"I can give you both, after a fashion." He held a key aloft.

Hope warred with caution as Erika regarded the key. Nothing had been handed to her since her father's death seven years ago. Besides Olan, there was no man left alive that she trusted. How could she trust a man she had first met over crossed blades?

Conor tucked her dagger into his belt and moved toward her. "Trust is not a simple thing for me, Angel, but I do hold high to honor. You would seem to have some of that. Therefore, a measure of freedom will be yours."

Freedom! Tears stung her eyes as the chains fell from her wrists and ankles. So intent was she on being rid of the iron fetters that she almost missed his words. "What do you mean, giving me a 'measure' of freedom?"

Instead of answering, he called for one of his guards. The soldier was shorter than Conor but just as bulky, with deep auburn hair contrasting his dark beard and unfriendly green eyes. She knew if Conor gave the order, the warrior would slay her without compunction. Or at least, he would attempt to.

Erika deliberately turned her back to him and faced Conor. "What do you mean by measure of freedom?"

She watched as he gathered the chains in his massive hands. "Freeing you from this pit is the only measure of freedom I can give you. I cannot have you disrupting the dun any more than you have. Padraig will guard you until I decide your blood-fine."

"And why should I pay a blood-fine when you know I did not raid the village?"

Any trace of humor he may have retained vanished. "Perhaps you do not have a true understanding of your plight," he replied, his eyes wintry. "At best, you are a hostage of war with no one to ransom you. At worst, you are one of the *fuidir*, with no rights save your life, which continues only by my goodwill. Your friends are few, your enemies as great. Your life is in my hands. You would do well to remember that."

Transferring the leg and arm shackles to Padraig, Conor grabbed the remaining length of chain that hung from the neck collar, wrapped it around his ample fist, then led her towards the door. Erika balked, suddenly not wanting to leave. "Where are you taking me?"

He drew her inexorably to the door. "To the one place I can ensure your safety. My chamber."

Chapter Six

Gwynna watched the silver-haired man sleep, unable to halt the strumming of her heart.

He was magnificent. Even battered and broken, his body awed her with its innate strength and beauty. She had refused to let him die, and it was a mixture of skill and will that brought him back from the brink time and time again.

How many hours had she sat beside him, urging him to live? How many hours had she listened to his disjointed ramblings, soothing him with words and touch? More than she had with the others, that was true. God help her, she had given more of her attention to him than the men of Dunlough, all the while believing he was their enemy!

It had been a burden on her soul, wanting the Viking to live, knowing that at any moment, Conor could order his death. She'd attempted to rationalize her want by hiding behind the healer's desire to help all, enemy or no. But the relief she'd felt at discovering the truth proved her rationalization for the lie it was.

She should have been afraid of him. He was a large man, acclimated to the ways of killing. His body bore evidence of the brutal existence he led. A giant with pale curls that flowed past shoulders twice as wide as she was, there wasn't an ounce of spare flesh on him. His face would have been harsh had it not been for the thick lashes that rimmed his eyes and the hint of softness around his lips. Yes, she should have been afraid of him. She had good reason to fear men such as he. Yet she did not.

Perhaps it was because he was powerless, on the brink of death as he was. Perhaps it was because she was the one in power, with God's blessing, holding his life in her hands.

Perhaps it was because of the dreams.

Delirious with fever, he had thrashed about on the pallet, calling out in a mixture of Norse, Gaelic and Latin. Gwynna hadn't been able to catch more than a few phrases, but she knew his thoughts were of his sister and her safety. His concern touched Gwynna, for it reminded her of Conor and his concern for her.

Turning to check his forehead for fever, she was startled to find the object of her daydreams staring at her.

His eyes. Sweet Lord, she had forgotten about his eyes. Blue as late afternoon sky on a warm summer's day, his eyes delved into her, uncovering her heart, her very soul, and claiming both for his own.

A smile split the close-cropped beard, lighting his expression. "Angel."

Gwynna couldn't hide the twinge of disappointment. Was he still under the spell of fever? His gaze was clear and steady, not glazed and pained. "I am Gwynna, my lord, not the Angel."

"Lady Gwynna." His voice was deep, rumbling from the depths of his chest, reminding her of waves crashing against the cliffs. He spoke her name again, slow, as though savoring each syllable. "I am Olan, and I am lord of nothing, save myself." He looked down at his mending body. "And perhaps not even that."

His gaze journeyed around the chamber, taking in everything before resting on her again. "Where am I?"

"You are in Dunlough, my home," she informed him. "You are safe."

Disbelief shadowed his eyes. "I traveled with others, a man and woman, Northmen as I am."

Gwynna noticed how careful he was not to reveal their relationship to him. But she could see the pinched expression that had nothing to do with physical pain. She gathered his large hand between hers, noting the long, calloused fingers.

"Your friend, Larangar, is dead," she said as gently as she could. "But Lady Erika is here, and well."

She would not tell him that his sister was locked in Conor's private chamber and had been for the past three days while Conor hunted down raiders to the north. She would not tell him that Erika slept in chains for two days prior to that. She would not tell him how close his sister came to being raped and killed. Gwynna remembered the anguish her brother had endured on her behalf. She would spare Olan that.

He blinked several times, and she wanted to weep for him, for causing him this pain.

His eyes found hers again. "I would see for myself how my sister fares." His free hand gripped the covers, lifting them away.

"Please don't!" Gwynna rose to her feet to stop him, knocking over her stool in her haste. Even if he could rise, he wore nothing save his bandages. Despite having seen that body injured and bleeding, it would be quite another to see it hale and hearty. Quite another.

Olan came to the same conclusion she had, for he fell back to the pallet, the cover tight to his body. "I feel as shaky as a new-birthed foal."

"Your wounds were grievous, my l—Olan." Gwynna hoped her face wasn't as flushed as it felt. "Many a time was it that I almost lost you."

The smile returned, illuminating his brilliant eyes. "Yes, I remember. I was on the path to heaven or Valhalla, I'm not sure which, and an angel blocked my way."

"An angel?"

He nodded. "An angel. But unlike any heavenly being I'd ever heard of."

Gwynna was drawn into the tale, mesmerized by cobalt blue eyes. "In what way?"

"The monks describe angels as golden-haired creatures of light, with wings upon their backs. This angel had hair as black as a raven's wing, and eyes as green as this land in springtime. Her beauty outshone the sun."

His quiet, compelling tone stole her breath. Could he be talking about her? True, she had dark hair and green eyes, but she was no beauty. "Go on."

"She was also different in that, instead of wearing white robes, she wore a simple dress soaked with blood."

He smiled at her startled gasp. "Yes, you were that angel. Each time I tried to continue on the path, you denied me passage." He gazed at her, his expression apologetic. "I was very angry with you."

Despite his warm gaze, Gwynna shivered. "I remember."

Even more than his sister, this Northman had fought her. She looked down at his hands, remembering how they had wrapped around her wrists as he raged with fever, leaving her bruised.

"I hurt you, didn't I?" he asked, his remorse clear. "Forgive me."

Touched by his concern, she leaned towards him, laying a hand on his in an impulsive move. "There's naught to forgive," she said. "You were wracked with fever and pain. As long as you fought, you'd live. Neither I nor your sister were ready to let you go."

His hand turned beneath hers, lightly clasping and leaving her breathless. His gaze was like a caress to her flushed skin. When was the last time a man had looked at her like that, she wondered. Had she ever been regarded in that way? She felt as if he wanted her to draw closer so that he could touch her, kiss her. Gwynna leaned towards him, closing her eyes...

A low rumbling sound rose between them. Startled, her eyes flew open. "What was that?"

Laughter, deep and strong, answered her. "My stomach," Olan said with rueful good nature. "I believe I will survive after all, if my hunger is any indication."

There were many kinds of hunger, she knew. At the moment, staring into the intense blue of his eyes, she was unsure if he was speaking of food.

She moved toward the door, of a sudden needing to put space—leagues—between them. "I will see to a meal for you."

"I would like to see my sister."

Gwynna froze, her back to him. She had dreaded this request, and now that it was upon her, she was struck by indecision. How would he react when he learned that he and his sister were little more than captives?

She didn't have to wait. "I cannot see her, can I?"

Turning to face him was difficult; seeing the look on his face was worse. "Perhaps, when you have regained your strength—"

"My sister and I are prisoners, aren't we?" he demanded. "We were captured."

"Conor thought you were responsible for raiding our village."

"Raiding the village?" he echoed. "We were protecting it!"

Gwynna remained by the door, poised to flee. "We know that now, Olan, but at the time, you were the only war band in the area, so of course Conor assumed—"

"We were not the only ones near the village," he cut in, his eyes fierce. "There were others, all Irish, led by a large man dressed all in black, with a scar on one side of his face..."

She must have made some sound, for his gaze sharpened, piercing her. "Do you know him?"

"He is my brother, Conor, ruler of Dunlough."

Olan stared at her. All the warmth they had shared earlier evaporated from his features, replaced by a coldness that permeated her heart.

"Your brother." He spat the words out like bitter ale. "The monster who stabbed my sister in the gut is your brother?"

Gwynna felt the blood in her veins turn to ice. "H-how did you know that?"

"My sister and I shared the same womb. Our bond is strong."

His gaze flicked hard over her, causing her to flinch. "Why have you saved us? Surely your brother does not mean us to live?"

Forcing herself away from the door, Gwynna drew herself to her full height. "Despite what you believe, my brother is not a monster."

"Is he the one called Devil?"

"Yes, but—"

"Then he certainly is not an angel, is he?"

"Neither is your sister," Gwynna burst out, and instantly regretted it.

Olan ignored her retort, though his eyes darkened in a potent mixture of anger and pain. "I would speak to your brother."

Heat suffused her cheeks. How had they become enemies? "Conor is out searching for the true criminals now."

"He knows that we did not plunder the village?"

"He knows that you helped the villagers fend off their attackers."

The change in his mood was immediate. "Then we are not prisoners, and you can bring my sister to me."

Gwynna twisted her hands into knots. "I can't."

The smile froze on his face. "Cannot or will not?"

"I cannot."

"Then we are prisoners."

"No," she began, but the protest was a feeble one.

"It is out of place for a lady to comport with captives," he said, his voice frigid. "We have nothing more to say to one another." He turned away from her then, a sheaf of his golden hair falling forward over his shoulder and obscuring his face.

Gwynna left the room, feeling as if she had lost something precious without knowing what it really was.

Chapter Seven

Erika bit back an oath. For the past three days she had been making short trips about the room. She knew every nook and cranny, just as she knew Padraig and another guard stood outside the heavy door. The taciturn man was taking his duty as her guard all too seriously, not allowing her to leave or anyone to enter, not even Gwynna.

Had she been healthy and unchained, she probably could have subdued both guards before an alarm could be raised. Yet even if she gained the hallway, Erika had no way of knowing where her brother was being kept. She would not leave without him, a fact the Devil of Dunlough was surely aware of. So she prowled the room.

His room.

The chamber was sparse, more suited to a cleric than a king. The few articles present, however, were sumptuous. Near the hearth, two finely hewn seats with dark green cushions flanked a small table boasting a chess set carved of ivory and obsidian, with a match in progress. A large, finely decorated chest held unadorned, dark clothing startlingly different from the multihued raiment of most Irish nobility, and grooming implements.

Then there was the bed.

The ruler of Dunlough did not have a straw pallet on the floor or a rough stone ledge. Conor had a bedstead, a low-slung wooden frame with four stubby yew posts delicately carved with the intricate swirls and beasts that were the hallmark of the island's artistry. The bed boasted an actual mattress stuffed with feathers, and blankets with exquisite embroidery along the edges. It was wide enough to sleep two adults comfortably.

Erika did not go near the bed after her initial examination of it. She had taken one of the chairs to the window, impeded by the chain connecting her ankles and shortening her stride to a hop. With a blanket and one of Conor's tunics to ward off the nighttime chill, the chair was a serviceable place to sleep. She would not sleep in Conor's bed.

Sleeping in his bed would mean yielding to the Devil of Dunlough in a way that was unacceptable. She would not willingly capitulate her body, a conclusion Conor would surely reach if he discovered her beneath his bedclothes. She may be trapped in his chamber, but she would not go freely into his embrace.

Erika's hands went to the heavy metal collar about her throat. Conor had promised her a measure of freedom. Surely that meant more than traversing his chamber?

Why his quarters? That was a question that had haunted her for the last three days. Did Conor have no wife? Surely if he did, the lady of Dunlough would be offended by her presence in this most private of places.

Erika's gaze returned to the bed. Was that the price she would have to pay for her liberation? Was that why she was now imprisoned in his private chamber?

Although she had never experienced intimacy before, what she knew of it confused her. She had seen conquering armies foist themselves on the hapless and been witness to the pain and suffering they inflicted. But Erika had also met a fascinating woman who actually charged men for the right to come to her bed. That woman had told her that joining with a man could be pleasurable or interminable, depending upon the man.

Which would Conor be? She couldn't help but wonder. Despite her inexperience, she knew firsthand the effect of desire on men. From her tenth year, many men had come to her father to offer for her. Erika's father, *Jarl* Thorold, had been a powerful and well-liked lord. With close ties to the rulers of Denmark and Norway, Thorold had no need to forge alliances through marriage. Doting on his only daughter, the *jarl* had granted Erika the right to choose her future husband when she came of age.

With all the brashness a ten-year-old could muster, Erika had declared she would wed the man who defeated her in combat. Motherless since the age of four, she had been raised by *Jarl* Thorold as he raised her brothers, in the ways of war. Wanting to please her father in all things, Erika soon became proficient in every Viking weapon but excelled with blades. Her success ensured that she would never have to leave her father.

In the winter of her fourteenth year *Jarl* Thorold died, and the darkest years of her life began.

Fear had driven her then, and fear drove her now. The cloying, gut-wrenching sensation had been a constant companion for her the last five years. She was afraid of death, afraid of being powerless. Afraid of losing her brother. Afraid of being captured, imprisoned. Afraid of being subjected to another's will.

Those fears had caused her to walk the warrior's path, to live a life that was not living. Knowing—and fearing—that the end of her journey would come sooner rather than later.

Now, all of those fears were personified in the man called Devil.

The overwhelming fact of her fate caused tears to well. Without her sword, she was powerless. Bereft of weapons, she was not the Angel of Death, fearsome warrior, but simply Erika Silverhair, a woman without defenses.

Ruthlessly she stamped the tears down. Tears had no power. Tears had not brought her mother or her father back. Tears had not freed Olan from their elder brother's cruelty. Tears had not kept her from killing to free her twin.

Tears had never helped. Erika had long ago learned the ability to cry silently and alone. Eventually she had learned how not to cry at all.

Commotion outside the window lifted her from her dire thoughts. Crossing to the aperture, she peered out.

What little she could see of Dunlough was impressive. A mixture of stone and wooden posts partitioned acres of neat, verdant fields. Some of the pastures held sheep, cattle or horses, and others were already sown with grains and vegetables. Conor's people, she observed, knew their duties and went about them with brisk efficiency even without the presence of their lord.

But their lord had returned.

Conor rode at the forefront of a column of riders snaking its way up the rise to the dun. He held himself proudly and easily astride a large mount as darkly shaded as his garments, his sable hair dancing about his shoulders in the breeze. In his somber tunic, Conor stood out from his men. He would have stood out in any case.

Watching him, Erika was reminded of the lead male of a wolf pack, and how that proud animal held sway over his followers by virtue of being the smartest and strongest. The lord of Dunlough was undoubtedly strong—crossing blades with him had proved that.

Defending the border between Connacht and Ulster was unquestionably a precarious duty, not for one weak in mind, will or body. It was patently clear to her that Conor mac Ferghal was weak in none of these.

As if drawn by the force of her thoughts, Conor reined his horse, his head lifting to discover her at the window. When their gazes met, something inside her tangled, struggling to break free. She remembered how it felt to stand in the protective circle of his arms, to absorb his scent and his taste. Her insides quivered in anticipation of being near him again.

After an indeterminate time, Conor's attention was snagged by one of his men. He looked away, breaking the enchantment that held her. With a flustered sigh, she sank onto the chair.

"Eye of Odin!" She covered her face with her hands. *What is wrong with me that I comport like a love-starved maiden in one of the* eddas? *Can I truly forget so easily that this man wishes me dead? That he has kept me in chains for five days?*

Anger surged through her. She grasped it fiercely, welcoming it for the weapon it was. She would need every defense she could summon, for a new fear was threatening to claim her—the fear of wanting.

"NOW, THERE'S AN UNCOMMON sight."

Conor handed his stallion off and turned to Ardan. "What was?"

Ardan nodded towards his chamber. "Seeing a woman leaning out of your window, eager for your return."

Wryness twisted his lips. "Eager to separate my head from my shoulders, no doubt."

Ardan didn't bother to smother his amusement. "Being trapped in your chamber for three nights is certain to make the Viking less than endeared to you."

"I don't need her to be endeared to me. Grateful will be enough."

Chuckles escalated into full-gale laughter. "Grateful! She'll be grateful, true enough. Grateful for the chance to put her hands to your throat!"

Conor had considered that. "As long as she doesn't have a blade hidden elsewhere on her person, I should survive the confrontation."

He moved toward the dun's entrance. "Do not worry, my friend. Erika Silverhair will not end my days, though she may be tempted to try."

Ardan shook his head, but tactfully changed the subject. "What do you plan for her then?"

What indeed? Truth be told, Conor had given little thought to the Angel's future. His thoughts had been preoccupied with hunting down his enemy. Early into the second day they had been successful in flushing the raiders out of their mountain fast. Ronan of Ulster had not been among those slain or captured, a truth that weighed heavy on Conor's soul. That guilt was balanced by the knowledge that none of his men had lost their lives. This time, at least, the demons that haunted him would leave him in peace.

Conor glanced at the window again. "I don't know yet."

They entered the dun. The main level was windowless, lighted by torches at short intervals along the walls. The smell of roasting meat wafted from the kitchens and out the door behind them. Servants waited for them with basins of water and towels to clean their faces, hands and feet, and cups of ale to soothe their parched throats.

The cool water did nothing to curb his reaction to the sight of Erika leaning out of his chamber window to watch his arrival. Her pale hair had glistened in the sunlight, floating on the breeze like a silver pennant. Her gaze had been so intent that it was a tangible thing on his skin.

Need slammed into him, hardening his flesh. Enemy or no, Conor wanted to sink his hands into Erika's hair and taste her fully, to join her in his bed and never let her out.

Ardan's soft curse brought him out of his musings. "What?"

"Careful, lad."

Conor paused, one foot on the stairs leading to the upper level. "That is too cryptic even for you, Ardan."

The eyes staring back at him were heavy with warning. "I don't like the look you're wearing. Remember who and what she is."

"A woman."

"A Viking woman who tried to kill you."

"Do you believe I could ever forget?"

Without waiting for a reply, Conor mounted the stairs to his chamber. Padraig, who had command of the dun in Conor and Ardan's absence, stood outside his door with another guard. Both hung their heads in abject misery. Gwynna was also there, with a servant carrying a basin of water and a stack of cloth. His sister was standing toe to toe with Padraig, haranguing him in that soft, quiet way she had that could reduce even the stoutest man to a quivering, useless mass.

Schooling his features into a bland expression, Conor approached them. "How fares our guest?"

"And how would I be knowing that, I ask you?" Gwyn wondered, her tone tart. "Your guards have not allowed me to enter. For all I know, she could be lying dead of a festering wound!"

Padraig turned helpless eyes to Conor. "*Tigerna*, I explained that your orders were to allow no one to enter. I did not think it safe to allow Lady Gwynna to go in."

"'Tis apparent he believed that Lady Erika would put a bandage to my throat and hold me hostage until your return," she retorted. She turned to Padraig, giving him a sweet smile that had little kindness to it. "I appreciate your concern for my safety."

The sentry blushed the color of his hair. "All is quiet within now, but the first night it sounded as if a *bhean sidhe* were trapped in the room. The second and third nights were most quiet, save for her pacing and muttering. When I brought her meals in, she never spoke a word, just followed my every movement with those damnable eyes of hers."

He shuddered, then made the sign to ward away evil. "Sure, if she needed a healer, she would have said," he finished.

Gwyn's answering snort made her opinion clear. For himself, Conor had to agree with her. Erika was proud to the point of stubbornness. She would not ask anything for herself, even to save her life.

"Thank you, Padraig. You may go." Both men bowed and retreated. Conor turned to his sister. He could see the argument brewing in her emerald eyes, and diverted it by asking, "What of the Angel's brother?"

Her ire softened. "He's recovering remarkable well, enough to demand to see his sister. He does not believe we have treated her fairly. Although I have attempted to disabuse him of that notion, my voice must have lacked conviction. He is quite angry."

Stillness gathered in Conor's bones. "Has he threatened or hurt you?"

"No. Olan has been most kind, given the circumstances. You cannot begrudge him wanting to see his sister's welfare for himself."

No, he could not. Had the situation been reversed, Conor would have been beside himself wanting to know the fate of his last remaining sibling.

He took the bundle of clothing and the water from the startled servant. "See to the Northman's needs," he told Gwynna. "We will reunite brother and sister within the hour."

Gwynna gave him a long look that he could not interpret before turning away. Conor waited until they were gone before opening his door, fully expecting to be attacked.

He wasn't. But if eyes were daggers, he would have died a thousand deaths.

Erika stood beside the window, her arms folded across her chest. She still wore the thin shift but had added a *leine* over it. The dark tunic falling off her sparse frame and the heavy iron collar did nothing to diminish the imperious tilt of her chin or the furious flash of fire in her eyes.

Conor had never seen anything so lovely—or irate. "You are well this day, my lady?"

"How can your mouth even form the words?" she asked, caustic. "You have trapped me in this room for three days!"

Glancing about the room, he noted everything was almost as he had left it. One of his chairs now stood by the window, and someone had advanced pieces on the chess set. The bed was untouched.

"Keeping you here was necessary, for your own safety," he replied, setting his burden on the table near the hearth. "Or would you rather I had kept you in that cell?"

"I would rather be free." It was not a request.

Conor had to admire her unflinching, if single-minded, resolve. He continued as if he hadn't heard her. "This is the best chamber in the dun. Only one other has a true bed, and it belongs to Gwynna."

He nodded toward the bed, knowing the answer before he asked the question. "Did you not enjoy sleeping in my bed?"

Amethyst eyes flashed with lightning. "You know well enough that I did not lie there."

"Whyever not?"

She stared at him as if he had taken complete leave of his senses. "Because it is yours."

The corners of his mouth twitched. "So is the *leine* you wear."

Cheeks flaming, Erika snatched the wool garment over her head and tossed it to the rug-covered floor between them. "There."

She stood there in pure Viking defiance, her hands on her hips, color high on her cheeks. She did not avoid looking at his ravaged face, staring at him full-on instead, firing his blood. She was magnificent.

He wanted her. Total and complete and sure. Wanted her pale fire warming him, her passionate nature fueling him. Wanted the purity of her emotions writ clear on her features to be for him and him alone. Wanted to be the one to claim and tame the legendary Angel of Death. What a fine match she was for the Devil of Dunlough.

He gave her a long, deliberate look. "If you refuse my *leine* and my bed because they belong to me, then you must refuse the shift as well, if you think on it."

A sharp gasp preceded a short word in Norse. "How dare—"

"Your reasoning is flawed," he interrupted. "If you refuse one aspect of my hospitality, you must refuse all."

"Hospitality?" Her voice rose as she gestured to her hobbled ankles. "This serves as hospitality in Dunlough? I am overcome by the way you honor me."

"Erika." His voice was low with warning.

She gave him a withering glance. "Three nights. I have been trapped here for three nights. And that heaping lump of clay you call a guard has not allowed anyone to enter, not even Gwynna with news of my brother!"

"Had you but asked him, Padraig would have told you how your brother fares."

She sniffed. "Had I but asked him, Padraig would have spat on me."

Conor's eyes narrowed. "You have a low opinion of the people of Dunlough, Angel."

"I have not seen enough of your people to form an opinion," she retorted. "Of the women, I know only Lady Gwynna. Of the three men I have met, one tried to kill me and another tried to rape me. The third, who guards your door, would have slain me without hesitation if you had but half-formed the request on your tongue."

Her hands fluttered against the collar about her neck. "You promised me a measure of freedom, Conor mac Ferghal," she said, her voice low with intensity. "I would have you keep your word."

Conor would keep his word. He would give her the freedom she craved. But the desire he felt upon seeing her again became an implacable thing, holding him more fiercely than the fetters held her. The Valkyrie was his prisoner, yet he was chained by his overwhelming desire for her. As long as it held him, he would never let her go.

Chapter Eight

He would keep her, but how?

An idea came to him. "You are right, my lady," he finally said. "I did promise you a measure of freedom, and I am a man of my word. I will free you from your chains, and I will take you to see your brother."

Joy burst like sunrise over her features, blinding him. That joy was followed by wariness. "Why would you do this?"

Never trusting. He could not blame her for that. "To prove to you that the people of Dunlough are not the ogres you believe us to be. Besides, I would not want to be kept from my sister, were our positions reversed."

She considered that, her eyes never halting their frank appraisal of him. "I will not lie with you."

Had he been in the process of drinking ale, Conor would have splattered it over both of them. As it was, it took him a few moments to collect his thoughts. Blessed Danu, the wench was plainspoken!

Recovering, Conor managed what he hoped was a formidable frown. "Have I asked you to lie with me?"

"No."

"And what makes you think that I will?"

It was *her* turn to sputter. "Most men want that."

His frown almost slipped into a smile. "I am not most men."

Her brows drew together in consternation for a moment. "Ah, you prefer other men."

"What?"

His roar caused her to wince. "Do not worry. It is a common enough practice in some places I have been, but it is passing strange."

Conor forced evenness into his tone. "No. I do not prefer men."

"Boys, then?"

He threw his arms wide. "Just because I did not ask to lie with you doesn't mean I would not."

That stopped her. "But you will not force me to your bed?"

Laughter welled inside him, rueful and biting, but he didn't let it out. "Despite my frightening countenance, I have never had to force a woman to lie with me. Your virtue, if you have it, is safe from me. You will come to me willing."

"Never!"

"Life is too uncertain for absolutes, lady warrior. Now, if you wish to see your brother, I need to remove your chains. Then you may refresh yourself."

His no-nonsense tone and seeming disinterest reassured Erika, and she forced herself to relax. At the same time, she felt a curious disappointment. Conor wasn't interested in her. She didn't know why, but that rankled.

Pulling a key from his tunic, he moved towards her. She shrank back, and he stopped. "I cannot unlock your shackles from across the room, Erika."

"I know that," she retorted, more angry with herself for her momentary fright than with him.

"Then let me do the deed and be done with it."

Instead of answering, Erika folded her arms across her chest and slowly, deliberately, turned her back to him. Even though she could not see him, she could feel the air stir as he moved behind her to unlock the heavy iron collar. She was instantly on the defensive, but not from the threat of physical harm.

His presence flowed around her, raising the tiny hairs on the back of her neck. She forgot how to breathe as his fingers lifted her braid over her shoulder to allow him better access to the lock.

Instead of releasing the braid, he began to run the silken length between his fingers. When he spoke, his breath caressed her nape, sending a fire coursing through her.

"I admire your spirit, my Valkyrie. Had those raiders possessed even a third as much, it would have been a fair fight."

Still reeling from the feel of her hair in his hands, it took a moment for her to answer. "You went after the raiders who attacked your village?"

Dark satisfaction swept through him. "Yes, and let one live to take the tale back over the border."

"I should have been there!" she cried, spinning to face him.

Her outburst stunned him. Hands settled on slim hips as she glared lavender daggers at him. "And what good could you have done?" he retorted. "You can walk but little."

"I would not need to walk," she answered tightly, as if he had insulted her. "I would have been on a horse. I would have used a short bow or sword just as easily astride as afoot."

She glanced at Conor, and he was surprised to see tears glittering behind her lashes. "I promised your people vengeance. Why have you denied me?"

What a strange, fascinating female! Disappointed because she wasn't able to go off and kill.

"The outlaws we attacked were hidden in the mountains," Conor explained. "To exact your revenge, you would have to be well healed. Some of those passes are dangerous, even for men who have ridden them all their lives. You would not have been able to fight if you were not able to keep up."

Erika's belligerent stance relaxed, though her eyes were still reproachful. "I am Viking. We take revenge very seriously."

"I believe you."

"I want to know what happened. You will tell me every detail. Now."

The command in her voice amused him, and he saw no reason to rebuke her for it. "May I remove the collar first?"

She acquiesced, and he stepped behind her again. After he removed the heavy iron collar she stepped away from him, her hands clasping her bruised neck as she sighed in relief. He set the ugly circlet on the nearby table, disgusted with himself for leaving her shackled, causing her further injury. There would be no way to hide the unsightly gouges from her brother. If the Northman possessed even a portion of his sister's temper, Conor would be hard-pressed to quench it.

He began giving her an edited version of the battle until she demanded a blow-by-blow accounting. Every bashing and thrust and kill she wanted to know. He gave in, telling the tale as he would with his men 'round a campfire, leaving nothing out. She enjoyed every bit of it, causing him to enjoy it as well.

Satisfied, she sat in the chair, her movements slow. "It is just as well that I did not accompany you. You are correct in saying that I am not quite ready for combat." It seemed to rankle her to make that admission.

Conor knelt before her to remove the leg shackles, attempting with little success to avoid staring at the slender columns of her legs. She was near to fleeing his touch, like a nervous colt. He could not blame her for that—had she been privy to his thoughts, she would be bolting for the door.

The largeness of her frame extended to her feet, but they were thin and shapely, and seemed fragile inside the cumbersome metal. She gasped when he lifted her foot, grasping her knees together with linked hands. He respected her privacy, but it was a near thing. How simple it would've been to allow his hand to glide upward, to seek out the mystery she hid behind her knees. And perhaps he would reach it before she attempted to wring his neck.

He made quick work of the leg irons then sat back on his haunches, staring at the woman too desirable for her own good—or his. "I am glad to hear you admit you are not ready for combat. It means you are human after all." He placed amusement in his tone, knowing she would be offended.

The ploy worked. The silver head rose as she once again fixed him with a glare. "Are you mocking me, Devil?" Her voice was dangerously soft as her hand unconsciously strayed to her hip where the pommel of her sword would lie.

A lesser man would have taken her inquiry for the warning it was and retreated. Conor was not that man. "By the beard of St. Patrick, I would never mock someone with such an eagerness to fight."

His lips curved in a goading caricature of a smile. "Unless of course, I could defeat his good self. Or her self, as the case may be."

It was a challenge and Erika knew it. Her smile was like sunshine and her eyes flashed as she purred, "And do you think you can best me?"

Conor allowed his gaze to travel the length of her, noting the defiant tilt to her chin, and the still-sharp planes of her face and arms. "Now, of a certain. After you heal, more than possible."

Erika rose to her feet, her grin just as feral as his. "I accept your challenge—if you swear to free us when I am victorious."

So that was her game. Conor admired her cunning as he gained his feet. "I will accept your winning as Danegeld payment, and I will give you the freedom of the dun while you heal."

Erika gripped his hand. If she worried about how it engulfed hers, she gave no sign. "Not that I intend to lose, but what will you set the Danegeld for if I do?"

Your surrender. "I have not decided. I will think on it. But perhaps now you would like to see your brother?"

Her face lit up like dawn breaking across a lough. "He will live?" she asked, her eyes aglow.

Conor blinked at her. When she wasn't talking so calm about killing, she looked most female. "Yes. Despite our efforts to the contrary, you Northmen are resilient. If you wish it, refresh yourself, and I will escort you to him."

Erika hurried through as complete an ablution as she could manage with Conor present. How she longed for a bath. Quick dips in frigid loughs had been a staple of her life for the past few years. Most of the *bruidheans*, places of rest and hospitality for travelers, had been ransacked by the lawless or feuding clans.

As if reading her thoughts, Conor said, "A bath will be waiting for you, when you return." He handed her a robe of blue so deep it was nearly violet. "Let us go," he said brusquely, and opened the chamber door.

Following Conor into the hall, Erika looked about her with interest. There were four other rooms on this level that she could see, two each flanking his room. The hall was wide, with solid, stone walls and planked floors, and lit every few feet with torches. Conor placed her to his right then led her down a curving stair that opened into a massive hall. There were two hearths large enough to roast an ox flanking four long trestle tables. The packed dirt floor was strewn with fresh rushes and the double entrance doors were open to allow the smoke from the hearths to escape.

A handful of people dotted the great hall, servants cleaning the tables or serving a few latecomers. All activity jerked to a halt as Conor and his charge walked past. The stares ranged from curiosity to outright hostility. Erika lifted her chin high, determined to ignore them.

She didn't speak until they reached the second stairway. "Your people do not seem taken with me," she remarked, as if commenting on the weather.

"They have no love for outlaws or any who help them," he replied, his tone devoid of inflection.

"They must know by now that I did not raid the village," she protested. "I only wanted to help."

"Your help brought death to their friends and loved ones." Conor's voice was hard. He set a brisk pace up the stairs.

Erika puffed along behind him. Her circuits about the room had not prepared her for the amount of stairs they were climbing, but by Odin's blinded eye, she would not tell him to slow. "It was war," she argued, surprised that she had to explain it. "Perhaps the battle should not have happened, but surely they understand—"

"Death is death, Angel," he said curtly. "They understand that husbands will never come home again, fathers will not teach their sons to hunt, and some weddings will not occur. Would you be unaffected by your brother's death?"

"I would weep for Olan, but I know that if he died in battle, he would be taken to Valhalla with singing and feasting. For a warrior, you speak strange words, Devil of Dunlough."

"A blade is not the only way to settle a disagreement." His anger showed through in his voice, and he did nothing to temper it. How could she talk so calm of killing and death? What had happened to her that she could speak of it as some women discussed their weaving?

"Many are they who are quick to war, and they are the ones quick to die. Be sure of this, Angel of Death: I fear little in this world and I have stared Death in the eyes many times. When I pick up my sword, I use it—and not to wound."

He stopped before another door complete with a pair of guards. He dismissed them and they left, giving her more hostile looks. Conor opened the door and motioned for her to enter.

Wary, she peered inside, then hurried in as she caught sight of the man lying on the pallet before the fire. With a small cry, she knelt beside him.

Conor turned to leave, but paused, caught by a curious sound. Erika was speaking in her native tongue, but that wasn't what caught his ears. No, it was the way she touched the face of the man on the pallet, the way she leaned over him, the way her shoulders shook.

The Angel of Death was crying.

It caused a curious sensation in Conor, as if something thawed inside him. He supposed it was the anger draining out of him at the realization that Erika was not as callous as she seemed. That 'twas possible she had a heart. Deep in thought, Conor closed the door, leaving brother and sister alone.

Chapter Nine

"Who is it that brings tears to your eyes?" Olan demanded. "Tell me, that I may give him grief."

Her brother's voice, humming with menace, stanched her tears and forced a laugh from her. "Ease your berserker rage. My tears are for you, because you live."

With a sweep of golden lashes, the fury in his eyes diminished. "It was a near thing, Rika," he admitted, using slow movements to sit upright on the makeshift pallet. "I could hear the hoofbeats of the Valkyr, come to bear me to Valhalla. But into their path came an angel with raven hair and eyes as green as new-grown grass."

"The Lady Gwynna," Erika confirmed. "She is a gifted healer."

A curious expression crossed her brother's face at the mention of the healer, a potent mixture of anger and yearning battling for supremacy. Anger won out. "She would not let you come to me."

"Gwynna was not able, though she did try," Erika insisted. "She told me what little she could of your progress while I was locked away, and for that I am grateful."

Blue eyes, blazing like sapphires, pierced her own. "All I knew of you was that you were alive, and at times, I could feel your fear."

His voice was as hard as the tempered edge of a sword. "Have you been harmed? Did that scarred whoreson who stabbed you in the belly attempt to touch you?"

Erika hesitated. She had never lied to her brother, though she had omitted telling him things at times. "My only injuries were from the battle. One guard attempted to harm me, but Conor prevented it. And more than that, I was able to challenge him to a duel, to first blood. When I win, we will go free."

Her news did not have the reaction Erika expected. A short, bitter word broke free of her brother's clenched features. "That you even have to face this is more than I can bear," he said in a harsh whisper. "I have failed in my duty to you."

"No, Olan, you haven't! Do not blame yourself for this."

"How can I not?" Anger drove him to his feet, though he swayed with the effort. He raked his uninjured hand through his shoulder-length mane, away from his sweating brow. "This life we lead—this is no life for you!"

Concern rising like bile in her throat she rose to her feet, facing him. "But it is the life I chose."

"That does not make it right!"

The outburst must have cost him dearly. A moan escaped him as he closed his eyes, leaning his head against the wall. Erika hurried to his side. "Olan?"

"Allfather, God in heaven, give me strength," he prayed, so low she almost didn't hear him. Opening his eyes, he stared at her, and Erika saw the anguish apparent in his gaze. "Rika, I do not wish to argue with you."

"Then do not." She quickly poured watery wine for him, pressing the cup into his hand.

He swallowed deeply, then refused her urging to sit on the small stool. "It is not I who will argue," he said, his voice hard. "I'll stand toe to toe with you as I tell you what you do not wish to hear. And you will hear what I have to say."

When he took that tone, Erika knew better than to challenge her brother. That did not mean that she would be complaisant. She sat his mug on the low table then folded her arms, waiting for the speech she had heard so many times before.

Olan smiled faintly at the stubborn tilt of her chin, but his expression sobered when he began to speak. "I have never been happy with the path your life has taken," he said. "You deserve more than this."

With one massive shoulder he pushed away from the wall, cradling his mending right arm with his left. "I swore a solemn vow when our father made his voyage to the afterworld. I vowed that I would do whatever was necessary to see you safe and happy. I have put us upon this course, not only for the gold and silver we have acquired, but also with the hopes that you would find a place you love."

No longer able to keep silent, she cried out, "But I am content!"

Slowly, Olan shook his head. "You are not content. I know of the tears you thought to conceal from me in the early days of our travels. I also know the day you ceased to shed those tears. I am your twin, remember? I can see the sadness in you. I have lost the sister with the ready smiles and bright laughter, lost her to a woman who only knows death and destruction."

"Olan—"

"That is why we were heading to Donegal. Larangar wanted to go to Anglia to join Canute, with you protected as his wife."

Shocked beyond measure, Erika could only stare at her brother. She sank onto the three-legged stool, trying to assimilate his words. "We were going to leave *Iraland*?" she whispered, her voice catching. "You were sending me to Anglia as Larangar's wife *against my will*?"

"No, not against your will," Olan replied, flushing with anger. "Never against your will, Erika. You must know that."

"Then what is this plan you speak of, this decision you made concerning my future that you did not share with me?" She surged to her feet. "How could you do this to me?"

"Because I will not see you die with a sword in your belly!"

He leaned heavily against the wall, strength ebbing from him. Startled to see her brother so angry, she rushed to him. "Olan, please do not tax yourself so!"

"Do you not know how it plagues me each time you are injured, no matter how slight?" he asked, his voice rasping with each word. "I would take you away from that, Erika. Lars wanted that as well. He has...had...loved you long."

She should have been shocked at his words, she knew. But deep inside, she had always known the truth. They had known the dark-haired Dane for most of their lives—their fathers had been best friends and often went a-viking together. She knew Lars had held deep affection for her, and had often joked about claiming her for his own if he could ever best her in swordplay.

"I loved Lars, but I could not have wed him," she said, her hands resting lightly on his shoulders. "That is not the sort of love I bore for him."

"I know." Olan sighed. "That is why I did not tell you. If Larangar could not convince you to wed him and settle in the Danelaw, I would have taken you elsewhere."

"But the reason we did not go Anglia from the start is because there are too many men there who knew our father, who might be loyal to Gunthar," Erika protested. "The risk was, and still is, too great."

His face was becoming alarmingly ashen as he ground his words out. "I will find a place for you. I failed you with Gunthar, and I have failed you here. If we live through this, I will not fail you again."

Her heart hammering in her throat, Erika brought the stool to him so that he could sit on it while resting his back against the wall. "You have never failed me, Olan," she whispered fervently, tears pricking her eyes once again. "I have never blamed you for what happened at home. Please believe that."

She found a cloth and a basin of water, and set about mopping his perspiring brow. He sighed gratefully, but the look he gave her was one filled with an anguish years old. "I know you hold me blameless, Rika, but I blame myself enough for the two of us."

Erika had never before considered that her brother carried such a weight with him. Olan had always been light of heart, and save for his berserker rage, his anger was as fleeting as a summer squall. Her heart twisted painfully inside her, knowing that she was the cause of his grief. Her own unhappiness she could bear, but not his.

She sought to lighten his mood. "When I win my duel with the man called Devil, we will find a place to call home, I promise."

"What if you lose?"

Erika laughed, a sound like silver bells. "I have never lost, Olan, as well you know, even when it did not matter. I will not lose now."

"If our lives are at stake, perhaps I should be the one to challenge him."

"I do not believe our lives are forfeit," she replied. "When I challenged Conor, he did not have time to set a prize for himself. But I will ask next time I see him."

Olan raised an eyebrow. "You are this familiar with the man who wished you dead?"

Erika had the grace to blush. Olan's mood was lightening. She would not ruin it by telling him she had been living in Conor's bedchamber the last three days. "Our deaths are no longer uppermost in his thoughts," she said, hoping it was true. "And he did subdue the true raiders."

Olan perked up. "Did the raiders suffer greatly?"

"Absolutely." She related the tale to Olan, and soon they were both laughing with delight.

Chapter Ten

Conor was startled by the sound of Erika's laughter. It was a sweet, musical sound. He wondered what it would be like to share such a laugh with her.

The laughter ended with the opening of the door. Erika shot to her feet, preparing to defend her brother against harm. Conor held up his hands. "Ease, Erika. No one here will harm you."

She relaxed her fighting stance, though she remained standing before her brother, blocking him from Conor's view. The look she gave him was wary, yet pleading. "Is Lady Gwynna about? My brother needs her."

Before he could answer, Gwynna pushed past him into the room. Erika stepped aside as his sister hurried over, and Conor had his first good look at the blond giant sitting against the wall. He had been impressive lying facedown in a puddle of his own blood. Now, even half mended, the Viking was a force to be reckoned with.

He seemed not to notice Conor's presence, focusing instead on Gwynna. "*Mo aingeal.*"

My angel. Conor frowned at the endearment. How dare this man be so familiar with his sister? His hand clenched into fists and he stepped forward. The anxious expressions on the women's faces halted him. Perhaps the Viking was still delirious from his ordeal, and thought Gwynna someone else.

Erika stood in the center of the small chamber, wringing her hands. The love she bore her brother was unmistakable, as was the concern. Conor knew he could use that to his advantage. He also knew he wouldn't have to.

He moved into the room, coming to stand beside the fair-haired woman. The need to reassure her, to erase the pinched look from her expression and replace it with the laughter he had heard earlier, was strong, and he gave in to it.

"Gwynna is the best healer in Connacht." His hand, of its own volition, moved to rest on her shoulder. When she glanced up at him, startled, he continued, "Her knowledge of the healing arts is handed down through generations of Dunlough women and Druid healers. You need not fear for your brother's life at her hands."

A ghost of a smile flitted behind her eyes. "I have seen the truth—"

"*Diabhal!*"

More epithet than name, the word was uttered low and harsh by Erika's brother. The Viking, having finally noticed Conor's presence, climbed to his feet, his eyes blazing. Gwynna tried her best to return him to the stool, but the man had the width and breadth of a *cromlech*, as immovable as those stone tombs. Conor read the clear intensity of the blue-eyed giant and knew they would be soon to battle.

"Gwynna, take Erika and wait outside," he charged his sister. "Olan and I have something that we must discuss."

"No."

Both women spoke simultaneous warnings, emerald and amethyst eyes flashing.

"Conor..."

"Olan..."

"Wait outside," the blond man commanded, his eyes never leaving Conor's. "No blood will be shed while you are gone."

Gwynna turned toward Olan, her back spear-straight. "I did not pull you from death's embrace just to send you back again. If you re-injure yourself, your healing will be a long, painful one."

Conor thought it most amusing until Erika turned to him with equal vehemence. "Do not think to have my brother stand in my stead in our duel, or I will give you cause to regret it."

They turned and left, their positions clear.

The atmosphere in the tiny chamber dropped several degrees as the blond man's eyes turned upon him with cold intent. "I will champion my sister in this challenge of yours," the pale warrior said with the deep rumble of a tree caving under the weight of ice. "I will enjoy returning to you that which you dealt to her."

Conor felt the familiar bloodsurge grip him. "It will be my pleasure to give you leave to try."

The Viking smiled, as if pleased by his answer. "Whether I kill you or merely injure you will depend on your answer to my question," he said, his tone of voice and posture that of studied nonchalance.

"Indeed? And what question have you that decides my fate?"

"Just this: What do you intend with my sister?"

Liking the younger man's bluntness despite himself, Conor assumed a bland expression. "Why do you believe I intend anything towards your sister?"

"Everyone intends something towards my sister. Can you tell me you do not?"

That steady blue gaze measured him like a spice merchant selling his precious wares. Conor found that he could not have been dishonest with the Viking if he wanted to. "No, I cannot. I do have intentions towards your sister, intentions I feel you would not be adverse to."

"And they are?"

"To marry her and have an heir."

The words surprised him, surprised him further with their rightness. The Devil of Dunlough having sons with the Angel of Death. His people would be protected long after he was gone.

A guffaw split the sudden, brittle silence. Olan's shoulders shook with the force of his laughter, cutting to a hiss of pain.

Conor's satisfaction became consternation. "This is no jest. I mean what I say."

"I believe you do," Olan replied, laughter rippling his voice. "Yet the fact that you still stand tells me that you have not made your intentions known to my sister."

Surprised and unsettled by the Northman's obvious mirth, Conor could only stare. "Think you that Erika will not be amenable to my offer?"

The response was wry. "Amenable is not an adequate description of the Angel of Death."

"Why would she refuse me?"

That caused another pain-filled laugh. "Why indeed? Is it because she has refused grander offers than yours? Is it because she has bested all who have challenged her for her hand?" Cobalt eyes narrowed at him with murderous intent. "Perhaps she will refuse you until the bruises from the shackles you had her in are healed."

There was nothing Conor could say to alleviate the other man's anger, except, "How long before you are able to defend your sister's honor?"

To his surprise, Olan shook his head. "It is not my place. Erika challenged you, or you goaded her into challenging you. She is the one you will have to meet, and the one you will have to defeat, may God bless you."

"I found her to be a worthy opponent for the brief time our swords crossed. You believe she is that good, then?"

"She is."

Conor digested that bit of information. "Then you have no objections to me wedding your sister?"

"Erika is a strong woman and a strong fighter. She vowed long ago to wed the man who can defeat her in a trial of combat. If you believe you are such a one, I give you leave to try. Tell my sister your intentions."

A twinkle returned to his eyes. "But I do not wish to be around when you do."

"CAN YOU HEAR ANYTHING?"

The Valkyrie pressed her cheek against the smooth wooden door. Gwynna loomed behind her, straining to catch any sound emanating from the room beyond. There was nothing.

"That is a good portent, isn't it?" she asked. "After all, we'd hear shouting if they were coming to blows."

Erika paused, considering. "I have seen Olan give a great battle cry at the outset of a fight. But when he enters his berserker rage, he becomes extremely quiet."

A nervous giggle bubbled from Gwynna's lips. She should have been appalled to hear the Northwoman speak so calmly about her brother's killing tendencies. She should have walked away and never looked behind her. She should have never given birth to the fragile dream in her heart.

She cleared her throat. "Your brother, is he...is he quick to anger?"

"No," came the answer. "He is patient with the old and the young, but he does not suffer fools."

Fools? What manner of fools? Those touched in the head, or those set in their ways? Gwynna gathered her courage to phrase another question. "Has Olan ever s-struck a woman?"

The warrior-woman lifted her shining head from the door to regard her, her expression curious. "I have never seen my brother strike a woman. But I have not seen a woman give him cause to."

She must have blanched or made a distressing noise, for Erika was suddenly by her side, supporting her. "Are you unwell?" the Viking asked. "Who heals the healer when the healer falls ill?"

Gwynna managed to regain her footing, and a measure of her composure. "I am fine," she assured the silver-haired woman. "I just took an improper breath."

She smoothed her skirts and shook out her intricately styled hair. She knew enough, Gwynna thought. She would not pry further into Olan's life. She did not want to know if there was someone waiting for him... "Was Olan betrothed when you left your homeland?"

Lavender eyes regarded her in a steady manner that seemed to see straight through her. "You ask strange questions, Gwynna."

Feeling her cheeks flame, Gwynna made a great show of straightening her skirts yet again. "I am powerful curious about the life of the man I lo...saved," she stammered. By the saints, what had she been about to say?

Erika stared at her, and Gwynna felt as if every tumultuous emotion was illuminated in her cheeks. There was more writ there than she knew, for the Valkyrie said, "You favor my brother, don't you?"

As soon as she asked the question, Erika knew she had guessed correctly. The healer's cheeks paled, then flared with color.

"No! He is a warrior and I am a healer. I abhor what he does!"

Erika chose not to argue that point, though she privately believed Gwynna protested far too vehemently for the circumstances. She knew that women found her brother pleasing, and told Gwynna so.

The healer lapsed into a fit of coughing. Erika pounded her back until Gwynna was able to decry her assistance. "Are you certain you have no need of a potion or herbal?" she asked worriedly. "I know a small amount of herbology. I would not wish you to fall ill, while I did nothing to assist you."

"My thanks, but I need nothing."

Erika stared at the other woman with unabashed curiosity. Her color was still high, and her eyes shining with surprising anger. Why was Gwynna irate? Erika had not thought of the healer as being odd, or simple. Was that why she was unmarried? Surely the workings of marriage for Irish nobility could be no different than they were in her homeland. Gwynna was, like herself, several years past marrying age. But perhaps things were done differently here than in Denmark. After all, Conor was a prince of Dunlough, leader of his people, and he was still unmarried.

A muffled coughing sound came through the door, quickly silenced. "Was that laughter?"

Gwynna looked as perplexed as she. "Why would there be laughter?"

"I do not know." Even knowing how quickly Olan's moods changed, Erika did not believe he would be sharing jests with their jailer.

"How long has it been?"

"Too long." She made to push open the wooden door when it was suddenly pulled from her hands. She was propelled into the room, into Conor's arms.

She glared at him before disentangling herself and moving to her brother's side, examining him for signs of further injury. The casual rage he had displayed minutes before was replaced by amusement.

"What could have transpired here that amuses you so?" she asked.

Olan looked from her to Conor then back again, his eyes twinkling with mirth. "Did you know that the *jarl* of Dunlough is a weaver of tales? He told me a marvel of one just now."

"He did?" Gwynna's surprise was apparent, and Erika had to agree with her. The Devil of Dunlough did not seem the manner of man given to fancy. "What tale is this?"

"One that can be told at a later time," Conor said.

Erika gave him what she hoped was a quelling glance. "You look as if you've sat on a knife. Is that how you intimidate your followers?"

Gwynna gasped, and Olan made a choking sound, but Conor simply gazed at her, gray eyes glinting with cold amusement. "I hardly intimidate you, do I Angel? Not that I do not try."

"He always yells, as well," Erika informed her brother. "I do not believe the man knows how to speak in a normal tone of voice."

Conor leaned toward her. "Oh, I can whisper, my Angel, fair enough." His voice was barely a breath on her ear. "Though I usually save it for the bedchamber."

Erika flushed, and barely suppressed a shiver. She was suddenly uncomfortably conscious of the long length of him, standing indecently close behind her. Did he always give off this heat?

Olan must have noticed her shiver, for when he spoke to her it was in Norse. "Are you sure you mean to do battle with this man, whatever the consequences?"

Erika knelt beside her brother, giving him an affectionate kiss. "I am honor-bound to do this, Olan," she whispered back. "It is I who challenged him, and I who will face him."

She gave him an infectious grin. "You may have what remains of him when I am done."

Her quip was rewarded. Olan erupted with booming laughter, which quickly converted to grunts of discomfort.

"Give over, Angel, and let Gwynna see to her patient," Conor ordered, his tone biting.

Instantly she obeyed the tone of command in Conor's voice, returning to his side before she could stop herself. She drew up sharply. Conor was no *jarl*. She folded her arms stubbornly, ignoring a twinge of pain.

He matched her frown, then visibly relaxed. "Come, Erika," he said. "Perhaps you could use a meal. And something to divert your worry for your brother. I noticed pieces on the chess set were moved. Do you perhaps know how to play?"

"Almost as well as I handle my sword," Erika replied, causing Conor to grin.

"I do enjoy it when you challenge me."

She could not let even that remark go uncontested. "Be sure that I intend to win."

He took her taunt with an unexpected calm. "So do I, Angel. So do I."

Placing his hand at the small of her back, he turned her toward the door. Erika was reluctant to leave. Her time with Olan had been woefully short. She was not ready to leave him yet. With a frown, she dug in her heels.

Conor frowned back, placing his hands on his hips. He drew a breath, but before he could speak, Gwynna cut in. "I can tend to your brother much better with plenty of room," she told Erika, her fingers lightly running over the golden-haired man's bandages. "I swear to you, I will care for Olan as I do Conor."

"I hope not," Olan muttered in Norse, causing Erika to stifle a shocked laugh. Did her brother feel something for the dark-haired Gael? Did he know how Gwynna felt towards him?

Disconcerted, she acquiesced, following Conor out of the room. Perhaps, once their situation was not so dire, Olan would be able to return here as he truly was, a Viking noble-man with wealth enough to pay any bride-price.

Erika glanced at Conor as he led the way down the hall. After she won their duel, would he let her brother court Gwynna? Or would his anger at losing color his judgment?

A hard sigh escaped her. Blessed Freyja, but she was tired. The pounding in her head matched the throbbing in her leg. Did he have to make such long strides? She was hav-ing a difficult time keeping up with him. "Your sister is ac-customed to having her way, is she not?"

Conor looked down at Erika. "In Dunlough, her word is second only to my own. And sometimes, not even that."

"Why have you no wife?"

Erika only asked the question for conversation's sake. She needed to keep him talking until she could catch her breath and match strides with him again. But the simple question had the opposite effect on him.

Conor jerked to a halt, causing Erika to crash into him. Only his hands gripping her arms kept her upright. It was excruciating pain, for he seemed unaware how tightly he gripped her wounded arm. She ground her teeth to keep from crying out.

"I was wed once, but she was no wife."

The menace in his voice was palpable. His eyes were hazed over as if caught by memories. Obviously they were not pleasant, for Conor had the look of a man close to violence. What had his wife done to cause such fury?

Conor realized how tightly he gripped her arm, and quickly let go. He bit back an oath as she shuddered in relief. "Did I hurt you?" His voice was harsh as he loomed over her.

Weakened, she took a stumbling step back. "I...the stairs," she murmured thinly. "No idea there would be that many. Does your hall always slant like this?"

Suddenly she was off her feet, her face pressed against his chest. The man was like a wall. Ineffectually, she struggled. "Free me! I am no simpering maid to be carried like a sack of grain!"

"If I put you down, you would fall on your face," Conor growled, his strides eating up the length of the hall. "You were near to swooning!"

"I do not swoon!" Erika bellowed, and instantly regretted it. A moan escaped her.

His face darkened like thunderclouds as he kicked open a door. "Why did you not tell me you felt ill?" he demanded, entering her chamber—his chamber.

"I did not, until after we had crossed the hall," she answered, defensive. "Besides, I wanted to see my brother."

He laid her on the bed, and she immediately became lost in the huge softness. She closed her eyes, taking in the sensation of floating. If only it could ease the hoof beats in her head.

A cool, damp cloth was pressed to her forehead, and she nearly cried out in relief. The bed creaked, and she knew that Conor sat beside her. She kept her eyes closed, humiliated at being weak in front of him.

"Have you ever been injured before, Valkyrie?" Conor demanded.

She started to shake her head, groaned, then whispered, "Not like this."

He leaned over her. "I have seen men with gaping wounds continue to fight without feeling pain, then fall to the ground, dead. I have seen those thought dead come back to life. And I have seen those with minor wounds recover, only to sicken and die a few days later because they thought to return to their duties before they were true and ready. Your stubbornness could get you killed."

She could not check the tears this time, though she tried behind eyes clenched tight. "I am a warrior. I will not be weak in front of you!"

"Why?" he asked, astounded. "You think I'll belittle you for your pain?"

Her silence was answer enough. "Erika, you were wounded. You cannot expect to be hale and hearty in just a few days. A warrior should know when to admit to pain, so that it may be taken care of. A warrior not ready for battle but refuses to admit it can cost his side the fight."

He reached out to capture a lone tear that had gathered beneath her eye, surprised to see his fingers shaking but not surprised at the cause. Desire had him in as sure a grip as spring's hold upon the land. Huskiness limned his voice as he said, "I'd never belittle you."

She opened her eyes and he could see confusion and wonderment in them.

"Conor..." Her voice was soft, halting over the Gaelic as it was wont to do. "Am I a guest or a prisoner? Your...kindness is appreciated, but surely you do not treat everyone in my position this way?"

Her position was lying beneath him on the feathered mattress. Instead of answering, he stroked her hair. A pale ringlet lay across her shoulder and he picked it up, wrapping it about his finger. "Your hair is like moonlight made substantial," he whispered with wonder.

Again he touched her cheek. "I must know if there be a woman hidden within the warrior."

He kissed her.

He could not help himself. The deep amethyst eyes drew him in, and those lips were so inviting, maddening. It was the barest of touches at first, as he waited for her to flinch away from his ravaged face.

She did not, and it warmed him anew. With a low growl he deepened the kiss, wrapping her hair about his fist to bring her closer.

Surprised, Erika opened her mouth to protest, and Conor's tongue shot through.

Blessed Freyja, what was he doing to her? Fire coursed through her veins, pooling in her belly like molten fire. Her body clamored like bells warning of attack. The Devil was burning her alive. She moaned against his lips.

Abruptly, Conor pulled away from her. He surged to his feet, his breath coming in harsh gasps. "No, my sweet Angel, I do not treat everyone this way," he finally answered, his eyes glittering dangerously. "But you would do better to ask me what I will claim as my prize for defeating you in our duel. Sure you're wanting to know?"

Dread filled Erika's stomach even as she still burned from his kisses. She most assuredly did not want to know, but knew he would tell her anyway.

She was not disappointed. "When you surrendered your weapon to me, it was symbolic of surrendering yourself," he told her. "You gave your life over to me, to use as I see fit. You belong to me now, my Angel. If I decided to hang you, I could do so. But that is not what I choose.

"I choose to make the Angel of Death wife to the Devil of Dunlough."

Shock coursed through her, rendering her momentarily mute. But only momentarily.

"Nei!" The word burst from her lungs with enough force to drag her upright. "I will never be wed to you. Never!"

Easily, far too easily, he captured her thrashing fists in his massive hands. "Never is something you cannot guarantee, even if your name is Angel."

Furious, flailing, she fought against his merciless tone. "But the duel! You said you would let us go when I win."

"'Tis certain I made that wager to satisfy your honor."

"You will not defeat me," she seethed. "Thor will guide my hand!"

Conor laughed, a sound that chilled her soul and dampened her fury. "Aislingh said much the same, when she tried to kill me. Perhaps, had she prayed to your gods, her blade would have found my heart instead of my face."

He loomed over her, his face so truly fierce that Erika shrank against the pillows. "You and I, however, will have our battle of honor. Try to kill me then. But know this: I will be victorious. The Devil of Dunlough will have the Angel of Death for his bride!"

Chapter Eleven

"You cannot marry her!"

Conor sat upon the raised dais at the far end of Dunlough's main hall. Before him were gathered the heads of the prominent families of the *tuath*, as well as Gwynna, Ardan, Old Aine and Brochadh, the *tuath's* priest. They all stared at him with identical expressions of shock and revulsion.

Their reaction was tame compared to the lightning bolt that was his intended. Once the initial astonishment had receded, Erika hurled invectives at him, and when strong words in Gaelic and Norse failed to curtail her anger, she began to hurl objects. It was a measure of his wisdom that he'd chosen a strategic retreat.

Conor regarded the tribal elder who had made the vehement declaration. "Why can I not marry her?"

Again the gaping. "Because she is Viking!"

"I have noticed that," he replied, assuming a relaxed position on the ornate carved chair. Inside he was strung tight. Courtesy dictated that he inform the tribal elders, these men who had elected him as their head, of his choice for a wife. He did not need their approval, but life would be smoother with it.

"The Northmen have been in Ireland for more than two hundred years, and in that time have married into some of the greatest royal families. Erika and her brother are from a notable family in their native land."

He wasn't positive about that, but Conor knew the imperious manner so intrinsic to Erika's character did not belong to a scullery maid.

"But she is the Angel of Death!" another protested. "She attempted to kill you!"

"And I attempted to kill her. She will likely attempt to do so again, when we duel."

"Duel?" Gwynna finally spoke. "Did you say duel?"

Focusing on him, the gathering waited, impatient, for his words. "On Beltaine, the Angel and I will duel. If she wins, she and her brother will go free, and I will consider their debt paid. If I win, Erika Silverhair and I will be wed ere the day is out."

The uproar was immediate and intense. Conor let it run its course for scant moments before he spoke again. "Think on it: the Angel of Death and the Devil of Dunlough. Those names have been feared with good reason. They will be feared even more so, when they are joined.

"You have maintained me as your leader despite my late wife's attempt otherwise." He pushed his hair back from his forehead, noting those who still averted their eyes. "This token among others, I realize, has shriveled my attractiveness as a husband to your daughters. At least, that is what I have assumed, having seen no evidence to the contrary."

Silence greeted that last remark, and Conor let it sink in. He knew the women of his clan found his countenance displeasing. Then there was the matter of his demons. No, no one wanted to marry his daughter to the Devil of Dunlough, despite the ties such a marriage would give him.

Conor surveyed the guilty expressions of those gathered before him. He held them blameless, for he knew he had been less than civil, less than human, since Clontarf and his wife's perfidy. Not marriage material by any measure.

Yet it was time. He knew it in the depths of his soul. He had to ensure that something more than killing and battle was his legacy to his people. An heir would do just that, a son with the strength and the intelligence to stand tall against the chaos and evil that abounded through the island. Erika Silverhair could give birth to such progeny. He would wed her, whether the elders approved or not.

Still, he had one final threat. "If you do not approve of my decision, you may vote another as chieftain of the tribe. Dunlough can stand alone if need be."

Like a boom of thunder, incredulity raced through the gathering. It was not every day that a chieftain threatened to abnegate his duties. For the last seven generations Conor's family had led the tribe, and their *tuath* was one of the largest of the clan. The implied threat was that Dunlough would break away and form its own clanship, taking its fighting men with it. Reluctant to rule or no, Conor knew he could acquit himself when the need arose.

"Do you love her so much, then, this Angel of Death?"

Old Aine asked the question. Conor had no idea why the wise woman would pose such a query before the elders. But he was an honest man and therefore did not flinch as he answered, "No, I do not love her. But together we will forge strong sons to defend this *tuath* and protect the tribe.

Whether I am chieftain or no, I will have the Valkyrie for my bride."

He rose to his feet then stepped off the dais. "Now, I must beg your pardon. You may avail yourselves of my table. I must see my betrothed."

His "betrothed" was enraged.

Erika twirled her staff, her movements a deadly dance as she sweated in the practice yard. Faster and faster she whirled from stance to stance, a gleaming dervish of lethal intent. She pushed her body as far as it would go, then she pushed it more. Even then, when pain became her companion, she was unable to escape her seething thoughts.

The Devil had tricked her! And fool that she was, she had walked blindly into his trap. She thought the prince of Dunlough was an honorable man. She thought he would allow her to work her hostage-geld by using her skills in battle. Instead, he wished to wed her—to *wed* her!

Pivoting with a growl, Erika used the staff to attack a wooden shield attached to a five-foot-high post. Even four days later, she still smoldered. After his stunning announcement, Conor had given her the use of his rooms and leave to practice her skills. Yet Erika had been loath to leave the chamber, loath to see the expressions of the people of Dunlough, loath to see her brother, loath to see Conor. Why would a man chain himself with a woman he clearly didn't want, especially one who'd tried to kill him and given the opportunity would certainly put her hands to his throat the moment she saw him?

The staff wasn't doing enough damage. She tossed it down in utter disgust and reached to her sides for the twin short-swords. That Conor had seen fit to return her weapons to train with showed how confident he was of his victory. She would show him just how wrong he was.

With a chilling ululation, she attacked the defenseless shield. Within minutes, it was nothing more than splinters. Breathing harshly, Erika spun about, seeking something else to destroy.

"Erika!" Olan's voice broke through the red haze of rage that surrounded her. "If you re-injure yourself it will be even longer before Conor can fairly fight you. Is that what you want?"

"What I want," she began, balancing a blade in the palm of one hand, "is my freedom. What I want is to erase the self-satisfied, pompous smirk from his face. What I want—" and by this time she was yelling, "—is to wrap my hands about his throat!"

"Calm yourself, *wer-datter*," Olan cut in brusquely. "A warrior who loses his temper has already lost the battle."

Sheathing her twin blades, Erika walked to where her brother sat in the shade of a large tree. The past four days had done wonders for Olan, though she was sure that was due more to Gwynna's attention than to the healer's herbs. They had not discussed it, but Erika knew that her brother had never regarded a woman with the intensity he reserved for the dark-haired Gael.

His lack of fury when Erika had finally imparted to him the nature of her challenge was suspect.

"You knew, did you not?" she accused, standing before him. "Even before I told you, you knew what the Devil had in store for me!"

"I did not know Conor's intentions until he spoke to me in the chamber, the same day he told you himself."

"Oh, it's Conor now, is it?" she retorted hotly. "Are you so friendly with the man you vilely called *diabhal* not four nights ago?"

Crimson stained her brother's cheeks. "I laughed at him when he told me his intent. Laughed! You have been defending your right against marriage nearly half your life, and I told him so." He looked at her. "I do not need to ask you if you favor his wager, do I?"

"You do not."

Shifting beneath the shaded branches, Olan leaned towards her. "Would it be so terrible a thing, to be married to the mac Ferghal?" he asked. "He is *jarl* of Dunlough. This place, its lands, and its people would be yours as well. You would finally have a home. You would be safe."

Erika stared out over the practice yard. She was all too aware of how much her brother wanted her to have a place of her own, a place to live happily for the remainder of her days. "Do you really believe I would be safe here?" she wondered. "The people of Dunlough know that I tried to kill him once. They know I fought the battle that cost many of them husbands and sons."

She shook her head, answering her question herself. "No, I would not be safe here. Conor's people would not accept me, especially when their ruler hates me."

"If he hated you, he would not offer you the honor of marriage," he said in a reasonable tone.

"Honor?" The word was strangled and bitter on her tongue. "What does the man know of honor?"

"Do you still have your maidenhead?"

The blunt question blindsided her, and she could only stare at her brother wordlessly. Heat rushed to her cheeks and it was some moments before she could stammer. "Y-yes."

"Then surely that proves his honor to you."

Confusion rippling through her, Erika turned away from her brother, her eyes to the packed earth of the practice area. Olan's defense of the man she preferred to consider as her enemy felt like a betrayal. Yet his judgments of character had saved their lives more than once on their journeys.

How could he not understand the turmoil within her now? He had been imprisoned in Denmark because of her refusal to be forced into a marriage. They had turned their backs on everything they knew for her right to be free. Why would Olan repudiate that right now?

A sickening sensation coalesced in her stomach. Spinning about, she stared at her brother as if he were a stranger. "D-do you wish to be q-quit of me?"

Olan was on his feet instantly. "Never that, Rika," he said solemnly. "It wounds me that you would think so."

Contrition stained her cheeks. "I'm sorry, Olan. I know you have sacrificed much for me, and would do so again. But I have seen your regard for the princess of Dunlough, and would not blame you for wanting—"

One large hand cut the air between them, silencing her. "When you win your duel, we will ride away from here and never look back."

Considering the matter done, he unsheathed one of her short-swords. "Prepare to defend yourself."

Erika gratefully accepted the diversion of sparring with her brother, putting all thoughts of marriage and freedom from her mind. They exercised fiercely despite their mending injuries, so intently that they did not notice the gathering watching their display.

It was quite a crowd. Nearly all of Conor's men, tribal leaders and servants without pressing duty thronged the yard, watching the warriors in respectful silence. Everyone had noticed the short work Erika had made of the shield, especially Conor and his sister.

"Perhaps she saw your face on that target," Gwynna murmured to her brother. "And this is the woman you mean to do battle with, and take to wife?"

"'Twas she who challenged me," Conor declared. Under his sister's steady gaze, he added, "Perhaps I did goad her into it, knowing she would leap at the chance. Erika's honor forced her to do the only thing she could—bargain with her sword arm for her freedom. I would not begrudge her the opportunity, but I mean to keep her here, Gwynna."

"And if you lose?"

Conor snorted. "The Devil will not lose. Do not tempt fate by thinking such a thing."

Gwynna snorted in return, glancing pointedly at the splintered remains. "Very well, then. Let us cease this exercise before one of them is hurt." They started across the yard.

Olan blocked his sister's thrust then froze, staring over her shoulder. "Blood of Odin!"

Erika spun instinctively, her sword raised—

A scream split the air. The blade, flashing in the afternoon sun, stopped with just an inch to spare.

Conor looked down at Erika then at the blade pointed at his chest, an inscrutable expression on his face. "Think you to kill me now, and be done with it?"

Her hands shaking, Erika lowered the blade then sheathed it. "Your people would immediately hang me, and well you know it," she muttered, not looking at him. Blessed Odin, what was happening to her? She had nearly killed him again!

She retrieved the other sword from the packed earth where Olan had dropped it so that he could better hold Gwynna, who had fainted dead away. Her brother had already scooped the healer into his arms and sat her on the bench. He hovered over her, his face etched with such obvious concern that she had to look away.

Keeping her eyes lowered to conceal her flaming cheeks, she said, "I have told you that I no longer wish to kill you, and I mean what I said. Not that you do not deserve it."

The muttered aside bounced off him as he gazed at her. Even drenched with sweat and dust, with her hair in disarray, Erika was magnificent. He remembered how it had felt to kiss her, the tiny waves of shock that had coursed through him. The need to have her took him and held him fast. "Then you are near ready to spar with me, that we may settle this with honor once and for all?"

That brought her head up. Her eyes were so fiery, they could have roasted a deer. "Honor?" she spluttered. "You call tricking me into a duel honorable?"

"The contest is your idea. We can be wed this evening, if you like."

"If I like? If I like?" Heat rushed into her cheeks, and her eyes began to spark. "What I would like is to—"

She broke off the impassioned hope, darting a glance at the curious onlookers. Sighing with a visible effort to calm herself, she placed her hand on his forearm to draw him away.

Conor would not allow such highhandedness in normal circumstance, but the ease with which Erika touched him showed that she was warming to him. And if she could be warm, she could be blazing.

"Shall I tell you what I would like?" he whispered before she could speak.

Her lips parted as she gazed at him, wary. "What?"

"I would like to see your hair as free and wild as your spirit is," he told her, amazed at the huskiness of his voice. "I would like to guess at the mystery of your legs as you walk to me in skirts. I would like to kiss the laughter from your lips."

He dropped his face within inches of hers, so that their breaths mingled. "I would like to kiss you right now."

How came she to be in his arms? Erika was surprised by the husky, longing quality of his voice, surprised by the ease with which she went to him, yielded to him. Surprised and appalled.

She stepped away from him, away from his scent and his heat, away from the magic he worked on her senses. "Again, Conor, I ask you—let us settle this another way. Olan and I are more than skillful with our swords. If we could join your men—"

"My men serve me out of loyalty and respect," he cut in. As quick as Irish weather, the sun in his eyes changed to stormclouds. "In return, I give them food and clothing, a home, education for their young. I am there when they are born, I am there when they are wed, and I am there when they are buried. For this, they call me lord and follow me most willing. I'll not hire a blade whose loyalty is only to herself. You'll do the honorable thing, Valkyrie, and meet me on the field to settle this thing between us. My sister tells me that three weeks more, at Beltaine, is sufficient time for you to be well. If you are fit earlier than that, please inform me. For now, go with my sister to bathe and change. You and your brother will dine at my table so that I may ensure you keep up your strength." He stormed off.

Erika could only stare after him as the crowd dispersed around her. What was so wrong about offering her blade into his service? Most of the Irish, merchants and nobles alike, had been more than willing to accept it. Was it because she was a woman? If that were so, why was he so willing to do combat with her and take her to wife?

Shaking her head, she joined Gwynna and Olan by the bench. "I do not understand him."

Gwynna had recovered enough to watch her brother stalk away. "Conor values loyalty and honor the way most value silver and gold."

"Loyalty is important," Olan said carefully, "but does he not react overmuch?"

Gwynna's eyes grew misty. "He has good reason. His wife betrayed him by having another man's babe."

Frost ran through Erika's veins as she remembered the fierce look in Conor's eyes. "He told me his wife gave him the scar," she admitted. "He never said why."

"That is why. When we saw the babe had red hair, everyone knew it could not be Conor's. They argued, and Aislingh slashed his face with her dagger before falling upon it herself. The babe was sick, and died two days later. Conor has not been the same since."

Erika looked after Conor. Her anger left her, replaced with a heaviness she could not name. "Honor is important to me too," she whispered, almost to herself. "Besides Olan, honor is all I have left. I would have him know that."

"Perhaps you will have the opportunity to tell him," Gwynna said, just as softly. "We will dine soon. Time enough for a long herbal bath and finding the perfect gown."

Erika's eyes widened in alarm. "I will not put on a dress!" she exclaimed frantically. "I refuse to wear a dress!"

Chapter Twelve

Olan sat with Conor and Ardan at the head of the honor table, finding it difficult to wait for the ladies to appear. Memories circled his mind. Larangar falling, Erika taking the blow to her side. Fevered nightmares calmed by a woman he should not care for.

By Odin's blinded eye, what a road the Norns had them on! Although he'd enjoyed a variety of women in his travels, none of them had held his heart in her hands. None of them had stood between him and death, brought him back to the land of the living with knowledge and force of will.

Was what he felt simply gratitude that Gwynna of Dunlough had saved his life? Olan took a deep draught of his ale, discarding the idea. Gratitude was part of it, yes, but there was something else, something deeper. Something that made him feel...almost as he did when the berserker fit left him. Shaky, sensitized. Aware of the beating of his heart, her heart, the pulsing of her blood at the base of her throat.

He wanted Gwynna as he'd wanted few things in his life. Yet if—when—Erika won her duel, Olan would ride away with her and leave his unvoiced emotions behind.

But first, he would beat the Devil so senseless the Irishman would believe he'd been struck by Thor's Hammer.

Ardan was the first to break the heavy silence. "Your sister does not seem taken with the idea of being queen of Dunlough."

"She is not." He answered Ardan's question readily enough, but his eyes were on Conor. "I knew she would not agree to the idea."

The dark-garbed giant shifted on the bench. "I have to wonder why she is not already wed," Conor said, his eyes fixed to the opening through which the ladies would appear.

"It is the right she was given, by her birth and our father's decree, that she wed whom she chose," Olan explained. "She chose to wed the man who could disarm her or draw blood in a duel."

"And none took the challenge?"

Taking another long drink from his mug, Olan sat back, a savage pride swelling his chest. "Oh, there were suitors aplenty, from the time of her twelfth year. Even our close-kin Larangar tried for her hand. She bested them all."

All. The word seemed to ring in the hall. More than a few had turned their full attention to the honor table.

"The men of your country are weaker than the women?" Ardan asked. "Little wonder then, that we drove your kind out."

Olan let the incendiary comment pass. His eyes were on Conor. "It was Erika's right to learn the way of the warrior, and her right to have the freedom to wed the man she chooses. It was that right, joined with loyalty and honor, that caused us to leave Denmark."

Conor leaned forward, his interest piqued. "Go on."

"Our father was a powerful *jarl*," Olan began, as good with a tale as any of the Gaels. "We are his children by his second wife. Our older half-brother, Gunthar, always hated us, and that hatred blossomed after our father died. Gunthar had me imprisoned, and offered Erika's hand to anyone who would pay his price.

"She refused marriage unless I was released. Gunthar then threatened to have me hung if she did not wed. He gave her a week to make her choice, or he would make it for her.

"The night before Gunthar was to kill me, Erika freed me. It was the first time she'd killed someone, and she cried as she stepped over the bodies of men she had known all her life.

"We spirited away from home, aided by our friend Lars, who had been one of Erika's suitors. She'd hidden a store of weapons and coin away, and we gathered those and Lar's longboat and sailed around the coast to France. Five years we have traveled, from Constantinople to Normandy, selling our blades and protecting the innocent. We have endured, but it has not been without strife."

Fists clenched against the pain, he stared at Conor. "I will never forget that I owe Erika my life. That is the burden I bear, that she turned her back on all that she knew and loved, comfort and security, to see me free."

Conor and Ardan exchanged glances as Olan gulped his ale. Loyalty indeed. Leaving behind luxury and the sight of home to come to a land not known for its love of Vikings, to be forever on the road without a place to call home. All this, for the love of a brother. What would she do, Conor wondered, for the love of her husband?

"The last five years have not been easy for Erika," Olan said suddenly. "She does truly have a gentle heart, and I believe that she longs to put her sword away. That is why I hope yours will prove the better blade."

Ardan nearly choked over his ale. "You want the Angel to lose?"

"I want my sister to be happy," Olan retorted. "I want her to put down her sword and wash the blood from her hands. I want her to become the carefree sister I remember. I want her to be an angel of life, not the Angel of Death."

Conor regarded the younger man with narrowed intent. There was much of Erika in her twin, the same determination, the conviction and the deep love they had for one another. Yet he had seen the way Olan had watched Gwynna and realized that the Viking was infatuated with his sister, perhaps more.

"Do you tell me this for your own ends?"

The bear of a Viking leapt to his feet, oversetting his bench. Dogs and servants scattered, and several men-at-arms started forward. "You question my motive, Devil?"

His voice wasn't raised, but the soft menace of his tone was enough to cause some of the soldiers to stand back. His huge hands clenched into fists at his sides, the only outward show of anger. "I place my sister's life and happiness so far beyond my own that mine have no meaning. Whatever the outcome of your duel, I will ride away from here if that is what she wishes. Can you tell me that your motive is pure?"

That the Northman dared challenge Conor told him that the man spoke true. He waved away his men-at-arms and pushed Ardan back onto his bench. "Do you believe that Erika can be happy here?"

"That is up to you to decide," Olan answered, his blue eyes still flat with anger. "She has loved *Iraland* since she first stepped onto its soil, and does not want to leave it. I do not know what you intend by the marriage to my sister, but if you treat her as well as you treat your people, then I believe she will come to be happy here."

He resumed his seat, his eyes never leaving Conor. "If you do not, all the fires of hell will not keep me from putting my hands about your throat."

Conor knew he meant it. He felt the same for his sister. After all, he had killed her husband for daring to beat her. "And I make that same vow to you, my friend."

They shook hands, and the talk turned to things most men enjoyed, ships and horses and fighting and women. Over refreshed tankards, the tentative bonds of friendship were extended.

A sudden silence gripped the hall, causing Conor to look up. When he saw what captivated everyone else, he rose to his feet, aware of his mouth wide with surprise.

Gwynna and Erika paused at the foot of the stairs. Gwynna wore a sleeveless gown of emerald over a pale green underdress. Dark green ribbons were threaded through her black curls, and the gold belt about her waist was worked with emeralds. She was stunning.

Conor didn't even notice his sister. He only had eyes for Erika.

She wore a gown of deep lilac embellished at bodice and hem with silver thread. Her hair was a glorious crown of curls and braids that gleamed golden in the candlelight. A belt of worked silver was fastened about her slender waist, from which hung a silver-handled dagger.

Conor felt desire pull him, harden him. She was magnificent.

She was terrified.

The entire hall—soldiers, servants, and pets—stared at Erika as if she had suddenly sprouted horns. Even Conor was staring at her as if he had never seen her before. No, he was staring at her the way he had when he kissed her. Erika felt her cheeks burn. She felt naked in the dress, showing, she believed, much more of her figure than her trews did.

They had been dressed more than half an hour ago. The delay occurred when Erika tried to walk in her dress. She hadn't been in skirts since she was a child, and found it hard to shorten her stride. Already she had tripped several times, and the stairs were particularly difficult. She knew she would fall on her face before Conor's people and disgrace herself for all time. For the first time in her life, she wanted to run.

Conor and Olan came towards them. Gwynna squeezed Erika's hand reassuringly. "Do you think Olan will like this?" Gwynna whispered, straightening her skirts with her free hand.

Erika was surprised. Was Gwynna nervous as well? She decided to reassure her. "He wanted you when he first saw you, when you were drenched in his blood," she whispered back. "He will not want you less now." Gwynna made a choking noise, but she nodded.

Olan stopped before Gwynna. "The sight of your beauty has driven coherent thought from my head," he admitted. "Might I have the honor of escorting you to table?" Gwynna murmured her assent and slipped her arm into his.

Which left Erika alone with Conor. He continued to stare at her, as if he could not believe his eyes. She looked everywhere but at him. That didn't mean she wasn't painfully aware of him, however. The man did know how to over-whelm the senses. He was still dressed in black, but his tunic was worked with silver and gray that glinted off the silver in his eyes. She could also see every muscle in the man's legs. Oh, how she wished she had her breeches—or even her sword—to hide behind. "Say something, damn you," she hissed, her nerves at the breaking point.

He did. "Is this the same woman who tried to kill me?"

Erika felt the heat rush to her ears. If he had kicked her in the seat of her breeches, he could not have shamed her more. It was bad enough that his people did not know whether to poison her or run away screaming, but did he have to pour greater humiliation upon her? It hurt bitterly, and even more so to know that he could cause her hurt.

"I told Gwynna that this was foolishness," she whispered. She turned to flee.

She heard him mutter under his breath as he caught her hand. Before she could extract it and escape, he brought it to his lips.

"Forgive me, Erika," he said softly, his breath warm on the back of her hand. "That was not what I meant to say. It's just that I have never seen anyone more beautiful in my entire life."

Surely he was mocking her, but the touch of his lips on her hand was sending tendrils of desire streaking through the deepest parts of her body. It was even headier than the other kiss they had shared. She suddenly forgot the hall and everyone in it. She wanted him to kiss her again.

"Conor." Gwynna's low voice reached them. "Quit tormenting the girl and bring her to table."

Relieved by the distraction, she said, "I would propose a truce, at least for dinner. You cease trying to mock me, and I'll cease trying to kill you."

His lips curved minutely into a smile. "I accept your truce." He put her hand in the crook of his arm. "But if I may say so, if you lift the hem of your skirts you would walk much better."

She glared at him but did as he suggested and was relieved to discover she didn't trip once on her way to table. But if she thought she was being given a reprieve, she was mistaken.

He insisted on sitting close, so close she could feel his leg, solid muscle, through her skirts. And his arm, as it brushed against hers. But she was not so overwhelmed by his presence that she didn't notice he was careful to place her to his right, away from the ravaged side of his face. No torch glowed behind him, leaving his left in shadow.

She realized then that it had become a habit to him, to them all, to avoid the scarred side of his face. Only in anger did he face her full. And as careful as he was to shield his scar, his people were as careful to avoid it. Erika shook her head. Vikings wore their scars proudly and with honor, boasting of the battles they survived, the enemies they vanquished. Their scars proved them to be warriors.

But Conor's scar did not come from an enemy. It came from a wife, a wife who betrayed him.

The trenchers were served. "Where is mine?" she asked after noticing a maid place a trencher of choice cuts before the lord. The girl looked up, caught Erika's frown, and squeaked in fright before she scurried away.

"We will share, my lady, if you do not mind," Conor replied, his eyes alight with amusement. He broke off a piece of bread and offered it to her. "You may want to smile more. You near frightened Maire out of her wits."

She was not the only one. Erika knew there were strict laws regarding serving choice cuts of meat. Bards and brehons were given the finest cuts, then clergy, then the chieftain. Conor had the highest rank this night, since the elders and the priest had left soon after her embarrassing exercise in the practice yard. That meant he, and she, dined on the best cut of beef.

She took the proffered chunk of bread, noticing that her hand shook. Conor, blast him, noticed it as well. "Are you afraid, Angel?" he asked her, his voice pitched low so that only she could hear.

"I am not afraid," she whispered back, lifting her chin. "I am...uncomfortable."

Even that admission seemed to cost her a great deal. The Angel of Death was not one to display anything other than supreme confidence. Conor could understand that. He knew the energy it took to remain controlled and confident.

"Sure now, being the object of everyone's scrutiny is not uncommon?" he asked. Indeed, everyone focused their attention on the head table.

"No, it's not. However, this dress, sitting at the head table, the food... You honor me."

Conor heard the disconcertion in her voice and sought to ease it. "And I should. We did not begin well, you and I, and my anger earlier was not warranted."

It was the closest to apologizing that he could get, but it seemed enough. She plucked a morsel of beef from the trencher. "Unwarranted but understandable. I do not know why I seem to be making a habit of pointing blades in your direction."

She plopped the bit of beef in her mouth, licking droplets of gravy from her fingers. Conor's arousal grew almost painful. He would be hard put to await the duel. "The meal agrees with you?"

"It does," she replied. "I have not had so sumptuous a meal since I left home." A shadow crossed her face, and Conor knew she thought of her youth.

"Do you miss it, your homeland?"

"There are days when all I can think of is keeping my head," she answered, staring into the hearth. "But there are other days...I miss my father's laughter and my mother's songs. I miss riding through the hills in the summer and slipping on the frozen lakes in the winter."

"Do you ever think about going back?" Conor was touched by the sadness evident in her voice. Without thought he reached for her hand.

She rebuffed the comforting gesture by pressing her hands to her lap. "I can never go back. I would be killed if I did. But it matters not. Denmark ceased to be our home after our father died. Now home is wherever my brother and I are."

He'd have to have been a fool not to see the pain and longing in her eyes. His desire left him, to be replaced by a feeling much more tender and profound. "And right now, you are here."

The remainder of the meal passed in a blur.

"An mbeidh aon cheol ann anocht?"

Startled by the soft question, Conor turned to the woman beside him. The pale-haired beauty looked out over the feasters, a wistful expression on her face. He could not deny her, he realized. Not if it would bring a smile to her eyes. "Yes, there will be music tonight," he told her. "And singing and dancing and shouting and drinking and fighting. It is our way."

A smile flitted across her lips. "And ours."

Conor signaled the harpist to begin a light tune. "You told me that you know chess. Are you for a game?"

A place was set up for them, and the noise level in the hall rose another notch as Dunlough's people relaxed from the day's endeavors. Erika was a formidable opponent, taking the game as serious as he.

Now that her focus was away from him, Conor took the opportunity to learn more about his betrothed. "Did your mother approve of your warrior's way?"

"Mother died in childbirth when we were four," Erika replied. "Father did not wed again. He said watching a wife die for a third time would surely kill him. He didn't know much about taking care of girls, but he knew his women tended to die, being as fragile as they are. I didn't want to die as my mother did, so I decided to become a boy."

Ardan, who had remained nearby, nearly choked on his ale. "How did you do that?"

"She cut off all her hair, that's what she did," Olan interjected. "Not even six was she, yet used one of our father's daggers to do it."

He grinned at his sister, who glared back.

The glare was softened into a smile by memory. "Father threatened to feed me to Fenrir if I ever cut my hair again. He gave me the dagger as a rite of passage, then told me if I was going to own a dagger, I needed to learn how to use one. Training warriors was what he did best. So I became a warrior."

"Had you no aunt or female relatives to teach you?" Gwynna asked.

Erika shook her head. "My mother was captured by my father on a raid. Father only had brothers, and they were scattered to the four winds. But I had a nurse who looked after me until she died."

Conor exchanged looks with Gwynna, who blinked back tears. Erika had reached womanhood without the guidance of a mother and with a father who denied her the right to be what she was.

Erika realized that Conor and Gwynna were both staring at her in horror. Even Olan seemed chagrined. "We had a good life," she insisted, defending her father. "Father was happy that I was learning to take care of myself, and I liked to make him happy. Father did the best he could before he died. It is not his fault that Gunthar was such a pig."

"Gunthar?"

"He was our father's firstborn. He hated the fact that Father replaced his mother with ours, and as a result he hated Olan and me. Another reason I learned weapons was so that I could defend myself against his pranks. He never forgave me for being better at swords than him." Her eyes grew grim. "He had his revenge though."

Conor and Ardan had heard the tale from Olan, but they were riveted by Erika's blunt account. "How did he do that?"

Erika didn't realize she was holding Conor's hand in a death grip. It was her only outward show of emotion as she said, "When *Jarl* Thorold died, Gunthar the Spineless became *jarl*. We were fourteen. He accused Olan of treason and imprisoned him. Olan demanded the right to a trial or be met in combat. Gunthar refused, knowing the gods would be on Olan's side.

"Meanwhile, Gunthar arranged for me to be wed to one of his friends. By our father's decree I had the right to choose my own husband, and I refused Gunthar's request. He locked me in my chambers and threatened to kill Olan if I continued to refuse. I asked him to release Olan and I would consider his request, but he decided to starve me into submission. When that did not work, he tried to whip me."

Hard, metallic sounds jerked Erika from her commentary. She looked up and was surprised to see that both Olan and Conor had crushed their mugs in their hands. They wore identical expressions of anger. Even Ardan looked outraged, and Gwynna was stricken. "The scars on your back?" she whispered.

When Erika nodded, Olan made a strangled sound. "He scarred you?"

Her brother's voice was a harsh whisper. Erika knew that when Olan got that quiet he was about to go into the red rage. "Why did you not tell me?"

She stretched a hand towards him, feeling his anguish. "I thought it more important at the time to escape, Olan," she answered, begging him to understand. "It would not have taken long for the men loyal to Gunthar to surround us. I wanted to get us to safety."

Even through his beard Erika could see the tight clench of his jaw as he fought to subdue his anger. The tips of his ears were fiery, marking the effort a failure.

With a curse, his fist came crashing down on the table. Gwynna threw up her hands, as if to ward off a blow. The dark-haired woman scrambled quickly to her feet, breathed an apology, and fled.

Olan made to go after her, but Ardan restrained him. "Not while you're steaming like a horse that's been ridden too hard, lad."

"I wouldn't hurt her!"

The old warrior's eyes were agate-hard. "She's not after knowing that, I'm thinking. Calm yerself. Mayhap she'll return."

Olan sat down, stricken. He was no less so than Erika. A simple game of chess and telling tales had become a disaster. Had she upset Gwynna with her tale? Why did the Irishwoman think Olan would strike her?

Erika turned to Conor. "Forgive me. I did not intend my tale to spoil the evening."

Conor was silent as he tried to smother his own rage. The idea of Erika being whipped made his vision turn red. He was consumed with the need to bash someone's head in. How dare anyone hurt her? That he had once chained her and threatened to execute her was burned away.

He asked only one question. "Is this man dead?"

Erika looked at him in surprise. His expression and tone was the same as her brother's, but while she knew Olan's stemmed from the love and protectiveness he felt for her, she knew Conor felt no such things. His anger on her behalf confused her.

His gaze compelled her to finish the tale. "Gunthar made the mistake of binding me with ropes instead of chains. I had worked most of the braid away with my dagger before he came to whip me. He taunted me before applying the lash, which gave me time to free myself."

She would not tell them how Gunthar had looked at her with lust in his eyes. How he had pressed against her, his fetid breath on the back of her neck as he told her how he and his friend would share her.

"The lash only reached me twice—once on the back, the second time around my arm, when I grabbed it and jerked it from Gunthar's hands. I stabbed him with my dagger, took his sword, then went to free Olan. I had to kill two men to do it, men I had known my entire life, but they were loyal to Gunthar, not us.

"We took Olan's longboat and made it to Larangar's holding. We sank our ship in a fjord, making it seem as if we drowned and washed out to sea. Larangar gave us safe passage to France, then chose to sell his boat and stay with us."

She looked down at the table. "I did what I had to do," she whispered. "Larangar was more our brother than Gunthar ever could dream of being. I will be forever grateful to him for what he did for us."

After she ended her tale, Olan excused himself from their company. Erika longed to go after him, but did not. She knew that he walked a fine line between grief and fury. Seeing her would not alleviate it.

"He will be fine," Conor assured her, his voice gruff.

Blinking to dry the moisture in her eyes, she said, "Olan's feeling of responsibility to me is great. He believes he has failed to safeguard me, but he has not."

"When we are wed, I will be your avenger."

Erika frowned at the possessiveness in his tone. "I am my own avenger. And our marriage is not a given."

Conor frowned back. "I see I have many things to teach my future wife. The most important is to never disagree with your husband. You surrendered your blade to me. Our marriage is as good as done."

Her scowl deepened, and even Ardan moved back. "I surrendered my dagger, true, but never my sword. I will marry you only if I lose our duel. Is that why you are trying to break my hand?"

With a muttered curse he let go. Erika shook her abused hand to restore the life to it, then quickly hid it in her lap. The Devil didn't know his own strength, but she did. She would be hard-pressed to win her freedom from him. Why did he want to wed her anyway? She could think of no other reason, except perhaps the kiss they had shared. But surely he didn't have to marry her to kiss her, as he was already doing so now? Did he still mean to have revenge upon her for attempting to behead him? As his wife, Erika would be at Conor's mercy, and she would be honor bound to endure it without Olan attempting to kill him.

It all came to one thing: she could not afford to have Conor best her in their duel.

"Erika, would you walk with me for a time?"

Only a moment's hesitation brushed her before she decided to agree. She was more than tired of seeing the walls of her chamber. "I suppose it is not safe to go for a ride?" she asked as Conor sent a servant for her cloak.

"There is a full moon, and we are safe on Dunlough land."

A servant brought Erika her cloak, and she smiled her thanks. She followed Conor outside to a large wooden enclosure on the east side of the dun. A young boy rushed in ahead of them then returned, leading a large stallion the color of charcoal.

"Have you a mount for me?" she asked as he accepted a nudge of welcome from his mount.

"That I do. Rhory, if you please?" The youth scrambled back inside then returned once again, leading a pale, recalcitrant mount. "Tempest?" she whispered. "Is it really you?"

The horse gave an answering whinny, and came over to butt his nose against her shoulder. "Tempest!" she cried, throwing her arms about his neck. "I believed you lost!"

Conor approached, watching as Erika talked to her horse. His men had found the animal about two hours after the battle, and it had taken four of them to drag him in. The stubborn animal had fought every step of the way, as mean-tempered as a winter storm. Young Rhory was the only one capable of getting the beast to mind, and Conor left the horse to him. He was preparing to tell her what an evil mount she had, when she robbed him of coherent thought by hiking her skirts above her knees, tucking them into her belt and swinging onto the gelding's back without aid.

His eyes were filled with the image of her bare legs. They didn't seem to stop. He watched her muscles flex as she gripped the horse's flanks. For the first time in his life, Conor wished he were a horse. The state of arousal that had plagued him all night intensified. The need to snatch from her horse overwhelmed him. He fought the desire by gaining his mount and pounding out of the gate.

Erika followed, leaning over Tempest's mane, unable to hold back her laughter. It felt so good to be free of the dun, galloping through the meadow with a breeze bringing her the crisp fragrance of the night. She passed Conor with a peal of laughter, her hair slipping free of its elaborate design and streaming behind her.

When they came upon a crystal lake, she halted Tempest with a soft word. She slid to the ground, turning in a slow circle as she righted her clothing. The lake was in its own private glen. The full moon shone through the ring of trees, bathing its surface with a silver glow. Tiny pale night flowers danced in a gentle breeze. It was a place of magic.

Perhaps it was the moon. Perhaps it was the wine. It may have even been the heady fragrance of the night, or the man watching her. Whatever caused the emotion to rise within her she gave in to it.

Trilling in delight, she spun in a circle, her arms flung wide. Her laughter pealed like silver bells as she danced about the lake, with the pure unadulterated happiness of being outside.

Conor had forgotten how to breathe. Moonlight caught the Valkyrie's pale hair and the silver cords threaded through her dress, causing her to sparkle from head to toe. She seemed like a vision out of faerie, the moon goddess come to commune at her sacred pond. Something inside Conor, buried long ago, began to awaken, brought from slumber by the sound of Erika's joy.

She stumbled to a stop before him, and he steadied her with hands to her waist. Her smile of gratitude was like sunshine breaking through rainclouds. He felt grateful that he had done something to bring this gaiety forth. He couldn't help but smile in return, though the muscles strained with disuse.

By Asgard! Conor became a different man when he smiled. He didn't seem nearly so devilish. In fact, he seemed downright *appealing*. Did he realize the moon caught the silver flecks in his eyes, making them glow?

Guided by impulse, Erika leaned towards him, placing her hand against his scarred cheek. The touch sent a jolt running through her. The way his eyes widened and he caught his breath, she knew Conor felt it as well.

"You should smile more," she whispered, not wanting to break the spell of this place. "You are pleasing when you smile."

He wanted to laugh at that, the idea that his pillaged face could be anything but wretched to gaze upon. The wonder in her regard stopped him.

His eyes never leaving hers, Conor reached up and covered her hand with his own. Her skin was soft, despite the calluses on her fingers. Heat radiated from her palm down the length of him, stoking the fires of desire.

"You make me smile," he whispered in return, reaching out to caress her cheek. He was afraid she would bolt, but she only closed her eyes, leaning against his palm. "But I fear you have imbibed too much wine, if you find this battered face pleasing."

Sooty lashes swept up as she regarded him again. "My head is clear, and so are my eyes. I know my own mind, and I think you are handsome."

"Do you not see this scar?" His voice hoarse with demand, he pushed his dark locks back, exposing his blemish to the moonlight and her gaze.

Because he seemed to want it, Erika examined the flaw in his otherwise perfect features. It was a pale, angry mark, vicious and deep, that began at his hairline, running into the edge of his eyebrow and narrowly missing his eye. It coursed through his cheek, splitting his beard and ending beneath his jaw.

"I see it."

"Do you know why my wife marked me? She wanted to blind me, because a blind man cannot rule."

Why? The question danced on her lips, but she refused to give voice to it. She did not want to know the answer, and doubted he would tell her.

Reaching out, she touched her fingertips to the start of the scar. Conor flinched but otherwise remained silent and still. Her touch light, she trailed her fingers along the path of the gash until she reached its end. "It is a badge of honor and courage," she finally said. "You should be proud."

Proud? Honor and courage? The Angel was mad. That was the sole reason, Conor knew, why she could look at him, could touch him there of all places. And her madness was contagious, for he reveled in her touch, the feel of her hand upon his cheek.

"Are you mad or do you mock me?" His voice sounded foreign to him, stone grinding stone. "There is no honor or courage in what happened, and there is naught to be proud of."

Her eyes shimmered in the moonlight. "You are wrong."

He barked out a stark semblance of a laugh. "Now I know you are mad. No one but you would dare to tell the Devil of Dunlough he is wrong."

Her hands gripped his shoulders as she leaned into him. "I have told you my tale. Do you believe my dispatch of Gunthar to be lacking in honor?"

Just the mention of her half brother's name was enough to cause him to growl. "No. You did what you had to do. There is no dishonor in that."

"Do you believe what I did took courage?"

Was she now seeking compliments? "I have never thought you lacking in courage, Angel."

"I have survived and persevered, despite Gunthar's wishes to the contrary. That is something to be proud of, do you not agree?"

"You should be called the Angel of Confusion, for 'tis certain I cannot divine your meaning," he said, feeling a frown lowering his brow. "Speak plain, that I may understand."

She smiled up at him. "I have courage for facing Gunthar and honor for having bested him. I am proud that I have survived. The lash marks he gave me remind me of that. They are a badge of honor."

Her hand returned to his cheek. "Despite your wife's perfidy, you still rule. You have survived and your people have prospered. You have emerged victorious. Like my lash marks, your scar is a badge of honor and you should be proud."

She could not be real. There could be no other explanation. No one dared speak to him of Aislingh and her betrayal, and even if they did, they never would have told him the scar was a badge of honor. Of all people, this woman, this foreign woman who tried to kill him, understood and gave succor to his soul.

Still she smiled at him. The strokes of her hand against his cheek caused him to burn. He would swear he could smell moonlight in her hair, and her eyes were as dark as the pool behind them. He couldn't think. He couldn't speak. There was only one thing left to do.

The kiss was so feather soft, it took Erika unawares. Like butterfly wings, his lips danced across hers. The tingling sensation she had felt when she touched him became a torrent. One small part of her made a token protest, but she had been waiting for this kiss for days. She pressed against him, her hands snaking into his hair.

Perhaps it was the magic of this place, perhaps it was simply the time, perhaps it was the man, but Erika was suddenly filled with longing such as she had never known. She wanted to know what there was between a man and a woman that could make them forget anyone else was in the room with them. Perhaps Conor could teach her.

Someone groaned, and Conor realized it was himself. Her lips were blessed soft, and when he deepened the kiss and coaxed them open, she complied, eager. She moaned and melted against him as he explored the sweetness of her mouth with his tongue.

Leaning against him was like leaning against a rock, a living, breathing, scalding rock. As a warrior, Erika had never liked soft men, even when she took their coin. Conor was anything but soft. The entire length of him was hard muscle, and the calluses on his hands testified to the frequent use of his weapons. She ran her hands over his shoulders, his chest and his back, feeling the muscles beneath.

Suddenly, she found herself on the grass, Conor leaning over her. She reached for him, ravenous for the taste of his mouth. He gave her a demanding kiss that left her spiraling, as dizzying as her dance around the pond. Like a burning cinder, his kiss tumbled from her mouth to her neck, trailing across the edge of her bodice. When his hand found her breast, she knew joy. When he stroked the rosy nipple, she knew bliss. And when he took the bud between his lips, she knew ecstasy.

Reduced to instinct, she arched against him, moaning his name. Her exuberant response robbed Conor of breath. He throbbed with the need to have her. His hand found its way beneath her skirts, his fingertips blazing towards her molten center.

Without warning, Tempest neighed, breaking the spell of passion. Erika and Conor both rolled to their feet in seconds, both reaching for the daggers at their waists. But there was no band of outlaws. Just a band of wolfhounds.

Erika stepped in front of him, her dagger at the ready. Another time, he might have laughed at the idea of being protected by a woman. This time, angered at being interrupted, he jerked her behind him, commanding the pack to heel. The five dogs dropped to their haunches, awaiting their master's next command.

Conor forced himself to count to ten and took his time doing it. He was furious for losing control of himself. A minute later and he would not have been able to stop himself from taking her then and there. Where had his blighted honor fled?

He turned to Erika, who was soothing her horse, no doubt calming herself in the process. She would probably mock him now, and rightly so. He had taken advantage of her and the ale she had consumed at supper, and behaved like a dishonorable simpleton. He went to apologize.

"Stand up," Conor ordered brusquely.

She straightened, turning to face Conor. "Did I do something wrong?"

"You're falling out of your dress," Conor growled. "Fix it before I dishonor you again."

She complied, not even turning away. Conor had to, muttering an oath as he did so. "I am not dishonored," she told him.

"You should be."

"Why?"

He couldn't bear her nonchalance. "Do you know what almost took place here?" he bellowed. The horses snorted and a few of the dogs whuffed excitedly.

Erika had a good idea, but didn't know for sure. She folded her arms. "So?"

Conor didn't smother his oath then. "Are you telling me that this happens to you often?"

Had she lied, she would have been free—at least of marriage. The thought never came to her. "No. But I do not understand—"

"Your brother would have my head if he knew what I've done." He shook his head as he paced. "Damnation, he'll have my head anyway, if he can feel your stronger emotions as you say he can. I shouldn't touch you again until we're wed."

Confusion drove the last vestiges of passion from her mind. "But you liked it," she pointed out. "Didn't you?"

"Of course I liked it!"

"Then why can we not continue?"

"Why?" He stalked towards her, a ravening beast barely held in check. Grabbing her hand, he pressed it against his pulsating erection. "Because to continue would be to put this inside you. And that I will not do until we are in our marriage-bed."

Mortified, Erika snatched her hand away. She was amazed at his control even as she was grateful for it. Yet something in her could not resist goading him, arguing with him. "Why would it be necessary to be married? We are not married now."

"It is a manner of honor," Conor barked. "You will be my wife before I have you fully. 'Tis your honor I'm thinking of."

She didn't appreciate the gesture. Not when she was on the verge of discovering what so many other women on her travels giggled about. "But surely men do not marry women just for that? I've even met some women who say they get paid to please a man."

The idea of Erika spreading her thighs for any brute who gave her hack silver set his blood to boiling. "If you even begin to entertain such an idea, I will beat you," he said, a growl tightening his tone. "When we are wed, you will be queen of Dunlough. You will remain above reproach."

"What makes you so sure we are going to be married?"

Pushed beyond his limits, Conor crushed her to him and gave her a bruising kiss. When he released her, she sagged against him, her strength and mettle gone.

"You burn for me," Conor breathed against her ear. "If I were to reach under your skirts, I'd find you hot and wet and ready to receive me. 'Tis pleasure you're seeking and pleasure I can give. That I promise you."

He had the audacity to grin. "The last thing on your mind right now is fighting me."

That was true. All she could think of was the stunning, mysterious hardness she had felt through his *leine*. She was bursting with curiosity, but she could no more resist the barbs he threw at her than he could hers. "I will fight you, Conor," she told him, her voice weak, desperate.

He didn't smile, but his eyes were viciously alight. "I hope you do. When you yield to me, it will be that much the sweeter."

Unable to think of a fitting reply, Erika allowed Conor to lift her to her horse and lead her back to the dun. Handing their horses into a servant's care, he led her into the hall and to her chamber.

Each step nearer that door caused Erika's heart to flutter. Conor's hardness was still imprinted on her palm. Even as she had argued with him, she recalled its size, its shape, its hardness. She had difficulty believing that something so large could fit inside her.

"Cease."

Her thoughts scattered by the harshness of his voice, Erika slowly raised her eyes to his. His features were as chiseled as the stone behind them, as if it took every ounce of his will to hold himself in check. If he were Thor incarnate, lightning would be dancing a frenzied turn about the hall. "Cease what?"

"Looking at me."

"Why should I?" she demanded crossly.

"Your eyes are inviting me to kiss you and more."

"Oh." She blinked, then focused on him again. "Then why do you not?"

His lips twitched briefly in what others would have called a grimace, but she had come to recognize as a smile. "What a woman you are," he admitted, leaning closer. "Unlike any person I have ever met."

This time when he kissed her, she was ready with the offering of her lips. Erika felt the same thrill as he pulled her closer, his hands running through the silken strands of her hair.

With a moan she melted against him, hungry for something she could not name. His lips grew demanding, slanting over hers again and again in a sensual onslaught that made her spirit seize. She returned to him what she received, hungrily melding her mouth to his, her arms tight about his neck, her fingers caught in the dark fall of his hair.

Abruptly he broke the kiss, setting her at arm's length. It was a long moment before she could remember how to open her eyes. Her body shivered as the air did after a lightning strike.

"You can end this torment," he whispered, his voice rough as she'd never heard it, his eyes a wolf-like gleam. "One word, and I will send for the priest. We can dispense of this petty duel and make our chamber ours in truth."

"No." The word seemed to come from someplace deep within her, the place where sanity still reigned. Whether she was refusing to leave go the duel or the wait for the priest, she did not know.

He stepped away from her, the forbidding mask in place once more. She was immediately bereft, unable to staunch the moan that escaped her.

His breathing was loud and harsh as a horse pushed too hard. "There will come a day, my Angel, when you will forget how to say no."

He opened the chamber door, ushering her inside. "Goodnight, my lady. Find pleasure in your dreams. If you can."

Chapter Thirteen

A shadow fell across Gwynna as she knelt in her herb garden, startling her. "May I speak with you?"

Olan. She groaned in dismay. She was on her hands and knees in the mist-drenched soil, wearing a faded and oft-mended tunic, with dirt covering every inch of her frame. Not the image she wanted Olan to have of her.

She glanced up, as far as his thighs, then dropped her gaze. She had seen far too much of the man to be proper, even for a widow. And even for a widow, the memories made her blush.

"Can it wait a time?" *Time to put on another dress, scrub the dirt from my face, dip my fingers in* ruam...

"You have avoided me long enough," the blond giant said. He reached down a hand to pull her up. Instinct had her flinching, raising her arm in a defensive gesture.

The large hand withdrew as he stepped back. "Do you think I would hurt you?"

Horrified at her involuntary movement, Gwynna scrambled to her feet. "Olan, I am sorry!"

"So am I." His face became closed. His voice seemed so wounded it caused her to wince. "You fled the dinner table that night as if for your very life. You have avoided me for nearly a week. I have frightened and offended you, yet I shall do so no longer." He turned away.

"No!" Desperate, Gwynna reached for him, catching her hand on his elbow. "Please, wait!"

The huge man stopped, his eyes cast to the ground. "I am sorry, Gwynna. It is wrong of me to attempt to offer you what I cannot give."

Her heart leapt into her throat, then dropped to her abdomen. "What?"

She watched him shove his hands through his thick blond mane, hands that had never risen against her with deliberate intent. He had never hurt her, except in his delirium. She fixed upon that thought, resisting the urge to run away.

Every move measured, Olan guided her to the bench. "When I was wounded, I thought the Valkyries were coming for me. But you stood between life and death, and brought me back."

He sat beside her, not touching, not encroaching on her space. "It was the happiest day of my life, to awaken and discover that you were real. For the first time in years the days seemed brighter, and it was because I had seen your smile. I vowed to give you cause to smile every time I saw you, so that I could store away the memory like treasure."

Smiling, he turned to her, hoping she could see the sincerity in his eyes. "You have made me the richest man on earth."

She was weeping openly, her tears making tracks in the smudges on her face. Olan didn't mind. "You saved me, Gwynna. My life belongs to you now. And so does my heart."

Surprise lifted her eyes to his.

"Do not ask me to explain the how and the why. Know only that I speak the truth. I know it does not seem possible, but surely you recognize that there is something between us?"

Her dark green eyes filled with hope and trepidation, her voice catching as she asked, "What is this thing between us?"

"Whatever you wish it to be."

She shot to her feet, wringing her hands together. "It cannot be. We are too different, you and I. You are Viking, I am Gaelic. I am a healer, and you are..."

"Say it. Speak the words you mean, that I may hear them."

"Y-you are a warrior." She sounded as if she had to force the words out. "I heal people and you-you kill them. And you enjoy it."

"There is no joy in killing."

"But you are a berserker. Everyone knows a berserker enjoys killing."

Olan closed his eyes. It caused an ache deep inside, that she would think this of him. How could she think otherwise? She knew only that he was a warrior, had tried to kill her brother, and had bruised her in his struggle to survive. He could not hope that she held him high in her regard.

"Though it damns me, and causes me to lose your favor, I cannot be untrue," he admitted, opening himself to more hurt at her hands. "When those I love are threatened, the red rage consumes me. I do not cease until that threat is done."

Focusing on her, he rose slowly to his feet, still keeping apart from her. "There is naught I can do to change who I am. I am a warrior. I will always protect what is mine, what I love, with my sword and my life. Always."

"I-I understand, Olan." Miserable to the core, Gwynna kept her eyes to the earth. She knew she had hurt him with her words just as she knew she would give anything to take that pain from him.

He reached out to brush the tears from her cheeks. She saw his hand approach, knew it was his and not another's. By God, she tried not to flinch away from him, away from this man her heart yearned to yield to, but her body betrayed her.

His hand fell to his side, clenching into a fist. He was angry, she could feel it spilling into the space between them. Trembling took hold of her, so violent her teeth clicked. "Please," she whispered, "please don't."

"You cannot even suffer me to touch you," he whispered, his voice raw. He stepped well away from her. "I have exceeded my place. Forgive me. I'll trouble you no more."

"He nearly beat me to death!"

The confession tore from her, born of a desperate need to make him understand. If he were to hate her, she wanted him to have good reason.

She sank to the ground, her dignity in tatters. But what good would it do to have her dignity and lose this man?

"I was wed once," she said, as Olan turned to her. "He was a stern man, very disciplined with his men and his people. But what was not known, what I didn't discover until after the wedding was the exact measure of his cruelty.

"He-he lived to inflict pain. It was as necessary for him as eating and drinking. The servants shielded me from his temper as best as they could. He was not home often, but when he did return...I did everything he asked of me, but I was his property and he could do as he wished.

"One day he came home unexpected. I was here, for visiting my family was my greatest pleasure. He followed me here, so drunk he could scarce walk. But he wasn't too drunk to beat me. He struck me so fierce I lost my senses. When I came to, I was in my old bedchamber. I was told that Conor had discovered my husband kicking me as I lay unconscious, and beat him till he died."

"I must remember to thank your brother."

Olan's voice throbbed with ill-concealed rage. Closing her eyes, Gwynna lowered her head, unable to see the disgust she knew she would find in his features.

"Gwynna."

So couched in misery was she that she couldn't answer, couldn't look at him.

She felt rather than saw him kneel before her. "Gwynna, I'm going to touch you now."

Panic welled in her chest, but she fought it down. If he didn't grab her too tight, it wouldn't leave a bruise, or she could cover it with her sleeves, or she could plead an illness—

His hand cupped her cheek. Her eyes flew open. How could a warrior's touch be so comforting?

Gentle, his fingers slid down her cheek to her chin, tilting it up. His eyes were bright with a promise she didn't dare interpret. "Gwynna, you know what my sister endured. If you think I could ever do to you as was done to her, you're mistaken. You are *mo aingeal, mo leannán*."

Tears spilled unbidden from her eyes. *My angel, my sweetheart.* "Olan—"

"I'm going to kiss you now," he whispered, his breath warm against her cheek. "I've wanted to kiss you since I awoke to find you real. Do not deny me."

She could deny him nothing. Indeed, she offered him her lips, yielding to the inevitability of the moment. And what a wondrous, healing moment it was.

"Marry me, Gwynna," Olan urged, his voice rough. "I have little to offer you—a few gems, some gold, my name. And my love, my body, and my soul. I give all those to you free."

"You have more to offer me than I to you," she told him. "I live in my brother's house in shame. He cares naught, but many do."

"I am not one of the many." He shifted on the bench then got to his feet. "I am a Northman in a land with little love for my kind. Their regard means little to me. Only yours matters. Tell me what I can do to raise your regard for me, and I will do it."

She stretched a hand to him. "I was afraid to hope. I didn't dare believe..."

He captured her hand, engulfing it as he knelt before her. "I will ask you again, heart of my heart. I want to offer for your hand. I am Viking, a warrior, with no land to claim as mine. But I will claim you and your daughter as mine. If you will but say yes, if you believe you can love me—"

She was off the bench and in his arms, pressing rapid kisses to his cheeks and mouth. He caught her against him as he rose to his feet, taking her with him.

"I do love you, Olan," she whispered, resting her forehead against his chest. How could she have ever doubted that she would feel anything but safe and protected in his arms? "I have loved you forever."

"Gwynna," Olan began, "you must know that I vowed that I would find Erika a place where she could be safe and happy. I do not know if that place will be here, but if it isn't..."

She touched his cheek, tracing the moisture she saw there. "I know," she said softly. "You must see your responsibility to your sister through. 'Tis one of the reasons I fell in love with you, Olan. I'll be your wife, and I will wait for you."

She smiled. "Now take me in your arms and kiss me."

Chapter Fourteen

E rika turned away from the tender scene. She had not meant to intrude, but she had been rooted to the spot, mesmerized.

She was selfish, too absorbed in her own misery and quest for freedom to realize the hardship her stance had inflicted on those she loved. Larangar had loved her enough to sacrifice his inheritance, and it had earned him a grave on foreign soil without a legacy.

Now Olan had a chance for the kind of happiness they had not experienced since their father's passing. She could not begrudge him that. Her brother deserved joy more than she needed her petty dream of freedom.

Olan had found a place for himself, a place she wished she had. She could not deny him that place.

It was time to make a deal with the Devil.

Her footsteps took her along the back of the wall, where several thatched roof huts hugged the wood and stone perimeter. It was then that she noticed the shadow following her own. Erika spun to face the man behind her, recognizing Padraig. "Why do you follow me?"

Padraig's stony expression never wavered. "The mac Ferghal wills it."

Just the mention of Conor had her narrowing her eyes. "Why?"

"The *tigerna* needs no reason, and you'd do well not to question him."

Erika glared at the man, but the huge warrior was as inflexible as the limestone wall behind him. He may not know why Conor ordered her followed, but she could hazard a guess: to make sure she did not attempt escape, and to make sure she was not attacked.

While she could appreciate the need, the choice of guards was unpalatable. "What must I do to have you cease following me?"

Cold, flat eyes flicked over her. "Return to your chambers."

As an answer and a choice, it was unthinkable. Padraig obviously knew it as well, for he folded his arms across his chest and gave her a look that was half smirk, half dare.

Erika lifted her chin. Apparently, this man had no idea who he was daring.

She turned on her heel, heading toward the *lios*. "Where are you going?" he demanded.

"For a ride," she shot back over her shoulder, not even breaking her stride. Her braes had been returned to her, clean and mended, allowing her to exercise more freely. The sun-bleached leather tunic and the linen *skyrta* she had worn beneath had been ruined by her injuries. Gwynna had supplied a *leine* but had added her own feminine embellishments, much to Erika's consternation.

Rhory must have seen her coming, for he already had the gray stallion ready as she entered. Padraig caught up with her as she accepted the reins from the horse-boy. "You canna do that," he warned.

Settling her baldric so that the pommel of her sword rested between her shoulder blades, Erika swung astride her horse. "Thank you, Rhory." She gave the soldier a beatific smile. "Watch."

Tempest needed no urging to burst out of the wooden enclosure. Once outside, Erika brought the stallion to heel, waiting.

She didn't have long. Cursing rattled the timbered walls of the *lios* as Padraig galloped out. Erika smiled and waved as he barreled by, then urged Tempest forward at a sedate walk.

More curses fouled the air as the large warrior curbed his protesting mount. He said nothing to her, but if his glare were a dagger, she would be bleeding.

Erika's smile was guileless. "Conor said that I might exercise freely. We're not after going against the mac Ferghal's wishes, are we?"

For answer, he turned his mount towards the beaten path that led away from the dun. Before they had gone far, three more guards were accompanying them. At her questioning glare, Padraig said, "The mac Ferghal would not send his betrothed out without a proper escort."

Tempest laid back his ears as Erika drew short. "I am not Conor's betrothed."

Padraig and the other soldiers exchanged smiles. "You would not be after going against the *tigerna's* wishes, would you?"

Rankled to have her words thrown back at her, Erika clucked at her mount, sending him trotting down the rocky incline. Once they were on the flat, grass-covered plain she gave Tempest his head, letting him gallop flat-out.

Free! Laughter ripped from her as her cloak flapped about her on the mist-laden wind. How wonderful it felt to be free! She tilted her head upward, closing her eyes to savor the salty breeze that caressed her cheeks. It was a liberating experience, one she and Tempest had engaged in many times before.

The illusion was quickly dashed by the arrival of her escort. Tempest jerked to a halt, his ears flattening to his skull, as the warriors surrounded them.

"Where would you like to go, my lady?"

"To the village."

The journey to Dunlough village was too long, and not long enough to her. The village was nestled against low hills that sported at least six shades of green on its northeastern side. To the west, just beyond a stand of trees, lay the sea.

For a moment she closed her eyes, savoring the pungent salt scent. How the sea called to her, pounded through her veins. Would she ever ride the waves again? Only the Norns knew for sure.

She guided Tempest onto the muddy track that led into the village. That was too strong a term, for Dunlough village was little more than a grouping of rotund thatch-topped huts, liberally daubed and wattled to protect against the ferocity of the sea-wind in winter. Several still bore scorch marks in mute testimony of the raid weeks past.

People stepped out of their homes as they recognized Conor's men and her silver hair. Erika dismounted and, before she could change her mind, removed her sword. Leaving Tempest with an admonition to behave, she strode to the center of the muddy track and waited.

She didn't have long. An old woman in a drab ankle-length smock and girdle scuttled forward. She gave Erika a stern, assessing gaze, then broke into a grin.

"You came back!" she cried, reaching her hands out. She stopped, as if unsure of her action.

Erika took the bony hands in hers and returned the woman's wide smile. "I returned as I have promised, Goodmother, though not as I wanted."

The old woman gave a dry, delighted laugh. "But you did return." She turned towards the others. "Come see! Our Angel has returned!"

Curious and emboldened, the villagers came up to them until Erika was quite surrounded. She ignored the frisson of trepidation between her shoulder blades and stared into the faces of each and every villager. Most were children who stared at her in unabashed curiosity, some were women, and a few, far too few, were men.

"I made a promise to you when last I was here," she said, pitching her voice to carry even to the mounted guards. "I vowed that I would return, bearing the head of the man who had wronged you."

She held out her hands, palms up. "I have not been able to fulfill that *geas*, but I have returned. To ask your forgiveness."

A ripple of surprise ran through those gathered. "Why would herself be asking us for forgiveness?" someone muttered.

Erika lifted her chin. "Because I would have you know that I do not easily make a pledge, and I have never forsworn a vow once made. I will protect your village, and I will find the man responsible for raiding you."

"Of course you will," the old woman beamed, patting Erika's hand. "You are an angel, sent to protect us."

"And how will she be doing that, after she weds the *tigerna*?" one wizened fellow demanded.

Piqued, Erika's chin lifted even higher. "My marriage to your lord is not a given," she said as evenly as she could. How long was she obliged to point that out before people accepted it? "The *tigerna* will have my hand only if he defeats me in a duel. And I will not make it easy for him."

Laughter rang out, strong and true. She let it run its course, then added, "But if I do become the mistress of Dunlough, my duty to you is even more certain. A vow has been made. A vow will be kept."

The air vibrated with the solemn truth of her words. Then in an act that both startled and moved her, each villager bowed over her hands and kissed them.

"What are they doing?" one of the guards hissed to Padraig.

The red-haired giant took a moment to answer. "They're swearing fealty. To the Angel of Death!"

Once she realized their intent, Erika attempted to halt the villagers. They would not be dissuaded. Mortified beyond measure, she suffered through their undeserving attention.

When the last little one threw his arms around her neck, she was finally able to ask, "Is there a Múireann here? She that has a young son?"

"She is here," the old woman—Eithne—told her. "Caught in the grieving, she is. With her man gone, she's left to raise her son alone. We do what we can, sure, and the *tigerna* will not be having his people starve. But she's having a hard time of it, and that's the truth."

Eithne pointed her toward another forlorn-looking hut. With Tempest trailing behind her, Erika went to the hut and called out, "Múireann?"

A young woman came to the entrance of the hut. Likely no more of an age than Erika, she looked far older. Her flare of crimson hair had banked to the color of dull embers. Grief still clouded her gray eyes just as the clouds had chased away the sunlight overhead. They brightened in recognition.

"The Angel of Death," she whispered. One bone thin hand clutched the neck of her smock. "I spoke for you, before the tigerna."

Someone in Dunlough had spoken for her? She eyed the Irishwoman with renewed interest. "I thank you, for doing what so many others would not have done. My name is Erika Silverhair and it would please me to have you call me thus."

"Have-have you come for me?"

"Yes." Seeing the woman pale instantly, Erika reached out a hand to steady her. "Nay, not for that. I come because I know that your husband fell in battle."

Múireann nodded. "The day of the raid, my poor Owain—" She broke off, her hands gathering handfuls of her skirts. "Did you kill him?"

The blunt question, though expected, pained. "I do not know."

The grieving woman sniffed. "He was all I had, save for young Gil. I had brothers, but they and my father died in that horrible battle two years ago. Most of Owain's family went the same way, else the sea took them. Save for Gil, I have no one, and nowhere to go." She covered her face with her hands.

Her grief brought Erika's to the surface, and she found herself embracing Múireann in an attempt to comfort her. It was a foreign sensation, utterly discomfiting. Why would she feel such unease from a simple embrace? When the answer came to her, it was a revelation.

Until she came to Dunlough, Erika had never held or been held by anyone. Truth be told, no one had held her since her mother died, and she could barely remember her. The life of a mercenary left little time for comfort or comforting.

"I'm sorry, Múireann," she said, her words stiff with a nameless emotion. "But it is a credit to your husband that he died gloriously, in battle."

The Irishwoman gazed at her with red-rimmed eyes. "How can you say such a thing? There is nothing glorious about battle."

"In my country, it is a warrior's greatest hope, that when he dies it is with his sword in his hand and his enemy at his feet. For then the Valkyries come for him, to take him to Valhalla."

"What is Val-Valhalla?"

"It is a place of much celebration and feasting. All warriors who fell in battle are gathered there."

The woman's smile was wistful. "Owain would like that. But 'tis a small comfort to me now."

Erika touched the woman's shoulder. "I will do what I can for you."

With a shake of her head, the grieving woman stepped back. "What can you do for me?"

"Take you to the dun."

"What?"

The more Erika thought about it, the more she liked it. "You will return with me to the dun. You and your son will have a place there."

Múireann's eyes glimmered as hope revitalized her. "But the *tigerna*..."

Erika dismissed her objections with a wave. "I will deal with the mac Ferghal. Gather your belongings."

"Thank you, my lady, thank you!" After an impulsive hug of gratitude, Múireann rushed back inside. Erika turned, feeling very satisfied.

Then she noticed that all the villagers were gone. In the middle of the mud track stood Tempest, her four guards—

And the Devil himself, astride a sulfur-and-brimstone horse.

"Are you ready to deal with me now, Silverhair?"

Chapter Fifteen

C uriosity.

At least, that was what Conor told himself as he followed Erika and her guards. He was curious to see where she would go, what she would do, on her first day outside the walls of the dun since their moonlit ride.

He did not expect the journey to the village.

She rode at her ease in the center of his men, her back straight and chin high. Her demeanor was one of complete assurance. She would need that, he knew, to approach the village.

The people of Dunlough were most curious about the woman he had chosen for his new bride. While many accepted it as they accepted everything he did, some were still angry with the Angel of Death. He did not think any of his people would harm her or would be given the opportunity, yet until everyone, including Erika herself, accepted her role as mistress of Dunlough, she would be followed and protected.

It was apparent, however, that the Angel was becoming more acclimated by the moment. It had amazed him how the villagers welcomed her, how she coaxed laughter from people sore in need of it.

Seeing how she comforted the grieving widow made his heart swell with a proprietary pride. The Angel would make a more than suitable mate for him.

As soon as she realized he was the one who made judgments, not her.

When she caught sight of him and began walking to him, he forced his features into their usual state of menace. Difficult to do when he was fair bursting with admiration. Even though she knew she faced certain trouble, he saw determination stamped on her features.

Brimstone snorted as she approached. Erika quieted the horse with a hand to its shoulder. She fired his blood with a hand to his knee. "May I have a moment in private?"

She could have anything she wanted, if only her hand moved higher... "Tell me why I should not be angry with you."

Her hand gripped his knee tighter as she stared at him, a silent plea in her eyes. "Will you walk with me?"

He could not ignore her request. He slid off his horse and held out his hand.

She stared at him a moment, as if certain he would trick her but not sure how. Then she slipped her hand in his, and he began a sedate stroll, heading toward the copse of trees near the cliffs above the sea.

The breeze grew stronger as they neared the drop, catching their cloaks and unraveling Erika's braids. She lifted her hands to repair the intricate design, but Conor stopped her. "Leave it. It pleases me this way."

He expected an argument and was surprised when he did not receive one. Instead, she folded her arms across her chest and turned into the breeze, closing her eyes as the salty mist bathed her face.

Conor watched her expression soften to one of peace and felt blessed that he had brought her here, had brought this gift to her. He too loved the sea and often walked along this edge, letting the soft rumble of the tide soothe his soul.

"You belong to a beautiful land, Conor mac Ferghal."

Her voice flowed soft, reverent. If not for the sword on her back, Conor would have thought her an ordinary maiden swayed by the sight of beauty. The Angel, however, hailed far from ordinary.

"A beautiful land, true, but also bloody. We fight for what is ours, to keep what is ours—and what we believe should be ours."

She smiled, seeing the humor he hadn't intended to interject. No one thought him humorous, least of all Conor himself.

"How much of this is your land?"

Being near her without touching was difficult. He took her hand again, pleased when she gripped his. "Our land," he began with subtle emphasis, "begins at the sea and stops at Slieve Torc, where the lands of the mac Murrough clan begin. I fostered at Dun Lief, and if there be someone not of my clan that I trust, it is Niall mac Laighin. All to the north is ours, until the plain before the kingdom of Ulster."

"And they are your enemies?"

"Yes." The word rang harsh. He would not say it aloud, but he believed deep in his soul that Ronan of Ulster had felled his brother. The enmity between them had run deep, birthed during a summer festival near fifteen years ago.

He changed the subject. "What is your homeland like?"

She remained silent for a time, and Conor let her have it, for she leaned into him as she gathered her thoughts. "Like this one, in a way," she said at last. "Most of it lies between two seas, but there are many islands that make my homeland. Large tracts of forests filled with deer and wolves. Mostly moors, rivers, and marshes. I think there are more fjords than people, which is why we always traveled by boat. Olan and I learned to swim before we learned to walk. In summer, everything was green and wet. In winter, the north was all covered in snow and ice. Even the lakes froze over, and we would skate on them."

"What is 'skate'?"

"Blades made out of bone that we would strap to our feet to cross frozen lakes. And in deep snow we used ice-legs, made of leg bones from horses, to go overland."

Conor stared at her, wondering if she was telling a tale for his amusement. "You speak true?"

"I always speak true. If there is snow here this winter, I would show you how to skate." Her lips lifted in a smile. "I would challenge you to a race on ice-legs. It would be...rousing."

Her words warmed him, for Erika had just promised a portion of her future to him. She would not have if she were so set against their union.

"You do not have to challenge me to rouse me, my lady," he whispered, hearing the hunger in his voice and doing nothing to temper it. Using their intertwined hands, he drew her close to his side. "I am well-roused by the scent of your hair alone."

Blush-pink stole into her cheeks, highlighting the color of her eyes. "You mistook my words, mac Ferghal," she managed to say.

"Have I?" he drawled. "Perhaps then, rousing me is not your intent. Perhaps rousing yourself is what you're after."

The blush caught her ears now, turning them a sunset rose. "C-Conor—"

"Ah, 'tis not easy for you, is it now? Perhaps you need a bit of help becoming roused."

"Conor." Pink had risen to her forehead, into the veil of her hair. "Why do you tease me so?"

Conor didn't believe himself capable of teasing, yet here he was. How she provoked him! "Because the blush on your cheeks makes you more than comely and less the dreaded Angel of Death."

Her brows dipped in confusion. "But I am the Angel of Death. I cannot change that."

"And that is why, without reason or need, you vowed to protect this village?"

Her fingers tightened in his grasp, but he refused to let her go. "I am doing what is right."

"It is not for you to do."

"Then who is it for?" she demanded, turning to face him. "I made a vow—first to the villagers, then to Múireann. Her husband is dead. Not because he is an evil man, but because I mistook him for one."

"Erika—"

"I told Múireann that she and her son could come live in the dun," she blurted out. "She has no one now to claim her.

I want—I need—to make sure that she is cared for. I cannot shirk that responsibility."

"I do not expect you to." Conor captured her other hand, bringing her full against him. Lifted by the breeze, her hair whipped about them, seeming to cocoon them from the world.

Erika opened her mouth then closed it. Confusion again darkened her lavender eyes. "What do you mean?"

"By your actions this day, Múireann will be given into your care, as she will care for you. It is fitting, as you are about to become mistress of Dunlough. My people will be your people, and your responsibility."

Her lips pressed together, and Conor saw the old argument about to begin. "You have acquitted yourself well this day," he murmured, drawing her closer. "I could not have chosen better for a wife." Then he kissed her.

Any protest she might have made expired as her lips met his. She leaned into him, and when he released her hands, they found their way around his neck. Her sigh vibrated through him, causing his hand to tremble as it cupped the nape of her neck to deepen the kiss. He nibbled her bottom lip from the edge in before plundering inside, mating to her with his tongue.

Before sanity could be consumed by the passion raging through his veins, he pulled away from her. Her lips were still bowed for his kiss, her half-closed eyes soft as heather in a misty rain.

He reached up to smooth back a pale curl. "You have done what should be done." He cupped her cheek. "You will make a fine mistress of Dunlough."

The dreamy expression left her eyes. "Conor, I know nothing of running a household. I have done neither spinning nor weaving since I was a child. I cannot be a wife to you or mistress of Dunlough!"

At least she wasn't prattling on about freedom. Did that not mean she grew accepting of the idea of being his wife? "You can be mistress of Dunlough. And you will be wife to me."

She pulled away from him, protest in her eyes. "Why? Why do you want me so? Surely there are other women you want more, women who would joyfully become wife of the leader of Dunlough?"

Her questions seeped into the heat that had risen in his mind and his loins. Why did he want her as he did? "It is enough that I wish it," he said in his most commanding tone, a tone that made many a man cower.

His intended did not even blink. "There must be more," she insisted. "Is it because—because you have come to love me?"

The question pricked what little conscience he had left. He could not lie to her, yet he could not tell her the truth. What was the truth, at any rate? That having the most feared Viking woman in Ireland at his side would make him invincible? That he wanted her as he had never wanted another woman but would never admit it and thus give her power over him? Or that he was incapable of love, and if she needed that, she was doomed to an unhappy existence in Dunlough?

A sigh lifted from him, carried on the ocean breeze. "Erika, I would have no lies between us. I do this for my people."

Erika stepped back. She didn't know what she expected him to say, but that certainly wasn't it. "Your people?"

Silver eyes regarded her somberly. "Not of my choosing am I the leader of my people. I am king of my *tuath*, chieftain of my tribe and adviser to the over-king of Connacht. My people expect me to protect them and their children. I do that of my own free will, but there will come a time when I will not be able to do so. I must see to the future. To do that, I need sons. Strong men unafraid to fight for what they believe in and wise enough to use words first."

He stepped closer to her, his gaze unwavering. "I would have those sons of you, Angel of Death."

You knew, she told herself. *You knew it was nothing more than that.* Yet the knowledge struck like a blow.

She lowered her head, the better to conceal her hurt. It was all she could do to speak. "The Devil and the Angel. An alliance between us would give many cause to fear."

"And many cause to rejoice." His hand cupped her cheek. "You will be a queen in Dunlough, a great lady. You will be accorded every respect. You will be welcomed and protected, and cared for. Our sons will rule this land."

I will be without friend, for Olan will surely wed Gwynna and leave to find his way. I will be kept in the dun with no light, no sea spray. I will be protected only because of my ability to bear children.

A love match had never been her wish. Her only requirement for a husband had been for a man strong enough to defeat her in battle, strong enough to protect her from any threat. Her childhood heart had always assumed that the champion would be someone she could love and who would love her in return. Reality was beginning to prove different.

Her distress must have been obvious, for Conor pulled her back against him. "Erika. For all the books I have been blessed to read, the poetic words escape me. You and I are alike in many ways, but the greatest is in our desire to protect those unable to protect themselves. You will be able to do more with Dunlough behind you than you would on your own. Our marriage will benefit us both. Then there is this."

He pulled her back against him and kissed her again, a rough, fiery plundering of her lips and mouth. This time a moan escaped her, and Conor himself groaned in dark satisfaction.

As soon as he was sure she was nearly senseless, he broke the kiss. His satisfaction grew as she whispered his name, her voice throbbing with want. She clung to him on that windswept overhang as if he was all that stood between her and being lost at sea. And perhaps he was.

"What is between us will be enough," he said, his voice ragged. "We have fire aplenty, and the desire to keep our people safe. It will be enough."

Would it? Erika wanted to believe him, wanted assurance that the rest of her life would not be a cold existence. What would become of them years from now, when passion died?

Desperate for assurance, she asked, "What if I cannot bear you sons? Will you set me free?"

For a long moment he gazed at her, his eyes shuttered and unreadable. Erika knew that she had gone too far. Before she could apologize, he stepped away from her, dropping his hold as if she'd burned him.

When he spoke his voice was wooden. "If it's freedom you're after, fine. Bear me a son. Then you will have your freedom."

Chapter Sixteen

"Mac Ferghal, there is something I need to discuss with you."

The solemnity in the younger man's voice had Conor drawing his mount to a halt. At last, the reason for this aimless wandering about the northern rim of the *tuath*. "Does this have anything to do with my sister?"

Olan had the grace to flush, as he shifted his reins from one hand to the other. "It does, at that," he admitted, then fell silent.

Conor let him have his peace. There was no need to rush the man into a statement that would alter his world. If there was any among the people of Dunlough who deserved love and happiness, it was his sister. He, who knew loneliness better than any, had felt his sister's sadness like an axe blow. If this Viking was as capable of bringing light back to his sister's eyes as he seemed to, Conor would give his consent of marriage without hesitation.

And if it meant that Erika would remain near to Dunlough no matter the outcome of their duel, so much the better.

It still chafed, her request for freedom. He'd offered her the place at his side and passion aplenty as they made their sons, and she'd rebuffed him. Would her blighted freedom keep her warm at night? Would it keep her safe? Why was it worth more to her than the security of Dunlough?

He followed Olan down a sloping hill toward a copse of trees. They were at the westernmost portion of Dunlough land, near the cavern-pocked shore. There seemed to be purpose to the Viking's wandering, and since his men had startled several deer for the evening meal, Conor saw no need to pull back.

"I love the lady Gwynna and want to wed her."

Conor halted his mount and fixed the younger man with a stare. "Do you, now?"

Blue eyes stared at him without flinching. "I do, and she feels the same." His tone dared Conor to say different.

He didn't accept the dare, not outright. "And what can you, a Viking without a home, offer a princess of Dunlough?"

Olan dismounted and Conor followed suit, waving his men to stay mounted with weapons at the ready against unwanted intruders. The Northman moved into the stand of trees, keeping his eyes to the ground as if he searched for lost treasure.

"I know you think me as unworthy of your sister's affections as I know you are of mine. But while your reasons for the match with my sister are a mystery only you are privy to, my reasons for wanting your sister's hand are as plain as the light of day."

That much was true. Conor knew the way his sister looked at the blond giant whenever he was near, and Olan shared that intensity. "Did she tell you of mac Broin?"

"Yes." The younger man's features grew as harsh as the wind howling from the sea on a dark winter's night. One hand curled into a massive fist. "It is good that this man is dead, though I feel a need to disturb his eternal rest."

Conor shrugged. "Who said he was resting?"

Olan laughed, clapping him on the back with enough force to cause him to sway forward. "As you have taken care of your sister, so shall I. This I can promise you. And more."

With a soft exclamation, the Viking picked up a dead stick of wood, and Conor could see runes lightly carved on one side. Olan then pushed aside dead leaves, and using the rune marker, began digging through the dirt. He soon replaced the twig with his hand and a disreputable dagger.

It was not long after that he uncovered a hinged casket, about the breadth of his massive hands and twice as high, and a well-worn leather pouch. Olan gathered his findings in his arms and rose to his feet.

"It is true that I have no place to offer your sister that I can claim, except my heart," he said, his voice solemn. "But perhaps these can be a small token to you of the esteem in which I hold Lady Gwynna, and the initial portion of her bride-price."

Conor took the proffered gifts. The casket was intricate, carved with symbols he recognized as eastern. Some of the carvings were chased with silver, some with precious gems. The box alone was fit for king or queen. Balancing the chest on one arm, he lifted the lid.

A tangle of gold and silver gleamed up at him, sitting upon a kingdom's worth of stones, polished and not. Conor's artificer would salivate upon catching sight of such a treasure, eager to coax them into intricate works of art.

Olan reached into the box, lifting a fistful of chain and coins from inside. With his other he rooted among the loose stones until he found two matched emeralds the size of a babe's fist.

"All the rest of the box you may have, as a first payment on land to settle my wife," he said with arrogance, polishing the twin gems on his tunic. "These I would gift to Gwynna, if you agree to have us wed."

"Think you to buy my sister?"

The tips of Olan's ears turned a fiery red. "You may think I jest when I say this, but I have loved your sister since the moment I awakened to find her real. I will protect her and our children yet to be born with blood and bone and flesh and muscle. I love your sister as I have never loved anyone. Can you say me the same about my sister?"

His reply was swift and brutally honest. "No."

"And yet you would still wed Erika. Why?"

Why, indeed? It was a question that had haunted him since Erika had first asked it, a question that crept upon him unawares. Why was he so adamant in his intention to have the Angel of Death for his bride? Was it because she fired his blood as no woman had done? Was it because of the proud, regal way she carried herself? Was it because she was the one woman, save his sister, who did not quail when she looked at his ravaged face?

Or was it simply because, in the darkest reaches of his blighted soul, he recognized a kindred spirit in the Angel of Death?

If wishing weren't so futile, he would wish that he had some of the younger man's passion. Wish that his impending wedding had come about because of love, passion or even money. But those things were not a part of him. He had been hopeful and loving once, until guilt and betrayal carved it out of him.

"Your sister and I will be a good match," he said after an indeterminable moment. "I will not be harsh with her."

Olan snorted. "I can see why Erika is so eager to wed you."

The sarcasm at any other time would have bounced harmlessly off him. Today, it rubbed him raw. "Your sister has no place and no people. Every tribal ruler and over-king from Dubh Linn to Sligeach wants the Angel of Death. I can change that. I can give her a home, a people, a name. A place she can be safe. A husband who is not weak."

Olan's expression was passing close to a smile. "There is truth in what you say. But I have told Gwynna and I will tell you: if Erika wins your duel, we will leave here to find a place for her. If she loses and still wishes to leave, I will do whatever I can to achieve that wish. I owe her that much."

"And if she loses and decides to stay?"

"Then I will give her into your care and welcome you as a brother."

Unlike most of his kind, the Northman seemed to be without guile. Perhaps over time, they could become friends. But Conor was not free with his trust. "You would give her with such ease?"

Instead of answering, Olan took the box from him, set it and his cache upon the ground, then charged into him, catching him solidly in the midsection with his massive shoulder. Conor landed with a grunt but taking Olan with him, rolling down the dew-drenched hill to the flat plain.

With his men cheering him on, Conor pummeled the younger man with abandon, receiving more than a few well-placed blows in return. His Gaelic blood sang in his ears. There was nothing more he enjoyed than a good tussle, except a good tumble with a willing woman and a tall pint of ale.

They wrestled to a draw when they were too winded and their eyes too puffed to see clearly. Wiping a trickle of blood from his chin, the Viking asked, "Are you ready to cease questioning my motives, Devil, and say me yea or nay?"

Conor staggered to his feet, squinting at the younger man through swollen eyelids. "If you hurt her..."

"I make the same promise to you."

A smile tugged at the corners of Conor's mouth. "As long as we understand each other."

He helped the younger man to his feet and clapped him on the shoulder. "Come, let us return to the dun. We can discuss marriage portions over a pint. All this talk of marriage makes a man thirsty."

"TELL ME ABOUT CONOR."

Erika nearly bit her lip in a futile effort to snatch the words back. But it was too late.

Gwynna looked up from her sewing, surprise clearly stamped upon her features. "What do you wish to know?"

Disconcerted, Erika put down the tangled mass of wool she attempted to card and got to her feet. What did she wish to know? What he had been like as a child? What manner of man he was? Why he never smiled?

What she knew of Conor only served to confuse her more. He was a harsh man, a fierce warrior, yet the love he held for his people and his sister shone like a beacon fire on a cold night. At times, he seemed to hate Erika almost as much as he wanted to marry her, yet his touch and his kisses were heaven.

"Erika?" Gwynna touched her arm. "Let us go outside. I always find fresh air a good companion to conversation."

Relieved to be free of her failed attempt at spinning, Erika followed the dark-haired woman down the stairs and out of the hall, where Padraig and another guard joined them. Spring had rolled upon the land, and it seemed that every living thing rejoiced in the fact that Beltaine was less than two weeks away. According to Gwynna, the holiday was always a festive occasion in Dunlough. With every member of the clan gathering from the four corners of the land, drawn by the duel between their chieftain and the Angel of Death, Dunlough would be bursting at the seams within days.

Glad to be outside, Erika closed her eyes and inhaled the crisp afternoon air, allowing it to clear her mind as well as her lungs. "You and Conor are very close, as I am to Olan."

"Yes," Gwynna smiled, "we are, at that. Murrough was fifteen years older than Conor, twenty more than me. Murrough was sent to fosterage near Clonmacnoise before I was born. Though Conor and I were separated by our sex, we were bound tight by our blood."

"What was he like as a child?"

"Like most boys, I would believe. He laughed and played and fought. He was a quick learner and loved going to the monastery, even at a young age, to learn from the monks there. There was talk that he would perhaps join the brotherhood."

"Conor a priest?" Erika couldn't help her disbelief.

"I know, 'tis difficult to credit, but I tell you true. Of course, the desire to be in a room filled with books warred most constant with the call of the sea, with traveling. He convinced our father to forgo the last years of his fosterage in return for spending time on a merchant boat. He left when he was sixteen, and traveled the world for near six years."

Her eyes clouded with memory. "I had been wed three years when Conor returned, and came to see me. I had learned by then what to avoid doing or saying to set mac Broin to anger, and I had learned to conceal how he released that anger on me.

"So it was that Conor, who knew and loved me as none other had, never knew my misery. Until I returned to Dunlough for a visit while mac Broin was away, and he came looking for me.

"He beat me unconscious. Conor came upon us, and from what I was told, killed mac Broin with his bare hands. Conor saved my life, but I believe that was the day he began dying inside."

Erika was silent. Even though she had overheard Gwynna's conversation with Olan, the Irishwoman's tale of her first marriage had Erika wanting to do battle. Instead, she attempted to concentrate on Gwynna's words. "You said Conor began dying inside. Why do you say this?"

Green eyes misted with tears. "Many reasons. For one, Conor never forgave Murrough for wedding me to mac Broin. They argued most fierce about it. For another, I had concealed my misery too well, for Conor believed he could find the happiness he believed I possessed, and wedded mac Broin's sister, Aislingh.

"They had been married for a year when Conor saved my life. Their marriage became strained after mac Broin's death, but no one knew the extent until we lost our brother Murrough and his heirs in the battle near Dubh Linn two years ago."

She turned to Erika. "Conor came home a different man. He'd never wanted to rule Dunlough, but he wasn't given a choice. Never once did he shirk his duties, for he loves our land and its people most dear. But something happened between Conor and Aislingh, what I do not know. All I know is that she became even less civil to him, then dishonored him by giving birth to another's babe."

Erika felt a cold knot form in the pit of her stomach. She knew the end of the story. Aislingh had taunted Conor one last time, then attempted to kill him and only succeeded in slashing his face instead. She and her babe had died, but she had taken a piece of Conor with her. Would the shambles of Conor's first marriage overshadow his second? What would befall her if she lost their duel?

She must have made a sound of distress, for Gwynna clasped her numbed fingers. "I do not tell you this to dismay you, but to benefit you. Conor is a good man, a proud man.

He knew how to laugh once. I believe with all my heart that he will again, and it will be because of you."

Panic clamped an iron fist around her heart and she had to force words out of her throat. "Gwynna, if I win the duel, I intend to be quit of Dunlough."

The older woman's eyes were solemn. "I know. And Olan will go with you."

Misery replaced Erika's panic. She loathed breaking this kind woman's heart, any more than she wanted to wound her brother. "Forgive me."

Gwynna managed a tremulous smile. "There is nothing to forgive. You must do what is right, what is in your heart. And yet I hope, when you think of places you wish to call home, you will think of Dunlough."

Erika turned to the scenery once more so that Gwynna would not be able to see the battle she waged with herself. Intrinsic to her nature was the belief that the Norns dictated her life, and the life of all Vikings. She had fought against that, taking up the sword instead of a loom, freeing herself and fleeing her homeland. What if the last seven years of her life, her journeys through Europe and the Far East, had been under the direction of the Norns, to bring her here?

Shaken by the import of her thoughts, Erika closed her eyes. "I am honor-bound to fight this duel. I cannot turn away."

Gwynna's response was cut off by the arrival of their brothers. Their guards carried a brace of deer, and the two men looked as if they had been in battle.

"What befell you?" Gwynna demanded, taking in their satisfied smiles.

Eyes narrowed, Erika sheathed the dagger she had drawn at their approach. She should have known that Olan would avenge her when he could. "They befell each other."

"What?"

As Conor and Olan dismounted, Erika explained, "They were fighting. Each other."

Gwynna turned to the two men, folding her arms across her chest. "Does she speak true?"

Conor looked at his sister with his one good eye. "Gwyn, we are unharmed—"

"Unharmed? One eye is twice the size of the other and you say you're unharmed?"

Olan was not wise enough to stay out of the discussion. "Come now, love, it was just a friendly—"

"Do not dare to placate me!" Gwynna shook off his hand and fixed him with an emerald glare. "Not two months past did I drag you from the clutches of death, and this is how you thank me?"

She released a stream of Gaelic curses that left both men blushing and Erika choking with laughter. She was unable to interject a word, but it wasn't necessary, in any case. Gwynna was saying enough for both of them.

Olan gave Conor a long-suffering glance. "Why did you not tell me that my betrothed is as fierce as a wolf?"

"Would you have believed me? Your wedded life will not be dull."

Gwynna broke off her tirade with a gasp. "Betrothed?"

Olan gathered the dark-haired woman in his arms. "I have asked your brother for your hand, and he has agreed."

Astonishment dealt a blow to the pit of Erika's stomach, causing the air to leave her lungs on a gasp. She turned to Conor. "Is this truth?"

Silver eyes on the couple, he nodded. "It is. The brehons will arrive just before Beltaine, and all will be formalized then."

"Why?"

His gaze swept hers. "You question my motives, Angel?"

Erika forced her fists to loosen, for she did indeed question him. Questioning everything and everyone had saved her life on more than one occasion. "I simply wonder why you would do such a thing."

He placed an arm about her shoulders, turning her to face the couple. "That is why."

She watched as her brother and Conor's sister embraced. Their blissful expressions were almost painful to behold.

"Our siblings have found happiness in each other," Conor said, his voice for her alone. "I will not deny my sister that gift, even if it is denied me."

What meaning should she glean from that? Did he mean that happiness would be denied him because of her actions? Or that it would be denied him always, no matter the outcome of their duel?

Questions seething through her, she raised her eyes to Conor's. For the first time, she delved beyond the enemy, the warrior, in search of the man.

And found him.

Something indefinable but familiar lurched within her, so deep she never sensed its presence before now, had never needed it before now. It shouted with silent joy, a rapture so potent it was dizzying. She would swear that the wind echoed that ecstasy, whispering one word.

Home.

Chapter Seventeen

Beltaine arrived, and with it the day of the duel. Anticipation gripped Conor. Before the day ended, Erika would be his.

"Do you realize all the bards in Connacht can speak of nothing save this duel?"

Conor turned to the man beside him. Niall mac Laighin, chieftain of Dun Lief, was a barrel of a man ten years Conor's senior. During his fosterage at Dun Lief, Conor had worshiped the very ground Niall walked upon. That idolatry had tempered to respect and then friendship after Conor's return from his travels.

Niall fixed Conor with a knowing grin. "'Tis certain we'll be overrun with odes ere the evening is out. The Devil of Dunlough and the Angel of Death. This day will be spoken of for years to come."

"If we get through it." Conor seethed with nervous energy. He was more than ready to dispense with this senseless duel and take Erika to wife.

"You seem disquieted, my friend," Niall observed. "Do you fear your lady Angel will fail to appear?"

Conor ignored the multitude arrayed behind them in the practice field and concentrated upon the path leading from the dun. "The sun is not yet at its zenith. Erika will appear."

Although he knew Erika would keep her pledge to duel him, Conor remained discomfited. Hard put to explain why, even to himself, he nevertheless knew he stood at a significant turning point in his life.

Something had altered between him and the Angel, more than the transition from enemies to allies. Each moment he spent with her, Conor became more aware of the change. Staring into her eyes, he could sense something ancient and powerful stirring deep inside him.

"I have heard news that might be of interest to you." Niall broke into his thoughts. "It is said that Magda journeys to Dunlough."

"Magda?" Conor's pulse raced. "Murrough's wife?" He had not seen Magda since her period of mourning ended and she quit Dunlough to return to her relatives in the south.

"The same," Niall confirmed. "What will you do?"

What indeed? Conor pushed away memories that threatened to cloud this important day. He could ill afford to be plagued by guilt before his contest with Erika. Too much was at stake. "Magda was once mistress of Dunlough. I will not turn her away."

Gwynna and Fionnuala, Niall's wife, joined them. The flame-haired mistress of Dun Lief had lost none of her beauty in the course of her fifteen years with Niall. Though both had tempers as charged as lightning, theirs was a happy union that produced four strapping sons and three daughters as lovely as their mother.

Fionnuala slipped her hand into the crook of her husband's proffered arm and gave Conor a smile. "Gwynna has informed me of how exciting life has been in Dunlough of late, though I can scarce believe it. I would have you tell me true, Conor. Is the Angel of Death as magnificent as is said?"

"More, but I will let you judge that for yourself." Conor nodded toward the path. "She comes."

The crowd fell silent as Erika came into view, followed by Olan and Múireann. Her gleaming hair pulled back into the single braid, she wore a pale *leine* and braes embellished in the Gaelic style. Over her right shoulder, the jeweled pommel of her sword fractured the sunlight.

"Mother of God," Niall whispered. "No offense, my friend, but I may have to change my wager."

"None taken." Others had the same thought, Conor noted. Most of the women seemed to be casting their lots with the Valkyrie.

"She really means to duel?" Fionnuala's voice was just as hushed as her husband's.

Conor felt a smile tug his lips. "It is a matter of honor, and for my lady, honor is everything."

Niall finally tore his gaze away from Erika and faced him. "How will you let her go if you lose?"

"Who has said I intend to let her go?"

He stepped into the circle created by the crowd as Erika stopped before him. The chief brehon and the priest stood between them. Both men looked decided uncomfortable, no doubt remembering how Conor had ordered the marriage contract be written so that Erika became his wife of the highest level, his equal. The lawgiver cleared his throat, then spoke. "There have been questions surrounding the legitimacy of the contest today. The law is clear: no woman shall take up arms and go into battle. The church agrees on this."

Murmurs arose from the crowd. Conor felt his guts clench. He had not waited so long to be denied now. But the brehon's pronouncement was absolute. If he decided against the duel, the duel would not take place. At least, not while the brehon remained on Dunlough land.

"However," the brehon continued, and the crowd fell silent, "this is an unusual circumstance. The rights given the woman by her father is a *geas*. An oath true and sworn cannot and should not be broken. The duel to first blood or disarming will commence, and may God have mercy upon them both."

The priest blessed them, and both he and the brehon stepped back. Erika drew her sword free and passed the baldric to her brother. She twirled the leather grip on her palm, the jewel on the pommel catching the sunlight and breaking it into a thousand bits.

His eyes never leaving hers, Conor drew his own blade. Instead of his heavy broadsword, he chose a lighter blade with hilt and pommel layered with gold and silver wire and studded with gems. Despite its pretty trappings, the blade was sharp. And tested.

So that only she could hear, Conor pitched his voice low and said, "Despite the brehon's pronouncement, you can end this now."

To his surprise, Erika grinned. "I shall not. Besides, I am told it has been years since your last thrashing."

Conor threw back his head with a shout of laughter, no doubt stunning many in the gathering. "Audacious wench! We shall see who receives the thrashing. Defend yourself!"

Erika expected him to move first and was not disappointed. But the blow, designed to knock the blade from her hand, wasn't nearly as heavy as she'd anticipated. She blocked it easily and sent it back to him, with heavier weight.

He parried, understanding. Erika was showing him she could give as good as she received, or even better. He remembered the last time they had crossed swords, remembered that her skill was true and to be respected. He would be ware, but since their duel was not to the death, he would enjoy himself.

When Conor pressed the attack, Erika nearly laughed with glee. Finally he treated her as a warrior and not a woman with a sword. He was proving himself quite a challenge, especially to someone who defended herself almost daily for the last seven years. It was a challenge she would meet and win. For now, she would enjoy herself until it was time to give the Devil his due.

Back and forth they went, the Angel and the Devil. The bards would sing of it for years to come, how two elemental forces contrived for dominion over each other. The worst of it was their smiles. Neither stopped grinning at the other, no matter how fiercely their blades clashed. They smiled at each other with every feint, laughed outright at every parry. It was, they would say, the strangest courtship ever known, but completely appropriate for the two warriors.

No one was sure quite what happened, and arguments would rage over meals for months afterward. One moment Conor was pressing his attack against Erika and the next he was toppling over backward, Erika falling with him. Both swords went flying, glinting in deadly arcs and causing the crowd to scatter lest they be impaled.

For one electrified moment all was still. Then like a wave, people rushed forward.

Conor gave a diligent fight for breath, for Erika's knee was perilously close to that most sensitive of places. She stared down at him, worry darkening her eyes. "Conor?" She patted his cheek once, then harder. "Are you all right? Did I hurt you?"

He groaned. "I beg you to move your knee, unless 'tis your intent to emasculate me. And what right have you to be concerned with my health after you tripped me?"

That got Erika off him quick enough, though her knee in his stomach forced another groan from him. "I tripped you?" she repeated, ire making her accent thick. "I did no such thing. 'Twas you who tripped me!"

Ardan was at Conor's side, helping him to his feet. He brushed the older man away. "Are you insulting me, woman?" he demanded, causing more than a few people to back away.

Erika leaned towards him, her chin jutting out defiantly. More people stepped back. "If you ask whether or not I question your veracity, you have the right of it!"

Niall was the only one brave enough to step between the two. "Arguing like husband and wife, and not yet married." He laughed heartily. "Not an auspicious beginning, but one keeping in character, 'tis certain."

"I'll not be married to this lout, not unless I—" Erika's hot rejoinder squeezed off with a gasp. "He is awarded the victory?"

The brehon stepped forward, standing safely between Ardan and Olan. "Your blade flew first."

"Of course you saw my blade fly—I wanted to teach the man a lesson, not cut him in half. But he let go his own blade first when he tripped over his own feet!"

"Do you claim I am cumbrous as well as a liar?" Conor's query was soft and widened the circle around them even further.

Heat rushed into Erika's face, clouding her vision as she reached for her brother's sword. "As sure as a true arrow finds its target, you—"

"Erika!" Olan's voice cracked like a whip, halting her forward progress. His hands settled on her shoulders. "Look."

She allowed herself to be turned and saw her and Conor's swords. Both swords were embedded in the grass, hers some distance away and vertical, Conor's nearby and at an angle. Her blade could not have been upright unless she released it while upright, just as Conor's had to have been thrown as he was falling.

"Your blade arced several times before it landed," Olan informed her. "Conor's did not."

Olan was right. She had released her blade first, and in so doing, had forfeited her freedom to the Devil of Dunlough.

"Erika."

She turned at the sound of Conor's voice. His expression was a mirror of what she felt, disappointment. "I am sorry. This isn't how I wished it to end. If you wish it, we'll fight again."

"No." She shook her head to emphasize her words. "The Norns have decided, and it is done. I will marry you." She turned away. "I would have married you regardless."

"You look as if you've been struck on the head," Niall observed to Conor as they watched Erika walk away, Fionnuala and Gwynna following. "What did she say to you?"

"You would not believe it. I am not sure I believe it. But there will be a wedding today."

"I wish you well, and luck with my sister." Olan clapped him on the back as the crowd cheered around them. "You will need it."

"Do not think you are done," Conor retorted. "We'll go into this madness together. There will be two weddings this day."

Niall shouted with laughter. "This calls for ale, and plenty of it!"

Chapter Eighteen

Erika discovered that wine eased her trepidation considerably. One cup as Múireann hurried her through a steaming bath, still another as she dried her hair by the fire. By the time she slipped into a deep violet gown of linen with bell-shaped sleeves, and the sleeveless overcoat of lavender, gray and green, she was almost giddy.

Almost.

Fionnuala and her maid joined her as Múireann fastened a heavy silver girdle low on her hips. "You are a sight," the Irishwoman remarked, taking a chair before the hearth and availing herself of the wine. "I can see why Conor is so taken with you."

"Conor taken with me?" Erika could scarce believe it. She looked at the woman through a mass of hair. "Surely you jest with me."

"I do not." She sipped her wine. "Even now, songs are being composed about the beautiful Angel who dared challenge the Devil."

The idea of bards singing about her alarmed and pleased Erika simultaneously. "I am not beautiful," she insisted. "And Conor is not taken with me. That is not why he weds me."

"Then why does he?"

"What reason does a man want a woman for wife? The Devil of Dunlough wants the sons the Angel of Death can give him."

"I've no doubt of that, but perhaps there's more." Fionnuala's maid put a bowl on the table before her, and she placed the tips of her fingers inside. "Perhaps it is also because you are the only woman besides myself and his sister who can see past Conor's scar to the man beneath."

Erika frowned as Múireann finished her hair. "I am well and done with this talk of no one being able to gaze upon Conor. He is a handsome man."

The other woman smiled knowingly over the rim of her cup. "Do you think so?"

"He needs to smile more, to be sure, and he can be quite intimidating. Not that I am intimidated by him," she hastened to add, "but if he did not go about like a thunderstorm about to be loosed, he would certainly be more pleasing to others."

"So you are pleased with your choice of a husband?"

"Forgive me, I did not realize I was given a choice."

Fionnuala accepted a cloth from her maid. "Leave us." When the two maidservants were gone, she turned to Erika and said, "Most women in Ireland do not have a choice, Erika Silverhair. You have been more blessed than most women of our time, for you have decided your own way."

"Have I?"

"You didn't battle Conor a second time, did you now?"

"It would not have been the honorable thing to do," Erika said, the excuse sounding thin to her. But the other woman was right, and she knew it. "Long ago, I vowed to only marry he who could defeat me in battle. A vow has been made. A vow will be kept."

Fionnuala rose to her feet, lifted the bowl and crossed to where Erika sat. "This is *ruam*. It is a stain made from berries that we use to color our fingers and lips for special occasions."

She lifted Erika's hands, gave them a gentle squeeze and placed them in the bowl. "I know that much has happened in your life, more than you may wish to share with a stranger," the older woman said. "Do not worry—you may tell me your tale in your own good time, perhaps when you visit me at Dun Lief."

Removing Erika's hands from the bowl, Fionnuala patted them dry with a soft cloth. "As I said, I do not know you, but I do know Conor. He may seem a harsh, forbidding man, but his circumstances have not been gentle to him."

"I do not consider him forbidding, but I do understand."

The other woman's smile was warm. "And I can tell you, today is the first time I have seen him smile or heard him laugh in almost three years. For that alone, I will be forever indebted to you."

Discomfited by Fionnuala's words, Erika stared down at her red-tipped fingers. She found it difficult to believe that she was the cause, but she knew that Conor's demeanor was greatly improved compared to their first meeting. "My lady..."

"Fionnuala. We are equals."

Erika inclined her head in acknowledgment. "I am honored by your words, but I cannot credit them. Conor was...understandably less than courteous when first we met. We both were. Once we ceased wanting to kill one another, it is natural that his mood lightened."

To her surprise, the red-haired woman laughed. It was a rich, booming sound, full of life and warmth. Erika couldn't help but smile in return.

"I have no doubt that you and Conor will do well together, perhaps in spite of yourselves," Fionnuala finally said, carefully drying her eyes. "It will not be easy—Irishmen are stubborn, wild men. Niall and I did not mesh well at all in our first days. As true as rain is wet, I hated him."

"You hated your husband?" Erika had seen the way the couple regarded one another and could not believe there had ever been any animosity between them.

"Ours was an arranged marriage, melding two powerful families. He is a decade older and was set in his ways even then. It took long months to bend him to my will. But bend him I did. And so will you, with Conor."

Erika snorted her skepticism at that, but Fionnuala brushed it aside. "Mark my words. Be honest to yourself, and to him. You will have a long, blessed life together."

There was a knock at the door then Múireann entered, her eyes round. "My lady, the *tigerna* bade me bring you this."

Hands trembling, the maidservant stepped forward and deposited a small, elaborate casket in Erika's hands. Curiosity lifting her brows, Erika turned to the table, set the box atop it, then lifted the lid.

Purple caught the light and fractured it into a million shards. Inside the casket, on a folded swath of gray silk, lay the most beautiful neck-chain she had ever beheld. The links were of twisted strands of silver highlighted with thin threads of gold. They coiled like plaits, ending in clasps that cupped the bale of the silver pendant that held the massive amethyst crystal.

"Sweet Freyja."

Breath bated, Erika lifted the beautiful pendant from its display. Substantial and cool in her hands, the purple quartz swung freely in the light, mesmerizing her. The bauble was like a living thing in her hands, power and beauty and grace, ferocity and brilliance and ice, all combined.

It was Fionnuala who fastened the heavy silver clasp, settling the neck-chain onto her collarbones. The older woman stepped back, her eyes wide with awe. "You were beautiful before. You are stunning now. It is perfect for you, Erika. Perfect."

Erika's hands fluttered against her collarbone as Múireann held the bronze mirror so that she could view her reflection. She had never owned anything so lovely. That Conor had gifted it to her made something thrum deep inside her. Was she so mistaken about the man who would be her husband? Could he care for her?

She was prevented from articulating her thoughts by Gwynna's arrival, with the priest and Fionnuala's maid behind. "Erika, Abbot Brochadh has come to hear our confessions before we pledge our troth."

Erika privately liked the dun's priest, though she rarely saw the man and knew he was not enamored of her. His personality was pleasant and the manner in which he helped the people of Dunlough pleased her.

The russet-haired man took the carved chair near the hearth that Múireann offered, and the goblet of wine Fionnuala's maid handed him. Fionnuala went first, as befitted her rank, and then Gwynna.

It came Erika's turn. Brochadh gave her a genuine, if somewhat wary, smile. "Shall we begin, my lady?"

With a nod and a deep breath, Erika launched into her confession.

Her voice was quiet and matter-of-fact as she recounted every man she had killed since choosing the warrior's way at fourteen. Eyes fixed on the priest, Erika was nonetheless aware of the horror Gwynna and Fionnuala felt with each word that left her lips. It saddened her that their regard for her might be tarnished, but she had done what she had to do, and most of the men had needed killing. Punishing at the very least.

An hour and two glasses of wine later, her confession was done. It was some moments before Brochadh could find his voice. "Do you enjoy being the Angel of Death?"

"I take no joy in killing. It is what was given to me to do, and I have done it well. If I can prevent horror by my presence or my name, then that is a good thing. It is the same for the Devil of Dunlough."

Brochadh nodded, as if her words were expected. "And do you believe the *tigerna* to be a capable man, able to defend his people and his *tuath*?"

Erika paused. There was something in the careful wording of the priest's questions that puzzled her. "There has never been a question of that, not to me," she finally said.

"If you believe him capable of protecting his people and his home, how much more will he protect his wife, the mother of his heirs?"

Too late Erika saw the trap opening before her. Must be the wine, making her addled. "You wish for me to put away my sword."

It was not a question, but Brochadh answered her. "It is not seemly for a woman of rank to go into battle, or even to touch an instrument of death. The Church forbids it."

Erika thought about that for a moment. She was still too Nordic, too Viking, to ponder the ramifications of the Church. How could God damn her for being what she was, and doing good with it?

Brochadh gathered her hands in his. "I listened to you, my lady. I know you take sorrow in killing. I also know you did not have much in the way of choice. Now you do."

Yearning pulled at her, sweet and strong. Putting away her sword...it was the secret dream buried in her hearts of hearts, a dream she never believed would come to light. Doing battle had been a part of her for so long, she did not know anything else.

"Has Conor asked this of me?"

"Nay, my lady, the *tigerna* has not asked this," he said, his eyes lowered.

The priest seemed so distressed that Erika longed to cheer him. "I will make a vow, that you will not see me draw a sword. Will this satisfy you and the Church?"

"Of a certain," he replied, vastly cheered. "Thank you, my lady. Your new path will not be regrettable, I promise you." He left.

Fionnuala smiled serenely. "I noticed that you neglected to mention that you would not draw a sword when Brochadh wasn't looking."

A shrug lifted Erika's shoulders. "If the priest did not notice the oversight, far be it from me to point out the faults of a holy man."

Gwynna's laughter echoed theirs. "You will be more than a match for my brother, Erika. I welcome you as my sister."

Touched beyond words, Erika found herself initiating the hug with her new sister. "Thank you."

Fionnuala broke the emotional silence by clapping her hands. "It is time."

Gathering her sword, Erika moved towards the door and her rendezvous with destiny.

Chapter Nineteen

His bride came to their wedding armed.

Conor saw his sister descend the flower-lined path to the verdant plain first. She wore a deep tunic of green banded with gold, her dark curls adorned with delicate white flowers. He heard Olan, standing beside him, gasp for breath and whisper something in Norse. Conor smiled to himself. Gwynna would overrun the young Viking if he did not learn to control his impulses.

It was the last coherent thought he had.

Erika made her way towards him, a vision in silver, gray and lavender. Held before her was her naked blade, point towards the earth and festooned with flowers and ribbons. The amethyst pendant nestled in the hollow of her throat as if it belonged there. The gem highlighted the deep color of her eyes, making them a mystery. The afternoon sunlight flocked to her until it seemed she glowed, from the artful array of braids, curls and purple ribbons adorning her hair, to the silver beads on her slippers.

He watched as she smiled to everyone she passed, robbing all of speech. When she reached him, she bestowed upon him a smile so brilliant he forgot the effrontery of her sword. He wondered, dazed, if he courted the danger of going blind. She stood to his left, urging him to poetry, her beauty stealing through him like a fog.

Radiant.

His mind latched on to that word. Yes, she was radiant, more luminous than the moon, brighter than the sun. He gloried in her presence, finding her scent beneath the perfume of flowers. Tonight she would be his. Tonight, after the feast of Beltaine, he would claim her.

Beautiful, untouchable. Yet she suffered his touch, seemed to glory in it. Why?

The question shook him, releasing a flood of others. Why did she suffer his touch? Why, after pursuing her quest for freedom with single-minded intent, why did she capitulate?

What did she want from him?

And the deed was done. For good or for ill, the Angel of Death was joined to the Devil of Dunlough in holy matrimony.

Whatever their feelings for their new mistress, the people launched themselves into celebration with exuberant wholeheartedness. It was Beltaine, after all. The great festival heralded the rebirth of the earth, and the Celtic spirit in all was unleashed with a zeal that would have been debauchery anywhere but in Eire.

Tinder for the great bonfire that was the hallmark of the festival day had been laid after the completion of the duel. Horse and foot races and feats of strength—not to mention great barrels of wine—kept the crowd occupied and the mood festive. Now was the time for feasting, singing and drinking. With sunset would come the lighting of the bonfire and the time for lovers new and old.

The hall overflowed with revelers. Conor surveyed the gathering with satisfaction. For too long Dunlough had been overshadowed by grief, death and war. Today changed that. His bride changed that, starting with lighting his dim corner of the hall and deliberately sitting to his left, in full view of his ravaged face. Those simple acts won her the admiration of his people—their people.

Over the rim of his tankard he watched her converse with Fionnuala. Conor was glad that Niall's wife had befriended Erika. His bride knew little of managing a household, much less one of Dunlough's size and stature. The mistress of Dun Lief would be a welcomed aid.

The dun was rowdy. Erika grew more intoxicated, her eyes rounding with each passing libation.

A tittering sound had Conor turning. Did his wife just giggle? "Something amuses you, my lady?"

A weaving hand gestured towards a darkened corner. "Your people dance passing strange."

Gaze following her unsteady gesture, Conor realized that the couple in the corner participated in a dance as old as time, the only rhythm that of their bodies. "Passing strange, indeed." He shifted to block her view.

Undaunted, she peered around him. "I wish to dance," she stated, her voice imperious with wine. "Will we dance that way?"

Heat assailed him. The image of Erika writhing beneath him caused his hand to tremble as he reached for his goblet. He couldn't keep the huskiness from his voice as he said, "In time, my lady wife, we shall indeed dance."

The new mistress of Dunlough smiled and clapped with delight. Conor damn near found himself smiling in return.

Her eagerness drove blood into his manhood, making him achingly erect. Nothing would do but satisfaction, and now.

He shot to his feet, need making him clumsy as he overset his seat. Music and revelry ground to a halt. Erika rose to her feet as well, her smile for him alone. "Now shall we dance?"

The need to throw her over his shoulder and carry her to their chamber drowned out all else, including good sense and decorum. He reached out, hands settling on her waist—

"It is time."

Aine's voice cut through his fevered senses, reining in his ardor. He couldn't help his muttered curse of frustration, however.

Niall, damn his hide, noticed his state. "Let us light the bonfire before you quench your own," the older man jested. "You'll dance soon enough." Ardan and Fionnuala joined his laughter with their own.

There was nothing for Conor to do but follow the old woman out to the bonfire site, Erika weaving along beside him. Most of his people, it seemed, were paired off. Those maidens still awaiting marriage contracts had already been secluded by their protective mothers.

Impatient, he hurried through his duty, giving his speech and laying his torch to the kindling. Tradition held that conceiving a child at Beltaine was a good omen for the year to come, and he meant to do his part.

As soon as the fire sprouted Conor turned away, seizing Erika's wrist and all but dragging her toward the dun. Niceties and tradition be damned—he wanted his wife, and he wanted her *now*. No one would gainsay him.

Except his bride.

She dug her heels in as people streamed around them, ribald comments and well-wishes coloring the air. "I do not wish to go inside as yet."

Petulant as a child, Conor thought, feeling the frown stealing over his features. "Whyever not?"

Her lower lip pushed forward in a pout that would have been amusing at any other time. "You promised me a dance, and I shall have it."

"So you shall." He turned to the dun once more. "In our bedchamber."

"No."

"No?" Surprised that she dared again to contradict him, he let her go.

With a trill of laughter she spun away from him, graceful despite the amount of wine in her blood. "If you think marriage will make me meek and biddable, you are mistaken. Just because you won our duel does not mean you shall have me so easily. You shall have to catch me first."

She gave him a measuring stare that fired his blood anew. "If you can."

Taunt still ringing in his ears and too dumbfounded to do aught else, Conor watched her traipse down the path to the lake.

"I'd be after catching her, were I you," Niall remarked, his wife tucked close under his arm.

Conor glared from his friend to Fionnuala's all-knowing smile. "Did you coax her to this?"

Niall's wife gave him an innocent stare. "And would I be doing that to your good self?"

"In a moment."

Laughter boomed from Niall's barrel-like chest as he gave Conor a push down the path. "Let your bride lead you on a merry chase, my friend. Have no care for your bedchamber. My lady wife and I shall see that 'tis used proper and get ourselves a Beltaine bairn."

Still laughing, they turned away. Conor did not conceal his growl of frustration and he headed in the direction his wife had taken. A merry chase indeed. There was nothing merry about trying to run with an erection.

ERIKA BROKE THROUGH the stand of trees circling the pond, pausing to catch her breath. The crisp night air sobered her enough to make her question her sanity, but not enough to return to the dun and seek Conor out. Besides, she was enjoying herself.

Nervous energy skittered along her veins as she found the supplies Múireann had prepared earlier in the day and set them out. More than once in the course of the day she had overheard speculation concerning the virgin sacrifice to the Devil of Dunlough. She knew now, for instance, that no woman had been in his bed since Aislingh's death more than a year ago. Many of the dun's women had wondered if that would serve to make a normally painful event even more unbearable.

A mixture of emotions clogged Erika's being. She wanted Conor's touch, craved it with everything within her. At the same time she feared the warnings of women more knowledgeable than she. Would Conor hurt her?

Branches snapped as her new husband burst through the trees, outraged and triumphant together. He certainly looked as if he meant to do her harm, if his expression was any indication.

"So, my Angel—you wish to dance?" His voice hummed with want. "Then dance we shall."

Before she could react he swooped down on her, clasping his hands about her waist. Lifting her, he spun about in a maddening circle until laughter escaped her and they were both dizzy. Yet he planted his feet firmly, and it was a measure of his strength that he was able to set her down slowly, imprinting the front of her body with his own and leaving her unequivocally aware of his aroused state.

"If you wanted to lead me on a chase, my lady, you should have picked another destination," he chided her softly. "This is the first place I thought you would go."

"That was my hope," she admitted as his gaze took in the cushioned pallet, jug of wine, and candle and tinder. "There was magic here, the night you brought me."

Her eyes lowered as she confessed, "I thought if we returned, I might feel it again."

Sword-roughened hands slid up her arms to cup her cheeks. "Beltaine is a night of magic. Perhaps enough remains for us."

The touch of his lips forced her eyes shut against the flare of passion that swept through her. His kiss was a slow melding of mouths that left her breathless. She pressed against him, reveling in the feel of his masculinity, aching for something she could not name.

She barely noted her silver belt falling to the ground, followed by her over-tunic and gown sliding down her arms. It wasn't until she stretched out on the cushioned pallet that she realized the moment was at hand. Involuntarily she stiffened, then forced herself to relax and hoped he would not notice.

Conor did indeed notice. "Erika."

Loath to interject reason at such an unreasonable time, he knew if he didn't make the effort now, he would not be able to later. Besides, his honor demanded nothing less.

He shifted away from her. "Erika, if you do not wish to do this, we shall cease."

Pale brows knitted. "Why?"

Now his brows knitted. "I told you before, I will not take a woman against her wish."

"It is not against my wish." Yet, her rigid body denied the declaration.

A flash of insight had him leaning over her, caressing her cheek. "You are afraid."

Scarlet crept up her neck to her cheeks. "I am...uneasy. Several of the women told me the first night is not joyous for the woman, especially if she has never... They said it would be best to lie as still as possible, that you would be done soon enough."

She took a deep breath, then burst out, "If it is so painful, why do some women take coin for it? Surely the payment is not worth the agony?"

Conor struggled for words to reassure her. His last virgin had been his last wedding night, a fact he did not care to recall at the moment. He had not given a thought to his partner's pleasure before. Now he found himself wanting to hear Erika's breath catch with pleasure, feel her body hum around his as she found her fulfillment.

"I will not lie to you," he said. "There can be some discomfort when the maidenhead is breached, but it eases."

"Do you think it will be worse than a sword thrust?"

Conor felt his lips twist at the ludicrousness of it all. Only his wife would liken deflowering with a sword thrust and mean it literally.

"There are few things worse than a sword thrust, and a wedding night is not one of them," he assured her. He cleared his throat. "There is also the fact that you have led a life that most women have not. It is possible that your maidenhead was broken before."

She stiffened, and even in the dark of the night he could see the flash of her eyes. "I have said that I have known no other man. Do you not believe me?"

Of course he believed her. The trepidation in her eyes, the instinctive stiffening of her body were true. "I believe you. It was but a thought, that the harshness of your existence until now may have done damage. I will endeavor not to hurt you."

She stared at him for the longest time, then cupped the nape of his neck, drawing him to her. Wordless, he took the offering of her lips. Under his gentle coaxing, her mouth opened for him as a blossom for the sun, and he drank his fill of her nectar.

When her arms went about his neck, drawing him even closer as she matched the depth and intensity of his kiss, Conor couldn't restrain his groan of pleasure. He had to have her. He would go mad if he didn't.

Rising to his knees, he ripped away his wedding finery. Erika's gaze was a physical touch to his burning skin and he felt himself swell even more with his need for her.

Her gaze moved from his throbbing arousal to her own body. "Are you certain you will fit?" she asked, worry leaching the passion from her voice. "It seems impossible."

"Aye, if there's one thing I'm certain of this night, 'tis that we'll fit well together." He lay beside her, claiming her lips as his hand slid from the base of her throat to the rising swell of one milky breast. A soft sigh escaped her as his forefinger teased he delicate pink bud to life, and she pushed her body against his in a wordless entreaty for more.

And more he gave. He forged a trail of kisses from the cleft of her throat to the rise of her breast, branding first one, then the other with his tongue. As she writhed beneath him, his hand commenced a slow glide down her belly to the crisp hair at the juncture of her thighs.

The soft touch at the molten center of her core caused Erika to emit a muted shriek of pleasure. "What do you do to me?" she asked, breathless. "It is beyond anything I have ever felt!"

He kissed her again, his mouth demanding as it slanted over hers. "I am using the magic of Beltaine to claim you as mine," he whispered, his breath hot against her cheek. "I will bind you to me with chains of pleasure. You cannot escape me."

"I-I have no desire to escape," she confessed, "only to feel—more..."

"More you shall have."

His hands and mouth seemed to be everywhere at once, tasting her, stroking her. Instinct claimed her as her hips strained against his hand. It was as if she were caught in an elemental storm, buffeted by winds of the purest ecstasy she'd ever known as she hurtled towards the edge of the sea. Fervent hunger rose within her, drowning out all but his name as she reached the ends of the earth and catapulted off into the stars.

In the depths of her release, she felt Conor move above her. "Hold onto me, my Angel," he compelled her, then entered her with one surging thrust.

Everything froze. Her heart, the night, their bodies. He filled her so completely she could scarce draw breath.

"Erika?" His voice was a strangled whisper. "How do you fare?"

"It is not a sword thrust," she said, her voice thin. "It is more like being impaled by a spear. Are you done?"

A shudder passed through him, echoing in the depths of her core. "Nay, my sweet, I am far from done."

Concern for him caused her to forget her momentary and now dissipating ache. "But you sound as if you're in pain."

A groan broke from him. "A moment... I did not expect you to be so tight."

He withdrew from her, slow and measured, and Erika drew in a deep breath of relief. Just as slowly, he flowed back into her. Prepared for pain, she was surprised to discover none. Indeed, in its place was a curious rippling sensation that made her want to melt like springtime snow.

She shifted beneath him, causing him to settle even deeper. A mewling sound collected in the back of her throat as a wave of pleasure washed over her. When Conor attempted to withdraw again, she clamped her arms about him, silently urging him to stay.

He groaned again. "My lady bride, just deflowered and already demanding. I could not be dragged away from you now even if my limbs were chained to a thousand galloping horses. Wrap your legs about me, sweet Angel. Burn me with the fire of moonlight."

Erika complied and cried out at the pleasure that consumed her. Conor moved against her, his thrusts increasing in depth and speed as desire flared even higher. She quickly learned the pleasure of matching his thrusts, her fingernails digging into his back for purchase. Fire coursed through her, burning away all coherent thought, shrinking all of existence down to where she and Conor were joined. The flames became a searing white-hot conflagration that exploded into a thousand sparks, blinding her.

Conor felt the heat of her fulfillment explode outward, consuming him. With a hoarse, triumphant shout, he gave himself to the flames, spilling his seed into her in a violent eruption seemingly without end.

For an eternity Conor lay above her, his face pressed against the curve of her neck. His senses were in shreds. He'd known it would be good between them, but this joining was unlike anything he had experienced before. On a fundamental level he was no longer the same.

One coupling, just one, and the Devil of Dunlough had given his soul to the Angel of Death. He did not particularly enjoy the knowledge.

Disquieted, he withdrew from her, got to his feet and crossed the clearing to the pond. He scarce took the time to hold his breath before plunging his head into the cool water. As an attempt to restore his senses, it was poor indeed.

He tossed his hair back from his eyes and discovered Erika watching him, her cloak clutched about her as a shield for her nudity. "Did I..." Her voice ground to a halt. She took a deep breath and began again. "Did I disappoint you?"

"How can you ask such a thing?"

Unable to look at him, she gestured toward the pond. "You were so quick to cleanse yourself, to rid yourself of my touch."

Her bluntness would be the death of him. "Erika, look at me. Do I seem disappointed?"

She lifted her head, her mouth rounding as she regarded his awakened arousal. "It was a failed attempt to curb my hunger for you," he told her, as blunt as she. "I would take you again, if you were ready."

For answer, she dropped her cloak. "I am ready. I want to touch you as you touched me, kiss you as you kissed me—"

"Take me as I took you?"

He meant it for a jest, but Erika cocked her head, seriously considering his question. "I suppose it is near to being astride a horse. Do you not think?"

Think? Thinking was impossible when all his blood coalesced in his turgid flesh. "There will be time enough for that," he said as he reached for her again, buried himself within her again. "Our wedded life has just begun."

Yet time, he knew, was not on his side. The day his seed took root in her womb was the day that time would start to count against him.

He could not afford to become attached to his wife. Enjoy the passion, yes. Secure an heir. But if there was anything he knew about Erika, it was that she would never relinquish her desire for freedom. And when she completed their bargain and walked away, he had to ensure she would not take his soul with her.

Chapter Twenty

Erika froze, her blade at the ready. Her enemy was almost in her grasp. Just a few heartbeats more...

Someone sneezed, shattering the tense silence. The hen squawked and flutter-hopped out of her reach. A decidedly unladylike curse escaped Erika as she chased after her quarry in the kitchen yard. Several of the dun's children, attracted by the clamor, laughed with delight as their mistress chased the terrified bird about.

Erika blew her bangs from her sweating forehead after the hen eluded her yet again. "Do you think you can do better?" she challenged her young spectators.

The children nodded enthusiastically. She couldn't resist a smile. "Very well. The first to capture yon bird receives a ride on Tempest."

The idea of riding the Angel's warhorse proved irresistible, and soon the yard was filled with shrieking laughter as the children joined the merry chase.

Damnable minutes later, Erika pounced on the hysterical fowl. Grasping the fattened bird securely beneath her elbow, she prepared to sever the head with her dagger.

"Milady, no!"

Múireann's warning came too late. Erika quickly realized that hens took great offense to being decapitated. The dismembered bird fought her more viciously after she killed it than before. By the time it ceased its death throes, she and a goodly portion of the yard were drenched in blood.

"By Odin's one eye, 'tis easier beheading a man than this foul-tempered fowl," she exclaimed, wiping her forehead with her sleeve. "How do you do this several times a day?"

Múireann released her laughter with an explosion of sound. "First, 'tis simpler to twist their necks, or put them in a bag before beheading them."

"Twist their necks?" Erika felt her stomach churn at the thought. "Well thank goodness I do not have to entertain such a deed again."

She thunked the bird down on the worktable. "I have dispatched the enemy. Now what must I do?"

She watched Múireann attempt—and fail—to school her features into a semblance of seriousness. "Now you must pluck it."

"Pluck it? You mean I must *pull* the feathers out?" Her stomach rebelled anew. "Can I not just skin it with my blade?"

"No my lady, we will use the feathers, with fresh herbs and straw, to stuff the mattresses. Your mattress."

"Oh." Erika felt heat flame her cheeks. Last night in their eagerness she and Conor had ripped their bedding, sending feathers throughout the room. Attempts to gather the airy bits resulted in a wrestling contest that in turn became another interlude to pleasure.

Heat increased in her cheeks, and in the sensitive place between her thighs that Conor knew so well. What was happening to her? From the moment of the consummation of her marriage, she had become a wanton. No it was before that, on the moonlight ride when she discovered caring beneath the Devil's stern exterior.

Now she could not even look at her husband without remembering and wanting. Damn his hide if he didn't exacerbate matters with the sensual twist of his lips that twisted her insides into knots, and knowing the exact moment she was alone.

Oh, he ambushed her several times a day. 'Twas obvious pleasure was not only to be had at night. Before she could open her eyes from sleep he was inside her, waking her more thoroughly than the sun could. Then after a long ride he would corner her in the *lios*, and she'd spend hours picking straw from her hair. In the exercise yard. At the pond. In the hall before their chamber.

Yes, being wed was certainly no hardship. And much more pleasurable than a sword thrust after all.

Shaking her head to clear it of such distracting thoughts, she bent to the task at hand. With a deep breath she grasped a handful of feathers and gave them a tug. The lifeless body quivered beneath her hold but would not relinquish its natural covering.

Her stomach tumbled again. Air pulled into her lungs to press upon her trembling insides, and she strengthened her hold. Pulled. Felt the feathers give way reluctantly, strength in such fragile matter.

It was too much. Dropping the bird on the worktable, Erika ran to the far corner of the yard, leaned over and vomited her breakfast into the grass.

Múireann was beside her, holding her hair, offering a damp cloth. She took it gratefully, wiping her sweat-drenched face and hands before taking the proffered cup of water and rinsing her mouth.

"How is it," the older woman wondered, "that the Angel of Death can strangle a man with her hair as rope yet come undone at plucking a chicken?"

Drained, Erika straightened with a sigh. "I've never been in a kitchen. While we traveled, 'twas Olan or Larangar who dressed our catch. Any birds we had were taken by arrow and skinned by knife. We had no use for feathers while we roamed."

She eyed the bird and suppressed a shudder. "I do know that I will never attempt this again. Such a feat is clearly beyond me. You will have to find another way for me to contribute to my household."

Múireann gave her a knowing smile. "Perhaps there is another reason for your weakened stomach? As much as you've been about with the *tigerna*, you should be with child."

"I know." Unfortunately, Erika had to disappoint them both. "My courses began yester morn."

She failed to keep the desperation from her voice. It had been ever on her mind, the need to contribute, since Olan and Gwynna had left for their new holding of Glentane the day after their wedding, a month gone. While passing strange to be apart from her brother after so many years, Erika found herself missing her new sister and her fount of knowledge. With her wedding to Conor however, it rightfully fell to Erika to oversee the managing of Dunlough's daily activities.

While it was all well and good that the dun's servants feared the Angel's wrath should they relax their standards,

Erika yearned to make a contribution to her home. She wanted to belong, to be needed.

She wanted Conor to need her.

The admittance didn't shake her as it once would have done. Rather, it filled her with an odd, quiet desperation. While she lived for the joy she found in Conor's embrace, she knew they needed more between them. Given their proclivity, it would not be long before she was with child. And once she was with child, her final days in Dunlough would begin.

Neither of them mentioned the bargain they had struck before they were wed. It was a bargain made from fear, mistrust and need. Despite the passion they shared, the vow hung between them, dormant, needing only the sign of her pregnancy to give it life.

"You do not need to prepare the food for the dun, my lady," Múireann assured her. "Sine rules the kitchen and would have it no other way. Besides, the herb-lore you are learning from Old Aine is a task given to every mistress of Dunlough."

Erika had surprised herself with her grasp of Aine's knowledge. She was proving to be an apt pupil, combining the aged healer's knowledge with her own recollections of wonders she had witnessed during her travels. The healer did have a steady stream of visitors to her hut near the lough, wanting everything from love potions to cures for fainting spells. If she performed even a portion of Aine's duties, it would secure her place in Dunlough.

She wasn't sure when her thoughts of freedom had transformed into thoughts of making her life in Dunlough permanent. Perhaps during the magic of Beltaine. Perhaps during the nights since, when Conor gave her pleasure so potent she could barely breathe from the memory of it. All she knew was that she wanted this to be her home, but she didn't know how to tell Conor that. Didn't know if he would be amenable to her staying. Yes, he'd made her his wife but that ensured the legitimacy of their children. All knew that he wanted heirs more than he wanted a wife. What if he sent her away despite her wanting to stay?

She buried the remnants of her morning meal beneath dirt and grass. "You are right, Múireann. And 'tis certain I would enjoy memorizing tonics and poultices more than plucking and puking."

"Milady."

Gil, Múireann's son, stepped forward, prodded by his fellows. "You promised us a ride, milady."

"So I did." She put her hands to her hips, surveying the ragged line of children. They retreated several paces. "A promise has been made, a promise should be kept. Is that what you believe?"

"Aye, milady."

"Then I am well-pleased. A promise is sacred, and should not be taken lightly whether it's to your friends or people in need. Since you all believe the same, you all may have a ride."

The children accepted this with boisterous approval, all except young Gil. "The girls can't ride!"

"Whyever not?" Erika asked.

"Because they're girls!"

Several other boys nodded their agreement to this logical pronouncement. The girls of their number looked mutinous, but most were close to tears at being denied.

Erika faced young Gil. "So you say that the girls may not ride, because they are girls?"

"Aye milady."

"But I also happen to be a girl."

His eyebrows shot into his scalp. "No you're not. You're the Angel of Death."

Smothering a smile, she replied, "That I am, but I was a girl first. And if I can ride a horse, so can they. Do you not agree?"

Gil had no choice but to agree. With children holding to her gown, her arms and her braids, and Múireann following, Erika headed around the yard to the front of the dun—

And stopped short at the sight of Conor with another woman in his arms.

CONOR HAD KNOWN THE day would come, and still he was unprepared.

He had been exercising in the *faitche* behind the dun, getting pummeled by his men. Difficult it was, keeping his mind on bashing a man's head in when all he wanted was to tumble his wife.

Madness, that's what it was. Married little more than a month, and still he thought with his nether regions. He could not get enough of his Valkyrie. In the morn, his cock would stir before the real cock could crow. After the noon meal he eased his digestion by easing into her gossamer heat. And at night—ah, the glorious pleasure to be had by candle-light.

It would have been easy to escape the madness had his wife not been so willing. Yet his bride matched him hunger for hunger, fever for fever. Her touch on his skin caused a fire to roar inside him that had yet to be quenched. The way her eyes darkened just before she achieved her pleasure near un-did him each time. He was nigh to believing his bride a faerie queen come to drain him of his very life-force.

At the rate they progressed, it would not be long before she ripened with his child. The image of Erika round with his bairn caused something to seize in his chest, something not unpleasant. It was sobered by the knowledge that when she began to increase, her time in Dunlough would commence to decrease.

He wanted her to stay, damn the fates. But she'd gone on so about her freedom up until their wedding that his pride wouldn't allow him to ask her to remain in Dunlough. He'd not beg a woman to stay at his side. And if Erika could give birth to his son and still want to leave, she wasn't someone he'd want to keep for a wife at all, was she?

"Someone comes!"

Grateful for the interruption, Conor tossed his sword to a guard and moved to the gate, Ardan beside him. He won-dered why no outriders had announced the caravan's pres-ence, and made a note to restore discipline with a good pum-meling.

Four men on horseback escorted a cart made handsome with gilded appointments. Two occupants stood at the fore:

a guard to drive the team of horses and a slight figure wrapped in a cloak of many colors.

Something about the multihued garment brought to mind the sounds of battle, the moans of death, the screams of denial. Clouds skittered across the sun, casting shadows that settled upon him like an iron weight, unshakeable.

The cart stopped at the gate, and the figure descended. Heart thudding, Conor stepped forward to greet his late brother's widow. "Magda. Dunlough welcomes you."

Murrough's widow was a small woman with flawless cream skin and hair that still burned bright although the edges were dimmed with gray. The emerald eyes stared at him without mirth, though the remainder of her expression made the attempt.

Memories assaulted him. Blood soaking everything, so much blood the earth could not hold it, like a waterlogged field after a heavy rain. Staggering about, a quiver's worth of arrows protruding from his *bratt*. Ardan coming to him, gray-faced, telling him what he already knew: Dunlough's ruler and heirs were gone and the survivors waited for his word. His word, for he was now king.

Head shaking in denial even as the bodies were laid before him: Phelan, Teigue, young Murrough. Then Conor's brother, brought to him in pieces, felled by two men with axes before they were dismembered in kind.

Magda put her tiny hands on his forearms. "Conor. Welcome me as your sister, for 'tis true I shall always be."

Wooden, he encircled the slight woman with his arms, noting the careful way she avoided looking at his ravaged face. He felt her fragility and the strength that had borne three sons and the loss of her husband.

He remembered the day, that horrid day he had returned to Dunlough. Magda and Aislingh both waiting at the gate. Aislingh's joy at seeing him, the last time he would see delight for him on her face. Magda's pale face becoming paler, for she knew before he could tell her. Knowing she knew but having to tell her anyway that her king and the three princes she had birthed him had come home for the last time.

Remembered always, the look she had given him before asking the question that continued to burn him: *why didn't you save them?*

Accusations did not color her features now, just the resigned look of sadness of every woman whose men are warriors. "It has been long since we have seen you," he said for want of anything else to say.

"Too long," she agreed, giving him a smile, a smile he was greedy for. "My heart will always be here, 'tis true, but it was time for me to go. Yet I had to return to wish you well, when I heard your good fortune."

Erika. Erika would have to be told that Magda had come, that a place would need to be prepared for the former mistress of Dunlough. Then he remembered her words on the bluffs overlooking the sea, when she'd told him she knew nothing of running a household.

But Magda did.

Erika would need her counsel in managing the dun. Even if his brother's widow would be a constant reminder of his failure, he would have her here as long as she wished to stay. For if Erika learned to manage the dun, one of her reasons for leaving him would be allayed. And he wanted her to stay, without doubt.

"Conor?"

The sight of another woman in her husband's arms caused a curious sensation deep inside Erika, a painful thump she'd never felt before. It made her yearn to reach for her sword, to defend herself.

The woman was beyond beautiful. She was tiny, not quite hitting Conor at the center of his chest. Creamy skin never abused by sun and wind, brilliant red hair that dimmed everything around her, and eyes the color of prized emeralds. The smile she gave Conor was too private, the way he held her too personal.

Erika remained frozen in place, dimly aware of the children and wolfhounds buzzing about her. She felt like a great lumbering beast, ugly, ungainly and boorish. Doubting that the woman before her had ever been other than perfect, Erika passed a grime-encrusted hand over her unraveled braids and down to straighten her skirts, stopping when she encountered the dried streaks of blood.

Mortified, she stepped back, intending to retreat into the dun or back to Denmark. At that moment the couple caught sight of her.

"Erika?" Conor strode toward her, scattering children and hounds alike. "Are you injured? What befell you?"

His hands settled on her shoulders, his concern loosening her tongue. "I fought your dinner. The dinner won."

For a moment his eyes sparked silver with mirth, then just as quickly shuttered. "Come. There is someone for you to meet."

Despite her reluctance, he guided her to the petite woman. "Erika, I would like you to meet Magda of Roscommon, widow of my brother Murrough. Magda, this is my wife, Erika."

Cool appraisal hit Erika as the Irishwoman gazed at her, from her soil-covered feet to the bloodstained smock to her dirt-smudged face and unkempt hair. She knew without the words that the widow was less than impressed.

"So this is the infamous Angel of Death?" Magda asked. Even her voice was beautiful, soft and lilting. "You look older than I imagined. The tales did not give truth to your beauty—nor to your prowess in battle, I'm sure."

Erika forced her hands from the crusted gown. While Magda's voice was pleasant, there was an undercurrent to her words that felt like barbs. And even though the widow smiled, it was a smile that did not reach her eyes.

Must be the grief, nothing more, Erika thought. It must have been devastating, to lose husband and sons the same day. She remembered how bowed with grief she had been over her father and could not begin to perceive the depth of Magda's sorrow. Two years would not be enough time to sublimate a loss of that magnitude.

Magda spoke again. "And none of the stories mentioned that you had children."

"Children?" Erika stared blankly at the woman. "Oh. No, they are the dun's children. I promised them we'd go riding."

"Riding?" Magda's voice was incredulous. "How do you find time for riding, when there is so much to be done running your household?"

Despite the dulcet tones, the censure was all too evident to Erika's sensitivity. Her back stiffened, and she said, "The people of Dunlough know their duties and do them well. I have complete trust in them."

"Well of course you do, and didn't I train them myself?" Magda answered smoothly. "Yet even I, who was mistress here twenty years, would not leave them to their own devices. You must ensure the standards are maintained, for Dunlough is renowned for its hospitality."

Conor finally came to her defense. "She did passing well with the feast at Beltaine."

Erika flashed him a grateful smile, a smile that faded as he continued, "I am sure, however, that there are a thousand daily tasks that my lady has yet to experience. Your advice would be appreciated."

A brilliant smile lit the Irishwoman's features, and she bowed her head in demure acceptance. "Of course, Conor, I will be happy to assist where I can."

She should be grateful, Erika knew. But dislike, intense and unforgiving, flooded her. She had always relied on her instincts, and her instincts sent a frisson of alarm through her and prodded her to say, "I would not want you to extend your visit just for me. I am sure you'll be anxious to return to your relatives soon."

Both Conor and Magda turned stone-like expressions her way, and she knew her voice had betrayed her. Magda reached out a small hand, and touched her larger, calloused one. "It would honor me to assist you. It has been long since I have had a purpose such as this."

Conor put his hand on the older woman's shoulder. The intimate gesture sent a shaft of something so foreign coursing through her that it took Erika a moment to realize it was jealousy. The bolt twisted further when he said, "Dunlough was your home for twenty years. It is still your home, and we wish you welcome."

Chastened and chagrinned, Erika swallowed her initial impression. "*Ceade mile faite.*"

Múireann took that moment to reappear. "Milady," she said, bowing to Erika, "a room has been prepared."

"Thank you, Múireann." She turned to her visitor. "Perhaps you wish to rest from the ardors of your journey?"

The two women turned up the path leading to the dun proper, Erika grateful that Conor did not accompany them.

Magda leaned close, careful to keep her cloak from touching Erika's blood-soaked skirts. "Is it true then, that you had to duel Conor, and wed him because you lost?"

The hushed horror in Magda's voice had Erika wincing. "It is so."

The older woman drew closer on the path. "It must have been horrible for you, to forfeit your freedom to wed the Devil of Dunlough."

Obvious sympathy had Erika wondering if she had imagined Magda's earlier censure. "Of a certain, it has been difficult at times."

"And overwhelming, to be sure," Magda said with understanding. "I cannot imagine having to forgo being—what are you called?"

"The Angel of Death."

"To forgo being the Angel of Death, to come and go as you please, being a warrior and a force to be reckoned with, reduced to being a prisoner of Dunlough."

"I am not a prisoner."

"Of course you are not. Being mistress of a political center like Dunlough is a different kind of freedom altogether. 'Tis certain to be a monumental adjustment to you, dealing with the dun and its master. Do you find it difficult to look at him?"

The blunt question took Erika by surprise. She rushed to defend her husband. "Conor is a handsome man."

"I meant no disrespect," Magda said, her voice reassuring. "He was quite a handsome man, a favorite of many a lady, until Aislingh carved his face in her madness." She paused. "You do know about Aislingh, his first wife, do you not?"

"I know." Erika's hands bunched in her skirts. She was more than ready to dispense of this duty, change her clothes, and take a much-needed gallop to the village and back.

"What a sad day that was for Dunlough," Magda continued. "It was devastating to Conor, so it was. Even more so, since he loved her to distraction."

"Conor loved her?" The question escaped before she could stop it.

"He did indeed. And swore never to marry again, because of it. That is why your marriage is such a surprise, though a pleasant one. I'm glad he realized that if Dunlough is to remain strong, he needs an heir."

The woman's perception was too much. "Forgive me, but I must clean my gown before the fabric is ruined. Múireann will see you to your room. If you will excuse me?"

Without awaiting an answer, she gathered her skirts and fled.

Chapter Twenty-One

E ven the Angel of Death knew when to admit defeat.

Spring faded into summer as Erika's marriage entered its third month. The bliss she'd experienced as a bride had quickly faded after Magda's arrival. The former mistress had moved from advising Erika to managing the dun. When Erika discovered that the servants reviewed her every order with their former mistress, Erika stopped giving orders altogether.

She kept her misery to herself, however, and filled her days with riding, telling stories to the dun's children, and studying herb-lore with Aine. True, she could have gone to Conor, but to what purpose? Would she say that Magda was too helpful? Erika had to admit that the Irish princess knew her duties and did them well, leaving Erika feeling decidedly extraneous. The only expectation that Dunlough seemed to have of her was to provide an heir.

By the saints, how she wanted to comply! More than anything she wanted to give Conor his heart's desire. Yet she was torn, for the bargain loomed in her mind: if she birthed a son, she would have to leave.

But she didn't want to. She had come to regard Dunlough as her home and could not imagine being anywhere else. Conor would not want her to leave if there was something she could do, something necessary.

Summer, like spring, was a green time, and Erika was dazzled by the variations of the color as she walked up the path to the dun. With the coming of summer, most of the dun's livestock had been moved to grazing grounds closer to the mountain. Some of the women were there as well, the better to make the butter and soft cheeses that were part of summer's food. They were guarded by youths old enough to defend themselves yet too young to go to war, and some of the men whose turn it was to remain at home.

War. Before, the word would fill her with tingling anticipation. Now it caused her worry. Would Conor have to fight? What if he didn't come back to her?

Urgency quickened her pace to Aine's hut, close enough to the dun for its protection, yet far enough away that the old woman could "hear the earth think", as she put it. The earth and timber dwelling seemed to grow from the land surrounding it, covered as it was by grass, flowers and plants. But there was peace here, a calming power that never failed to soothe Erika. Today she hoped it would aid her.

She rapped her knuckles against the doorframe before stepping inside. "Good-mother, may I have a word with you?"

The old woman looked up from the bundle of herbs she was wrapping. "Of course, child."

Erika settled on the wooden bench that had seen better days. She retrieved needle and thread, to continue stitching the herb-bags she'd begun earlier that morning. Usually this task was a mind-numbing exercise of pain as she stabbed her fingers more than the cloth, but now she brought all her will to the task as she struggled to put her request into words.

"What bothers you, my lady?" Aine asked, her green eyes alight with her inner strength. "'Tis obvious that something weighs heavy on you."

Looking everywhere but at the woman beside her, she replied, "In my study with you I have learned that there is more practical than magical in your remedies."

She could feel the ancient eyes on her, assessing her. "'Tis true enough. But what is practical to some can seem magical to others, like a great tree growing from so tiny a seed. Are you in need of magic?"

Being subtle was difficult for Erika, so she dropped all pretense. "I wish you to give me a tonic to quicken my womb."

The request hung in the air between them like a poisonous fog. Old Aine turned on the bench, piercing Erika with her squinted stare. "I know of your foolish bargain with Conor. Are you anxious to leave your life here?"

Erika couldn't subdue the flush that stained her cheeks. "No, I like being married to Conor. I just..." She faded, looking down at her fingers as she twisted them into knots in her lap. "He wants a child so much. I want to be able to give him that."

A gnarled, pale hand reached into her lap and squeezed her numb fingers with surprising strength. That simple gesture released the iron control Erika held herself with.

"I have tried, Aine! I have tried to do as Magda bids, to learn what I must as Conor's wife. I have tried to prepare meals, I have tried to sew, I have tried everything. I can do nothing a woman is supposed to do in a household. I would like to be able to do this one thing!"

"My lady, it is still early in your new life. You must give your body and yourself time to adjust. You will conceive when it is time."

Erika turned on the bench, grasping the old healer's arm. "Please, Aine, you must help me. I must be able to do this. I must!"

Green eyes stared into lavender for an interminable time. Finally the old woman sighed. "All right. I will help you."

"FAR BE IT FROM ME TO intrude where I do not belong—"

"When has that ever stopped you, Niall?"

Niall coughed once, then squinted up at the graying sky. The rhetoric of the meeting was enough for one day, and Conor had called its end, leaving them to stretch their legs. "Never, when I deem it important."

Conor heard the seriousness in the older man's tone and paused. "What is it?"

"How long do you intend to keep Magda here?"

The question surprised him. "Why do you ask such a thing?"

"A dun cannot have two mistresses."

"My dun does not."

"And you are certain of this?" Niall's voice was skeptical. "Magda was princess here for two decades. Your new wife is a Viking mercenary. Whom do you believe your people follow?"

Surprised and disconcerted, Conor replied, "They follow my wife because she is my wife. I do not expect her to change from Angel of Death to princess of Dunlough overnight. If Magda can help her learn her duties, is that not a good thing? Besides, Erika has not complained."

Niall gave him a level look. "Would she? To you? About your brother's widow?"

He could not refute Niall's words, and the logic behind them. However, he tried. "This is Magda's home. I cannot send her away."

"Forgive me, Conor, but Murrough is dead. No amount of wishing and keeping her here will bring him back. Having Magda act as mistress here only sows discord in your home. Unless..." He paused. "Unless you have tired of your wife already, and mean to put her aside?"

Anger pulsed through Conor, and he clenched his teeth. "Only the friendship I bear you keeps you on your feet, Niall."

The other man smiled. "So that's the way of it, then. You are besotted with your wife."

"Besotted? I think not."

"Think what you like, but it was only when I questioned your need for your wife that you threatened harm."

Conor stopped denying. "Erika is a fever in my blood. I thought my need for her would wane, yet it increases. When I cannot have her, I become surly. But our time is limited."

"Why?"

"She means to leave after she births me a son."

"'Tisn't true!"

Conor nodded. "It was a vow we made before we wed. She can have her freedom when I have an heir."

"And she agreed to this?"

"Freedom is important to Erika. Important enough to duel for, do you not remember? And we are both of us honor-bound to keep that vow."

Niall frowned. "And 'tis certain you do not entice her to stay with another woman under your roof."

"What can I do? I cannot throw Magda out." The guilt at even the thought threatened to crush him. "I will not throw her out."

"I know, my friend." Niall clapped his shoulder. "I would just urge you to caution. Having loved and lived with my Fionnuala for the last fifteen years, I can tell you women are handful enough without hurting their feelings. Once you do that, there's the devil's own mother to pay. I do not envy you and your decision. I do not envy you at all."

Chapter Twenty-Two

Conor mounted the stairs to the bedchamber, fatigued in body and mind. It seemed more possible that war would be waged yet again, and Dunlough's warriors would join those of Glentane and Dun Lief to heed the request of the King of Connacht. While thoughts of going to battle resigned him, thoughts of what he would leave behind plagued him.

Gwynna and Olan had come for a visit and announced their impending parenthood at dinner. Erika was quick to embrace both with joy at the news, and he'd managed to mutter something congratulatory. Yet as Erika returned to her seat beside him, her hand went to her still-flat stomach. A look of such intense longing crossed her face that it caused a most painful twist to his insides. He'd reached over to clasp her hand, and she'd returned the gesture with a desperate embrace. Moments later she'd excused herself by pleading a headache, a plea Conor knew to be false but allowed to pass.

Could Erika be upset that she had yet to increase? It concerned him, yet it did not. It would take her time to become acclimated to the role of wife. And the longer it took her to conceive, the longer she would remain. Was it possible that Erika wanted to carry his bairn? Why? To leave—or because she wanted their child as much as he?

Thoughts jumbled, he pushed open the door to their bedchamber, then stopped in surprise.

Candlelight glowed from every corner of the room, casting light on a steaming bath. Sitting on a stool at the head of the bath was his wife, welcoming him with a warm smile.

He stepped into the room, closing the door behind him. "I thought you were sleeping your headache away."

She rose and crossed to him, and he saw that she wore a thin shift that outlined every curve of her body, and the necklace he had gifted her with on their wedding day. "I didn't have a headache," she confessed, not the least ashamed of her falsehood. She gathered his hand and led him forward. "But you seemed weary with all the talk of wars and rumors of wars, and I want to give you surcease tonight."

Conor tore his eyes from his wife's beguiling form and looked at the steaming bath, wanting nothing more than to bathe his cares and strain away. Taking his silence for agreement, she unfastened his belt, placing it on the waiting table, then helped him from his *leine*. The simple act of unfastening his belt had unleashed his hunger for her, and he settled his hands on her shoulders to draw her near.

She slipped away from him with a light laugh. "Bathe first, my lord."

Disgruntled, he glanced at the bath with several vegetable-looking things floating in it. "Think you to make of me a stew?"

"They are just herbs, to ease you," was her answer. "Though I will make a stew of you if you do not get in."

So he complied, enjoying her light banter and the heat on his skin, knowing it to be a precursor of the heat he would find inside her. He sat waist-deep in water, his arms draped over the sides, his legs slightly bent. "I do not suppose I could entice you to join me?"

She laughed again, kneeling beside him, and her mirth soothed him. "There is not room enough for us both, though the idea is a tempting one."

"You could sit on my lap."

Her eyes darkened, and Conor thought he'd won. Then she shook her head. "Allow me my way tonight?"

"As you wish, my lady." He settled in the water. "But you are in my debt."

Erika moved behind him to sit on the stool he'd seen earlier. "You shall collect soon enough," she said, her hands running through his hair, pulling it over the lip of the bath, untangling it. Conor closed his eyes in pure delight, almost groaning as warm water sluiced over his scalp.

Why was she doing this? She had never attended him before—unless he took too long to undress before bedding her—and he had never expected her to. What had he done, or hadn't done, to receive such blissful attention?

"Why do you tense?" her voice whispered over his left shoulder as she massaged his hair.

"I do not."

"Then why are your hands fisted?"

Caught, he forced himself to relax, his fists to open. "I wonder why you do this."

Her hands stilled in his hair. "Does this not please you?"

He heard the genuine surprise in her voice, and beneath it the hurt, and near groaned again. "It pleases me much. My true question should be what have I done to deserve this, that I may do it again?"

The ministrations of her hands commenced again. "You are you, Conor mac Ferghal. I want to do this for you. Is that not reason enough?"

Thrown, Conor remained silent, though inside he marveled at the woman who was his wife. How could she have known that he needed this—needed her? He didn't care whether she knew how to make candles, stuff a mattress, or pluck a chicken. If it ever came to it, and he was unable to defend Dunlough, knowing she was within its walls was a sweet relief.

"Erika?"

"Hm?"

"Tomorrow, if you will attend me at council?"

A gasp answered him, and a minute twinge of pain as her fingers tightened in his hair. Before he could demand to know what befell her, she answered, "It would honor me."

"Good. We will begin after the morning meal." He settled deeper in the bath. Her hands in his hair were as gentle and lulling as being in a *curach* on the still waters of Lough Dun. He could imagine himself in the little boat, waves cradling them as he rested his head in Erika's lap and played her a tune on his harp...

A sharp cracking sound had him lunging from the water, reaching for his sword. Laughter stopped him, and he turned around.

Erika still sat on the stool, her hands covering her mouth, her eyes dancing with mirth. "We are not being attacked, my Devil. 'Twas but a snore."

Heart still pounding, he pushed his wet hair from his eyes and returned to his previous position. "If you are weary, my lady, we should end this."

A fist connected with his shoulder. "Do not think to lay that devil's sound at my door. 'Twas yourself that snored, and loud enough to wake the dead. 'Tis right obvious you are tired. Perhaps sleep is all you need this night?"

Lightning quick he turned in the bath to grab her, but she had already stepped away. Miffed, he stood, planting his hands on his hips as the water sheeted off him. "Do I seem as if sleep is all I need?"

Appreciation sparked her eyes as they dropped to the center of his anatomy. "Far from it, my lord."

The husky murmur swelled his erection further, pushing the tip snug against his navel. He held out a hand to her. "Come here."

As if in a dream, she shook her head, her gaze never leaving his arousal. "Only if you let me finish your bath."

"I am done with my bath, and with waiting." He paused, and her gaze moved to his face. "I want you, Erika."

A small sound escaped her as she dropped the cloth she held. Her breathing came faster, causing her nipples, firm and proud, to push against the delicate barrier of her shift. It was a moment before she found her voice. "If I—if I could dry you?"

With a nod, he stepped from the water and moved to stand before her. She retrieved the cloth she'd dropped and stepped behind him to dry his hair. He could feel the heat of desire rising from her, and the gossamer glide of her shift on his back near undid him. Tremors shook her fingers as she rubbed the cloth in a slow, amorous manner over his shoulders, down his back to his buttocks, down one leg and up the other.

Conor forced himself to stand still, to accept the torturous ministrations that seemed so important for her. The cloth, damp now, slid down his left arm as she crossed in front of him. Then across his chest to the right arm, the heavy-lidded expression she wore stealing his breath.

Sweet skies, she made love to him with her hands, her heat combining with his to evaporate the water on his skin. The cloth slid down his chest, bypassing his turgid center, and she knelt to dry the front of his legs. She made his battered body feel more precious than any treasure.

Warm breath on his thighs almost brought him to completion. His erection didn't want to be dried. It wanted to be wet, to bathe in the warmth of her mouth. But she had never done that to him and he had never told her of that ultimate pleasure. Then her hands closed about him, both hands not enough to cover the length. The half-formed request died before reaching his lips as his hips moved forward, pushing his hard length through her hands. He thought he would die.

And then she kissed him.

Knees close to buckling, her name on his lips was a groan, a plea, a prayer. Then a benediction as her mouth drew him inside. She was unskilled—the brush of her teeth told him that—but her fervor was enough to kill a lesser man. He was sure he himself saw the lights of heaven.

Harsh groans tore from him, and he attempted to back away from the exquisite pleasure. She stopped him with fingernails digging into his flexing buttocks and the gentle press of teeth on his vulnerability.

When he stood still, she paused long enough to ask, "Do you like this?"

"Like it?" His voice was a strangled groan he didn't recognize. "I'm close to dying from the liking of it. Who told you of this?"

"A whore in Constantinople," was the blithe reply. "She said it could drive men to madness. Are you mad?" She licked him.

"Delirious." Another harsh groan shook him, deep and rumbling, as his hips flowed forward on instinct. "Erika, stop. I am close to spilling in your mouth."

She paused again, looking up at him in mischievous pleasure. "Will I like that, do you think?"

Breath whooshed out of him on something close to a laugh. "I do not know, *mo aingeal*, but you are close to discovering it for yourself."

"All right." And damn him if she didn't latch onto him in earnest, demanding with lips and tongue until he shouted.

She gagged and withdrew. He dropped to his knees, weak-limbed, the final spurt of his seed spilling to the rug. He thought he'd been struck blind with pleasure until he realized his eyes were closed. Dragging them open, he discovered his wife beside him, wiping her hands and mouth with the drying cloth she'd used earlier.

Her smile was satisfied as she poured a goblet of wine. "You're salty, like sea-spray. Not unpleasant at all. Next time, I will be prepared for the amount."

"Next time?" Conor near dropped the wine she passed him. "Next time?"

She took the goblet back, taking a long draught that fired his senses. "Surely there will be another time? You were pleased, and I enjoyed giving you pleasure."

She enjoyed pleasing him. With such ease and truth the words came from lips that had just ravished him. "Have no doubt, my lady, I enjoyed receiving it. Now I shall return the favor."

Rising, he lifted her to her feet and crossed to their bed. Her cheeks flushed with pleasure as he ran his hands over her curves through the diaphanous material of her shift. Even that flimsy barrier was too much and he grabbed a fistful and drew it over her head, the motion causing her to sit on the edge of the bedstead.

Kneeling between her thighs, he cupped her face in his hands. "You are beyond imagining."

As she flushed pink with flustered pleasure, he slid his sun-darkened hands down the pale column of her neck to the twin globes with their rosy peaks, teasing them both with the tips of his thumbs. She moaned low in her throat, head tilted back, her breasts thrust outward in a silent entreaty he could not deny.

His lips closed around one nipple, her appreciative moan gratifying and hardening him. As he laved her with his tongue, his free hand slipped down her belly to the pale hair at the juncture of her thighs. The immediate rush of heat and intake of breath inflamed him, as did the welcoming shift of her legs to give him free rein.

She was ready for him, wet and warm. His thumb found the sensitive rise of her flesh even as two fingers slipped inside, delving into her softness. Breathing his name, she arched against his mouth and his hand, her body tensing with longing.

Not stopping the motion of his fingers, he raised his head to look at her. Her cheeks were flushed with passion, her eyes dark as the evening sky. The stark desire on her face, pure and unfeigned, pleased him.

"Now, my angel, it is time to please you as you've pleased me."

Erika didn't have to wonder what he meant. His lips replaced his thumb on the throbbing flesh between her legs, and she collapsed backwards with an inarticulate cry.

Waves of pleasure tossed her as Conor drank from the fount of her desire. Her hips rose of their own accord, her shoulders pressing into the feathered mattress, her hands digging into the bedcovers, his shoulders, his hair. If she didn't anchor herself, the pleasure was sure to carry her away. As it was, the rhythmic laving pushed her to the edge of a precipice, dangling her over the edge.

"That's it, my sweet," he whispered against her center. His fingers continued their relentless advance and retreat inside her. "Leave go."

When his teeth grazed lightly over her engorged crest, her hips convulsed. As he drew on her, pleasure slammed into her with the force of two armies colliding. Reflex caused her legs to clamp about Conor's shoulders, his name a warbling cry on her lips as ecstasy launched her off the cliff and into the stars.

She didn't know how long she danced among the stars before her body glided back to earth, her senses in shreds. Dimly she became aware of Conor's mouth leaving her, the dip of his weight as he climbed onto the mattress, the heat of his body as he settled beside her.

Languid, she turned her head to look at him. Clear gray eyes stared back, sparkling with satisfied warmth. She would swear that his lips curved in a grin.

Heart thumping wildly with pure nameless emotion, she reached out, touching his lips. He caught her hand and kissed her palm. "My Devil, if this is hell, I will stay here forever."

His chest heaved, causing her to sit up. "Did you just laugh?"

"I did not."

"I believe you did."

"You believe wrong."

"We'll see about that!" Erika pounced on him, her fingers searching out the sensitive areas on his body. He rolled away but she followed, not to be denied. Victory was hers as she straddled him, tickling his ribs and coaxing a true guffaw from him.

"I've done it!" she crowed. "I've made the Devil laugh!"

"And so you have." He gazed up at her, eyes darkened, his hands on her thighs. "Such a momentous feat deserves a reward. Name your pleasure."

Her pleasure was lengthening beneath her. "You."

The look he gave her made her insides go weak with want. "Then take what is yours."

With his hold to steady her, Erika impaled herself, melting around the warm, delicious length of him. How he filled her, expanded her. Completed her.

Deep, so deep she could taste it, she felt him. Then he shifted, flexing his hips to settle her more firmly. In an instant her world exploded, in quick, violent waves that momentarily blinded her.

The swift fulfillment only served to fuel the flames of her desire even more. "Conor, come with me. I want to—I need to feel you with me..."

He rose to sear her breasts with the rippling pleasure of lips, the exquisite pressure of his teeth. Head tossed back, hands clamped to his shoulders, she rode him, urging them both on to glory. His fingers dug into her hip bones as a hoarse shout tore from him. His joyous release welled so deep inside her that she cried out, arms flung wide with the searing overwhelming pleasure of it.

Depleted, sweat-slicked, they collapsed against each other. His arms closed about her, cocooning her in the afterglow of their still-joined bodies. Sated satisfaction slid towards sleep as she kissed the taut skin over his heart. "We have done it," she whispered. "We have made our child."

She registered the tightening of his arms around her and nothing more as sleep claimed her.

Chapter Twenty-Three

Magda caught Erika at the entrance to the dun's smaller meeting hall. "The men are at council."

"I know they are, thank you." Erika forced civility into her tone. Dunlough's former mistress had given her hostile looks all through the first meal of the day, a meal she and Conor had arrived to late. If her expression had been identical to her husband's well-sated one, Erika knew everyone at the table—perhaps everyone in the dun—knew why they were so exhausted.

Displeasure turned down the corners of Magda's mouth. "If you know they are at council, then you must also know they are not to be disturbed."

Erika stepped back, surprised at the other woman's decidedly waspish tone. She watched Magda make a visible effort to calm and say, "Perhaps things are different in your homeland, that women sit at councils of war, though how a lady could stomach such talk is beyond my knowing."

She gave a delicate shudder. "Of course, I realize that you are lacking full knowledge of our customs, having spent your time in our fair land engaged in bloodletting. It is a joy to me to impart to you the knowledge I gained as mistress here."

There was not a day that passed that Erika didn't hear what Magda had done as mistress of Dunlough, and she had heard enough. "I am glad, Magda, to give your life some joy. My duties as mistress are plentiful, and your assistance with

Cook and the housekeeping earn you my heartfelt thanks. In fact, if you would be so kind, assist Cook with bringing refreshments to the council. My lord expects me, and I do not wish to keep him waiting in matters of war."

Done, she moved past the startled—and blessedly silent—woman and entered the chamber. Smaller than the main hall and free of the perpetual cloud of smoke, this chamber held a single table running the center of the room. Around this sat Conor, Olan, Niall and three others she did not recognize. The latter were recently arrived, if the dirt-caked look of their clothing was any indication.

All had turned, stood, when she entered the room. The strangers stared with surprise, and Erika wondered if she had stained her smock yet again. She almost bobbed her head to check when Conor stood, his eyes lightening as they rested on her. When he held out his hand she stepped forward to take it, and smiled for him alone.

He led her to the place beside him at the head of the table. "Lady wife, this is Domnall mac Cormac, emissary to Taig of Connacht. With him are Cormac Roe, and Lughaidh, both of Belanagare. I present to you Erika ni Conchobhair, princess of Dunlough."

She had not heard her new name and title since the ceremony of their marriage, and it startled her at first. Domnall was a slender fellow with intelligent blue eyes beneath his auburn hair, his strong chin devoid of beard as was the wont of a few nobles. Cormac the Red was true to his name, with a shockingly bright beard and mane of hair. Lughaidh was as dark as Cormac was red, with a stature that could have called to mind Danish blood.

Domnall blinked several times before bowing to her.

"They sing of your beauty, though I must say, mere words do not do justice to the actual seeing."

She was aware of Conor tensing beside her, probably as uncomfortable with the flowery comments as she. "As for seeing, I see that you have traveled long and hard to reach this council. That bespeaks the seriousness of your news?"

"You speak true, my lady," Domnall replied. "Though my tale may not be suitable for your delicate ears."

Delicate ears! Her hand began to curl in a fist until Conor covered it. He leaned forward. "The Angel of Death will hear what you have to say."

The emissary swallowed before saying, "The fighting near Dubh Linn is increasing and has sparked fighting near the mouth of the Shannon. Power struggles between the Ard Ri's surviving heirs and the former high king have fractured what was even then a precarious alliance. Some of the Munster tribes have engaged our people near Clonmacnoise."

Clonmacnoise was not so terribly far from Glentane. Far enough to be safe, yet close enough to worry.

"The King understands the need to be ever vigilant against Ulster," Cormac Roe said, "but he believes the presence of the kings of the north—and the Devil of Dunlough in particular—will turn the tide."

"Meanwhile we leave our homes defenseless," Niall observed.

From the few years she had spent traveling Ireland, Erika knew the remark was not cause for treason as it might have been elsewhere. Taig ruled Connacht because the province wished it so. Provincial kings ruled by tradition and agreement and strength of the tribal chiefs, local kings and rulers of the larger duns and raths.

Conor, as chief of his tribe and ruler of one of the largest local kingdoms, and Niall, a powerful chieftain in his own right, were a reckoning force. The Connacht King had to ask for their assistance. Their first thought would always be to their *tuaths*, then their tribe, then to their over-king. If Niall decided not to join this fight, then the men of Dun Lief would not go. It was almost certain, Erika knew, that if Conor refused, Glentane and Dun Lief would remain behind as well.

Erika waited with interest for Domnall's reply. "*Tigerna*, the King does not request that you empty your fields or leave your homes unprotected. Yet he is firm in his belief that a showing of strength by the rulers of the north would be a fine showing indeed."

The three northern rulers exchanged glances, and Erika realized that an accord had already been reached, most likely before the emissary and his companions had been spotted on Dunlough land. Conor confirmed it when he said, "Taig will have his showing, and we will have ours."

Doubt was clear on Domnall's face. Erika realized that their showing was why Conor had asked her to be present. She turned to her husband. "What would you have me do?"

"That which you do so well," Conor answered.

"Fine. Who am I to kill?"

BY MIDDAY, ALL WAS prepared for departure. Erika, who well knew the necessities of a traveling army, oversaw the preparations. Magda, after greeting the men from Roscommon, was notably absent.

Erika stood with Gwynna and Fionnuala at the entrance to the dun, as they and their captains prepared to return to their respected homes. "You rendered Domnall mac Cormac speechless?" Fionnuala asked. "I didn't believe such a feat possible!"

"When Conor asked me to be the Angel of Death, I asked him whom he wanted me to kill. Lughaidh cursed, Cormac spewed his wine, and Domnall just gaped like a dying fish. And since Conor didn't intend for me to kill anyone, all our husbands just smiled!"

The image had them erupting with laughter, laughter they needed to cover the worry Erika knew each of them felt. Their men were capable warriors, honed in battles and border skirmishes. That did not mean they would worry less, however.

"I do not know what you have done," Gwynna remarked, "but you are to keep doing it. I believe I saw my brother smile."

"Conor has always smiled," Erika insisted beneath her blush. "Though truly, not with what most would consider gaiety."

"I concur with Gwynna," Fionnuala said. "Today you have come into your own as mistress of Dunlough. Remember yourself, and know you have but to send word, to either of us."

Touched, Erika embraced the older woman. "I know, and I will. I promise you that."

She saw them to their respective entourages and husbands, and looked for her own. He was already astride his night-dark stallion, overseeing the contingent of Dunlough men. The black *leine* he wore contrasted sharply with the saffron yellow of his men, and her heart swelled with pride to behold the man she'd wed.

His gaze caught hers and he urged his mount up the slope to where she stood. She couldn't resist touching him, resting her hand on the powerful muscles of his thigh, reveling in the flexing of muscle and sinew and bone beneath her hand. "My lady, I entrust the safety of Dunlough and its people to you. You will be the Angel, but you will have a mixed company of soldiers from each of the duns with you. Do not endanger yourself or the future of Dunlough." He gathered his reins.

"That is it?" she asked, incredulity causing her voice to rise. "That is all the leave-taking I am to receive from you?"

"What more is there to be said?"

What indeed? Tender expressions of heartfelt devotion? The feelings swelling in her chest were too fragile to be set free, even more so that she could not be certain of his response to them.

Averting her gaze, she muttered, "Perhaps no more to be said, but surely more to be done."

Conor stared down at his wife. How she had blossomed during her short time as mistress here. He was loath to leave her, to miss any moment away from her side. The quicker done with battle the quicker he could return.

He lifted her hand from where it burned the skin of his thigh and brought it to his lips. "Take care of our land and our people while I am gone."

Dropping her hand, he wheeled his mount around and dug his heels into its flanks, lest he do something he'd never done—such as throw her over his shoulder and carry her off like plunder.

Keep going, he told himself, feeling the normal frown pulling his features. Keep going and do not look back, do not see the way the sun glistens through her hair, the tender expression in her eyes, the firmness of her breasts beneath her tunic—

Cursing to wake the dead, he startled the men around him by wheeling his horse in full stride and turning back from whence he came. His wife saw him, must have read the intent in his eyes. At the right moment she launched herself at him, vaulting up even as his arm settled about her waist to haul her before him. To the cheers of their men, the Lord of Dunlough carried his wife off to their private glen.

Her laughter vibrated against his chest, her hair streaming like sunlight over his shoulder. His heart swelled with a heady, rich feeling it took him several moments to recognize: happiness. He set the feeling free, allowing it to burst from him in laughter to match hers.

Once the dun disappeared from view, he slowed the horse to a walk. "Swing your leg over and lean forward."

Without question she complied, and he yanked the hem of her skirt up, exposing her thighs and pert behind. His hands on her bare flesh had her peeking at him over her shoulder. "What do you do?"

"I'm attempting to ease the fever you have caused in my veins," he answered, easing her back and down.

"But we're on a h...ah." Her protest died as he slid into her soft heat.

He anchored her with one hand on the flat of her stomach and urged his mount into a steady trot that did his work for him. "How can I give you a proper leave-taking when I do not wish to leave at all?" he asked, passion roughening his voice as he curved into her. "How can I ride away from the memory of last night and your mouth and heat?"

"Conor." She leaned against him as he dropped his hands to her waist, her hands digging into his thighs, no longer needing the horse's movements as guide. His hair fell over her shoulder like a sable waterfall as he leaned forward to trail kisses along the column of her neck, her jaw, then to her lips.

His hand slipped beneath her skirts, his fingers finding the slick jewel at the center of her pleasure. "By the saints, I'll never have enough of you."

He wasn't deep within her, but he was deep enough, stroking her, inflaming her. Within moments she shuddered about him as he spilled inside her, their cries of completion mingling on the summer-laden breeze.

Sated by the proper farewell, he righted their clothing then pulled her back against him with both arms wrapped about her. He rested his cheek against the back of her head. "This memory and last night shall be like a sumptuous feast, giving me sustenance while I am apart from you."

She turned as far as she could, giving him so deep a kiss that his toes curled. "So it shall be for me as well."

Conor turned Brimstone back to Dunlough. "I will rest easy, knowing that Dunlough and the others are in your capable hands. But have a care for my battered soul and be not overzealous in making the presence of the Angel of Death known."

His hand settled on the rise of her stomach. "And if 'tis true that the heart of Dunlough's future beats beneath your breasts, you are to cease."

She laid her hands atop his, clasping them. "I promise. Will you promise something to me?"

"If I can."

She reached up to remove a chain from inside her tunic and turned to place it around his neck. "This is for you."

Curious, he lifted the chain in his hand. It was a pale cord wrapped in silver wire, from which hung her cross and hammer. That she would part with her battle charms for his sake pleased him beyond measure. Then he realized the silken cord was not the ribbon he thought it, but hair.

She smiled when he looked at her in wonder. "I know I cannot ride into battle beside you as is my wont, so I will leave that to Ardan. With this you can take a part of me with you, and I shall be there in spirit. All I ask is that you bring my charms—and yourself—back home hale and whole."

"I will."

It was a promise he made willing, and was glad for the making of it. This vow he would keep.

For the first time in over two years, he felt hope.

Chapter Twenty-Four

Erika sat astride her mount on the rutted and well-worn path that was the road north to Dunlough, three guards with her. The secluded glen and trips to the village had been her comfort during the month of Conor's absence, as Magda had continued her subtle attacks. Now, even that small measure proved fleeting.

Above her, the sky churned in a frightful swirl of black and ash-gray clouds. The air was heavy with anticipation of the tempest, so much so that the very land seemed to quail beneath the promised onslaught. Yet the sky served as manifestation of the tumult churning inside her.

Someone close to her was dying.

She had felt it in her dreams. Had dreamed of a wolf with the bloodied, broken body of a raven in its jaws as it loped along a blood-drenched plain. Had dreamed of Valkyries descending from Asgard to gather those heroes slain in battle, lightning flashing on their helms.

Word had already reached them two days ago of the terrible battle fought at the center of the island. The carnage supposedly rivaled that of Clontarf. No one knew the number of dead, only that hundreds were.

Was Conor among them? Erika's heart asked what her mind could not, answered what her mind could not. The Devil could not be among the slain. Every fiber of her being thrummed with the knowledge that her husband still lived.

Yet her mind and her heart needed the proof, needed to see him astride his huge black stallion, needed to touch him, to hold him. Only then could her body cease its frantic trembling. He had promised that he would return to her. He had *promised*.

She huddled in her cloak, scarce able to believe that this was late summer. Her guards, affected by her somber mood and the unnatural sky, gave her a wide berth. It seemed as if the entire world held its collective breath, waiting.

Padraig reined in beside her. "All is in readiness, my lady."

Erika could not look at him, could not tear her sight away from the path that the men of Dunlough would return on. "Where is the good-mother?" she asked, meaning Aine. While many others, led by Magda, had dismissed her warnings as nonsense, the healer had corroborated them.

"She is within, my lady, awaiting your word."

Curiosity limned his voice, but he wisely did not give utterance to it. Yet even she had to wonder at Aine's obsequiousness. The Druid woman was still a force to be reckoned with, and not even Magda dared to gainsay her. When they were in the presence of others, the ancient healer deferred to Erika in all things, a fact the people of Dunlough instinctively emulated even as they questioned it. Erika, irritated by the need for Aine's blessing, used it to her advantage, ordering Padraig to clear half the main hall to make room for the wounded that were sure to come.

A cool wind laden with the salty scent of the sea, or blood, caught her sun-kissed braids, causing her to shiver inside her cloak. "Thank you, Padraig. Go to your rest now."

The stern warrior didn't budge beside her. "You should come inside, my lady, out of this strange weather."

Touched by his kindness, Erika laid a hand on his arm. "I cannot," she whispered, "not until I know—"

"Then I will wait with you." His hand covered hers briefly before dropping away.

Her throat constricting with emotion, Erika returned to her vigil, thankful that it was no longer a lonely one.

Soon, sooner than she had believed, a shout went up. "They come!"

Forgetting to breathe, Erika craned to see. A first she could make nothing out of the graying afternoon light. Then coming up the dip in the road she saw them: Dunlough's men.

Usually there was cheering and bawdy songs as the men marched triumphantly home. Now they were quiet. Too quiet.

Where was Conor? She pressed her legs against her mount, straining for a glimpse of a huge black beast, a dark-haired man.

There! Conor's horse. But no one rode it. Why wasn't he on his horse?

Something was in the center of the silent procession. A collection of shields, being held shoulder-high, with something lying upon them. Another few heartbeats, and she could discern a bundle, covered with a cloak.

A decidedly human-shaped bundle.

"Conor!" Denial shrieking past her lips, Erika kicked her heels in Tempest's sides and went thundering down the path, dimly aware of the dun emptying behind her. She could not tear her eyes from the interlocked shields with their terrible burden. A splash of dark flickered in her vision as she slipped from her horse and ran headlong into the returning men. Was it Conor's black *leine*, at the head of the shield guards?

It was. She changed course, still running, decorum be damned. Nothing mattered except reaching her husband and proving her dreams false.

Colliding with the solidity of his bulk was the most wondrous feeling in the world. Only the weight of his arms surrounding her eclipsed it.

"Conor!"

"Erika?"

His voice was distant, as if he awakened from a dream. Then his embrace tightened about her. "By the saints!"

As abruptly as he'd embraced her he pushed her away. "No, I can't touch you."

Erika stared up at him. Dirt and gore still covered him, but she didn't care. He was alive and she would ensure that he remained that way.

She cupped her face in his hands. "I don't care about the stains. I need to know you're all right—"

Laughter rang, dry and hollow. It was a sound that chilled her soul. She noticed for the first time how bleak his eyes seemed, how desolate. "I'm not all right. I'll never be all right.

"Ardan's dead. And I killed him."

Shock turned her blood to ice, eclipsing the joy she'd felt at holding him in her arms. "No." Her eyes stinging, she turned to the cluster of shields beside them. "Not Ardan."

"*A bhean uasail.*" Erika turned to the warrior calling her by the formal title of lady, never loosening her hold on her husband. She didn't ever want to be away from him again.

It took her a moment to remember his name. "Fionn. Tell me, what happened? What of my brother?"

"We left him and his men at the divide in the road to Glentane. Our Ardan took a terrible sword thrust to the chest, a blow that was meant for the *tigerna.*"

"So he died defending his lord, with honor." Erika turned to Conor. "You cannot blame yourself for that."

His eyes were bleak, his expression remote. "I can. I do."

Gripping his shoulders, she forced him to look at her. "Ardan gave his life for yours. Do not belittle his sacrifice."

A low moan answered her. It took a moment to realize that the sound did not come from Conor. Cautiously, she moved to the cortege. "Lower the shields. I want to see him."

Several of the warriors looked at her numbly, then looked to Conor. He nodded, and they carefully eased their burden to the grass. Kneeling and taking a deep breath, she lifted the edge of the blanket.

Blood caked the shield, but some of it was red, not brown. The old warrior's face was mottled red, but his skin was still warm to the touch.

"Mother of God!" Erika whispered. She turned to Conor, who was still watching her with despondent eyes. "Conor, come see! Ardan isn't dead!"

Her exclamation sent a murmur through the gathering. Conor knelt beside her. "Not dead?"

Smiling, she caught his hand, dragging his fingers to Ardan's neck. "Careful. Do you feel that?"

She watched his face, saw the realization lighten his gaze. "That is his lifebeat?"

"Yes. He's survived the journey home. That means that he may be able to survive completely."

She took his hands, wanting to reassure him, protect him, revive him. "I do not know if we will be successful, but Aine and I will do all that we know to make sure Ardan lives."

Silver eyes stared down at her. "Whatever you must do, do it."

"I will. I swear it."

With that promise given, she turned to the people gathered around them, commanding them to action. Three of the warriors cut Ardan free and carried him inside, Erika and Conor hurrying after.

Throwing off her cloak, Erika quickly cleared off one of the trestle tables. "Put him here. Take care not to jostle him overmuch." She continued with her orders as she checked Ardan for further wounds, her voice flowing with command, not pausing to marvel at the quickness with which her orders were obeyed.

Besides the wound just above his ribcage, there was a deep gash on Ardan's right temple, which probably had much to do with his unconscious state. His breathing, while light, was steady, not rattling, and no blood poured from his mouth. She breathed a silent heartfelt prayer of thanksgiving that there were no more injuries. She could tend the head injury easily enough, but she had never attempted so serious a wound as the one on his chest.

"Rhory, find Old Aine and bring her to me. Múireann, have the cook bring boiling and fresh water, and mead. Sibheal, where are the fine needles and boiled thread I asked for? Magda, did you tear the bandages?" Turning to the table, she pulled free her dagger, to slice the yellow *leine* away from the wound.

"Who are you to order me about?" Magda sputtered. "I am a princess, not a servant. Besides, the man is already dead!"

Quick as silver lightning, Erika turned to face her detractor. Her blade gleamed in the candlelight, its tip steadily pointed at the red-haired woman's pale throat.

"Though you are no longer mistress here, you have responsibility to those once your people," Erika said in the sudden quiet, her voice ringing with chilling gravity. "I have not the time to argue with you, my lady. You will either help us save Ardan and the other men of Dunlough who once served you, or you will retire to your room."

Averse to saying more than she had already, Erika turned back to the table, if only to hide the paroxysm in her hands.

She had pressed a blade to the throat of a princess of Ireland, a feat that would little help her situation. There was sure to be a law against such a thing.

She could ill-afford to dwell on it now. Even if she were to be banished from Dunlough, she would keep her promise to Conor and do all in her power to save Ardan.

Behind her, Madga audibly swallowed then chimed, "Come, Conor, I will see to your needs."

For the second time in as many minutes, Erika came close to violence. It took a supreme effort not to turn and throttle the Irishwoman. If Conor went to her now, Erika would never forgive him.

Knowing that everyone watched her, she began slicing away the top of Ardan's tunic with more calm than she felt. Save his life, she thought to herself. Perhaps later there would be time to save her heart from breaking.

"Leave go, Magda," Conor's voice rumbled as he moved to stand beside Erika. "There are many here more injured than I. See to their needs."

Erika released a breath she didn't realize she held. She knew she had done herself no favors by drawing her blade on Magda—the violent rending of cloth being torn into bandages assured her that she had made an enemy for life.

"My lady." Aine's voice washed over her, calm and soothing. "I am here."

Grateful for the ancient woman's presence, Erika ordered everyone to their duties as she continued to carefully pull the *leine*, bloody brown instead of saffron yellow, away from the wound. "Conor, can you tell us what happened? Was it a sword or an axe blow?"

Her husband stood beside her, staring down at the still form of his dearest friend. His hair was matted to his head; Erika could see dried blood on his temple. His eyes were dark with inner turmoil as he answered. "I-I do not know. Everything happened so fast...I think it was a sword, meant for me, but he—he stepped in the way. His death is on my hands."

His voice was wooden, lifeless. Yet there was an undercurrent to his words, anguish so deep it was nearly imperceptible.

Not to her. Erika could feel it, see it. Conor had lost enough. By all that was holy, she would not have him lose a man who was more than a good friend but was like a father to him. She would battle Hel and hell if she had to.

"Conor, stand by his head. We may need you to hold him down as we work." If Ardan showed any signs of struggling, it would be a sign from heaven.

"Will you not give him a potion, to make him sleep?" Múireann asked from her right.

"I don't dare," Erika whispered, even as Aine shook her head. "He is weak enough already."

Aine's soft voice brought her back to the task at hand. "Tell me what you see, child."

Cleansing her hands as Aine had taught her, Erika then dipped a clean cloth into another basin of warm, herb-steeped water. Carefully she wiped at the wound, but Ardan did not stir. "It's a sword thrust, Good-mother," she said. "It's crusted with dirt, cloth and dried blood."

Her hands shook as she retrieved a small knife with a thin, sharp blade. Expelling a breath, she forced her hands to steady and cautiously widened the wound.

Múireann gasped, then made a gagging sound. Erika was about to order her away when blood welled, angry-red, from her incision. "Ah!"

She could feel people pressing in on her. "What is it?" Conor's voice, harsh and grating, sliced through the murmurs.

"The wound's not deep," Erika explained. Hope tinted her voice. "The blade was stopped by his ribs. And there's no smell. That is a good sign."

Aine nodded. "So there are no foul humors, at least not yet. Are you ready, my lady?"

Hesitating, Erika glanced at her husband. He looked down at her, and in the steel-gray eyes she saw silent pleading, as well as resigned hopelessness. He believed Ardan would not live.

If she was the only one to believe Ardan could survive, so be it. She would believe enough for all of them. She could not, would not falter. "If I could have room and more light, I am ready."

Everyone stepped back a respectful distance. Some held candles and torches near. One soldier stood on the table in front of her, holding two torches aloft. The firm set of his face suggested he would not move until she told him to.

The dun fell silent as the severely wounded drifted to sleep and those already tended gathered to watch her and the old healer perform a miracle. Time ceased to be a concern, the agony in her back a distant memory as Erika, following Aine's quiet instructions, meticulously cleansed away every minute trace of grime. The Druid woman had stressed repeatedly the necessity of cleanliness, a tenet that had been shared by only a few other healers Erika had encountered during her travels. But she trusted the old Druid as she trusted few people in her life, and she had seen enough people, supposedly healing from their wounds, sicken and die. She would not give Conor that false a hope; it would devastate him.

Finally she began the methodical, excruciating process of patching Ardan's innards together. Calling for more light and blinking through her fatigue, Erika slowly set her stitches into the pale skin. She was grateful to Aine and Múireann that they refused her entreaties to cease her needlecraft; her sewing had transformed from clumsy tangles to delicate, orderly stitches.

"It is done." Releasing her breath with a drawn-out sigh, Erika attempted to straighten and nearly toppled over. Múireann was by her side, steadying her.

"Come away, my lady," the woman pleaded through her tears. "You have done your best, and that is all that we could hope."

Erika took a proffered goblet of mead from a servant, managing an exhausted smile of gratitude before she drank. "There is still much to be done, Múireann. We must salve and bandage both wounds, and move Ardan to a pallet near the fire."

Startled green eyes met her own. "You—you mean Ardan will live?"

Not wanting to inspire false hope yet needing to offer comfort, Erika chose her words carefully. "The next few hours will be telling. We must make sure he takes mead, and a wee bit of the herbal if possible. If Ardan survives the dawn, I believe he will have a chance."

Murmurs of relief swept through the dun's people. Múireann stared at her in wonderment. "You're not the Angel of Death!" she whispered in awe. "You are the angel of life, sent from God Himself!"

It seemed as if others were in agreement. Uncomfortable with the sudden reverence, Erika said, "Godsend or no, we still have much to do. Sibheal, help Múireann bind Ardan's wounds. Use that salve—yes, the dark green. I will see to the others."

But first she would see to her husband. Grabbing a bowl of fresh water and clean cloths, Erika turned to tend to Conor's injuries. He was gone. Anxiety rippled through her as she cast about for him.

He stood near the door, talking to the priest. Gathering her skirts, she hurried to join them. Abbott Brochadh was speaking, and it took her a moment to realize he was giving Conor names.

Names of men of Dunlough, now dead.

Stricken, Erika watched Conor's face as each was spoken. It was as if each were an arrow loosed, striking his heart with mortal accuracy. His face could have been as solid and immutable as the crosses of the ancient Celts. It seemed as if darkness gathered in the planes of his face, changing him.

Claiming him.

When the priest finished speaking, Conor raised his eyes, staring directly at her. Erika's blood ran cold, and she instinctively stepped back.

His eyes were empty.

Without uttering a word, he spun towards the door. Erika, galvanized by the movement, made to go after him.

"Conor, wait!" Strong arms grappled hers. Padraig. "Leave go!"

"I cannot, my lady. No one follows the *tigerna* at times like this. Not if he values his life."

Exhausted by her work, she ceased her struggles and turned to stare at the commander. "Conor has done this before?"

The warrior nodded, his eyes dark. "Since Clontarf."

Fear gripped her heart. Not fear for herself, but fear for Conor. "Where does he go, and how long is he gone?"

Padraig's face was pinched with fatigue and sorrow. "My lady, do not ask me."

Erika grabbed his forearm. "Please, Padraig. I must know."

Her desperation must have been evident for he continued, "The *tigerna* does not leave the tribe's lands. Some say he joins the *bhean sidhe* on Slieve Torc, adding his grief to hers. Some say he races through the fields in the dark of night, or stays in a cave."

His words came with difficulty, as though reluctant to betray his lord. "It is like a madness, my lady, the way his mood darkens. Like a fever runs its course, so does this. It may be one day or four, but it does pass."

Four days? Every part of her being yearned to dislodge Padraig's hold, to follow Conor into the darkness. He was out there in the night, hurting. He needed her.

She gave Padraig a long stare that would countenance no disobedience. "You will send one guard after him. I would know where he goes."

Padraig opened his mouth and Erika narrowed her eyes at him. He hesitated, then bowed to her. "I will see to it, my lady."

Sighing, Erika turned back to tend to the remaining injured. She needed to rest, but these men needed her. It would also help distract her from her worry over her husband. He would come back to her. He had promised, and she intended to hold him to that promise.

Chapter Twenty-Five

"So you have come for me, then?"

Erika jerked upright, startled by the rasping voice. "Ardan?"

The grizzled warrior stared back at her, his moss-green eyes unnaturally bright. "Sure and you know who I am, if you've come to lead me home?" He smiled weakly. "But 'tis good to know that heaven has a sense of humor."

Looking up, Erika saw that Múireann had returned, and pulled up a chair on the other side across from her. The older woman's eyes welled with tears as she stifled a gasp with her hands.

Apparently Ardan thought she was an angel, not *the* Angel. Erika touched his forehead; it was warm, but dry. Had the wound in his chest become festered? She prayed against it.

"How do you feel, Ardan?"

"If I did not know you for one of the angelic hosts, I would swear that I am being tortured in hell." His eyes strayed to the crackling hearth. "I'm not in hell, am I?"

Smiling despite the circumstances, she answered, "You are not."

"Then might I trouble you for a drink?"

Múireann hurriedly poured watered mead into a cup and passed it to Erika, who, with Padraig's help, lifted Ardan enough to help him sip. He gagged, but managed to down most of it. "I don't suppose heaven has something stronger?"

Her smile grew. "No, I don't suppose it does."

Closing his eyes, the warrior sighed. "Una and my boys, are they here? I will see them soon?"

Erika cooled his forehead with a damp cloth. It was a moment before she could speak past the tightness in her throat. "They send you their love, but say you are still needed in Dunlough."

"Conor."

"He needs you, Ardan," she said, clasping his hands in hers. "Come back to him."

He opened his eyes, his gaze steady and clear as it fixed upon her. "'Tis you he needs, my lady."

Unsure if he was truly with them or not, Erika tried to ease the hammering of her heart. "C-Conor needs me?"

"He does. Darkness dogs his every step. Losing Murrough and his sons took much from him, sure it did. Aislingh could not understand it, and then she betrayed him. You *can* understand it. You are a light against that darkness. You can help him escape it."

"How?" The word tore from her. "What can I do?"

Green eyes burned fiercely into her own. "Help him remember how to laugh. If 'tis too much to ask that you love him, at least care for him."

"I do."

"Then you are helping him already. Promise me that you will not give up on him, even though he has given up on himself. Never surrender."

Tears spilled onto her cheeks. "I won't if you won't."

"Done, then." He settled back, closing his eyes. "Now let me sleep."

Erika looked at the slumbering man, feeling as if her heart would burst. "I won't fail you, Ardan," she whispered. "I won't fail Conor either."

Resolved, she rose to her feet, untying her bloodstained apron and tossing it onto the chair. Padraig rose with her. "My lady?"

"Prepare my horse. I go to bring Conor home."

"Not alone."

She knew better than to argue. "Three others. No more. We ride at once."

THE DARKNESS CAME FOR him.

He had been fighting it for hours, days, an eternity. But the demons of guilt were as voracious as they were cruel. Their claws were embedded deep in his soul, and he knew they would never let him go.

Dead. So many of them dead. He was supposed to protect them, supposed to keep them safe, with his own life if necessary. But he had failed them, failed them all, and he would suffer eternal damnation because of it.

Already he could hear them, the demons, their call as persistent and irresistible as the *sidhe*. He belonged to them, they whispered, he was a part of them. They had given him his name. Surely he wanted to come to them? All he had to do was let go, to surrender to the murky void, and all would be well.

Yet something kept him from taking that final, fatal step.

Conor rode through the night, pushing his mount in a merciless drive to escape. Even then, he was powerless to out-run the demons that pursued him.

They wore familiar faces, his demons. Faces of men he had played with as a boy, trained with as a youth, fought with as a man. Murrough, chieftain of Dunlough, with young Murrough after him. His youngest nephew Brochan, fostered where he himself had been, and the son he'd never had. Phelan, who had a warrior's size and a poet's soul. Their faces taunted him the most, for when they needed him most he had failed them.

The fighting had been brutal, axes and swords. The sweet green grass had decayed into the brown of drying blood. In the trees, blood had dripped from branches like a red rain. It had been blinding, but not too blinding for Conor to miss the axe-blow that had severed Murrough nearly in half, another blow that had taken Phelan's head.

Conor had found Brochan, had believed he was spiriting the boy to safety until they were caught in a storm of arrows. It didn't matter that he had been felled, had nearly died. He had lived, and his brother and nephews had not.

When his mount began to stumble from the exertion, Conor slid from his back. Landing on his knees, he grabbed huge fistfuls of the chill, fragrant earth, struggling to find purchase, something to keep him rooted. His demons roiled about him, feasting on the agony in his soul.

It welled within him, that agony, struggling to break free the pitiful barrier of flesh. His muscles bunched with the urge to succumb, to allow the demons to ravage him. The emotion welled from the deepest corner of his core, gathering strength as it sought to escape. And escape it did, blistering from his throat, riding on a sound that had never before been uttered by a human.

THE UNNATURAL SOUND stopped Erika and her guards in their tracks on the majestic slope of Slieve Torc. Lore said that the spirit of Dunlough, the *bhean sidhe*, resided in the prehistoric stone cairn at the top of the mountain. Erika had heard her soul-chilling wail two days ago, a wail that supposedly heralded a death. Was that where Conor would be?

As if in answer to her unspoken question, the moon broke free of the clouds, bathing the cairn in its pale light and illuminating a path through the dense undergrowth below. Not heeding Padraig's caution, Erika kneed Tempest, turning the horse up the silvery path.

Erika heard Conor before she saw him. Heard the brutality of his pain and knew she would give anything to assuage it.

She halted, waiting for Padraig to draw along side. "I will go alone from here."

"*A bhean usuail*, I cannot allow it. The *tigerna*—"

"Needs me," she finished for him. "I must do this, Padraig. For Ardan, for me. And for Conor."

"My lady." Worry was clear in his features.

Tempest shifted beneath her in the moonlight. She calmed him with a light touch, though inside her heart roiled with fear. Conor needed her. And she needed him.

"Padraig." She waited until she had their attention. "I will go alone to Conor. We will return, as he always does."

Reluctance limning his features, Padraig acquiesced, fading into the shadows. Erika knew he had not gone far. Padraig's loyalty was unquestioned; he would not leave until he was satisfied. But he would not interfere.

With a word, she urged Tempest into the copse of trees. It was cool this far up the side of Slieve Torc, and their breaths steamed in the night. The full moon hung above her left shoulder, casting a silvery glow to everything about her and creating shadows that should have been menacing. But Erika knew the true menace was the darkness that laid claim to her husband.

Resolved, she straightened in her saddle. She was the Angel of Death, a fighter. She would fight for her husband. She would bring him home.

Or die trying.

"DAMN YOU, MÓRRIGAN!" Conor bellowed at the frigid, black sky. "You could have taken me! Why them? Why Ardan?"

Not even the wind answered him, and it only served to sear the agony into a blistering rage. "Where are you, war-goddess? Do you cower before this mere mortal? Have you no courage in your damnable black heart to face me?"

The provocation proved successful, answered by the sound of hoofbeats, the emergence of the moon. Mórrigan and her minions coming to do battle. Conor felt his lips peel back from his teeth as he unsheathed his sword. He would go, but he would not go peaceful.

It would be over. At last.

Hoofbeats came closer, the moon brighter as he readied himself for his final battle. Something silver flashed through the copse of trees, coalescing into a spectral beauty with streaming moonbeams for hair, astride a pale horse breathing fog.

He was not surprised at the form his adversary had chosen, but the twist of pain he felt at the sight did surprise him. "So Mórrigan, you've chosen to face me as the Angel of Death. If you believe staring at my wife's visage will sway me from this course, you are mistaken."

The pale apparition dismounted, silver hair gleaming in the moonlight. "Conor, I'm not the Mórrigan. I'm Erika."

"You lie!"

"I do not." The specter's words were quiet, compelling. Her hands went to her cloak, sending it billowing to the ground. It was followed by her baldric and sword. "I am your wife, and I've come to take you home."

Laughter tore from him, brutal and harsh and mirthless. The Mórrigan stepped back, and he laughed anew. "And what is your home? A cold black place filled with the screams of the damned? Can it be any worse than what I endure now?"

"Conor, listen to me. Look at me." Her dress fell to her feet and she stood, glorious and nude before him. "I am real. I am your wife."

"No!" His words were a snarl of denial. "Enough of this—it ends now!"

Brandishing his sword, he raced across the clearing. The Mórrigan made no sound, did not reach for her sword. Did nothing but stare at him with his wife's eyes.

A cry of anguish tore from him. He could not do it. Merciful heaven, he could not strike down the witch that wore his wife's face.

The hand clasping his sword fell to his side and he dropped to his knees, the defiance drained. "Do what you will," he whispered, weary in mind and soul. "I am beyond care."

Movement, the Angel of Death coming closer to him. She knelt before him, one hand reaching out to touch his marred cheek. The rush he ever felt at his wife's touch coursed through him, illuminating his dark misery. She melted against him, pressing kisses over his ravaged face. He pushed his fingers into her hair, drawing her closer, needing her touch and her scent. "Erika."

As quick as he grasped her he pushed her away. "Return to the dun."

"I will. With you." Her voice was cool as moonlight.

"No!" He stumbled to his feet and away from her. "I was near to killing you—do you not recognize that? You were close to being beheaded!"

"Yet I was not."

How could she be so calm when he was seething inside? "Leave me be!"

"No." She rose and came closer, and the tremble in her voice reached him. "I will remain with you, Conor. You will not turn me away. I will not let you."

Her essence stole into him as she stepped close behind him, cooling the madness that burned his soul. He turned into her, pressing his burning cheeks into the softness of her hair. "Angel of Death, become angel of mercy. Will you show me mercy? Can you heal me?"

She stroked the dark silk of his beard. "I would like to try."

With a groan he crushed her against him, capturing her mouth in a kiss that hovered on brutal. His hands were clumsy on his clothing and he heard the rip of fabric. He knew he should slow his pace, but need rode him with the desperation of a drowning man reaching for a rope just beyond his reach. "Touch me, *Aingeal*," he commanded, his voice grating. "Burn me with your light. Make me forget."

She came to him, molding her body to his, lightning melding with thunder. It was she who pushed him to the dew-covered grass, she who rose above him, straddling his thighs, her hands wrapped about his hardness.

He could not bear the waiting. Grabbing her waist, he surged inside her with one swift invasive thrust, causing her to gasp. There was nothing gentle about this joining, and beneath the storm of need the part of him that could still reason despaired for causing her pain.

"Conor, look at me."

He did, and what he saw stole his breath. Her pale skin was aflame with desire, her eyes glittering with the same need he felt in himself. He kept his eyes on her, needing the glory of her flesh in the moonlight to banish the darkness. Fingertips scored his chest as she rode him, meeting him wildness for wildness, needing the comfort as much as he. They were warriors, their passion warring with tenderness. Need drove them, the need to be united, to be lost and found in each other.

He matched her stroke for relentless stroke as she moved above him, head tossed back, breasts thrust upward. Her pace increased, and passion blocked all but her image from his mind. When she arched backward, his name tearing from her throat, he was engulfed in silver flames that seared his heart, mind and soul. His release, when it came, was violent, shattering, bursting over and around them like thunder.

Spent, they collapsed against each other, their breaths mingling on the night air. It was a long moment before they could bear to part, but the night air forced them into their clothing. Conor wrapped Erika's cloak about her then settled her against him tight, unwilling to be parted from her for long. "Why did you come?"

"You needed me."

He did, and most desperate. "I didn't believe you were real. What would you have done if I had not stopped? What would I have done had I killed you?"

"Yet you didn't. Think on that instead."

He shook his head, unable to put into words the horror he felt at how close he had come, how his madness had near driven him to...

Her hands on him were soothing, comforting. "Tell me, what drives you so?"

"I will not speak on it."

"Even to me?"

His sigh trembled. "How can I be called Devil, and not face my demons alone?"

Erika cradled his cheeks in her sword-calloused hands. "I am your wife. You no longer need to face anything alone."

The words were a balm to his soul, and he closed his eyes in gratitude for the gift. Be they truth or falsehood, he needed to hear them.

Defenses crumbling, he gathered her hands in his, needing the contact but unable to look in her eyes as he prepared to bare his soul to her. His gaze remained fixed to the darkness.

"I see them sometimes, riding through the mists. The spirits of my clan, the princes of Connacht. My foster-brothers, my cousins, my friends. I remember how they lived, and I remember how they died."

Once begun, the story spilled from him, an unstoppable torrent. As he spoke, a gentle rain, whisper-soft and full of mist, gathered around them. He told her everything, unburdening his soul the way he had with none other.

"You are wed to a weak man, lady warrior," he said finally, when her silence had become unbearable to him. "Will you mock me now, or will you call a *brehon* to pass judgment upon me?"

"I will not mock you, nor will I send for a law-giver."

He snorted in disbelief. "I do not need your pity, lady wife."

"And you shall not receive it." The solemnity of her voice softened the harsh words. "We are warriors both. It is who we are. Death will always be around us, but it does not mean that we have to enjoy it. Nor does it mean we are unaffected by it. If I lost Olan, I would be beside myself."

"And if you lost your husband?"

He hadn't meant to ask the question, but he could not take it back. Until now, he feared nothing, but he feared the answer she would give. "Never mind, Erika. It is not a question that deserves an answer."

"I would be devastated."

Conor's breath caught. "What?"

She smiled at his surprise. "The last five years of my life have been full of wonders and fear. You have taken away that fear, and given me magic to replace it. I cannot imagine life without you."

Stunned, Conor caught her against him. "How is it that you are mine?"

"Do you not remember? I lost a duel."

The reminder stirred his ever-present guilt. "Erika..."

She touched her fingertips to his lips, silencing him, then kissed his apology away. "I am capable of jesting, as are you."

He held her away. "Is this a time of jesting?"

"Our people would not want us to wail and gnash our teeth in constant sorrow," she said. "They would want us to celebrate their lives, because they live on in our hearts."

Then she told him what he needed to hear. "Our Ardan lives on in Dunlough. He sleeps now, but he spoke to me."

Ardan lived. Air whooshed from his lungs as he engulfed her in his arms, rocking her. Words couldn't come to him, so he pressed kisses to her cheek, forehead, and the side of her neck, breath surging in and out with the force of his emotion. "Thank you," he whispered, his voice rough. "Thank you for saving him."

Erika let her tears fall even as she gave him a gentle smile. She was the thankful one, for in saving Ardan she had saved her husband.

"Let us return to the dun. Our people await us."

After a long moment he released her and rose, helping her to her feet. She was grateful for the assistance. Now that the danger was past, weariness settled over her like fog above the lough. It was all she could do to gather her sword while Conor gathered the horses.

He lifted her to her saddle. She reached for the reins and would have toppled to the ground had Conor not caught her. "Erika!"

She managed to give him a smile through a yawn. "I am simply weary, my lord. It has been an unending day."

"Then we shall stay here, so that you may rest."

"No." Her hand rested on his forearm. "'Tis true I could be anywhere with you, but I would prefer to have you beside me in our bed. Besides, I promised Ardan that I would bring you home, and he means to see that I keep that promise."

Her jest was rewarded with the faint glimmering of a smile. She had felt the darkness drain away from him, lightening him. Saving him. Conor lifted her to his rested stallion, and vaulted up behind her. She settled against the comforting solidity of his chest with a sigh of contentment. Gladness filled her, and she rested her head on the warm, wide expanse of his shoulder as fatigue dragged at her. "Conor, will you promise me something?"

She felt him grow still. Dragging her eyes open, she raised her head. His jaw was firmly set, his eyes once again shuttered. "What does my lady wish?"

Another yawn escaped her, and she muffled it in the fabric covering his chest. "We are together, you and I. That matters a great deal to me. Promise me that when the time comes for grieving, we will grieve together."

Grieve together. Conor held his wife as she slipped into a blessed slumber. He gave Brimstone his head, letting the stallion pick his way down the mountain path. Padraig and three others materialized out of the night, surrounding them. He surrendered Tempest's reins to one and concentrated on holding his wife close.

Dawn began its banishment of the night as they returned to Dunlough. Erika stirred just as Conor debated giving her to Padraig while he dismounted. "Why do we stop?"

"We are home." He paused to savor the warmth that filtered through him at the phrase. "Can you stay your feet long enough for me to dismount?"

She slid to the ground, rubbing the sleep from her eyes. When he stood beside her, would have gathered her in his arms again, she turned to him. "Let us see how Ardan fares."

His heart hammered, cutting off any reply he could have made. He wanted to see his captain, true, needed to see that his friend would indeed survive. If Erika's assurances proved false, he did not think he—

A hand slipped into his own, cool and comforting. Fortifying. Erika would be at his side, regardless the outcome. With a deep breath, he stepped into the dun.

The main hall was dark save for the area before the main hearth. A pallet had been created, and stools ringed it. Múireann and another woman were there, with two of the shield guards, keeping vigil.

His feet felt like *ogham* stones as he allowed his wife to pull him forward. Do not let him be dead, he thought to himself. Do not let him be dead, do not let—

"So you've come back then, my angel?"

Erika knelt beside the pallet, brushing Ardan's hair from his face with a tender gesture that tugged at Conor's heart. When had Ardan's hair gotten so much snow in it?

"I have indeed returned, as promised. And I've brought someone with me."

The wounded soldier raised his eyes. His face wreathed into a smile. "Ah, there he is. We did us a good turn, didn't we?"

The rough voice, though weak, was the sweetest music Conor had ever heard. "That we did," he answered, kneeling beside his wife, staring into his friend's face to keep from staring at the blood-soaked bandage on his chest. "You did us proud. Everyone brought honor to Dunlough."

"C-couldn't let you fall," Ardan said, his voice fading. "Needed to make sure you got home safe to the Angel..." His eyes closed.

Panic hit him square in the gut. "Ardan?"

Erika's hands covered his. "He sleeps. He will be thus for several days, as he heals." She lifted the bloodied bandage on

Ardan's chest, and Conor's stomach lurched at the sight of the puckered, angry wound covered in a green, slimy substance.

"I need to change this dressing," she said, struggling to get to her feet. Her knees buckled, and Conor swept her into his arms. "Put me down, Conor. I must see to Ardan and the others!"

"I'll tend him, my lady, and the rest," Múireann said before he could argue with his wife. "You'll be beyond weary, that's for certain."

"But the dressing must be securely fastened around him, after you put the salve on," Erika protested.

"I will help," Padraig said, echoed by the other two guards.

"Fionn and Séanán will assist Múireann," Erika mumbled in a mixture of Norse and Gaelic that proved how tired she was. "Mind you, Ardan is a wounded man, not a sack of grain. Padraig, I command you to take yourself off to sleep or I'll have your ears for breakfast!"

Conor's translation combined with Erika's commanding, though sleepy, stare hastened all to do as she bid. Once she was certain all was progressing as she wanted, she slumped against his chest and fell headlong into slumber.

She didn't stir as he carried her to their chamber, or as he undressed her and put her to bed. He sat beside her, fingering the silk of her hair. The hollows beneath her eyes looked as if they'd been smudged with ashes.

Realizing then how she had pushed herself to the limits, he felt guilt that was soon consumed by pride. His wife, so long an instrument of death, had embraced the cause of life. Instead of fighting to kill, she now fought to heal.

How fierce she was, daring what so few, man or woman, would. His wife had stared down a princess of Roscommon, battled for a life and wrestled him back from the brink of insanity.

She had healed him. He felt the knowledge of it sink into his bones. Since she had invaded his life, it had become worth living. He had begun to think about more than the past, more than ghosts and demons, more than his failures. He had begun to hope and to need.

Even now, need welled within him, deep and sure. It was not the white-hot flash of lust, or the steady flame of the desire he ever felt for her. This need was more fundamental, more abiding.

He needed her to love him.

His hand froze in its journey through her hair, waiting for his heart to resume its normal pace. Conor mac Ferghal, the mighty Devil of Dunlough, wanted his wife's love.

Could she love him? His mind latched onto the notion with hunger for proof. She had given him her battle charms, had clung to him with such relief when he returned. She had ridden out into the dead of night, not knowing what to expect, to bring him home. She gave her body to him again and again, taking and giving pleasure as if it was the only sustenance they needed.

"Conor?" Her voice was full of sleep as her hand reached out, seeking him.

"I am here, *mo aingeal.*"

"Come to bed. I cannot sleep until you do."

He refrained from informing her that she'd done just that, and obliged her by pulling the *leine* over his head and slipping beneath the bedclothes beside her.

She curved against him as he gathered her close. "I will make a bargain with you, Devil," she whispered on a yawn. "I'll make a *leine* for you of my own hands, one that befits your rank, and you'll wear it and leave go the horrible black."

Did she realize what she asked? He glanced down at her. Her eyes were closed, her hand a sleep-filled movement in the hair and scars on his chest. He could scarce think, and realized he didn't need to. If she asked it of him, he would do his best to see it through. "I will."

She gave him a sleepy smile. "Thank you." Her hand stilled upon his chest as she once again settled in to sleep.

He pressed a light kiss to her forehead, closing his eyes as contentment drove the last of the darkness from his heart. Sleep would come easy for him tonight, and every night hereafter, thanks to his Angel.

She was courageous.

She was magnificent.

She was his heart.

Chapter Twenty-Six

She was pregnant.

Erika stared at Aine in surprise. "Are you certain?"

The old druid's expression was amused. "Can you not tell the difference in your own body?"

Thoughtful, Erika lowered her eyes to her still-flat belly. "My courses have never been regular," she admitted. "I thought I had eaten bad cheese."

She thought that Magda had poisoned her. It was not something that she had proof with which to substantiate. She knew the day she drew her blade on the crimson-haired princess that she had made an enemy, one who was sure to retaliate.

Thoughts of Magda couldn't halt the smile spreading through her. She was with child. Conor's child. She looked down at her hands, instinctively cradling her womb. What would a child born of the Angel of Death and the Devil of Dunlough be like? Would it have her pale features or Conor's dark ones?

Impulsively she threw her arms about the old woman's neck. "Thank you, Good-mother! I must give Conor the news!"

Heart light, Erika flew out of Aine's hut. Finally she would be able to give the man she loved his dearest wish.

Joy swelled inside her as she ran, laughing, crying and calling Conor's name. This time of day he would be in the *faitche*, practicing weaponry with his men. Not the best time of day to interrupt, but she found she didn't care. She scrambled up the slope to the field, her legs barely keeping pace with her heart. Then she saw him, her Irish thunder god, turning as she called his name. Alarm colored his features as he dropped his sword and ran to her.

Giddy, almost incoherent, she crashed into him, all but leaping into his arms. He held her close and she could feel his heart beating a pounding pulse. "What is it, are you all right?"

Laughter bubbled out of her. "I am more than all right. We have done it!"

Alarm turned to impatience as he stared down at her. "By all that is holy, what has been done?"

She gave him a smile that began deep in her heart. Cupping his dear face in her hands, she whispered, "I carry your child."

Time seemed to suspend itself. She saw the moment her words registered, saw the spark that flared in his silver eyes a moment before hearing his intake of breath, feeling his hands tighten on her waist.

"My child," he whispered, and there was such wonder in his voice that tears came to her eyes. "Well done, *mo aingeal.*"

"I could say the same to you, *mo diabhal*," she whispered tremulously. "I thought it well done indeed."

Dunlough's soldiers gathered around them, relaxing their defense. "What news?" one called.

Conor set her down slowly, then lifted his head to his men. "The lady of Dunlough tells me that there will soon be an heir."

Cheers greeted his pronouncement. "A *ceili*! A *ceili* to celebrate!"

"Aye, there will be singing and dancing, and ale for all!"

The men dispersed to spread the news, leaving them alone. As they began to walk back to the dun, Erika placed a hand on her still-flat womb. "I didn't know at first. Aine had to tell me."

His arm still circled her waist, his eyes bright with pleasure. "If Aine has said it, it must be so." His grip loosened as his expression lost some of its pleasure. "You will have to forgo being the Angel of Death for a time."

She found the news didn't cause her the upset it might have even a month before. "I know. It does not distress me."

His lips twitched with his version of a smile. "We will find something else to occupy your time."

"As long as it does not include chasing foul-tempered hens about the kitchen yard," she said, and earned a truer smile.

He stopped, turning her to face him. "Oh, I'm thinking of something a sight more pleasant."

The imprint of his thighs upon hers left no doubt of his meaning. "Can we still do that?"

"Do you not want to?"

"I always want to," she admitted. "I just did not believe it possible."

"'Tis more than possible, my lusty wife," Conor said, his voice grazing her ear as he rocked against the cradle of her thighs. "Shall I prove it to you?"

She sighed and leaned against him, melting at the core. "Yes, please."

Arm in arm, they entered the dun. Even the sight of Magda's disapproving stare did not daunt Erika today. The former mistress of Dunlough sat in a prominent place that afforded her a clear view of the main entrance and the hall leading to the kitchens, a basket of mending at her feet. Her eyes widened as Conor guided Erika to the stairs. "And sure herself's not tired at this time of the day?"

"My wife needs her rest now more than ever," Conor declared. "I go with her to ensure that she receives it."

"Conor." Erika smothered a reproachful laugh as they mounted the stairs.

He was unapologetic. "You will be receiving, and soon. I promise you that."

Receive she did, for a glorious interlude. Replete, they collapsed against each other, languidly basking in afterglow. "I'm glad you've proved me wrong, husband," she said with a sigh. "I must admit, not being with you like this would be hard to bear."

Conor held her close. "Remember you said that. While we've months to go before we have to cease, it does not mean we should shirk our time together."

"Good." She grinned. "For this is one duty I've no plans to shirk."

Her husband leaned over her, his lips tugging upward. "It gladdens me to see you happy."

Fragile feelings threatened to break free of the cage of her ribs. She brushed her knuckles down his cheek. "And you?" she breathed. "Are you happy?"

He captured her hand, pressing a kiss against her palm. "I cannot recall a moment I've been happier."

Her heart threatened to overflow. "Oh Conor, I—"

A timid knock sounded on the door. "Away from that door if you value your life!" he roared.

Erika's giggle over the abrupt sound of retreating foot-steps soon became an outright guffaw. "It would seem our duties come looking for us, after all."

His sigh was rueful as he climbed from the bedstead, reaching for his *leine*. "It does indeed. There'll be no rest for you now, not until after the *ceili* tonight. Perhaps not even then."

Her pulse leapt deep inside as she pulled her robe on. "I hope not."

Silver eyes blazed anew at her soft words. "Perhaps we could take a few moments more?" he suggested, reaching for her.

Laughing, she danced around him while pulling her hair into a haphazard braid. "I'll not be keeping you from your duties," she told him with mock severity. "And you'll not be keeping me from mine. I've a *ceili* to prepare for, remember?"

"I remember well." He opened the door for her then followed her through. "You'll not overdo it."

Erika knew a command when she heard one. "I won't," she promised. "I doubt if Magda will let me, at any rate."

Some of the acerbity she felt must have been obvious, for he paused, drawing her near. "Has Magda not been a help for you?"

Hesitant, Erika bit her lower lip. The Irishwoman never had more than two words to say to her of late, not that she minded overmuch. Still, she didn't want to be enemies with

Conor's sister-by-marriage, for his sake as much as her own. "I did hold a dagger to her throat, you know."

"Yes you did." He looked horrified and amused together. "I suppose it will take her some time to recover from the shock."

"I suppose it will," she equivocated, still unsure of his mood. What would he do if she said that she'd had enough of Magda's help?

"I know herself's not had an easy time of it," she finally said, her tone careful. "Even though she hasn't been here for two years, it must be difficult for her not to assume her former status."

Conor halted his descent and backed her against the stairwell wall. "Are you diplomat as well as warrior? I noticed you did not answer my question."

Though her head reached his shoulder she felt trapped by his size. Even so, she hesitated. "What question was that?"

He leaned closer to her. "Did you know that your nose turns red when you attempt to avoid questions?"

Heat crept up her neck. "It does not," she retorted tartly. "And I'm not avoiding questions."

"Then answer me, now and true. Is Magda not a help to you?"

If she said no, would he send her away? Everyone would suspect, and rightfully so, that it was because of her that Conor would send Magda away. Erika didn't want it thought that she could not suffer a widow and Dunlough's former mistress in her home. It was a matter of pride.

Looking him full in the eye, she said, "I have learned much from Magda." That was true. "I would not have been able to manage many things without her." Like the constant feeling of inadequacy and frustration. "I do wish things would improve between us." *If only because you wish it.*

To her credit, she didn't blink as Conor gave her a measuring stare that surely cowered many a man. Finally he stepped back, and they continued their descent.

At the entrance he paused again. "Until tonight, my lady."

It was indeed a night of music and singing and dancing.

And miracles.

Dunlough celebrated as it had not since the wedding feast. The scribe read from the annals, and a bard sang of the strange courtship of the Angel and the Devil. After the bard, soldiers traded war stories, and Erika even gave them a tale of being beset by thieves while guarding a spice merchant on the great road to Rome.

Conor watched the proceedings with an indulgent, pleased expression, though he did not partake in any of the boasting himself. Erika was conscious of him sitting behind her like Odin watching over humanity but not interacting with it.

When hand-clapping joined the sounds of harp and bodhran and pipes and foot-stomping, Erika turned to her husband. "You do not join the celebration?"

He waved a hand to the shifting bodies before the hearth. "The people enjoy themselves. Their joy is my joy."

Her heart clenched at his casual words. How many nights had he sat this way, keeping to the shadows, with his people yet so removed from them?

She slipped her hands into his, tugging him to his feet. "Tonight, your joy is their joy."

Conor let himself be led into the throng of dancers, who greeted him with smiles and thumps on the back. He pulled his wife close. "Do you know what you're doing?"

She smiled and spun around him. "No, but you've done so well teaching me other things, sure you can teach me this?"

Never one to refuse a challenge, Conor led her a merry step that had them both breathless. Erika didn't know the dance of the Gaels, true, but she'd managed to survive her nineteen years by studying people, and she proved to be an apt pupil.

With reluctance, Conor gave way when Ardan intercepted them. In the two months since his wounding the commander had recovered well, and even seemed to flourish under Erika's care. And if his dancing was any indication, he seemed to be growing younger as well.

Accepting a much-needed ale, Conor returned to his seat. Magda soon joined him, and they watched the celebration in an easy silence.

"How good it is, to see Dunlough rejoicing again," his sister-by-marriage said.

"I agree." He couldn't keep the pride from his voice. "Erika has done much to lighten the pallor that has been here too long."

He watched as his laughing wife was passed from Ardan to Padraig. Magic was certain in the air, for his commanders' previous contributions to celebrations had been draining the ale barrels as quick as possible.

Magda shifted beside him. "In the rush to prepare, I forgot to give you my sincerest well-wishing. It must please you, knowing that you shall have an heir at last."

"It does." He let the satisfaction of it seep deep. He'd been damn near to constant smiling all day. Yes, Dunlough's mood and his own were much improved, and he knew he had his wife to thank. She'd healed them all since that disastrous battle, body and soul. If his people had been standoffish to her before, they near worshipped her now.

"I thank you, Magda, for helping Erika adjust to her new life," he said. "She tells me you have been a great help to her."

The woman beside him gave a start, then settled again. "It has been a pleasure to help her, you must know that."

"I do. And I thank you again. She'll be needing your aid more than ever, in the months to come."

He noticed that she shifted on the bench again, discomfited. "Something troubles you, sister?"

"I'm concerned, right enough, but I don't know how to say what needs to be said."

"Say it plain and true."

Before answering, she looked out over the gathering. "Conor, it distresses me to say this, to even suggest that anything untoward has occurred..." She paused. "Yet perhaps I, of all people, am the one who can say it."

Her fingers bunched the fabric of her skirts. "Oh Conor, are you certain the bairn is yours?"

The fraught words sucked the joy from him like wind from sails, leaving him adrift. If anyone else had asked such a question of him, he would have backhanded the fool over the bench for even thinking such a thing. Yet it was Magda who posed the question, a question he hadn't realized had been buried in the deepest, darkest corner of his soul until she spoke it.

She laid a hand over his now-clenched fist. "Forgive me, Conor," she whispered in misery. "I would not ruin this glorious day for anything, but after Aislingh..."

Conor didn't hear another word over the rush of blood beating against his ears. Erika was not Aislingh! Teeth clenched, he searched for his wife, her silver mane standing clear in the crowd. She finished her dance with Padraig by changing places with a blushing Múireann.

As if aware of his heated gaze, Erika lifted her head to stare at him. The smile on her lips faded as her eyes widened in surprise. He watched her gaze narrow as it moved to the right of him, to Magda. She started to push through the crowd, heading towards them.

"I'm sure there is no cause for concern," Magda reassured him as she rose. "Sure, she's had little time for liaisons even if she does ride out each day all about the *tuath*, and has since before you returned from battle. I suppose it is how she eases the pain of not having her freedom. Though 'tis true, she'll have it again, once the bairn is born." With another apology she took her leave.

Erika made her way through the crowd at last, her stance warrior-like as she stopped before him. "What has happened?" she demanded. "What news did Magda bring you that distresses you so?"

"Nothing that has not been said before," he said, biting off the words. There was no way he could recapture the good humor he'd enjoyed earlier. He could not believe the worst of Erika, did not believe the worst of her. Yet the idea, once planted, refused to leave him be.

And even though he knew his Valkyrie would not have dishonored him or herself, there was still the matter of her freedom. How could he have forgotten the vow they'd made—her freedom for a son?

Because he'd thought it didn't matter anymore. That no matter their bargain Erika would choose to remain. She had begun to make a place for herself, a future for herself. Was freedom more of a lure than Dunlough, than their child, than himself?

He rose then stepped away from her, needing the distance to clear his senses of her. Having Erika leave now that he was beginning to live again, to feel again, would be akin to having his arm ripped away. Having her stay when she wanted to be anywhere—wanted to have anything—but what he offered, was far worse.

"I think I will retire now."

In a moment she was by his side, her brows dipped in concern. "Are you not feeling well?" she asked. "You seem out of sorts."

He heard the concern. How true it sounded. Yet he knew it for a lie. Knew that all she had done since becoming his wife had been for this moment, the fulfilling of their vow. He knew for certain how single-minded she could be when pursuing the fulfillment of her vows.

Grief howled through him, bitter and swift, before he shut it away behind two years of resolve. The bairn was all that mattered. Not Erika, not her freedom, not even his joy.

He would see Dunlough's future born, see his wife leave and then his duty would be done.

Chapter Twenty-Seven

Erika soon discovered why bards did not sing of the joys of pregnancy.

As soon as her eyes opened to the new day she would retch. If she attempted to ingest anything more savory than bread and cheese, she would retch. Only a special elixir provided by Aine and imbibed twice daily got her out of bed at all.

The only positive she could see from being with child was that her slumber was deep. So sure was it that she was almost always asleep when Conor came to and left their chamber. Only his rumpled side of their bedstead proved to her that he did sleep beside her each night.

In the month since the *ceili*, her husband had firmly retreated to his former taciturn self. His days were spent in training and judgments and overseeing the stock, long hours that apparently left him little time to see to his wife.

No, that wasn't entirely true. Conor did show interest in her welfare. He posed repeated questions to the three people closest to her—Aine, Múireann and Padraig. Through them, he knew when she needed more stuffing in their bedding, ordered her baked fish prepared without the heavy sauce and seasonings, and ensured that she retired at midday to rest.

Without doubt, he was a concerned father-to-be. If only he showed a modicum of that concern to his wife.

Erika had no answers as to why he had withdrawn from her. Her confrontations with him were over before they began, terminating with him quitting her presence with the excuse of pressing business about the *tuath*.

She had had enough. In her heart of hearts she believed Magda had something to do with Conor's retreat into stoicism. She'd seen the Irishwoman talking with Conor the night of the dance, and knew that his demeanor had drastically changed afterwards. Unfortunately, Magda had soon hied herself off on a visit to former friends about the holding, leaving Erika with a mounting frustration.

It was time for Magda to leave. The widow had done little but snap at her heels like Fenrir gobbling up the world. She was Loki's sister in spirit and deed, and had done more harm than good since her shadow darkened the door to the dun.

The decision was sure to cause strife, Erika knew, but it was preferable to what she endured now. With the former mistress returned to her southern relatives Dunlough would finally settle, and she and Conor could get about the business of building their future together.

Erika paced about her chambers, her stomach roiling unceasingly. Magda had returned yester eve, and she'd summoned the widow to her chambers for a much-needed reckoning. It was not a conversation she looked forward to, but knew it a necessary evil to be borne. She just hoped the maidservant would arrive with her calming elixir before Magda did.

The elixir and Magda arrived together. The servant sat the tray down on a near table then left. "Well." Magda's smile was strained as she lifted a mug from the tray. "You wished to speak with me?"

"Yes." Erika reached for her own wooden goblet and took a sip of the overly bitter brew to calm her nerves and keep her hands from circling the other woman's throat. "The truth of the matter is, Magda, that I have been unfair to you."

The Irishwoman seemed taken aback. "Unfair to me? How?"

"I have taken advantage of you and your knowledge. For that, I offer a most humble apology. You are a guest here; it is time I treat you as such."

Magda's jaw dropped open in an entirely unladylike manner. "But-but I—"

"I'll not hear another word," Erika smoothly interjected. "It has been an unnecessary burden on you. I am grateful for the gracious manner in which you have undertaken my education, but it is a burden you no longer need carry. It has caused you to tarry longer here than you would have otherwise, I am sure."

Her voice hardened. "I know you said something to Conor the night of the *ceili*. It matters not what was said. All that matters is that it upset him, and that I'll not have. I'll not have you or anyone else affect his happiness. It is time for you to leave."

For a moment, such blind rage suffused Magda's face that Erika instinctively reached for her dagger to defend herself. Then the older woman smiled, a curving of lips that chilled Erika to the depths of her soul.

"You poor, foolish barbarian. I wanted to spare you the harsh truth, for 'tis not my place to speak it, but you must know. Conor sent for me, to run his household and to raise his heir."

The flame-haired woman smiled again as she stepped closer. "Do you remember the bargain you struck? Your freedom for a male child? Ah, I see that you do. Conor will uphold that bargain, you can be sure. Can you really believe that a murdering mercenary can remain as mistress of Dunlough? Such a thing is impossible for the leader of northern Connacht. You will never be accepted, but your get will. Conor realized this long ago."

"You lie!" Her vehement declaration lacked conviction, and Erika knew it.

Magda knew it as well. "Do I?" she wondered, chuckling with indulgence. "Tell me this: has Conor asked you to stay? Has he ever told you that he loves you? Of course he hasn't. And he never will."

Erika did reach for her blade then, and lunged toward Magda, wanting nothing more than to rip the smaller woman's throat out. Instead, she tangled in her own skirts and fell to the floor, hard.

Mocking laughter came to her through a sudden haze of pain. "No, Conor will never love you, Viking whore! In fact, with thanks to the elixir you just imbibed, he may come to hate you, for destroying his child."

"No!" Erika tried to scream a denial, but pain forced all air from her lungs.

"Oh yes." Magda retrieved the damning cup and walked to the door. "Pity that you'll not be able to recall our talk, if you even survive. I would have enjoyed seeing your face as you told Conor what transpired here, and seeing him not believing you. A good day to you, Angel of Death." Her laughter lingered even after she left.

Stars danced before Erika's eyes as another wave of pain hit her, clawing at her insides. Clawing at her child. She tried to climb to her feet using a nearby chair for leverage, and only succeeded in toppling over again.

Panic squeezed the air from her lungs, making it impossible to scream, to call for help. She had to get aid; if she didn't, Conor's babe would die.

Her fingers clawed the floorboards as she dragged herself to the door, a door that suddenly seemed a league away. She wasn't going to make it; she would never reach the door...

Her hand connected with wood. Survival instinct flowed into her veins, momentarily overpowering the poison and giving her strength to stagger to her feet. To open the door and stumble out.

"Help me." In her mind it was a scream, but her body continued its rebellion, the plea only a whisper. The hall reeled around her as her body cramped again. She retched, the force of it kicking her from her feet, sapping her strength.

She was dying, taking another life with her, a precious life. The last unclouded part of her mind railed against it, but the poison was stronger than her will. Her hand moved feebly to her womb as she begged for forgiveness, forgiveness she knew would not come.

THE SCREAMING COULD be heard everywhere about the dun. Urgent, grieving shrieks that clammed the skin of all who heard it.

Conor ran into the dun, a brace of soldiers with him, weapons drawn. Something was wrong with Erika; he knew it to the depths of his soul. He shouted her name, pounding up the stairs in the direction of the screams.

Múireann stood at the head of the stairs and 'twas she who screamed, horror limning her features as she stared at the floor.

Erika lay crumpled facedown at the top of the stairway, her hair spread about her like a pale silk cloth. Still, so very still. Falling to his knees, he turned her over, ignoring the palsied tremor of his hands. On the front of her gown a scarlet flower blossomed, increasing with every heartbeat.

It wasn't a flower.

"Erika?"

Slow, oh so slow, her eyes opened, washed out with pain. "C-Conor. The babe...must save..." Her eyes fluttered shut.

"No!" Gathering her in his arms, Conor raced to their chamber, shouting orders at the top of his lungs. He laid her on their bed as his people scattered for water and linens and Aine.

Erika thrashed on the bed, moaning with pain. The blood had become an angry vermilion stain, soaking her robe and the front of his tunic, and still it would not stop. He took his dagger, slicing the front of her dress, looking for a wound, praying there was a wound.

"Kill me," she whispered, her voice frantic. "T-tried to—" She heaved beneath his hand, rolling to her side to vomit, to utter a weak scream.

Aine came into the room, followed by servants carrying the necessary supplies. They tried to make him leave, but he refused to go farther than across the room. He needed to be there, just in case.

It was a nightmare that would not end. Erika alternated between Gaelic and Norse, breathless pleadings that they save the baby, cries for forgiveness. Each whimper tore through him like a sword strike, bleeding his soul. There was nothing he could do for her save add his pleas to her own, to whatever gods would listen, that they save her and their child.

Those pleas were in vain. Erika lost the battle to keep their babe. Aine won the battle to keep her from bleeding to death. A final, pain-filled shriek of denial rang through the chamber, slamming into Conor, sending him to his knees.

Gone. Everything, all his hopes...gone.

People milled about the room, Múireann and Aine and the priest and Olan, who nearly killed a horse in his race to his sister's side. Feeling like an old man, Conor climbed to his feet. "Did anyone see what happened?"

His question was greeted with silence. Anger surged through him, temporarily holding the grief at bay. "All of you were in the hall. Did you not see anything?"

None answered. "Get out," he ordered. When no one obeyed his command, he drew his sword. "Get out, all of you! Leave now!"

He pushed people to the door, throwing some bodily into the hall. At last he slammed the chamber door and bolted it, resting his head against the smooth wood. The cool surface did nothing to quell the demons rising within him, the specters of death that had haunted him for two years.

He had failed her. He had been so consumed with distancing himself, with shielding his soul against her inevitable departure that he had not been there when she needed him most.

Images danced through his mind. Erika, handing him the tiny dagger as a gesture of trust. Giving him her sword during their marriage ceremony. Yielding her body to his, surrendering the freedom she valued above all else. She did all this, based on a promise he had made, the one promise he should never have made.

The promise to protect her.

He had failed Erika and their child. Failed to protect them, just as he had failed to protect his older brother and three nephews during the fighting at Clontarf. His mind roiled with images, all awash with screams and blood. And above them all, Erika's cries and pleas echoed in his mind, his soul.

He brought his hands up in a futile attempt to ward them off. Blood caked his fingers and arms. Erika's blood.

With a cry of impotent rage, Conor drew his dagger and plunged it into the door again and again, as if he could slay the voracious demons that taunted him. The cry tore from him, from the deepest, darkest chambers of his spirit and rose to an inhuman roar that echoed through the chamber and out into the night.

Falling to his knees in exhaustion, Conor looked towards the bed. Erika had not stirred during his outburst. The thought that she might be dead near slammed him into the floor. What would he do if she were dead?

With his heart in his throat, he moved to the bed and dropped to his knees. Pale hair lay against an even paler bandage about her forehead. Her jaw line was livid with deep purple bruises, and shadows were heavy beneath her swollen, red-rimmed eyes. The slow rise and fall of her chest was the only indication that his wife still lived.

Even in slumber, sorrow was evident in her features. Had Erika ever been happy here? She had come to Dunlough a prisoner, was almost raped and had been forced into marriage by losing a duel to him. He had told her he could never love her, that he wanted an heir, not a wife.

No, Erika had not had an easy time here. Did she still dream of freedom, of a life away from him? Would she choose freedom now, since her sole reason to stay had just been taken?

As if sensing his distress, she moaned, her head moving side to side as she struggled to awaken. He was about to leap to his feet to summon Aine when her hand flailed out, catching his forearm. "Conor."

He covered her hand with his. "I am here."

Lashes fluttered against the sooty hollows beneath her eyes. "No...leave. You. Promised..."

Blessedly, unconsciousness claimed her before she could utter more. In rising horror he stared down at his slumbering wife, unable to believe her words, unable to hear, see, or feel beyond the flash of pain that consumed him.

He had lost everything.

Conor held the limp hand between his own, rested his head on the mattress, and cried.

"EASE, MY LADY. EASE."

Light beckoned, promising solace. She knew it for a lie. Only the darkness could contain and conceal the pain, the grief and the terrible, terrible emptiness.

Pain flailed at her relentlessly, and that alone forced her eyes open. Aine's face swam into view, Múireann's beside her and weeping silently. She rolled her head in slow agonizing movements on the pillow. Her brother sat at her bedside, not her husband.

Conor's absence scoured her. She saw the grief on her brother's face, knew he must have felt indirectly some of what she endured. Knew the answer to her question but had to ask it anyway. "I lost the babe, didn't I?"

Múireann's sobs grew louder as tears spiked her brother's lashes. "I am sorry, Rika."

She closed her eyes, wanting nothing more than to will the blackness to return, to capitulate to the darkness and void. She could not, not until she knew... "Conor?"

"He is not here."

Conor was gone. Olan's presence washed over her, his hands attempting to draw some of her pain away as they had done since she was a child. "Where?"

"You must rest, my lady," Aine admonished her, tilting her head for a sip of something too bitter to be water. Even that small movement left her gasping, the gasping leaving her blinded with agony. Olan's hands tightened on hers, and the physical anguish abated slightly.

"Fighting broke out in the east, near Dun Lief," he informed her. "Conor rode out two days ago."

Two days. He had been gone two days. She had been in darkness at least that long. Was the fighting truly so fierce, or was that merely a reason to escape? "What befell the door?"

Olan turned to the heavy oak, now pitted with deep gouges. "Conor did, after you—after Aine—" He broke off, his hand trembling in hers. "You have not stirred for three days. Three days have I sat beside you, praying that you would not die. Conor should have been here."

She struggled to make sense of her lost time. Conor had been there, the first day. Then the call to arms from Dun Lief had arrived. As Ardan had yet to recover fully, he could have sent Padraig to lead Dunlough's men, but she understood that he would need to go. His demons had come back, and the heavy door was not catalyst enough to help him battle them.

Images and sounds filtered through her mind, wordless pleas and curses, and a piercing roar of denial. "You must go to him, Olan." She reached out, her hand clasping the sleeve of his tunic. "He will surely blame himself."

"And well he should—"

"No, the fault does not lie with him," she interrupted, her whisper halting the beginning of his tirade. "It is mine."

Aine rested her hand on Erika's forehead. "My lady, do not say it—"

"I must have done something wrong. You told me it was still much too soon, but I wanted to give him what he wanted most of all."

She turned back to her brother, feeling fatigue battling the pain and the grief. "He will blame himself for this, as he blamed himself for Ardan's injury, and his brother and nephews. Promise me that you will go to him, Olan, that you will stand with him."

Olan's face remained flushed with his anger. "Because you ask it, and only because you ask it, will I go. When you are rested, you will be taken to Glentane."

"Glentane? Why?"

"Do you think I can allow you to remain here? After all that has happened?"

"But Dunlough is my home..." Her voice faded as she saw the look in her brother's eyes. "H-he didn't—didn't—"

"No." Olan leaned close to her, his free hand cupping her cheek. "He did not suggest it. In truth, he seemed to think you asked him to leave."

She moved her head restlessly on the pillow. "Leave? Why would I ask him to leave? This is my home. He is my home."

"Ah, you've fallen in love with him, haven't you?"

"Yes." She felt tears gather behind her eyes. Truly, she loved Conor, and it hurt all the more that she had failed him. "Bring him back to me, brother."

"May I hurt him first?"

Erika tried to smile, even though she knew Olan was serious. "What is between Conor and me will be dealt with between Conor and me. Just bring him back."

"I will." He stood, bending to brush his lips against her forehead. "Recover swiftly, sister. I want you on your feet when I drag your worthless husband home to you."

Erika awaited her brother's departure before succumbing to tears. She wept bitterly for what she had lost: her babe, her husband, her hope.

"What did I do amiss, Good-mother?" she asked through her tears. "I did all that you instructed to keep the babe safe. Why did this happen?"

"Hush, child," the healer whispered. "It will not do to overset yourself. Do you remember what happened?"

She tried, but memories eluded her. "Everything is blurred, like half-remembered dreams. All I can remember is feeling tired and..." She paused, about to say *alone.* "D-does Conor blame me?"

"Of course not. It is as you say, that he blames himself. Neither of you are at fault. Nature does this at times, for reasons we do not know. Though I must tell you, there were moments I feared I would lose you as well."

Erika rested her hands on the bedclothes above her empty womb. She felt as if she had indeed died. There was one more question she had to ask, one she had to know the answer to. "Good-mother, I will be able to give Conor a child, will I not?"

Moss green eyes regarded her solemnly. "Time will show the truth of it, my lady. We near lost you and your body will need much time to recover from that."

Numbness pulled at her as she took hope from the healer's words. She had no other choice. If Aine did not believe she could still be a true wife for Conor, there would be no hope for them.

With that despairing thought still in her mind, she tumbled into sleep.

Chapter Twenty-Eight

"If there is someone else here who needs killing, let us do and be done with it. I for one wish to return to my wife."

The goad found its mark. Conor whirled and struck the Viking such a blow as would have felled another man. Olan did not even sway.

"Hit me!"

The younger man folded his arms across the metal links covering his chest. "No."

Infuriated, Conor moved through their uneasy men until they were toe to toe. He had endured more than a month of Olan's censure, then Niall's when the ruler of Dun Lief discovered what had befallen Erika. His emotions were strung tighter than a harp's strings, and the routing of raiders had failed to appease them. "Hit me, damn you!"

Blue eyes flashed with a searing rage before the pale lashes swept down, smothering Olan's fury with calm. "There is nothing I would enjoy more at this moment than to beat you senseless. For the blow you just gave me I should kill you. That you treat my sister as less than a servant, I should kill you. That she could ask me to protect you even while she believes you have spurned her, I should kill you. Yet I cannot."

"Why?"

"Because my sister, despite you, despite herself, has fallen in love with you."

Breath left Conor in a rush, leaving him light of head. "What do you say?"

"Are you deaf as well as stubborn? My sister loves you."

Conor thought that his knees would give way. While he'd hoped for Erika's heart, he never believed it would be given to him. "Are you certain? How do you know?"

Olan folded his arms across his chest, his eyes still hard with anger. "She refused my offer to move her to Glentane. When I asked her why, that is the reason she gave."

Erika loved him. The news warmed the dark recesses of his heart with hope. She loved him and didn't want to leave him.

Conor strode to his horse, then stopped to face the Viking again. "Why did you not tell me this before now?"

"You were not ready to listen, and I needed the bloodletting as much as you. I wanted you to hurt as Erika hurt. And your guilt hurts you worse than my fists ever could."

IT WAS MIDAFTERNOON of a brilliant fall day when Dunlough came into view. In the month that he'd been gone the harvest had begun and the herds brought back from the summer fields. Life continued, and the thought renewed his hope as he dismounted and headed for the dun.

But it wasn't his wife who greeted him at the door. It was Magda. "Conor! Welcome home. I have much to discuss with you—"

"It can wait. Where is my wife?"

"She's gone."

"Gone?" The word swept into his soul like a winter squall, driving out all else. "When?"

"As soon as she recovered from the babe." Magda sidled next to him. "'Tis right sorry I am about the bairn. A pity it is, knowing how Erika worried herself so."

Words took their time sinking into the coldness that surrounded him. "She was worried?"

"And sure she was, over the wee bairn. I heard herself on more than one occasion, wondering what could befall the little one. 'Tis no wonder she fretted herself until she fell ill. After she recovered, she took herself to the old woman's hut. She has not returned to the dun in days, at least a week."

Conor spun away from her, not wanting to hear another word. Erika was gone. Olan was wrong. She had wanted to leave all along, and left as soon as she was able.

What reason did she have to stay?

Ardan greeted him as he rode toward the gate. "Did you kill everyone that needed killing?"

The censure in his captain's eyes was obvious and unforgiving. Conor could accept it, had censured himself often enough in the last six weeks. He wanted to set things a-right, but to do that he had to find his wife.

"Where is my lady? Magda says she has been gone a week. Did she—did she go to Glentane or Dun Lief?"

"Lady Erika is at neither of those holdings."

Hands fisted at his sides, Conor forced his emotions into the void that had served him so well in the last two years. "Where is she?"

Ardan's expression was accusatory. "She took your leaving hard, believing you abandoned her. Blames weighs heavy on her, and she believes you blame her as well." He paused. "Do you blame her?"

"No!" The denial was quick to his lips. She had been so joy-full when she'd first told him of her condition.

Then he remembered the pleas, the pain-filled, weak pleas that he save their child. Pleas that still echoed in his soul and would forever more. He needed to see her.

"Ardan." He clenched his jaw. "Tell me."

"She is at the village."

"The village?" It took a moment to realize that she hadn't gone, that she remained on Dunlough land. Then he turned to the gate, calling for a fresh horse.

He spent the time it took to reach the village proper making decisions. They would start anew, he and his wife. They would put the past behind them, concentrate on living each day as it dawned.

The salt-laden breeze intensified, heralding his arrival at the village. At this time of day the village should have been bursting with activity, men coming in from the sea with their catch, children scampering about in play or work, women dressing the catch or sitting before their huts doing their chores.

Now, a lone sentry served as guard, and the single lane was empty. Where was everyone?

"*Tigerna*." The guard greeted him with a proper bow. "Welcome home. The mistress will be glad to see you returned."

Would she? Conor held the question back by pressing his lips into a frown. "Where is my lady wife?"

"At the overlook."

He kneed his horse in the direction of the cliffs, wondering how many others he would have to question on the whereabouts of his wife, and how many more censorious replies he would receive before he saw her.

Topping the rise, he saw Erika sitting at the base of a spreading yew in the dip of the land. Gathered around her, their faces bright with rapt attention, sat the children of the tribe. On her lap was what appeared to be a cloth bundle until a tiny pale fist and arm flailed at her hair. Erika captured the little fist in her hand, leaning forward to kiss it before tucking it back into the blanket.

The image near felled him. The Angel of Death as a mother. In less than half a year's time it would have been his bairn in her arms.

His fingers tightened on the reins as he fought to dampen the tumult of emotions that churned within him. She seemed well recovered since he'd seen her last. She looked happy. Had she even grieved the loss of their child?

The question shamed him. He wouldn't have these doubts if he'd been here, with her as he should. He would have noticed something amiss. He would have gotten to her in time. He would have saved their child.

Would she forgive him for that? Would her love for him redeem him in her regard? Or was all lost?

There was but one way to find out.

Erika felt him before she saw him, a disturbing ripple on the wind. Over the heads of the children she watched her husband riding up the rise like an approaching thunderstorm. Her heart leapt, as it always did to see him returning to her. It quickly fluttered still as his features became more distinct. He didn't look happy. He looked irritated.

Smiling had never been easy for Conor. She reminded herself that of late, she had given him nothing to smile about. If he had grieved the deaths of his men, surely he had grieved over the loss of their child? Surely that was why he had left, and stayed away. The alternative—that he had hoped she would leave, that he couldn't bear the sight of her—had her lungs constricting painfully.

Still holding young Turlough in her arms, she rose to her feet. "I'll finish the rest of the story tomorrow," she told the children, speaking over their chorus of disappointment. "Our men have returned, and we should prepare for them."

The children gleefully scattered as she gave them various duties. Conor had topped the rise by then, reining in his horse.

Time seemed to suspend itself. Erika just stared at him, at the man who had the power to hurt her as no one else could. He was dirt-stained and sweat-soaked, and new lines creased his eyes. He seemed exhausted, mentally and physically. Above all he seemed to be holding himself in check. The air felt as charged as a summer sky giving way to lightning.

Erika's heart plummeted. She had hoped that time and distance would heal the breach between them, that he would be able to forgive her for taking away what he wanted most. The look in his eyes said otherwise.

As if sensing her distress, Turlough stirred in her arms and began to wail. Conor's eyes darkened further, and the brown beast he sat astride pawed the grass.

Quickly, Erika handed the crying child to Bebhinn. "Take him to his mother," she whispered to the girl, who nodded and scurried away. She gathered folds of her skirts and turned back to him as he dismounted. "Welcome home, my lord."

He ignored her lackluster greeting as he dismounted, standing close but still far away. "You were not at the dun," he said. "Magda told me that she has not seen you for more than a week."

Harshness weighted his voice, causing her to hesitate. It would do her little in the way of good to tell him she had quit the dun as soon as she'd regained her feet, spending her recovery in the solace of Aine's hut. The dun had become oppressive to her, and Magda a presence she avoided at all costs.

"I returned to my studies with the Good-mother when I was able," she finally said. "A sickness befell the children here and it caused Thala to deliver early…"

Her voice cracked and she fought to subdue it. She would not recount to him how it was duty alone that had kept her by Thala's side, or the jealousy and sorrow she'd endured when the woman had birthed a healthy son.

She raised her head. "The sickness has passed, thank God, and we did not lose any of them. Thala and her son are doing well also."

Conor's anger fled him. How difficult had it been for her, to help a mother through a difficult delivery? He had not seen such shadows beneath her eyes since she was first captured. The bones at her throat stood out in harsh relief, mute testimony to what she had endured.

'Twas obvious that she'd suffered, and the renewed guilt he felt over that near consumed him. 'Twas obvious she'd suffered and too much.

He held out his hand, intending to lift her to his horse. "We return to Dunlough. I will have one of the villagers bring your things to you."

"But there is still much to do—"

"You have done enough!"

Pale skin paled even further, but all she said was, "I must look in on Thala before we go."

Without a word, she turned and walked down the path, leaving him to follow. After pausing long enough to call himself twelve kinds of fool, he did. He saw her stop before one hut, taking a deep breath before stepping inside.

After a time she came out, followed by Eithne. The old woman thrust a bundle at him with gnarled hands. "Mind you now, herself's worn out caring for the children and poor Thala. Don't let her overdo the welcoming of you."

He took the bundle, relieved to see it was clothing and not the bairn. After securing it to his mount he turned to his flushed wife to help her mount, then vaulted astride behind her. She sat as straight as a yew tree though she bade a warm farewell to the villagers.

Not halfway on the slow journey to the dun, Erika settled against him and fell asleep. Conor slowed his pace even further. It felt good to be close to his wife again, to hold her in his embrace. Yet he could feel her thinness, her fragility, even through two layers of clothing. He made a silent vow to take better care of her.

She stirred as they entered the gates, then straightened away from him. When he stopped, she slid to the ground without assistance. She looked at the dun's entrance with an expression of intense dislike. As quickly as it appeared it left, leaving Conor to wonder if his fatigued mind played games with him.

In a fluid motion he dismounted, standing beside her. "Are you well?"

She sighed, straightening her shoulders as if to bear a heavy weight. "I am. The Good-mother has aided me."

Before he could ask her what Magda had done to aid her, she continued. "You must be tired after your journey. I'll send for hot water for a bath."

Conor itched with the desire to take his wife into his arms, but he refrained. The cool aloofness had returned to her eyes, and he had no weapon against it. Had it only been a season ago that she had run out of the dun to greet him? A season that she had come to him, banished his madness with her pure light?

They entered the dun. He was relieved to find the main hall scarce. There was a decided relaxing to his wife's shoulders as they mounted the stairs to their chamber, only to return again as they were left alone within.

Conor watched her close, awaiting some evidence of her supposed regard. Yet his lady wife's eyes were hooded and she appeared uncomfortable to be in the same room as he.

Want rose sharp within him, the want for more than pleasure. He wanted Erika's forgiveness as much as he wanted her love. Wanted to know there was still hope for them despite their loss. Yet she couldn't even look at him. What would she do if he attempted to touch her?

Impulse suited thought as he raised a hand to touch her hair. Erika flinched as if awaiting a blow. He dropped his hand, a sick feeling twisting his guts. His first night home in nearly two months and his wife could not suffer his touch.

A thought came to him, unbidden. Aislingh had been much the same way when she began to betray him.

Conor stepped back from her. No, he could not, would not, think that of Erika. His Valkyrie was not Aislingh.

"I must see to the dun," he said, his voice stripped bare.

"Shall I—shall I wait for you?"

Her voice shook. Did she ask out of want or out of fear? He could not discern and decided not to test her further. His battered pride would fracture if she fled him.

"There is no need," he said at last, folding his hands behind his back against the urge to bury his fingers in her hair. "'Tis certain I will not be done until late. I will sleep elsewhere, so as not to disturb your rest."

Erika nodded once, eyes downcast. He left, not wanting to see relief in her eyes.

Chapter Twenty-Nine

Her life had become a living example of the Christian hell.

Erika walked the path near the high edge of the lough, Múireann by her side as she sought medicinal plants among the weeds and grasses. It was the only task she could manage, for all her energies poured into holding back tears.

In vain, she had waited for Conor to return to their chamber, waited until an exhausted sleep took her. This morn the place beside her had been untouched. Only his rumpled *leine* of the previous day had convinced her that he was indeed home. But where had he spent his night?

The question dogged her. She'd fled the dun as early as she could, feeling the pitying looks of the household like nettles stinging her skin. They knew, every single one, that the Lord of Dunlough had not passed the night with his lady. They might even know whose bed he had shared.

She could not endure much more of this. She felt more like a foreigner with each passing day. Her role was undefined and unacknowledged; her attempts to find her own way met with failure. Her one shining moment of saving Ardan's life had been eclipsed by the miscarriage. She needed to know if she belonged, if she was necessary. She would put the question to Conor; his answer would determine whether she could find a place here or somewhere else.

The thought gave her pause, a heavy feeling growing within her. She did not want to leave. She loved Dunlough and its people. She loved Conor. She wanted—needed—the joy Gwynna and Fionnuala shared with their husbands. Without it, she would surely go mad.

"Sure we have enough by now, my lady," Múireann protested as the sun drew high overhead.

Erika straightened her aching back. "I must replace the tonics we used at the village. We must have enough to last the winter." *Whether I am here or no*, she thought to herself.

Múireann sighed, but resumed her harvesting. Erika did not blame her. She would not have thought that such a lack-adaisical activity would be such a painful process. A scream slashed through her thoughts. Múireann dropped the collection of plants she was carrying. "What is that?"

Erika had already discarded her basket and unsheathed her dagger. "Run to the dun and get Conor. Quickly!"

Gathering her cumbersome skirts in one fist, Erika ran at full speed to Lough Dun, the direction the screams were coming from. The shrieking continued unabated, sure to bring every warrior in the *tuath* running. She crashed through a stand of yew trees, unmindful of the branches scratching at her face and arms, and burst through the other side.

A woman knelt on a steep overhang above the lough. Over her screams, Erika could hear frantic splashing in the water below. "What is it?"

The woman raised a tear-streaked face. It was Maire, one of the villagers. "Oh mistress, Bebhinn fell in!" she cried, grabbing Erika's skirts. "Please save her—she's all I have!"

Erika didn't hesitate. Taking a deep breath, she leapt off the bank and into the lough. The shock of hitting the frigid water threatened to steal the air from her lungs. She flailed about, failing to find the child. She knew she did not have much time. The run to the water had left her winded and fatigued. The folds of her dress were already heavy with water, jeopardizing her ability to stay afloat.

She broke the surface long enough to catch her breath and get her bearings. A small hand pierced the water less than ten feet away before slipping beneath the dark surface. Erika quickly shed the constricting smock, then dove and swam toward the spot. Her outstretched hand connected with something soft and yielding. Wrapping both arms around it, Erika again headed for sunlight.

The sodden bundle struggled in her arms, kicking and thrashing with strength born of the instinct to survive. A blow struck her squarely in the right eye, causing Erika to release the child. The little girl managed to remain afloat for several seconds before the water reclaimed her.

With a cry of denial, Erika plunged beneath the surface again, snagging the child before she disappeared into the murk. Coughing and spluttering, she resurfaced with the now-unconscious girl and paddled to the bank. To her horror, the bank was too sheer to climb. There was only a small rock protrusion and a tree root.

Her muscles trembling in protest, Erika managed to wrestle the still child onto the tiny ledge. Remembering what her father had taught her, she eased the girl onto her side and pushed on her stomach until water spewed from her mouth.

"My lady?" The hysterical woman's voice floated down to her. "My Bebhinn—is she—"

Erika looked at the little girl. Her skin was pale, but her chest rose and fell evenly. "She lives," Erika called, "but I cannot climb up from here. Múireann went for Conor—see that they bring rope and dry clothing!"

She heard the woman scramble to her feet and run off and she sighed, lowering her head to the rocky outcropping. Now that immediate danger was over, reaction was beginning to set in.

The shallow end of the lake was much too far away. She would not abandon the little girl, who was becoming paler by the moment. Even without the child, Erika knew she would never be able to swim that distance. It was taking all of her energy to hold on to the root and the outcropping. Coldness sank into her muscles, into her soul, sapping the rest of her strength and her mind. She did not know how much longer she could hold on to the ledge. She said a fervent prayer that Conor would come soon, that he would not let her die this way.

CONOR SLAMMED HIS HEELS into Brimstone's flanks, outpacing the soldiers accompanying him. His heart had yet to recover from Múireann's hysterical report there was trouble at the lough and Erika had gone to investigate armed with just a dagger. Then came Maire, screaming that her child had fallen into the lough and Erika had gone in after her.

He was off his horse and bellowing Erika's name almost before the animal scrambled to a stop. He couldn't see sign of her or the child. The bank was devoid of life; everything was still. His heart seized. What would he do if she were hurt? *Don't let me be too late. Dear merciful heaven, do not let me be too late.*

There was a flash of light at the far end of the lake. He sped along the bank. Dropping to his knees, he peered over the slope. What he saw stole his breath.

A small child lay on a minuscule rock ledge, unmoving. Erika was up to her chin in icy water, one hand on the child, the other gripping a root. "Erika?"

She raised her face, and Conor could see the stark fatigue and strain in her eyes. She managed a fragile smile with lips turned blue with cold. "My thunder god comes for me," she said in Norse.

The sight of his wife clinging to the tiny ledge was enough to drive him mad. Without thought, Conor leapt into the water. The brisk temperature shocked the breath out of him, but he righted himself and broke the dark surface. Slinging wet hair out of his eyes, he swam over to his wife. She stared at him with confusion, as if she did not recognize him. "Why in the name of all that is holy did you jump in the lough?"

"It is the d-duty you have given me, to protect these people, with my life if necessary," she said in a mixture of languages difficult to understand. "I am a s-servant of Conor's people but it is service I give most willing, for I have come to love them."

Even as his heart soared that she would put his people's welfare above her own, it pounded with fear at the cold that was spreading from her lips to her cheeks. "Do not think that you are not held in the same high esteem," he told her.

"I am not," she said, her voice just above a whisper. "Yet it would be bearable if my husband but gave me some token of his favor."

The cold of the lough receded. "You believe you do not have my favor?"

"Conor is a f-fine man, full of bravery and strength and honor. I am more blessed than most, and I sh-should be c-content." Her eyes closed. "I wish to rest now."

"No!" Keeping one hand on the ledge, Conor wrapped the other about Erika's waist. "Wake up!" he ordered, shaking her. "Do you hear me, Erika? Open your eyes now!"

Her eyes opened, much too slow for his liking. "Conor?"

"And who else would be holding you like this in a cold lough?"

She gave him a wan smile. "I suppose you are going to shout at me again."

"I am. But I will wait until you are dry."

"You are most k-kind."

Her dry tone made his lips twitch, until he saw that she wore nothing but her shift. "What befell your dress?"

"Y-you're shouting."

He wanted to strangle her and kiss her at the same time. In a quieter voice he repeated his question.

She stared at him with eyes glassy from cold. "The water wanted it. It would have pulled me down, but I was able to discard it."

And thus become chilled that much the sooner. A cold fist of fear formed in Conor's gut. "You brave, foolish woman," he said, though he felt near to tears. "What am I to do with you?"

"Y-you should not have jumped in," she said, her words slurring together as if she'd partaken too much ale. "You could become ill."

"And you could not?"

"Our f-fjords are like this most of the y-year. I am u-used to it."

She was not used to it. He could see that clear in her eyes, the way she no longer trembled from the cold. "Ardan is bringing rope. You are to hold to that ledge and not let go. Do you understand me, wife? You are not to let go!"

It took much too long for her to answer. "I do not know if I can promise you that, but I will try."

Conor was snarling with impatience by the time Ardan arrived and dropped the rope to him. Wrapping a good length about his arm, he reached for Erika, but she shook her head. "B-Bebhinn f-first," she said. "I d-d-don't know how bad she f-fares."

Fear tightening his chest, he managed to tie the rope quick and secure about the unconscious girl's chest, a difficult process with one hand free. He'd be damned if he'd leave Erika behind, however. "Pull her up and quick now!"

That done, he turned back to his wife. If possible, she was even paler. "Hurry, man, with that rope! My wife needs out of this water now!"

The rope returned. "Now, my lady, take the rope and up you go."

Pale hair was plastered to her head, making her eyes stand out huge and vulnerable. "I'm afraid my fingers disobey us both, for I cannot seem to move them."

He reached over and pried her hands free. Their iciness sent an answering stab of ice into his soul. Wrapping one arm with the rope, he placed the other around his wife. "We're both of us coming out of this damned water now."

Her smile was sad as she closed her eyes. "I want to help, b-but I cannot seem to make my limbs move. It seems that I fail you yet again."

He kept silent lest he loose a snarl of rage at her reckless behavior or a howl of anguish at her condition. The journey to the top of the embankment seemed to take an eternity, but at last they made it. Hands pulled them over the ledge and blankets were piled over them. Conor ignored them all, his need to see to Erika overriding everything else.

Her head pitched forward against his chest; she didn't even have the strength to shiver. "Conor is angry with me yet again," she whispered. "It seems that is all I am capable of doing, angering him. Tell him I am sorry for that. Tell him to forgive me."

She went limp in his arms.

EXHAUSTED FROM HER ordeal, Erika slept a feverish sleep through the night and most of the next morning. Conor spent the majority of that time berating himself for the weight he had settled on her shoulders. Múireann, Padraig and Ardan all told him how she had quit her sickbed to tend the ill in the village, working without rest to save the children's lives. That dedication had almost cost her life.

She took too much upon herself, he realized as he sat at her bedside. She was mistress of Dunlough, not a servant. A princess of the *tuath*, not a soldier. While his heart swelled with pride at how she threw her whole heart into the protection of their people, his heart also skipped at the thought that one day she might succumb because of it.

"Conor?"

Erika blinked, attempting to sit up. He splayed one large hand on her chest, pushing her back down. "How do you fare?"

"Well enough," she answered, then spoiled the assurance by shivering. He lifted her, bedclothes and all, and carried her to the hearth, settling her amid the warm furs waiting there. He picked up a serving tray sitting near the fire then returned to her.

"This is a broth Aine said will warm your insides," he told her, lifting a wooden bowl from the tray. "Are you able to hold it?"

She reached out with both hands. The broth sloshed in her grasp. Conor wrapped his hands around hers, guiding the warm liquid to her mouth. Her eyes fastened to his as she sipped at the liquid. "Argh." She shuddered. "Sure, and ale will warm me faster?"

"Perhaps," Conor said. "But this is better for you. Have another taste."

She let him tip the broth to her lips again, and again her eyes watched him. What transpired behind that lavender gaze, he did not know.

When she finished half the bowl, he took it from her, returning it to the tray. "Are you warm enough?"

"Yes. But I am ready to return to my duties."

"You are to rest."

"I cannot. There is much to do, and I would see how Bebhinn fares."

"Others will do what needs to be done," he told her, noting that her eyes were still ringed with sleep and fatigue. "As for Bebhinn, she is well. She did not take much water."

"Thank the gods. My father taught me how to push the water out."

He reached up and touched a lock of her hair. "Your hair is all entangled. Shall I comb it through for you?"

Her eyes widened in surprise. "If it pleases you," she whispered, dipping her head.

He left her but a moment to retrieve her comb. Pulling a stool behind her, he took a seat then lifted a lock of hair in his hands. She stiffened at once, then pulled the blankets close about her. Shivers caught her again as he lifted her hair, revealing the curve of her neck. "Should I return you to the bed?" he asked. "I thought the fire would be good for you."

"I am well," she replied, her voice just a whisper. After a pause, she spoke again. "Why do you do this?"

"Because it needs to be done. Because it is my duty to care for you."

"Duty." She huddled deeper into the bedcovers. "You do not have to do this, Conor. I am sure there are other duties about the dun that are more important."

"At this moment, nothing is more important than ensuring that you are well."

She fell silent, neither moving nor making a sound as he worked her silver mane free of tangles. He enjoyed the simple pleasure of touching her hair, seeing how the firelight cast shadows and shimmers through it. But concern for her health overrode his enjoyment, so he lifted her in his arms and carried her back to the bed.

She struggled to get up. "There is much to be done."

"It will not be done by you, not this day."

She turned on her side to face him full. "So are you still angry with me?"

"Should I not be? No sooner than you regain your feet, but you must stave off a plague and rescue drowning children, never once thinking of how you risk your life. How many times do you think you can throw yourself into death's path before he will catch you?"

"And what of you?" she asked, her cheeks pinking. "Do you not do the same, again and again, in the hopes that he will catch you?"

"I am the Devil of Dunlough. It is what I do."

Her gaze was heavy on his skin. "Your people need the Devil of Dunlough, true enough. But they need Conor mac Ferghal more."

Right uncomfortable were her observations, making him defensive. "What they need is promise of the future, which can be achieved through my sword or my son. For now, my sword is all that I have."

Blood drained from her cheeks, and Conor recognized his harsh words for the accusation they were. "Erika, forgive—"

"There is nothing to forgive, Conor," she whispered, closing her eyes. "I know I have failed you."

Her words, so soft, so sure, pierced his soul like arrows. "Failed me?"

"I know I have not been the wife you wanted. I know that I did or didn't do something that caused you to turn away from me even before—"

She swallowed the tremor in her voice. "I know you blame me for what happened to our babe. I know how important the child was to you. If I could have given my life for his, I would have."

Though she whispered, her voice was like a shout in the still of the room. Her words resurrected the fear that even battle could not slay. He had been near to losing her. He had ridden away like a coward after her miscarriage so that he would not have to see her die.

"I would not ask that sacrifice of you," he managed to say, struggling to keep the horror of such a thought out of his tone.

She did look at him then, her eyes dark and solemn. "You would not have to ask it. I would have done it most free, to give you that which you desire most."

"No!"

His bellow, summoned by the fear her words wrought, tore from him, stunning them both. Fisting his hands to keep them from shaking, he said, "You have done enough."

He had meant to reassure her, but his words had the opposite effect. She paled, as if about to faint. "It's done then?"

"What's done?"

Agitation marked her features as she quit the bed like an arrow loosed from a bow. "You've chosen her?"

He was becoming dizzy, trying to follow her path and understand her questions at the same time. "Chosen who? And for what?"

"Do not pretend to misunderstand me!" she demanded, pacing before him with wobbling, angry steps. "You know of whom I speak. Did you think I wouldn't know, that I wouldn't care?"

"*Tá tú ag glagaireacht!* You must have hit your head when you leapt into the lough yester eve."

"I am not talking nonsense, you oaf of a man!" she exclaimed. Her frenetic pacing carried her to one of the chests on the far side of the room. "The whole dun knows you have not been to our bed since your return. And this—this treatment of me now is a mockery born of your guilt, nothing more."

She flipped the chest open and rummaged in it, never once halting her tirade. "I have endured much, but this goes too far!"

Upon finding what she sought she straightened, then crossed to him. "If you believe I will be docile and idle while you take another woman to bed, you are mistaken."

Of a sudden Conor found himself juggling a mass of metal rings as Erika thrust the shackles into his arms. "It is bad enough that she is mistress in all but name. If you give her that name, I become less than a servant. I'll not be second to anyone! I would rather be put back in chains."

Head buzzing as if he'd drank too much ale, Conor could do naught save stare at his wife as she retreated from him. "You think I have taken another because you miscarried our babe?"

"Did you not?" she asked, her voice cracking. "You made me a solemn promise, Conor mac Ferghal. You swore to me that when tragedy claimed the next soul of Dunlough, you would not leave me. On your honor and your life you swore that to me. I asked you not to leave, and when I awakened, Olan told me you were gone."

Anguish coursed through him, bitter poison. His suffering was far from over. Her words flayed his soul as she continued, "When I awoke and found you gone, I thought—I knew—that I had failed you."

Her violet eyes were stark as she beheld him. "I became angry with you, Conor. For a time, I was near to hating you for breaking the vow we'd made. Then the children of the village fell ill, and I had to go to them. Tending them, I understood why you had to go, but not why you had to stay away. Until yesterday."

His fingers dug into the pile of metal in his hands. "So you believe I have turned to another? To Magda?"

All the fight drained from her as she collapsed onto the side of the bed. "I cannot do this, Conor," she whispered. "I have tried to find my place here, to no avail. You will not allow me to fight. Magda rules your household. It will be years before I achieve Aine and Gwynna's skill for healing, so your people don't need my skill with herbals. If you refuse our bed, 'tis obvious you don't need my body either. I am set aside in all but name."

He was shaking. From fear or anger he could not tell. How had they gotten so far apart that she could believe he wanted her out of his life?

"I do not want Magda for wife," he managed to say, every bit of control he could summon thrown into his voice. "I do not want another in my bed or as mistress of my household."

The shackles bit deeply into his hands. He wanted to tell her that she was what he desired most, his angel, and his heart. He couldn't. Not until he knew that she would stay, consent to be his—forever.

"What do you want, Erika?" he asked. "If it is in my power, I will give it to you."

Her shoulders lifted in a bone-weary sigh. "I want you to forgive me for all that I have done. I want to be necessary to you and to Dunlough. I want to bear you the child you desire."

Unshed tears spiked her lashes as she looked up at him. "But if I cannot bear you another..."

He lowered his head, blinking against the sudden pain that shafted through him. Blessed Danu, he had driven her away without conscious aforethought.

"Then you will have your freedom." The cuffs dug into his palms as he held them in a death-grip. "All you have wanted, since before we were wed, is your freedom. I will give you that. I'll not hold you—not by vows, not by these damned shackles!"

With every ounce of strength he possessed, he jettisoned the heap of metal rings out the high window. "You are free, if that is what you want."

His heart pounded like a thousand horses galloping. If she asked for her freedom he would give it to her. Sweet skies, if it was the one thing that would bring a smile back to her eyes he would do it. How he would be able to live with her gone, he did not want to contemplate.

Looking at her, at the sadness that slumped her shoulders, was akin to looking into his soul. He saw the sadness and the anguish, the resolve and resignation. Beneath it all he saw a deep, elemental need. A need, he realized, that mirrored his own.

Before he could speak, she reached out one pale, slender hand to him. "What I want, what I've always wanted, is you."

"Me?" It wasn't that simple. It couldn't be that simple. "When every right thing I have attempted to do for you becomes wrong? Why would you be wanting me?"

Her eyes swam with tears. "Can you not know? I love you."

It was that simple. His senses reeled as he stumbled to his knees before her. "Erika." Her name ripped out of his very soul as he wrapped his arms about her waist and buried his face into her lap, her empty womb. He wanted to give the words back to her, tried to say them back, but they were trapped by the powerful surge of emotion in his chest.

She curled over him, and he could feel hot tears scald the back of his neck. "I choose free to stay here with you, Conor—if you'll have me."

He raised his face to her. "Do you think I could be without you, you who have been the wellspring of my happiness these last months?"

"Conor." She threw her arms about his neck.

"Ah, *aingeal*." Rising to his knees, he buried his face in her hair. "I need you sure as a homeless man needs a place to lay his head and food to line his belly. You've given me back my soul, and I thank you."

She answered him, but he couldn't ascertain her meaning through the tears and tremors that shook her. Truth to tell, he wasn't dry-eyed himself. Crying females made him uncomfortable, right enough. The Angel of Death reduced to tears undid him.

For a long moment they were silent, grieving together. He consoled her best as he could, with gentle touches and light kisses to her forehead, eyelids, cheeks and jawline. Using the pads of his thumbs, he brushed away the tears that tracked her cheeks. He brushed a feathered kiss across her lips, intending only to soothe. Her lips opened beneath his in invitation to give and receive succor, and he accepted.

The kiss deepened, opening a pathway to the passion that always simmered between them. He wanted to give more than take, to show her by actions what he could not with words.

Slow and gentle, he marked kisses down the slim column of her neck, dipping his tongue in the pulsing hollow at the base of her throat. She sighed, trembling, then angled her head to bare her throat full to him.

When her hands dropped from his shoulders to the belt about his waist, he drew back. "Nay, my lady wife. This is for you."

Her hands fell away as he molded his palms to her thighs, pulling the fine material of her shift up her legs with the upward motion of his caress. Once she was free of the garment, he returned to the fullness of her lips and throat.

Still kneeling before her, he cupped the silken rise of her breasts in his calloused, battle-roughened hands. The rosy peaks swelled at his touch, blossoming beneath his tender ministrations. Lowering his head, he placed kisses to one hardened peak then the other, then laved each with his tongue.

Erika gasped then arched her back, presenting her bounty for his feast. He bore her back on the bedstead, shifting until they were side by side. As he continued his impassioned worship of her breasts his free hand tracked a path down her ribcage, skittering to a stop on the now-flat plane of her stomach.

Her hands threaded through his hair. Raising his head, he saw the misty understanding smile she gave him. His heart surged in response, and his hand continued its southern journey until it reached the pale curls that hid her secrets.

With gentle strokes he found the core of her femininity and slipped a finger inside, just a light caress. She warmed at his touch, her essence drenching his finger as she moaned his name. He continued his slow, tender loving until she shuddered and gasped her release.

Pleased to have pleased her, he raised his head to kiss her, long and deep. Her hands once again went to his *leine*. "I need you, Conor," she whispered. "I need to feel you inside me."

Wanting nothing more than to join her, he nevertheless hesitated. "Are you certain? I do not want to hurt you."

She stared back at him with love in her passion-heavy eyes. "I am."

After removing his *leine*, he found himself trembling as he guided his arousal to her heat. As nervous as the first time, he bathed himself in the waters of her passion. Then with a long, careful stroke, he slid home.

Her soft sigh welcomed him, her thighs circling his hips and settling him deep. Shaken, he paused to rest his forehead against hers, savoring the pleasure and rightness of their joining.

He loved her most thoroughly, withdrawing until just the tip remained inside her soft folds then sheathing himself again to the hilt. Again and again he advanced and retreated with measured stroke, giving in to a joining truer and more profound than any furied coupling.

Release was a deep outpouring of his soul, accepted and reflected by hers with soft world-shaking exclamation. Together they floated in a cocoon of sensation and emotion, at last united body, mind and soul.

Chapter Thirty

Conor set the missive on the table before him, rubbing at his eyes. Fall was completing its inevitable change to winter. Soon, fierce rains would lash the westernmost shores. It was a time when those most sensible remained in their homes eating, drinking and bedding their women.

"Is something amiss?" Erika asked, looking up from the *leine* she embroidered with painful precision. She was well recovered from her ordeal in the lough four days' past. Her skin fair glowed in the hearth light.

"It's an urgent summons from Taig, to join him."

The *leine* fell forgotten in her lap. "He's not thinking of waging war during winter, is he?"

"It does not say." Conor sighed. By the saints, he hoped not. He looked forward to exploring the wonders of his wife's love, not hieing about the countryside beating sense into those too foolish or too ambitious to stay home. "With luck, he wants nothing more than to discuss strategies for the spring."

He rose then crossed to where she sat near the fire. "I would take you with me, but winter travel is not good at even the best of times."

She set her sewing aside then rose to her feet, stretching before leaning into him. "I would beg off in any case. Gwynna is near her time and I must go to her."

He wanted to be there with her, with them all. "Will you fare well?" he asked, threading a hand through her hair.

"I am in fine spirits," she answered, her voice soft. "I will be well in Glentane."

He gathered her close. "Then we can travel south together for a time."

"Will you be away for long?"

"If it were within my power, I would be gone but a moment," he answered, want coloring his voice. "I am loath to be apart from you."

Her arms tightened about him as she laid her cheek against his heart. "I love you."

It still stunned him to hear the words. Not five days past he'd wondered if she could even suffer his touch. Thank God he had been wrong.

He placed his forefinger beneath her chin, lifting her face to his. "Say it again."

Laughter spilled from her, causing her eyes to dance and break up her words. "I wouldn't have taken you for a vain man, needing flowery speech to swell your chest. But I tell you true, Conor mac Ferghal: I love you. I love your prowess in battle and bed, the silver of your eyes and the smile made all the more precious for its rarity—"

He cut off her words with a deep, slanting kiss that had the room tilting at a crazed angle. Then he realized that they'd fallen back against the wall.

Erika righted herself first, fixing him with a stern stare ruined by the blush staining her cheeks. "'Tis a wonder you didn't crack your head open," she scolded. "Are you certain enough of what I feel for you?"

He glanced at her through lowered lashes. "There's one thing more you could do to convince me."

"What? Oh." Her ears crimsoned. "Have we time enough for that?"

"Not the time I want to take," Conor said in disappointment. "We should be on our way while the weather holds. Can you ready us for departure within the hour? I mean to make it a quick journey."

"Yes, the faster gone, the faster we shall return. If I may request it, I would like Ardan to remain here. He's near himself again, but I'd rather he not ride about the countryside if the winter rains come sooner. Besides, Padraig needs the exercise."

Conor barked a laugh, sure the commander wouldn't appreciate the inference that he'd grown comfortable in his duties guarding his lady.

"Done. I need Ardan here to oversee the final harvest. Fionn and Cian will accompany you." He gathered her close again. "Take your sword, but no looking for battles, wife. The sooner gone, the sooner returned."

She smiled. "And the sooner you'll be out of the black and into your new leine. We'll have a homecoming feast to celebrate."

"We will indeed." He opened the door for her. "See to our preparations while I talk to Ardan and Padraig."

After Erika disappeared upstairs, Conor went in search of Magda. He found her in a side chamber on the main level, her maidservant and two guards, Renald and Crutchin, with her.

Conor hid his dislike behind an impassive mask. He liked the two men little, as they had little care for his standards of work and exercise.

"Leave us."

Magda looked at him with reserved curiosity. "You wish to speak to me?"

Conor wasted little time. "My lady wife is appreciative of the assistance you have given her, Magda. Rest assured, when I am confident that my wife has fully recovered, you will be able to regain your status as a guest in our house, and my wife will visit such thanks upon you as she sees fit."

Magda lowered her head. "There's so much left to teach her, and difficult to do, with herself riding about instead of tending the hearth as she should."

He felt a spark of anger and sought to subdue it. "My wife has done what has been needed."

"For Dunlough, or for herself?" she wondered. "She is gone so long, with no accounting for her whereabouts. Is it certain, where she goes?"

"You would do well to guard your tongue."

"Forgive me, Conor," Magda said, contrition limning her voice. "I've no wish to speak ill of anyone. It is the love I bear you as a brother that urges me to speak of rumors that continue of the woman you have taken to wife."

"I thought you above such petty deeds."

"Even rumors at times possess a kernel of truth. You are wrong if you believe I take joy in telling you this. I tell you so that you may be ware."

"Then tell me and be done with it."

"It is rumored that the Angel of Death is in league with Ronan of Ulster."

Conor stared at her a moment before roaring with laughter. "That is the great rumor you have to tell me? It is one I have heard before, and even considered myself before I wed her."

"And why did you consider it? Because of the raid on the village? A raid conducted by Ronan, knowing you would go after him. And it was happenstance that herself was nearby, and attacked you?"

Conor had heard enough. "You go too far, Magda. I'll not have you disparaging my wife. Others have been judged and sentenced for less than you have said this day."

Her face paled. "Conor—"

"I will not have it said that I threw my brother's widow from her wedded home," he cut in. "Yet Erika is mistress here now, and she will stay. I will stop in Roscommon on my way to Taig, and will notify your kin of your impending arrival."

She looked as if she were about to speak then changed her mind. At last she nodded. "I will do as the *tigerna* wishes."

Conor sighed. He should have done this long ago, before it reached this level of difficulty. "I know this has not been an easy burden for you to bear, Magda. And I thank you for doing it. I am sure you are more than ready to return to the friends and family you left in Roscommon."

"You are right, of course," she said, her eyes lowered. "I do miss my home. It will be good indeed to get back to it."

He stared at her lowered face, wishing he had the proper words to say, and still feeling the need to apologize to her. Instead he said, "I wish you good day" and quit the chamber in search of his wife, hoping to leave the guilt behind.

EVEN BEFORE HE ACCEPTED the missive, Conor knew it boded ill.

His last instructions to Ardan were to inform him of anything untoward. He had not been able to explain what made him uneasy, only that something had. He knew Magda was less than accepting of his decision to send her home, and his guilt increased his concern for her.

The missive did not concern Magda, however. It concerned his wife.

Abbott Brochadh's precise lettering stared back at him.

This was found half-burned in your chamber. Forgive me, my lord, but Ardan bids me urge you to return home at once.

With shaking hands he read the second, cruder note, charred about the edges.

...not easy for you. You have done well, my love. Soon the time for action will come and the Devil of Dunlough will die. Then we will be together again.

Blood pounded in his ears. This could not be truth. Erika would not betray him. She had no reason to betray him.

Neither had Aislingh.

The thought chilled him, and opened the floodgates to more. Erika withdrawing from him, spending less time in the dun, even before she'd lost their child. Why? Was she going to the village, learning herb-lore and visiting Dun Lief and Glentane as she said? Or was there another reason?

No. Erika loved him. He heard the words from her own lips; she had proven it in a myriad of ways.

Yet he had also heard her say that she had not been the wife he wanted. Did she not ask him for forgiveness for all that she had done? Was that not a confession, an admission of guilt he didn't want to see?

She had been so eager to kill him at the first. Then all she wanted was to escape, to reclaim her freedom. How sudden it seemed that she'd resigned herself to their duel, to her fate. Had she lost a-purpose, because she'd been ordered to wait, to kill him at an opportune time?

Then why hadn't she? Why was he still alive? Sure, it would have been difficult to explain his death by stabbing or strangulation. Poison would be a much bet—

He froze. Erika was studying herb-lore with Aine. Poison would be a part of that study.

Blessed Virgin! A sick feeling settled in the core of his heart as he crushed the missive in his hands. Was Erika out to betray him, to end his days when he was unsuspecting? Had her words of love been false, part of a plan to ensure his downfall?

There was only one way to be certain. He had to return to Dunlough.

As quick and polite as he could, he made his goodbyes to the royal court. He rode for Dunlough, pushing the horses as much as he dared. A day's ride away, he came across the body of the messenger, lying in a gully beside the rutted path that served as a road to the dun.

"Is that the messenger that gave you the letter?" Padraig asked.

Conor rolled the body over. "It is."

His belly had been ripped open, either by an axe or a sweeping sword. It was a painful way to die.

"What's that he's holding?"

Prying open the stiff hand, Conor retrieved a blood-soaked neck-chain. No, not metal, but silver cord, from which hung a silver cross and a gilded hammer.

Denial slammed into him, pounding between his ears. It corroded to an insidious doubt. He had given Erika back the chain, the last time he'd returned from battle. It was always on her person or his, never where someone could steal it.

Soon the time for action will come...

I have not been the wife you wanted...

The charms bit into his palm as he crushed them in his fist. Somehow, Erika must have known the news the messenger carried, had ridden to intercept him. Had killed him when she realized she was too late.

"Ah, no." Padraig's voice held a note of hushed horror. "Our *bhean aingeal* would not—this cannot be Lady Erika's doing. It cannot be."

Every movement slow, as if his muscles were bound, Conor remounted. Stillness settled in him. A fool was he to think that fate had been kind to him at last, that the gods would forgive him and give him happiness. It wasn't meant to be, if it had ever been.

"Bring the body. I want to reach Dunlough by nightfall."

ERIKA SMILED TO HERSELF as she let Tempest pick his way through a patch of clover. Gwynna and Olan, the healer and the warrior, now proud parents of twin boys. It made her heart light to see their love displayed for all to see. Gwynna, bless her soul, had been more concerned for Erika than herself.

True it had been difficult. Not as difficult as helping Thala deliver her child, but bittersweet nonetheless.

Things were different now. Happiness was hers at last. Conor knew how much she loved him, how she wanted to stay. And she believed that he loved her in return. He had not said the words, true, but he would. Especially if what she suspected was true.

The sun was near setting by the time she and her guards returned to Dunlough. Fingal and Crutchin were by the gate, yet neither returned her greeting. 'Twas then that she noticed the absolute stillness of the dun. Where was everyone?

As soon as she dismounted, she was surrounded by a phalanx of soldiers. "A *bhean usuail*, the mac Ferghal bids you join him in the great hall."

"Conor's returned?" Her heart skipped at the news as she handed her sword to a waiting sentry. It had been nearly a month since she had seen him off to Clonmacnoise, and she ached to be with him once again.

She hurried into the hall, only to stop short. Conor sat in his usual place at the head of the hall, opposite the entry. Standing before him were Brochadh, Magda, Padraig and Ardan. None of them smiled in greeting. She had never seen such an expression of ferocity on her husband's face.

"What is it?" she asked, striding forward. "What has happened?"

For answer, Conor gestured to Ardan. The commander stepped forward, uncovering the bundle on the floor between her and her husband. A gasp filled the hall as the face of a man, grayed by death, was revealed.

"Do you recognize this man?" Conor asked.

She had not heard that tone from him since he'd questioned her in the earthen cell. "I do not. Was he set upon by thieves?"

Instead of answering her he asked another question. "Did you engage in battle two days past?"

Erika looked at the priest, who looked saddened and disappointed. Why? Why did this seem an interrogation?

"We were set upon by thieves or raiders, a small band," she answered. "That is why I wondered if this man was their victim as well."

Murmurs rifled through the throng. Erika swung her eyes through the gathering before turning back to Conor. Something was amiss. "What happens here?"

Brochadh stepped forward. "Erika ni Conchobhair, princess of Dunlough, a charge has been brought against you."

"Charge? What charge?"

"Adultery, and murder to conceal said adultery."

Shock slammed into her, followed by utter disbelief. "This is beyond reason. Who brings such a charge against me?"

Her eyes swung to Magda, and fury gathered in her veins. "You. You have done this! I will rip your black heart from your deceitful body, you dishonest wi—"

Two guards halted her forward progress, relieving her of the dagger she didn't realize she'd drawn. Her accuser peered at her from the relative safety of Conor's side. "You see how quick she is to accuse me, I who have done nothing untoward?"

"Enough." Conor's voice, harsh and biting, silenced the hall. His eyes flicked over her like stones. "It is not from Magda that these charges come. There was a witness to the battle."

He turned to Fionn. "There are claims that someone cried, 'It's the Angel! Protect the prize!' Did you hear this?"

Fionn shifted beside her, uneasy. "My lady?"

Erika's voice was equally soft. "In all things, we must tell the truth."

"Aye, my lord, we heard the words. I thought it passing strange, then thought of nothing save protecting the lady."

Conor turned back to Erika. "Where is your cross and hammer?"

Her hands went about her bare neck. "You have them, do you not? I assumed you took them when last we parted."

"I did not take it." He loosed his fist, and the charms dangled into view. "I did find them—beneath the body of this messenger."

Voices rose in alarmed whispers about her. She took a step back, eyes fixed to her husband's stern visage. "Y-you believe me capable of *murder*?"

She could scarce force the words out, as if saying them lent legitimacy to these proceedings. She was amazed at how calm she sounded. Her true self shrieked with outraged denial, screamed in disbelief at the hard expression her husband wore, wailed at the agony his condemning questions lanced through her.

"Conor." Her voice broke on his name and she had to stop, to fight down the bile that rose in her throat, the combination of fear and disbelief and pain that he could believe this, that he could believe Magda's lies. "I have visited Glentane. I have visited Dun Lief. I have protected our people. *I have done that which you have given me to do.*"

"Then how do you explain this?"

He held a charred parchment towards her. She took a step forward, only to be restrained again.

Burgeoning anger hardened her voice. "I do not know what that is, as I have never seen it before."

"It is a letter, found half-burned in our chamber." He read it aloud. Each word slammed within her as she realized their portent.

"You think these—these lies were for me? You think I seek to betray you?"

"It is beyond the seeking now, Angel."

"You believe this? How could you believe this?" She brought her fisted hands to her heart. "By my life, I swear that I have not betrayed you."

"Be ware of what you swear, Lady Death. You may need to fulfill that vow."

Erika blanched against the vehemence of his voice. "Conor, please. If I could have a word in private—"

"What you have to say to me, you may say to my people." The Devil's face was stern and implacable, shorn from rock. "For 'tis true, you have dishonored their trust as well."

Stung, she raised her eyes to his, willing her husband to hear her, to believe her. "I have dishonored no one," she said, forcing her voice to firmness. "Everything I have ever claimed as mine has been taken from me. All that remains is my honor, and you would take even that?"

"You have given it away!" he roared. "You gave it willing to the Cur of Ulster!"

His words slammed into her battered heart like spears launched by an expert hand, causing her to stagger. Conor looked on, impassive. So implacable, so unreachable. So beloved.

Glancing about the hall, Erika realized that none of these people would come to her defense; none would dare risk the wrath of the Devil of Dunlough. It wasn't what she'd done. It was what she hadn't done.

She had been so quick to escape Magda's presence in the dun that she'd left the Irishwoman ample opportunity to turn the people against her. Flesh and blood she could fight, but words, thoughts, hatred—she was powerless.

Ardan and Múireann wore matching stricken looks, and everyone else seemed horrified and frightened. Only Magda's face glowed with malicious triumph.

Conor's expression wounded most of all. Gone were the lights of tender feelings in his eyes, as if they had never been. "You believe me capable of such treachery?" she choked out.

"You tried to kill him more than once!" Magda's strident voice shook the rafters. "And you killed his babe—if it ever was truly Conor's. Was it at the behest of your lover that you did these things—the lover whose child you carry even now?"

Gasps pierced the charged atmosphere, led by Erika herself. Her hands cupped her womb in a protective gesture. How could Magda know, when she'd only realized it herself?

She lifted her head, seeking Conor. He was frozen in place, his face drained of all color. "Is this true?" he whispered in a strangled tone.

"Conor—"

"Are you with child?" Her hesitation infuriated him. "Answer me!"

The dun waited with bated breath. All she had to do, Erika knew, was deny it and be welcomed back into her husband's bed. Then if a babe arrived early to the royal couple, all would be acceptable.

But she could not, would not lie. Not about this. Eyes never leaving Conor's, Erika spoke the words that would forever damn her. "I am with child. Your child."

The hall erupted with outrage, drowning out her words. She ignored everyone else. Their opinions did not matter. Only Conor's did.

She watched shock drive color from his face, and the anger of betrayal that quickly replaced it. He believed as the others did, that she couldn't be carrying his child, that it was impossible that she had conceived before he'd left to attend the King of Connacht little more than two months ago.

Anguish hit her low in the gut, almost doubling her over. He didn't love her. How could he, and believe the worst of her?

Forcing her back to straighten, she stared at the man who had broken her heart. "I know the Devil of Dunlough has little reason to trust women. I know there is naught I can say or do that hasn't been done or said, but I will say this: I am not Aislingh. I would never betray you. Even if I never had your love, I thought I had your trust."

He did move then, so quickly that she heard the thudding sound almost before his arm lowered. Gasps filled the hall. Buried in the packed earth before her feet, still quivering with furied force, was the tiny amethyst-studded dagger she had surrendered to him so many months before.

She staggered, pain blossoming in her heart as if he'd stabbed her instead of the hard ground. It was the final act. He would never believe her, would never forgive her. Closing her eyes, Erika let go of everything she possessed: hope, dreams and love. Even when her babe was proven Conor's, she could not stay here, not with a man who didn't love her, if he ever had.

"Take her to the pit."

Ardan stepped forward at Conor's words. "Sure you'll send her to her chamber?"

"Do not think to gainsay me!" the Devil of Dunlough thundered. His voice was unrecognizable, so twisted was it by fury. "Take her to the pit—and all else out of my sight. Now!"

His thunderous shout had the great hall emptying with alarming speed. Erika remained frozen, too numb to do aught but stare as Conor turned his back to her. *Fight*, a voice inside her screamed. *Fight and escape.*

Fighting would mark her forever guilty in Conor's eyes. Her sole hope was to wait, to bide her time until she could speak to her husband alone. Wait, and fight the grief that threatened to consume her.

With her fist pressed against her heart, it was all she could do to hold her spine straight and her head unbowed as Ardan and a pair of soldiers led her into the night, remaining silent until they reached the earthen cell. "And so it ends, the way it began," she whispered. "Even the gods would smile at the irony."

"My lady." Ardan cleared his throat several times before he continued. "Once his anger cools, he will see reason."

She wanted to believe it, was desperate to believe it, but the truth stared at her as cold and sure as death. "He'll not see reason about this, Ardan. The past is too close, still holds him. He thinks that I could, that I could—"

She swallowed, reining in her emotions lest she shatter. "Upon my soul, I have not done that of which I have been accused."

"I believe you, my lady," Ardan said in a gruff voice. "I know your love for him."

"It is not enough. Perhaps it will never be enough."

Ardan had no rejoinder for it, and true what more was there to say? She stepped into the dank, cold cell, struggling not to lose hope as the door slammed home behind her.

"I will bring a stool and blankets for you," Ardan told her. "I'll not deny you comfort while we wait for the Devil to come to his senses."

Conor. Anguish welled within her, potent and bitter. He thought her capable of the ultimate betrayal, of yielding the body only he had known to another. Of carrying another's child.

She cradled her womb, wanting to shield the tiny, fragile life inside her, to protect it from a world in which honor and love meant nothing. She wanted a son to grow in Conor's image, final proof of her veracity. She wanted a daughter to teach to be strong, courageous and unyielding to the weakness of the heart. She wanted to be far away from Dunlough and memories of what she had gained and lost.

The sound of the door opening had hope leaping in her breast. It died a quick death as Magda walked through.

Erika's first instinct was to put her hands to the witch's neck and make the world a better place. She remained seated, her hands on her knees as Renald and Crutchin entered with her, weapons drawn and torches high.

She felt the fury pounding behind her eyes. "You sent Conor that message. You killed that poor messenger and hid my neck-chain on his person."

Magda laughed, a chilling sound. "I would never kill someone by so foul a method. That's why I have Crutchin and Renald to do my bidding."

"Why?" Erika asked the question that burned her soul. "Why have you done this?"

"You do not belong here. I will always be the rightful mistress of Dunlough."

"Conor will hear of this."

Magda laughed anew. "Who will tell him? You? Do you think he will believe a deceitful Viking mercenary over his brother's widow?"

No, Conor would not believe his brother's wife capable of such treachery. It was far easier to believe it of his wife the mercenary. Every moment he did not come to her proved that. Despair settled deeper in her heart.

"Be done with your gloating, and leave me in peace."

"I cannot do that. In fact, I've come to help you."

Her disbelief must have been obvious even in the torch-light. "Believe me or no, it is your choice," Magda said. "You would never be happy here, even if Conor had asked you to stay. You live by your sword, and your freedom means much to you."

The Irishwoman stepped closer. "Conor does not love you, Viking. 'Twas obvious even before today. Even now, he ponders whether to hang you or banish you. Do you wish to abide in this pit until he decides? Would the legendary Angel of Death sit meek as a lamb or would she choose her life and her freedom?"

With Renald at the ready, Magda took another step closer. "Your stubborn mount awaits you just beyond the door, along with your sword and a bag of hack silver. Leave here, this place that was never your home. Leave Eire and never return."

Erika knew there was a caveat to Magda's offer, but found she didn't care. All that remained was the need to be as far away from Dunlough as Tempest could carry her.

She rose, towering over the men and the woman, who stepped away. That gave her the first real smile she'd had in hours.

"And sure the witch of Roscommon has no need to fear me?" she asked. "Though I must confess, the need to strangle you is like a fire in my veins. If your death would change what lies between Conor and myself, you would even now be dead."

Both men stepped further back, leaving Magda unguarded. "What fine guards you have, so eager to protect you. Fortunate for you my desire to be quit of this place is greater than my desire for vengeance."

Magda regained her aplomb as she stepped aside. "Then be gone."

Still uncertain and sensing a trap, Erika moved through the doorway. Sure enough, Tempest awaited her. Since she still wore the trews she'd worn earlier, it was a simple matter to vault astride, to put her heels to his flanks, to speed towards the opened and unmanned gate. She did not look back.

She forced her mind to subdue her roiling emotions. Freedom was all that mattered now. Dun Lief and Glentane were closed as options; she would not place friends and family in this breach. The village was also closed to her. Although near the sea, she could not hide there until a boat large enough arrived to offer transport, and she would not leave Tempest behind.

That left the north. If she could make it to Dun na Ghall, she could find a longboat, a Viking crew to take her to Anglia or Normandy. Places where she would be just another Viking woman, and not the cast-off wife of an Irish noble who held more to the past than the present.

So steeped in misery was she that she didn't acknowledge the absolute stillness of the night until too late and was ambushed. Screaming a defiant curse, she pulled free her sword and managed to fell three of her attackers until their sheer numbers dragged her to the ground. Blows rained upon her, and she curled into a ball to protect her unborn child even as she flailed out with feet to shins and knees, breaking several.

"Ease off, you bastards!" a harsh voice commanded. "The whore's no good to us dead!"

Stars danced before her eyes as the pack retreated, and she gasped in a pained lungful of air. It was too dark, but she sensed someone standing near her.

"So you are the legendary Angel of Death," the voice spoke again. The sound of it slithered over her skin like dead fish. "Bring a torch and let's have a look at our prize."

Erika realized then that she couldn't see clear because her eyes were nearly swollen shut. She discerned a pool of light, and a pair of legs, scabbed and sparsely covered with red-gold hair.

A fist gathered in her hair, wrenching her to her knees. She bit back another gasp of pain and widened her eyes as far as she could to regard the face of the man she would kill when she was able.

"I am Ronan the Red Hand, the man who will kill you and your precious Devil of Dunlough."

Ronan of Ulster. Despite her pain, Erika almost smiled. This was the man responsible for raiding Dunlough village. Norns willing, she would be able to fulfill her promise and deliver the bastard's head to the villagers.

"Too pale for my taste," Ronan was saying as someone bound her hands. "Don't know why the Devil chose you, but then everyone knows the mac Ferghal is mad. Let us see what has entranced him so."

His free hand slid over the front of her tunic. Revulsion filled her stomach at his vile touch then rose to her throat as he ripped the front of her tunic open with a sharp downward pull. When his hand touched her bare skin, she struggled anew, attempting to bite him and gain her feet.

He stopped her weak attempts with a ringing blow that toppled her onto her side. "I like a woman with spirit," he crowed, reaching for her hair again to pull her upright. His breath was fetid as he leaned over her. "'Tis my hope your spirit will last until you service the lot of us."

No! Her mind screamed even as the men about her cheered the news. She would rather die than let him touch her again.

"Of course, no celebration would be complete without our most honored guest," Ronan said. "How shall we ensure the Devil's attendance? What invitation can we send that he would not refuse?"

His hand tightened in her hair as he drew a wicked long dagger that was almost a short-sword. "Undeniable proof, that is what I need. And I know what will provide it."

Chapter Thirty-One

When tankards failed to numb his pain, Conor called for the barrel.

Drinking himself into oblivion wasn't occurring fast enough. The pain still twisted inside him, widening the breach where his heart had been, growing until he wanted to scream with anguish.

Erika had betrayed him. He had done right by imprisoning her. So why did he now feel as if he'd made the gravest mistake of his life?

She had professed her love to him, given of herself in a thousand ways that seemed to bear truth to her words. Yet she had stood in the great hall, damning herself with every question answered. Then she had confessed her greatest betrayal.

In that moment, Conor came close to hating her. History had repeated itself, giving him another unfaithful wife. Then she had read his very thoughts and insisted that she was nothing like Aislingh.

Enraged anew, Conor threw his tankard against the far wall. The act of violence dampened his rampant emotions enough that it begged repetition. A pitcher, a platter, then the table followed the tankard.

How could she claim the babe was his? He'd been away a month. Before he'd been away for almost two, subduing raiders near Dun Lief. The last time he'd lain with Erika had been when?

After she'd saved the drowning child. After she'd near driven him mad by risking her life. After he'd realized that he loved her and didn't want to live without her.

Exhausted, Conor sank into the remaining upright chair and buried his face in his hands. Aye, he loved Erika. He loved her as he'd loved none other. Even now, with his heart flayed open by the whip of her betrayal, he still loved her.

Had she betrayed him? The rational part of him wondered. He remembered the look of wondrous joy on her face as she'd cradled her womb. It was a look he'd seen once before, the first time she'd told him she carried his child.

Then he remembered the look on her face after he'd thrown the dagger. The horror and the anguish were unfeigned. By the saints, he hadn't even thought when he pulled the dagger from his belt. His hands shook as he recalled how close he had come to felling her.

Was she innocent? He had the missive. The dead messenger had been found with Erika's neck-chain in his hand. Why would he have her chain?

Why indeed? When Erika wore it, it was as he did—tucked inside her tunic. But she'd not worn it in some time, not since she'd first become with child. Had he misplaced it, left it where someone else could take it? Someone who wanted to discredit his wife? Who would want to do such a thing?

Magda.

Dread settled into his stomach and refused to let go. Why would Magda do this to Erika? Their strained relationship could not be so unbearable that his sister-by-law would resort to such harsh measures.

It mattered not. All that mattered was freeing his wife from the pit. Once he was reconciled with Erika he would deal with sister-by-law.

He flung open the chamber door and stepped out, near colliding with Aine, Ardan and Padraig. "So you've come to your senses then?" the old woman asked.

"Aye, that I have. I can pray that it is not too late."

He strode into the hall, the trio following. "Ardan, find Magda and bring her to me."

"Magda?"

"This is her doing, and I would have her tell me why—after I reclaim my wife."

Grabbing a torch, he walked out into the night, his stride eating the distance between the dun and the pit. A soldier intercepted him. "My lord, Lady Erika has escaped!"

A skittering sensation crept up his back. No one had ever escaped from the pit. The wooden frame was buried deep in the soil then packed with earth then covered with rocks. Brute strength would not open the door. Someone had helped Erika to escape.

Or convinced her to.

Soldiers converged on them. "Her horse is gone as well, my lord."

"Who guarded the gate?"

Padraig answered. "Crutchin and Renald."

Magda's soldiers. Too late, things became clear.

Conor turned for the gate, calling for his horse and sword. Dun Lief was closer than Glentane, but would she go there? Would she go instead to Olan and Gwynna? They would not make it easy for him to get Erika back, but no matter what it required he would do it.

A shout went up from the gate. A single rider rushed up the slope, a pale horse in full gallop. Conor recognized Erika's horse seconds before he realized it was riderless.

And covered with blood.

He ran forward as the animal entered the gate, snatching its reins as it reared with fright. Its withers had been sliced open. A pouch slipped to the ground, and one of the soldiers retrieved it as Conor calmed the bleeding animal.

Hands shaking, Conor opened the pouch and reached inside. Finding silk beneath his fingers, he grasped it and pulled it out.

It wasn't a scarf, or a rope. The strands beneath his fingers were spun moonlight, a braid as thick as his wrist.

Erika's hair.

Knees weak, Conor gripped the severed plait in whitened knuckles. He knew what had happened, as sure as if he'd seen it. Magda had urged Erika to flee, and she had—into Ronan's trap. Then the bastard had cut her hair.

Eyes closed against a fresh onslaught of pain, he brought the pale plait up and looped it about his neck. It lay heavily on him, like an iron collar, searing his skin. It would remind him, always, of what he now knew without doubt.

Erika hadn't betrayed him. He'd betrayed her.

"Tigerna?"

Conor opened his eyes, vision blurred against the tears that flowed unchecked down his cheeks. The yard overflowed with the people of Dunlough. Their expressions were neither reproachful nor accusatory, just expectant.

Rising to his feet, he stared into the faces of each one and spoke. "I would beg your forgiveness, each and every one. Today, I made the gravest mistake of my life. Tonight I ride to correct that wrong. To return my wife and my child to their rightful place.

"This will not be a battle for bards to immortalize. This will be a slaughter. Ronan and his men will die this day. Nothing and no one will stand in my way. I will even defy heaven and hell to bring my lady home. I will order none to go with me. I only ask that you do not visit the sins of the father upon my son, and allow him to be the ruler I wanted to be."

Ardan stood beside him. "She saved my life. I will go."

Another stepped forward. "She healed my son. I shall go."

"She taught my Bebhinn to swim. I shall go."

"She sat with me when I was ill. I will go."

"She delivered my bairn safe to me. I shall go."

And so it continued until every man and several women volunteered to go. "You are our lord; where you go, we shall follow."

Shouts shook the gates as the Devil swung astride Brimstone. Their approval touched him, strengthened him. He would not fail them. He would bring their angel back. Or die trying.

Chapter Thirty-Two

The Angel bided her time by contemplating the slow manner in which she would kill Ronan of Ulster.

Almost lovingly she stoked the anger, keeping it simmering. As long as she was angry, she lived. As long as she was angry, she conquered pain and fear. As long as she was angry, she had the strength to kill as many of these men as she could before she died. And the one she would certainly take with her was their leader.

Ronan was a thin redheaded man with a permanent sneer. That he had taken his blade and shorn her braid at her shoulders enraged her. That he had taken her to induce Conor to follow to his death angered her. Besides, she knew what he did not: Conor would not follow.

For a moment, anguish roared through her with the force of a bonfire, sparked by the memory of Conor's betrayal. Before the entire populace of the dun, her husband had denounced her, judged her guilty for that which she had not done.

Summoning the cold, deep part of her was difficult; it had been months since she had needed the Angel. But the warrior still lived within, heeding the call.

Ronan took that moment to stop before her and regard his prize. If he thought to see the Devil's bride broken, if he thought to see her weeping, if he thought to see her crawling, he was disappointed.

For one thing, she was upright. Despite the fact that she bled from several wounds, despite the fact that her garments hung in shreds and one eye had swollen shut, the mistress of Dunlough held her head high as any queen out for a stroll with her subjects. She caught his stare and bestowed a smile that did nothing to warm his heart.

She wouldn't smile long. The Devil's bride would pay for what he did to Ronan's Aislingh. Then Conor would pay.

Ronan gave the rope binding her hands a vicious tug. Angel stumbled but refused to fall. The look she gave him would have frozen flame.

For a long, yawning moment, he stared into the eyes of Death. Then he smiled. "Do not think to intimidate me, Viking wench. Not when your fate is in my hands. When I am done with you, I intend to sell you into slavery. A beautiful woman like you will fetch a high price, of that I am certain. And you will not have to worry about your husband finding you, for he will be dead."

The Angel stared into the face of her enemy, not bothering to conceal her disgust and hatred. "You gain nothing this day but your own death."

Ronan tossed his head back in a bark of laughter. "How bold you are, surrounded as you are by my men. Or does your confidence stem from the fact that your husband and his men will come for you?"

It was Angel's turn to laugh, a sound completely devoid of mirth. "You are mistaken, dog of Ulster. The lord of Dunlough will not come for me."

Ronan was incredulous. "The Devil not come for his Angel? Do you take me for a fool?"

"You are a fool." Her voice cut the air, whiplike, and Ronan stepped back as from a lash. "Conor mac Ferghal set aside his wife. He cares naught for her, nor for the Angel. He will not come."

The copper-haired man stared at his captive, searching for any sign of falsehood or pain. There was none. Instead, the shorn woman stared back at him with eyes resolved to her fate. She believed the Devil would not come for her. And now he believed it as well.

"You have just ensured your death, Angel." His gaze swept her from boots to hair. "But first, my men and I will take some solace in your flesh before we return your body to Dunlough."

The Angel laughed again, but this time there was mirth. Mirth made all the more chilling by her words. "Think you to frighten me, Irish dog? Me, the Angel of Death?"

On a night with no moon, she seemed to glow. She shook her shining head, her words still full of mocking laughter. "I do not fear Death. I welcome it. For then I will be truly free of this pain. 'Tis not I who will meet Death this night. If your men are blessed, their deaths will be quick. You, however, will die slow and painful. For the crimes you have committed, I will strip you of your manhood, then disembowel you with your own sword. Then when you can no longer scream from the pain, I will let you die. The last of this world your eyes will see will be me, taking your head from your shoulders with your own blade."

Silence, save the rushing of waves to the rocky shore below. And over it what could only be the wind, bringing the promise of rain, blowing with a sound that was almost a moan rising to a strangled shriek. Several of Ronan's men made the sign of the evil eye, and several more backed away from the Angel's soulless gaze.

The Valkyrie smiled. "The *bhean sidhe* is with me one last time. Those of you who wish to live, leave. Now!"

More than a handful obeyed the otherworldly order, turning and disappearing into the night. Many screamed as they went, but the screams were abruptly cut off when they reached the shadows of the trees.

Ronan spun in the direction of the trees. "What madness is this?"

The pale-haired warrior smiled. "It is Death, come for them. And for you."

IT TOOK EVERY OUNCE of willpower Conor possessed not to charge into the clearing. A brute of a man held his wife, her arms drawn up tight behind her. In the dawning of the gray day he could see the dried blood in her hair and about her mouth, the bruises marring her eyes and jaw, her ripped tunic exposing her skin from neck to navel. The desire to kill everyone who had looked upon her rose within him, a potent brew he could ill-afford to give free rein. Wits would win this day, not brute strength. When the day was won, then would he hack Ronan to pieces, and take his time in the doing of it.

"They die," he whispered to Padraig. "Every man there will breathe his last for what has been done to my lady. You will save Ronan for me."

"When?"

Conor's reply was stopped by Erika's voice, carried to them on the wind. "The lord of Dunlough will not come for me."

"Do you take me for a fool?" Ronan sneered.

"Conor mac Ferghal has set aside his wife." Erika's voice was cold, lifeless. "He cares naught for her, nor the Angel. He will not come."

The words slammed into Conor, shredding his heart. Erika believed what she said. She believed he would not come after her.

She was wrong! He wanted to scream it at the sky, reveal his presence and his love to her. Ronan was too close to her; they were too close to the cliff. He had to save her first. There would be time. If she forgave him, there would be all the time in the world.

"Nothing is more important than Erika's life," he breathed, knowing the men surrounding him heard and understood.

Men broke away from Ronan's band, heading toward Conor and his men concealed in the copse of trees. He did not have to give an order. Dunlough warriors fell upon those in flight, silencing them forever.

Ronan spun toward the trees. "What manner of madness is this?" His voice shook with a new emotion, different from the haughtiness: fear.

The wind once again brought Conor Erika's answer. "It is death, come for them. And for you."

It was time. "Ronan!"

Conor strode from the concealing cover of trees, sword loose in his grip, staring at the man he would kill this day. Padraig and Ardan flanked him.

"So you have come for your tainted bride after all, Devil?" Ronan's grip on Erika tightened. Whether she was surprised or glad to see him, Conor could see no sign. "Come no further, lest I slay your soiled angel where she stands."

Conor felt his lips pull back from his teeth. "For laying your hands on her, you will die," he said, his voice almost pleasant. "For cutting her hair, I will kill you slow."

"Such brave words for a man come to meet his death," Ronan laughed, a sound without bravado. "Do you not fear it?"

Conor shook his head. "I am wed to Death. I have no fear of it." He kept his eyes away from Erika lest he lose the iron-hard grip on his anger and charge his enemy. "It is you who should fear."

He took a step forward, then stopped as Ronan took one step closer to the cliff. "Leave the woman. I am the one you want to face. There is no sport in killing women."

"You'd be knowing the truth of that, wouldn't you? The Devil of Dunlough and his blighted honor." Ronan spat on the ground. "Here's what I think of it."

"Blighted or no, I have it. What would you know of honor? You turned Aislingh against me, and now you think to claim Erika? Why settle for my leavings when you can have me?"

He beckoned with his free hand. "Come now, Ronan. I know you and honor are not acquainted, but I challenge you nonetheless. Just you and me, as it should be. To the death."

"And leave your whore free to wreak havoc? I think not." He turned to his men. "Attack!"

The remainder of Ronan's men surged forward, believing themselves to be more than a match for three men outmatched seven to one. Angel knew just how wrong they were when the three stood their ground, calm, waiting, then began to move in a dance of death that made Ronan's men seem oafish.

Rain swept in from the sea, drenching all and muffling sound. It was time to act. Without warning she jerked her head back, slamming her skull into the face of the man holding her from behind, shattering his nose. Even as her captor fell she spun, drawing free the dying man's blade and completing her circle to face her enemy.

Ronan's frozen astonishment thawed with a mad laugh. "Think you to defeat me with your hands tied?"

Angel crouched, heady with the red berserker rage coursing through her veins. "I can kill you with one hand tied behind me," she said in a quiet, still voice. "Shall we see?"

"Your life ends now!"

Ronan raised his blade high overhead. Angel remained in a semi-crouch. With her hands tied, she wouldn't be able to gather the force she needed to separate his head from his shoulders. But let the overweening bastard swing down; she would roll under his swing then gut the raider like the swine he was.

Ronan's blade slashed down—

The shriek of metal on metal rang in her ears. Another blade had stopped Ronan's downward arc.

"I believe this fight is mine."

The Devil stared into the twisted features of his enemy, the coldness of his rage just held in check. He'd long waited for this revenge, Angel knew. She stepped out of reach of the blades but not before saying, "No. I want to kill him."

"It matters not to me which of you I kill first," Ronan declared, his jaw twitching with the strain of holding his sword to the Devil's. A maniacal grin twisted his face. "You will both die this day."

Never taking his eyes from his enemy, the Devil said, "Angel, take the dagger from my belt then give way. Mine is the greater claim."

Of course. His honor demanded nothing less. Reluctant, she acquiesced. "Do not be quick about it."

"I do not intend to."

The Devil of Dunlough pushed the raider away. "Enough talk. This ends now."

Their blades clashed together with the force of a lightning strike. "Wouldn't you like to talk about your wives, mac Ferghal?" Ronan taunted. "I have had them both, you know. Shall I tell you which was better?"

For answer, Conor struck him a heavy blow, meant to quiet the fool and settle into the fight, but the red-haired man blocked it with a faltering parry. "I'll not be as easy to dispatch as Aislingh was," he boasted. "Though 'tis true she deserved to die, for failing to blind you as I ordered her to."

The words did not surprise him but they cut nonetheless. Ronan must have seen something in his eyes for he laughed and said, "She begged me to release her, your precious Aislingh did. How she longed to be free of the dishonored Devil with no courage. It was simple to finish what Magda began, making your sweet wife betray you."

Cold slammed into Conor, stunning him. Even then, Magda had worked against him?

"Did you not know?" his adversary asked. "Magda's hand was in this from the beginning. And like Aislingh before her, your white witch was turned against you."

Ronan swung quick and wild, making himself vulnerable as he slipped in the wet grass. Swift and sure, the Devil brought his blade up, the tip sinking through Ronan's tunic, his heart and out his shoulder.

The Ulster raider dropped his sword and sank to his knees. The Devil leaned forward, to fix the dying man's eyes with his own. "The Angel is nothing like Aislingh." A foot to the chest freed his blade. "Nothing."

"You did not take your time."

Erika stood several paces away from him. Her right hand held a blooded sword, and her left the tattered halves of her tunic. She didn't look at him, but kept her gaze on the dead man.

"Dead is still dead." He pulled free his cloak pin and secured her tunic before swinging off his cloak and draping it about her. Now that the rage had left him, he saw anew the hurt she'd suffered, the purpling bruises to her eyes and jaw. Saw the ragged shorn locks that just brushed her shoulders and the absolute emptiness of her eyes. "Did he, did he—"

"No. Never."

He believed her. Near too late, he believed her. "Erika. Say that you'll—"

Something hit him in the back. He looked at his wife, saw her bruised eyes widen with horror scant moments before pain blossomed in his shoulder. He looked down.

An arrow protruded through his chest, just above his heart. Grimacing against the pain, he reached with numb fingers to break the shaft and pull it out.

"Don't!" Erika's voice shook as her hands covered his. "You could bleed to death before I get you to safety. Just keep your hand over—ah!"

Her words broke with a scream of pain. Her sword clattered to the ground, torn from her grip by an arrow in the muscle of her upper arm.

"Erika!" He took a step toward his staggering wife, but his legs buckled and he fell to his knees.

"Have no care for your Viking whore," Magda said, stepping from behind a standing stone. "You shall see each other in hell soon enough."

Conor wished for the rage, the cleansing purity of anger, but it did not come. Instead, a heavy stillness settled deep into his bones, numbing the physical pain. He had been wrong about so many things. "Why, Magda?"

"You dare ask me that, *Diabhal*? You stole my very life the day you let Murrough and my sons die. That is why I took yours."

Through a haze of pain he heard Erika's gasp. "You poisoned me! You came to my chamber and put something in the brew Aine gave me!"

Magda's laugh was frigid. "You were to die as well, but I failed to consider the hardiness of your peasant blood. When that failed to drive you apart, it became necessary to enlist Ronan's aid once again."

She turned back to Conor, freeing a dagger from her cloak. "Aislingh's betrayal and the Viking's quest for freedom made it simple to inflame the rumors of an alliance between the Angel and Ronan, and Ronan himself supplied the proof to turn you against your precious wife. Now you know what it feels like to lose everything. Even your life."

Conor tensed, waiting for the path of the dagger before striking.

A scream tore through the damp air, the chilling wail of the *bhean sidhe*. "You killed my child!"

Shrieking with rage, Erika crashed into the smaller woman. Fear rose like bile in his throat as momentum took them close to the cliff's edge. He stumbled to his feet and launched himself at his wife, wrapping his arms about her waist just as Magda disappeared over the promontory.

The sound of a snap reached his ears as he fell to the ground. Pain stole his breath and caused stars to dance a jig before his eyes. He heard Erika pleading, the sound of running feet, the slow thump of his heart. Hands were on him, severing his grip on his wife. "Erika? Erika!"

Then she was beside him, the morning rain pelting her cropped hair and mixing with the tears on her cheeks. Her hands cupped his face, but he could not feel them. "I couldn't save her, Conor. I tried to hold her but she let go."

It took tremendous effort to reach up, to brush his fingers along her cheek. He left a trail of blood in his wake. "You...you are safe?"

"I am safe. You saved my life."

Peace drove the last fragment of pain away. "My life for yours. A fair trade. And my...burden is gone. You, you are free."

Her face contorted in grief or pain he did not know. He wanted to ask her forgiveness, to tell her that he loved her. His hand fell through the remnants of her hair. "Erika. *Mo leannán*. I think I hear your Valkyries come for me. I was a f-fool to wait so long. I'm so sorry I didn't..."

The last thing he saw was her tear-streaked face.

Chapter Thirty-Three

"Conor, no!"

Her shriek of denial brought more Dunlough warriors running, but Erika paid them little heed. She couldn't take her eyes from the splintered remains of the shaft protruding from Conor's chest, close, so very close to his heart.

Ardan dropped beside her. "Sweet merciful heaven, no."

Blood was a shiny stain on the darkness of Conor's *leine*. His heart, his strong, proud heart was killing him with every beat.

"My lady. Oh God, no."

Ardan's anguished words galvanized her. She had to act. She had to act or Conor would die.

"Ardan, Ronan had a fire. See if it still burns. If not, you must start one."

He looked at her dully, his face streaked with rain and tears. "What can you do, my lady?" he asked brokenly. "He is—"

"Not going to die today." Somehow she forced horror and heartache away. She grabbed his tunic with her un-wounded hand. "He thought the same of you, and I brought you back. I will not let him die."

Ardan lowered his eyes. "Yes, mistress." He scrambled to his feet. Erika pulled at the ragged edge of her tunic to free a strip of cloth. She pressed it carefully against Conor's chest. "You will not die, Conor mac Ferghal. I will not let you."

Ardan returned. "By the saints, the fire still burns. And we found dry wood for it!"

"Thank you," she whispered, casting her eyes heavenward for a brief moment. She pulled a blade free. "Ardan, take my blade and one more. Put them into the fire until they become red with heat."

Padraig took his place. "What would you have me do?"

"Send someone to ride for Aine, and to Gwynna and my brother. I need four of you to help me move him closer to the fire."

He gathered a few warriors and they took hold of their lord. At Erika's word they lifted him, their movements gentle for men so rough. In moments they placed him beside the fire. He'd neither moved nor spoken, not even a groan. Had she lost him already?

No. She refused to believe it. She would save him. She would.

"Cut his *leine* away for me. I have to pull the shaft free when Ardan returns with the heated blades. I need cloth to bind the wound, a cart to take him home on." She looked up at the gray sky. "I need it to stop raining!"

As if obeying her scream, the rain eased to a mist, then stopped altogether. She pulled Conor's cloak from her shoulders and cast it over him, then prepared to rip the sleeve from her tunic.

"My lady!" Padraig's hand forestalled her. "You are wounded!"

Erika looked down at the remainder of the arrow protruding from the blood-soaked sleeve of her tunic. She had forgotten it in her grief, but now the pain returned with a vengeance. She gritted her teeth and set herself to ignore it. "My wounds matter not. We must see to Conor."

Padraig ripped his own sleeve free, several warriors joining suit. He then helped her raise Conor to a seated position, then he began to cut the *leine* away with unsteady hands as Erika cradled Conor close. Moisture blinded her, running down her face in an unending stream as she cried without sound.

Conor had neither moved nor spoken during her preparation. His face grew paler with every heartbeat. He couldn't die. What would she do if he died?

She pressed her lips to his cheek, just below his ear. "I know you came here to die, Conor mac Ferghal, but I will not let you. Damn your hide, the people of Dunlough need you, not your ghost!"

"The blades are ready, my lady," Ardan informed her.

She held Conor tight against her, stroking his hair, his beard, the scar that marked his ability to survive. "You will survive this," she whispered. "You must!"

She turned to the captains. "I cannot see as I should. Padraig, you'll need to help me hold him. Ardan, when I say, you are to pull the shaft out, from his shoulder. Can you do this?"

The men nodded. Using a scrap of fabric, she lifted one of the blades from the fire, feeling the heat radiating from the red-tipped metal to her palm. She pressed her lips against her husband's cheek, her breath drawing in raggedly. "Please forgive me."

Ardan pulled the remainder of the shaft free of Conor's shoulder blade. Erika quickly pressed the hot blade against the spurting wound, filling the moist air with the scent of burning flesh and blood. Conor jerked once before moaning and settling back into silence. It was Erika who cried out for having hurt him, feeling the pain as surely as if she'd seared her own flesh.

Her stomach protested the violent action, but she fought the reaction down, fought the palsy in her hand. She dropped the first knife to the damp grass and retrieved the second. It was the dagger she'd worn in her braid, the dagger Conor had embedded in the ground at her feet before banishing her. Her silent tears became huge sobs as she repeated the cauterization on his back, singeing blood and flesh.

Padraig surged to his feet to empty the contents of his stomach. Others joined him. Ardan, a pale shade of green, remained by her.

She could barely speak above the tears and grief that threatened to consume her. "Help me bind him, Ardan. My fingers are numb."

With Fionn's help, Ardan managed the binding, frowning to keep from weeping. Conor's face was ashen, as if death already claimed him. What would Dunlough be, without its Devil?

Ardan looked to Erika. She cradled her wounded arm in her lap, rocking to and fro as more tears rolled down her bruised cheeks. She had to be at the last of her strength after her ordeal, yet her only thought was for Conor. Ardan knew that if anyone could defeat death, and had time and again, it was the Angel. But what would defeat the look of utter rout in her eyes?

He helped her to her feet as warriors came to lay their lord on a collection of shields. "Have a care," she cautioned them, her good hand stretched out to them. "You must make careful haste, to get him into Aine's care. There is no Dunlough without the Devil."

She still trembled, a leaf caught on a blustery wind. She looked as pale as fog at the start of day, and just as likely to blow away. Her eyes were washed out with pain and tears. "This is my fault, Ardan," she whispered, her voice shaking. "He should not have come. Why did he come?"

He signaled to Padraig and Fionn as Dunlough's warriors laid Conor in the back of the just-arrived cart. "My lady, he was on his way even before he received your braid. He loves you, and it near killed him to realize what Magda had done."

"You're wrong, Ardan." She shook her head. If she noticed Padraig and Fionn flanking her, she gave no sign. "The mac Ferghal does not love me."

"You're wrong, I'd stake me life on that. God willing, the mac Ferghal will tell you true so there's no mistaking. But we need to make sure the both of you will survive that long."

"I'll return to Dunlough long enough to ensure that your lord lives," she whispered, swaying with the effort to remain upright. "But I cannot stay. You can see that I cannot stay, not now?"

Ardan's throat tightened. "I can see that you need Aine's touch as much as the *tigerna* does. You'll be staying at Dunlough. I'll not have a word otherwise. There is no Devil without the Angel."

At his nod, Fionn and Padraig immobilized her so that Ardan could break the arrow and pull it free of her arm. She gasped with pain before her eyes rolled back in her head. Padraig caught her before she fell.

Ardan ripped her sleeve to expose the ugly wound then used the soaked strip to slow the blood flow. "Will you put the blade to it?" Fionn asked.

"God, no." Ardan shuddered at the thought. "I'll not be risking the Devil's own wrath by marking the Angel's skin."

"Did you see how she commanded the sky to stop raining?" Fionn breathed. "And how the fire still burned despite the weather?"

"Aye, 'tis a right miracle," Ardan said. "Let us pray that the miracles are not done, and the lord and his lady will survive the day."

He spread his cloak over her, tucking it about her still form. He stepped back, clearing his throat. "Put her in the cart beside the *tigerna*," he ordered in hoarse tones. "Old Aine should be upon us soon enough. Once she makes sure they'll survive, we'll lock them in their chamber."

Both men looked at him as if he'd just danced a jig. "Sure, you're not serious?" Fionn asked.

"I am. I've never seen two people more in need of being locked together in me life. They love each other and need each other, and if it takes locking them in their chamber before they'll admit it, so be it."

He could hope they'd be too occupied with reconciling to wonder who'd given the order to imprison them.

"Bring Ronan's carcass as well. The Angel and the Devil promised his head to the village. That promise shall be kept."

Chapter Thirty-Four

Conor came awake with a start. Darkness greeted him, then pain. It was all he could do not to groan aloud. He was in his bedstead at the dun, and the place beside him was empty.

Physical pain paled compared to the hurt in his heart. Erika was gone. She had heard his confession, heard his pledge of love and rejected it.

He could send after her. He could have a brace of soldiers find her and escort her back. He could use force, put her back in chains to make her stay.

He would not do it. Bad enough that she didn't love him. He couldn't bear it if she came to hate him as well.

Perhaps it was too late for that. Denouncing her in front of all, not believing her in his heart despite what reason told him. Throwing her in the pit, allowing her to be captured, using her to get to Ronan... He had done everything to make her hate him but order her outright.

His heart seized as he recalled the scene at the cliffs. Hearing her declare with such calm that he would not come for her. The assurance in her voice had frozen his soul. If she didn't believe he would come after her, how could she believe that he loved her?

Yet she had loved him once. He clung to the knowledge. Sure he'd heard the words from her lips. Sure a kernel of tender regard remained despite his foolish attempts to thwart it.

She had been by his side as he fell, had saved him from death. She had worked with Aine to save his life. Had he not felt her tears scald his fevered flesh? Had he not heard her, deep in his unconsciousness, tell him that she would not let him die? Was that not enough to resurrect her love?

He put his hands to his head, the movement aggravating his wound and causing him to groan.

"You're awake."

Erika. She was still here. Widening his eyes, he could just make out her form, sitting on a chair by the hearth. "You are well?"

She looked at him across the expanse of floor, her cropped hair burnished copper in the firelight beneath the drab mantle that covered it. "My arm will heal."

It was as if she were on the other side of Slieve Torc, so distant she seemed. Was she angry still? She had every right to be, Conor knew. Would she be able to forgive him?

"H-how long has it been?"

"I think it has been three nights and four days since the battle on the cliffs."

"You are not sure?"

"I was not awake when we arrived ho-here," she answered. He couldn't see her eyes in the dim light, but she was so still, so careful in her words. "I tried the door when sunlight filled the room some hours ago. It is locked from the other side. It would seem that we are prisoners of Dunlough."

"Prisoners?" His chest throbbed and the room spun in maddened frenzy. It took several breaths before his head cleared. "Why would our people imprison us?"

She shifted in the chair then turned her gaze to the fire. "Not you, but me. Ardan's doing, I think. And Padraig and Fionn with him. They seem to believe you will change your mind, and made sure I would stay until you awakened."

She rose to her feet, lighting the oil lamps, brightening the room. He saw that she wore a traditional dress, not the trews, and that her right arm was in a sling held to her chest. The cuts and bruises were beginning to fade; the hurt in her eyes looked to be permanent.

"I need to give you answers, and then I will take my leave." Her voice just reached him across the room. Her back was pressed to the door as if she strove to go through it.

He said the first thing that came to mind. "So you—you believe this imprisonment of ours a futile one?"

"You know that it is, Conor." Her voice was slow, a weak thing. Her entire demeanor was one of defeat, and that scared him more than anything ever had. "I wanted to give you laughter. I wanted to find a place to belong. I have done neither."

You have. The words formed in his throat but became clogged on the crest of fear that rose within him. He could not blame her for still wanting to leave, but how could he let her go?

"I carry your child, Conor. I first showed signs at Glentane, after Gwynna's delivery. True, it seems a miracle, so soon after..." Her voice tangled to a halt.

"But the day after I saved Bebhinn from drowning, that is the day we made our child. I never betrayed you. I would not do that. I will never do that."

He believed her. Even in the great hall, while Magda's evil worked on his emotions, his mind had believed. His inability to trust had been greater than his ability to reason, and now he stood to lose everything.

"I will go to Glentane for the rest of my time. After I am delivered, you will have your heir, and I will be gone from your life."

Words. They were just words, yet they cut sharper than any blade ever could. Somehow, he found the strength to speak. "You would leave your child—our child?"

Erika closed her eyes, her mouth open in a wordless groan. Her hands—a warrior's hands, a lover's hands—curved over her womb in a motherly gesture that broke his heart.

"It will be the most difficult thing I have ever had to do," she managed to say, tears breaking free of her will.

"Then do not do it."

The words were finally free. He had spoken them, had finally begged her to stay. An agony to say them, a torment to await her reply.

Tears spiked her lashes as she shook her head. "I cannot stay, Conor." Her voice was a mere fragment of a whisper. "Not now. We are not meant to be. Not in this life."

His heart sank. "Why?"

Her smile was sad. "We were enemies. Better for you had we remained such."

"How can you say that?"

"Because you never believed in me!" she cried. "You never believed that I chose to marry you, that I wanted to be a true wife to you." She shook her head. "I wanted to love you,

Conor. I wanted to make your heart light, to make a true home and a true marriage. You would not let me."

"I *couldn't* let you!"

He struggled to rise, just managing to right himself and plant his feet on the floor, ignoring the shaft of pain that pierced his shoulder. Pain be damned—he would rather bleed to death than lose her this way.

"After Aislingh, I could never believe that happiness was supposed to be mine, that love was supposed to be mine. I knew naught but guilt and betrayal and darkness. I didn't believe, couldn't believe you could love me. I didn't think I deserved it. I know I don't deserve you."

"Conor..."

He plunged ahead. He had nothing left to lose. "Do you know where I would be without you? Do you?"

"Yes!" Her voice cracked. "You wouldn't have a hole just above your heart. You'd have your life, your health. You'd be happy!"

"I'd be alive. But what is health without a heart? What is life without someone to share it with?"

"You will have someone. You will have your son. He is what you desire most."

"And what do you desire most?"

"It matters not." She turned her face to the door, resting her forehead against the dark wood. The mantle slipped down her back, revealing her hair. The spiky ends had been evened out but did not even brush her shoulders. He would always blame himself for that.

"What do you desire most, Erika?" he asked again, his voice hoarse with persistence. "A place to call home? Done.

To have the adoration and respect of our people? Done and done."

He rose to his feet, his back flat against the wall to maintain his balance. His good hand stretched towards her, willing every ounce of emotion and love he possessed into his gaze. "My body, heart and soul forever linked to yours? Done and done and done."

She looked at him, her beautiful violet eyes blurred with tears. For the first time, Conor saw a flicker of hope, and it gave him strength to say, finally, what needed to be said.

"I have loved you long, lady wife. From the beginning I loved your bravery, your devotion and your strength. When you rescued me from myself, I became yours. I knew in my mind that you were blameless when Brochadh put the accusation to you. Yet in my heart, where I love you most mad, in my heart, I am a jealous fool."

"Conor." His name broke from her on a huge sob.

"I'll not let you go, Erika." The conviction of his words circled the chamber. "If you leave I will follow, to the ends of the earth if needs be, and I'll bring you home. Once I captured your body, but you have captured my heart."

"Conor, please—"

"Oh, but I wish to," he breathed, not bothering to dash away evidence of his own weeping. "I have much to atone for. When I heard you declare to Ronan that I would not come for you, I near died inside. Magda did her work well, but if I had but dared to believe what I felt, what I knew—if I had let go of the past long before now, her words would not have had the power they did.

"Forgive me, wife. Allow me to spend the rest of my life finding ways to make you love me again, to make you laugh again. I'll start by telling you that I will love you beyond my last breath. Do you believe me?"

"Conor." She covered her face with her hands. "Oh, Conor."

When naught but tears answered him, he said, "You have besmirched my honor. I demand satisfaction."

Surprise dragged her tears to a halt. "Are you challenging me to a duel?"

"I am."

She gestured the length of him. "Are you mad? You are in no condition to fight a duel!"

"True," he admitted. "A month hence, I will be fine."

A ghost of a smile dusted her lips. "A month hence, I will still be losing my meals. No more swords during pregnancy."

"A wise precaution." Conor assembled his features into an expression of gravity. "And then there is the birthing and weaning. That is near two years hence."

Erika dried her eyes with the back of her hand, then took a step towards him. "What will happen if I birth a daughter?"

"I will love my daughter and spoil her in full measure," he declared. "But since she will no doubt be as beautiful as her mother, I would like a son to help me fend off unwanted suitors."

Her tremulous smile was like a balm to his soul, restoring his heart. "That puts our duel near four years away."

"Aye, it does at that."

"What shall we do in the meantime?"

She was finally, blessedly, close enough to touch. Heedless of his injury, Conor captured her wrist and pulled her to him. "Will you forgive me?" he asked, his voice ragged. "Will you try to love me again? With but half your love, I would be content. Even half."

She touched his cheek with her good hand, her eyes spilling anew. "You have all my love, Conor. You always have. It is just that I thought you didn't love me."

He didn't want to let her go, but he was near to toppling over. "Sure I told you, at the cliffs? I wanted you to know with my dying words that I love you."

She made a sound half-laugh, half-sob. "I heard you apologize for *not* loving me."

"You'll never misinterpret my words again. I love you, *mo leannán*." He repeated the words in Latin and Norse for good measure, then sealed the pledge with a kiss.

His fingers touched her shorn locks, and another bolt of pain pierced him. "If I could kill him again, I would."

A touch stilled him. "No more," she whispered. "No more darkness and dwelling on things past." She took his hands, placed them on her belly. "Our lives are here and now. Our lives start here and now."

She was right. The past was gone, and with it the darkness. The future stretched before him, bright with promise and love.

Energy spent, Conor all but collapsed onto the bed. "I'll not have more hair than my wife," he declared, wiping sweat from his brow with the back of his hand. "Think you can trim it for me? And rid me of this beard while you're about it?"

Her eyes brightened, then dimmed. "I don't think I can ever point a blade in your direction again, after I sealed your wound."

He took her hand, drawing her down beside him. "You did what you had to do to save me, and I'm grateful. No more dwelling on things past. Your words, my lady. If the future starts here and now, we must do something to mark it. I can think of nothing more fitting, except perhaps a certain pale *leine* worked with silver?"

The smile went to her eyes, chasing the last fragments of pain and doubt away. "I would like nothing better than to mark the occasion," she whispered. "But between my arm and your chest, I don't think we make one whole person."

"You're wrong about that, my love." He held her close. "Between the two of us, we are complete."

Epilogue

S *even months later*

Erika awakened slowly, still in the clutches of sleep. With careful movement she turned onto her side, suppressing a groan at the ache deep in her womb. It was to be expected, after near a day spent giving birth. Expected, yet so very worthwhile.

Conor sat in a chair beside her, dressed in a blue *leine* embroidered with a gripping-beast design she'd sewn herself. In the curves of his massive arms he held the fragile forms of their twin daughters. His expression was a potent mixture of emotions: pride, wonder, love and joy.

Her throat tightened. She'd received those emotions in full measure in the months since they were freed from their chamber. True to his word, there was not a day that went by that Conor did not find a way to show her that she was loved, and she did the same for him.

He had been ever beside her, his presence constant since the first pains announced the beginning of her travails a day ago. How he'd endured her vituperations she didn't know. Some of the names she'd called him made her flush with shame. He had borne it all, soothing her when she needed soothing, urging her when she needed urging. She knew she could not have done it without him.

She raised her gaze, startled to find him quietly staring at her, his silver eyes shining. "Good morrow."

His gaze brightened, and she felt as if she'd just been kissed. "Good morrow, wife."

She gave him a wavering smile. "You're not disappointed that I didn't give you sons first?"

"Never." His eyes misted as he cradled their children. "Two daughters, two beautiful, perfect daughters. They'll not want for anything, and they'll be free to make their own destinies."

He gave her a warm smile, his eyebrows arching upward. "Though 'tis true I'll enjoy the making of sons, when you're up to it."

"Conor." Laughter was beyond her at present, but it colored her voice.

"I'll need the help protecting my daughters from every young prince from here to Constantinople."

Erika snorted softly. "I doubt that any will want to cross the mighty Devil of Dunlough. And for that matter, who'll protect my sons from every noblewoman from here to the Orient?"

He snorted. "With the Angel of Death as mother, our sons will be well-protected indeed."

"My days of fighting are behind me," she whispered, "now that I have what I fought for. I love you, Conor mac Ferghal."

The smile he gave her stole her breath. "And I love you, Erika ni Conchobhair. Not a day will go by that you'll not know it."

"Promise?"

"I do." He leaned forward most carefully, so as not to awaken the children, and kissed her. "A promise has been made."

She reached up, cradling the clean-shaven cheek of the man she would love forever. "A promise shall be kept."

Author's Note

Whiled this is very much a work of fiction and artistic license, I could not have created this world without research. I am forever grateful to the following works and writers: *A Social History of Ancient Ireland* by P. W. Joyce; *A History of the Vikings* by Gwyn Jones; *The Story of the Irish Race* by Seumus MacManus; and the *Book of Irish Names* by Ronan Coghlan.

Any inaccuracies are entirely my own.

About the Author

Mallery Malone is a pseudonym of award-winning author Seressia Glass. She lives south of Atlanta with her guitarist-machinist hero, gamer son, and two attack poodles. When not writing she likes to belly dance, watch anime, and collect purple things.

She can be reached on the web at www.seressiaglass.com[1] or via email at seressia.glasse@gmail.com.

1.   http://www.seressiaglass.com

Don't miss out!

Visit the website below and you can sign up to receive emails whenever Mallery Malone publishes a new book. There's no charge and no obligation.

https://books2read.com/r/B-A-WQWJ-YGNDB

BOOKS 2 READ

Connecting independent readers to independent writers.

www.ingramcontent.com/pod-product-compliance
Lightning Source LLC
Chambersburg PA
CBHW071153250626
47159CB00001B/72